DRAGON MATES: THE FALK CLAN TALES VOLUME ONE

BOOKS 1-4

C.D. GORRI

Dragon Mates:
The Falk Clan Tales Volume One
Discreet Cover Edition
Books 1-4

The Dragon's Valentine
The Dragon's Christmas Gift
The Dragon's Heart
The Dragon's Secret

by C.D. Gorri
Edited by Book Nook Nuts

To all my Dragon Shifter lovers, I hope you enjoy this limited edition series bundle!
& Remember, when he says *Es Meus*, it means you are his...and he is yours, too!
Xoxo, C.D. Gorri

Don't forget to sign up for my newsletter here:
https://www.cdgorri.com/newsletter

BLURB

Readers beware... here be Dragons! After 500 years of servitude, these sexy Dragon males must find and woo their modern mates. Read the Falk Clan Tales today and discover unique Dragon Shifters and their journey to true love.

Maccon City is in for a thrill when a group of sexy Dragon Shifters comes to town, seeking sanctuary and looking for their mates. Building a castle is the easy part, filling it with love is the challenge. *Will they succeed?*

USA TODAY BESTSELLING AUTHOR

C.D. GORRI

THE DRAGON'S VALENTINE

A FALK CLAN TALE

BLURB

She's given up on love, but he's just begun...

After five hundred years of servitude, Dragon shifter Callius Falk and his three brothers are finally freed from their bonds. Callius has one mission, to find his true mate.

Winifred Castillo spends her nights tending bar at *The Thirsty Dog*, a local favorite in Maccon City, New Jersey. After her boyfriend skips town with her rent money, she's sworn off men. For good!

But what's a Werewolf to do when a dark-haired stranger with golden eyes and rippling muscles claims her as his mate?

PROLOGUE

Callius Falk looked around the throne room with thinly veiled disgust in his golden eyes. At the sound of a throat clearing, *one of his brothers no doubt*, he stilled himself. It wasn't easy, but he bit back his anger.

This was no time for pride. Callius knew what he needed to do. He exhaled and dropped soundlessly to his knees. The cold, hard floor seeped through his leather pants, but he barely felt it. His mind was on more important matters.

He dipped his head low, placing himself at the feet of Dragomir, Chief Dragon of the Blackthorne Clan. His warden these last five centuries. It was symbolic of his subservience to the tyrant.

True, he was the stronger of the two, but he'd never get the chance to prove it. The Blackthorne Clan had over one hundred Dragons in the hold alone. Each was sworn to defend Dragomir, and each would die at his behest. Regardless of how lowly the man was. *Service above all.*

Dragomir's silver hair was his greatest prize. It hung long, way past his knees when he stood up. Seated, as he was, the glittering braid sat coiled on the embroidered rug that sat just underneath his throne. The swirling patterns of reds and golds was intricate as it was delicate.

Woven by a true artisan of the Clan, from the finest threads made from a secret mixture of molten gold, silver and other precious metals. Such a piece of true Dragon craftsmanship belonged hanging on a wall in a gilded frame, in a place of honor.

Not beneath *his* ever-increasing girth. It most certainly should not be used as a resting place for his ridiculous hair. Callius raised a sleek black eyebrow.

He often thought it rather effeminate of Chief Blackthorne to style his hair in intricate braids with golden ropes woven throughout. The several dozen pearls and precious gems he used for adornment only added to Callius' theory. The Clan Chief was a *dandy*. A *fop*. More concerned with his appearance than with ruling with a fair and just mind.

Callius kept his own hair short on the sides and in the back, though the top hung down to his chin in the front. Unlike many members of the Clan whose own braids hung down their backs in imitation of their leader. What was it they said about imitation and flattery? He sneered at the thought.

Disgust was just about all the feeling he had left for the Chief and his followers. The gilded throne Dragomir sat on with his soft and untrained body was encrusted with priceless gems and won with the blood and sweat of others in the Clan.

Inscriptions in ancient *Dracan*, the language of the Dragon shifters long since unspoken, marked the arm rests and legs of the throne. It was priceless.

A treasure forged a thousand years ago for the once great Chiefs of the Blackthorne Clan. It told the tale of how the first Dragons mated with human females who then birthed the first Dragon shifters. Callius doubted that Dragomir could even read it.

It was almost time. He could practically taste freedom. The scent was there. Just out of reach. He could not wait to leave the desolate castle and the Blackthorne Clan.

He wanted, no, *he needed*, a castle of his own. A place he and his brothers could call home. And of course, more than anything else, Callius needed a mate. A female companion worthy of his diamond rose.

The greatest gift he had to give. One to carry his young and bring them forth into the world. A female worthy to share in his treasure. And he would have hordes of it to give to her and his brothers. That was a promise.

Traditionally, the right to seek a mate was granted by the Chief alone. One thing he knew for sure, he would rot in that cell of a room for the rest of his days before he asked Dragomir permission to find his mate. He wouldn't give the Clan Chief that satisfaction.

Chief Blackthorne's heart was as cold as the ice castle they lived in. They were so far north that normals had very few settlements surrounding them. In the old days that had made trading difficult, but with the dawning of the 21st century much had changed. Computers ruled the world as much as man did.

Dragomir did not like the new age of websites and cellular phones. It made it too easy for his subjects, and their human wives and children, to be independent from him. He was a vicious and jealous ruler.

Callius had seen it in the way he coveted not only all the wealth and finery his clansmen gained, but also the wives of those he was to protect. Ironic, considering the circumstances of his own imprisonment. *I forgive you, father.*

Callius suspected that last bit accounted for the number of single Dragons in the Blackthorne Clan. That was why he'd decided long ago that he would not make his home in that place.

Finding a mate was necessary. He needed an heir. Callius did not have the luxury of time. He was almost six-hundred years old. If he did not find a mate, one who would faithfully carry on his line, he would miss the opportunity to reproduce, he would become *cold*. His fire would not last without a family to protect.

It was his only mission. Without a mate, he would die. Callius had no desire to die. He wanted, above all, to be free. And he would have freedom. For himself and his brothers. Even if he had to kiss Dragomir's feet to get it.

The four Falk brothers; Callius, Nikolai, Edric, and Alexsander, had been kept prisoner for too long. Freedom was a whisper away and he hungered for it like nothing else he had ever tasted.

And now, here he was, seconds away from it. He bit back a snarl and kept his position on the floor. His trained body unmoving even as the Chief's heavily perfumed hair threatened to make him gag. He was still as stone as Dragomir read the decree that would release the four of them. *Finally.*

For a moment or two, Callius thought he would deny them liberty, but the Chief merely snarled at him with thick pink lips. His round face reddened as he spoke his last parting words.

"A warning, Brothers Falk, do not come here seeking aid or shelter for you are banished forthwith upon punishment of death. Take your final leave!"

He turned his rotund head to where a waiting attendant placed a crème filled pastry inside of his mouth. Callius rose from his position on the floor, his eyes remained downcast as another servant came forward with a key.

The sound of his irons crashing to the polished marble floor of Castle Blackthorne sent waves of relief through his entire body. His brothers' chains followed suit. He could feel their anticipation. *Wait for it. Now.*

It's been too long since he tasted freedom. Cold wind rushed to meet him as he thrust open the heavy wooden doors of the castle. *His prison.* He exhaled slowly. His mind was still reeling from the realization that it was finally over.

Callius turned and looked at his three brothers. Their faces all wore the same rapturous expression. He felt it too. As if they were alive for the first time in centuries. With little ceremony or circumstance, their five hundred years of subjugation was over. *At last.*

Callius nodded his head, and the four brothers began their

Change. The shift from man to Dragon was instantaneous. Myth and magic merged into reality in that one glorious moment.

It was like a thousand tiny, little sparks burned throughout his entire body and then, *poof*, they were gone. Not painful but electrifying. It felt amazing and very, very right.

Callius settled into his enormous body with the same ease and comfort as when he changed clothes. He stretched his long neck and strained his ears to listen for anything amiss. He could feel his brothers' anxiety. It mimicked his own.

They were anxious for his signal. The need to fly far from that palace of horrors was strong. Callius did not dally. The Chief was notoriously fickle. He'd not give the man a reason to revoke their freedom. Without any further ado, he took flight.

His brothers were right behind him. Their enormous wings cut through the frigid air with powerful thrusts. Each second took them farther away from the place of their birth. The place that had become their prison.

The scales of Callius' Dragon were dark and coal-like in color. A glittering black against the white of the Northern sky. On his underside, they lightened from a dark bronze to a brilliant gold just above his heart.

His beast was heavily muscled. Power and magic radiated from him as he reveled in his first taste of freedom in half a millennium. He turned his enormous body in a celebratory circle, taking in his brothers with his enhanced vision.

His brothers' Dragons ranged in size and color. *Red, Green, and White.* Each one deadly, magnificent, and gifted with unique talents. They'd been forced to use those talents for the tyrannical Chief of Castle Blackthorne during their confinement. It was the most loathsome experience of their lives. *But no more.*

Callius was free at last. He loosed a stream of brilliant flame from his mouth, simultaneously sounding a triumphant roar. He was a *FireDragon,* but this was the first time in centuries that he used his gift without orders.

His ability to create and breathe fire was a rare and coveted talent. Even among Dragons. His brothers' gifts differed greatly from his, but each had a specialty. For the first time in ages, they would own their own talents. It was a heady feeling.

They flew off the Isle of Pain, where Castle Blackthorne stood, together, into the unknown modern world. Like four shooting stars.

The Blackthorne Clan lived in the northern-most region of the Arctic Ocean on a tiny island that, from Callius' present vantage point, looked like nothing more than a black rock against the white and blue background of the frozen sea.

He felt no remorse in leaving the place of his birth. On the contrary, he was exhilarated. One word rang in his ears and one word only. *Freedom.*

As the eldest living Falk, he was now responsible for his siblings. It was no great burden but could prove somewhat problematic. Especially since he could sense their restlessness.

He knew what he needed to do, *what must be done.* To put it mildly, a Dragon without a permanent home was a very, very unhappy creature. At that moment, the Falk brothers were without home, without Chief, and without Clan.

They flew for several hundred miles before he opened his mind to the easy telepathic communication he shared with his brothers while they were in their Dragon forms. It was time they talked.

Callius was a warrior first and, like all good soldiers, he knew they needed a strategy to succeed. He recalled the sneering comments of their former master, Chief Blackthorne and growled deep in his chest.

"You will crawl back to me, Brothers Falk. The outside world is a cruel and hollow place. I will find you in my service once more. Of that, I am certain."

Not if I have anything to say about it. He remained silent at the time, but his mind had roared his response. Dragomir Blackthorne was a cruel leader. Greed, lust, violence, and fear were the tools he used to keep his Clan in line.

Callius despised him. He would chew off his own claw before he allowed himself or any of his brothers to go back there. *No. We will succeed.* It was time they make a plan.

Brothers, we need to talk. The world is changed, but our needs remain the same. A castle, a Clan, and a companion each. These are our needs.

Aye, but where will we go to find them, Cal? The next eldest and Callius' longtime war companion, Edric, spoke first.

His scales were a brilliant red on his back and lightened to orangey gold on his chest. They were as bright as his flame-colored hair when he walked as man. He had three horns spiraling out from the crown of his serpentine head.

On two feet, he wielded a knife better than anyone Callius had ever seen. On four feet, he did something few had ever managed. He manipulated the weather. Callius had seen him create lightning storms with just the beat of his wings.

They'd been through much together. Waging war for a tyrant for five-hundred years had taken its toll on them both. Callius was certain Edric was as sick of death as he was. Perhaps more so since their last battle. But it was over now.

Of all his brothers, he was closest to Edric. If anyone understood what Callius wanted, it would be him. Through their telepathic connection he could not only hear their voices, but he could also feel their feelings.

I do not know where my wings shall take me, but this I do know, we four brothers are now the Falk Clan. Together we shall be equals. I will find us a castle. One where we can come and go and share the fruits of our labor. What say you? Callius felt the approval in their hearts as he spoke in their minds.

Aye, a castle is a thing we all need. But what of a companion, Callius? Shall you find a mate as well? One who is worthy of the diamond rose?

Yes, Edric, I will find both my mate and castle. We shall have a home. All of us. I shall present a worthy female with the diamond rose and she will be mine.

You do that, brother, find a mate and a castle, but I will go explore. Do not expect me home so quickly. Alexsander, the youngest, was never one to shy away from his real feelings.

As a boy, he always yelled the loudest and fought the hardest. Callius suspected it was the only way he felt that he was heard. He looked at him now. *A man. A Dragon.* No longer a boy.

Alexsander's translucent-white scales made it almost impossible to find him as he spun and dipped in and out of the surrounding clouds. His youngest brother had felt the cage around them much more keenly than the rest. He saw his adolescence behind stone walls.

As do I. Like Alexsander, I wish to visit the places I have only glimpsed at in the last five hundred years. I've sent you the accounts and coordinates. You've only to use the cellular phone to look them up.

Nikolai's green Dragon was the closest in size to Callius'. His genius brother spent the past five-hundred years buried inside of books and computers. *A tomb of information.*

That was what he called his work room. He fattened the coffers of their jailer and managed to whittle out a slice for the brothers as well. Chief Dragomir allowed them their small personal ventures. What was a few million to a Dragon anyway? Now, Nikolai wanted to stretch his wings. Callius would not stand in his way.

And I too would like some time, brother. Edric's voice was solemn. Unexpected, true, but he deserved his liberty. They all did.

Callius' golden Dragon eyes landed on each of his brothers. He opened his long snout, row upon row of razor-sharp teeth glistened against the black of his scales, then he loosed a roar of blue and red flame against the whited-out sky.

He would miss them. They were his flesh, his blood, and his constant companions these five-hundred years. But he understood.

Agreed. Take care, my brothers. As eldest, this is my pledge to you, I will find us a castle and claim my mate! Then I will send for you.

Choose wisely, brother. The diamond rose is special.

Farewell and much luck to you on your quest!

Yes! May you be successful!

Somewhere over the vast Atlantic Ocean, the brothers parted ways. It was bittersweet as all partings were. Only the idea that, one day, they would live in a castle of their own kept Callius on a steady course. His purpose grew stronger with every passing moment.

An idea of Castle Falk began taking shape in his mind's eye. Not an old stone mausoleum like the one he came from. No, he wanted something new and modern. A haven where they could protect their own and come and go as they pleased. No master, all equals. Yes, it would be a fine thing indeed.

But first things first, he reminded himself.

Find a mate and claim her.

CHAPTER

ONE

"**D**ammit," Fred struggled with the three cases of booze she lugged up the cellar stairs to the main floor of *The Thirsty Dog.*

Being a Werewolf definitely had its perks! Increased strength, sense of smell, and enhanced vision to name a few, but none of them helped her as she banged her elbow on the door frame while exiting the musty old basement. If anything, she only hit it harder. *Ouch!*

It wasn't her fault that she couldn't see over the cases of long necks, was it? What could she do about her height? Not a damn thing!

Fred often joked about being vertically challenged. She was short. Period. *Especially for a Wolf.* At five-foot five-inches tall, she was the runt of the Pack. Not a bad height for a *normal*, but next to her six-foot plus Packmates, she was seriously lacking.

Her weight was fine. She maintained a solid buck forty. She was as fit and muscular as any Wolf in Maccon City. And that was without exercising at one of those twenty-four-hour gyms that were all the rage.

Fred got enough exercise between her two jobs and full moon

19

runs with the Pack. She had no extra time for running on treadmills and Zumba classes.

Not that she was complaining. That was how she liked it. *Keep moving, stay busy, no worries.* Something her older brother used to say.

"Fred! Let's go! We got customers!" Mike, the seventy-five-year-old Wolf who owned the place, yelled at her from across the bar.

He was tall, well over six-foot. Long, lean, and muscular without a single gray hair on his head. He looked more like forty than seventy-five, but that was the same with most Wolves.

Fred didn't care about his looks. He was a good boss. Better than most, and that counted for everything! He paid her on time and treated her with courtesy and respect. Heck, he'd given Fred her very first job in town! She owed Mike.

"I'm coming already! Hold your horses!"

The roar of the crowd from the main room of the bar was like a smack in the face as Fred rounded the corner. *Ugh!* She wished she had remembered to put her ear plugs in.

Her Werewolf hearing was super-sensitive. Most of the time it didn't bother her, but tonight she had one hell of a headache.

Cheer up, girl! Noisy means crowded. Big crowds meant big tips. And she seriously needed the money.

Saturday nights in Maccon City tended to be slower in the winter. But even with snow on the ground everyone seemed to be out tonight! It was Valentine's Day after all.

Cheesy paper-Cupids with bows and arrows decorated the doors. Red streamers and glittery heart-shaped confetti covered every inch of the place.

Mike even had buckets by the front door filled with long-stem roses. The bouncers gave one to every woman who walked in. *Happy Valentine's Day!*

The fact that the town served as the headquarters for the Macconwood Werewolf Pack accounted for most of the supernatural customers. Pretty much every Wolf in North America made their way to Maccon City at one time or another.

Werewolves liked paying their respects to their leader and this was his hometown. There were always a couple of Wolves she didn't know in the bar. Heck, Fred had been a visitor herself only six years ago.

She liked the Jersey Shore town so much that she stayed. Finally taking her brother's advice to "put down roots". *Damn, she missed him.*

She'd been shiftless for so long. No direction. No family. No home. Loneliness was becoming too familiar, but just lately she was thinking about getting a degree in counseling, buying a place, settling down. But that was never gonna happen! Not now.

Fred usually worked two jobs at a time. She used to work one day a week at a local realtor's office, but it wasn't her speed. Meanwhile, she was doing 12-hour days, six days a week at *The Thirsty Dog* until she found another gig. That was just to make ends meet.

She didn't mind hard work. Of course, she wanted to finish her degree and get a "real job" someday, but that was in the future. For now, she was happy she finally found a place to fit in.

Of course, that happiness was fleeting. That was before the latest in a long line of disastrous relationships blew up in her face. Ugh. She really hated men.

She shook her head in an attempt to get back in touch with reality. These musings of hers were doing no one any good. Fred took a deep breath. She needed to get back to work and in truth, she did like this job.

The Thirsty Dog was a cool place. A real favorite with the locals, Werewolves and normals alike. Mike prided himself on the fact that he served two types of crowd, and *no*, not the obvious two. He offered a place for sophisticated palates to try some truly unique liquors and for others, who were not so discerning, to just hang out.

Serious drinkers could quench their refined thirsts with his unique collection of locally distilled liquors, wines, and craft beers. Younger, party crowds could find entertainment of all kinds on the premises. The place had pool tables, virtual gaming stations, multiple dartboards, a punching bag, a DJ booth, a stage for bands, and a newly finished dance floor. Werewolves certainly loved to play.

The lights were always dim, the bathrooms were impeccably clean, Fred would know, and the black leather stools looked damn fine next to the polished pine wood bar. Just last year, Mike ripped the ceilings open to reveal the steel beams that held the place together.

He said it gave the place an edgy, industrial look. A large mirror lined the back wall behind the bar. That's where he showcased an assortment of high-end liquor, with a focus on local breweries and distilleries, lined the shelves.

Fred's absolute favorite was produced by Mason Lane. He was another local Werewolf. The founder and owner of a successful line of artisan distilled whiskey right out of Maccon City. She'd only seen him once or twice. The dude liked his privacy.

He called his whiskey *Bite*. And it certainly had one. Fred couldn't keep it on the shelves! *Top quality, organic ingredients, non-GMO, crafted by artisans.* Liquid gold.

Werewolves preferred high quality food and drink. Especially older Wolves. Their heightened senses made the super-processed foods of today difficult to swallow. Fred had to admit that once she began to eat organic foods, she could actually taste the chemicals in regular food. She couldn't even begin to justify the consumption of meat from animals kept in pens and fed GMO corn, grain, and who knew what else. Not to mention the number of insecticides on non-organic produce.

Mason Lane had it right when he created his label. It was the cleanest, finest whiskey Fred ever tasted and she pushed it at the bar for that reason alone. It was simply better. Especially to the Wolves in the area, though to be fair, normals loved it just as much.

A flood of just turned twenty-one-year-olds let the cold night air in as they crammed into the bar. Fred guessed their ages from the "I'm 21 today! Buy me a drink!" sash that one of the girls wore over her clothing.

Not that there was much clothing. Black lycra, red lipstick, a few Valentine's Day flashing necklaces and not much else. She grinned at Mike then nodded at them. He clapped his hands and grinned. He was seeing dollar signs and an opportunity to keep the Wolves in the bar entertained. *Wolves loved to play!*

Fred rolled her eyes at the guys who were already sniffing around the cloud of hairspray, perfume, and *ew*, was that *KY jelly*? *TMI, girl-friend*! Her Packmates were down to party, the guys especially tended to be players of the highest order. Werewolves had loads of energy and needed to blow off steam regularly, but they were honest about it. Fred respected that. They treated their women right and only messed around with those that knew the deal.

It was dangerous for a Werewolf to get in too deep. Protective instincts took over and before you knew it, *bam*, you were married and mated! Not that Fred needed to worry about that. She never dated other Werewolves.

But these ladies were more than happy to get all that masculine attention. And, *really*, it wasn't all their fault. Normals tended to be naturally receptive to the virility of Werewolves. They had natural charisma. Their physical attributes were simply a bonus.

Not too many ugly, flabby Wolves walking around. Especially, not in Maccon City. Fred rolled her eyes. She certainly didn't mind the fact that she had toned abs and clear skin as a supernatural bonus, but she never flaunted the way her male counterparts did. The hams! But boys will be boys, playas gonna play and all that. Werewolves were no exception.

On the bright side, hot young girls meant tons of men looking for a no-strings hook-up. Those men usually paid for the drinks. They also left large tips to attentive bartenders.

So, *yeah*, Fred thought, *come on in and get your drink on, ladies and gents!*

"Hey, girl! How 'bout a round of *Bite-Bombs* and *ooh* could you put extra cinnamon heart candy in them like last time? Thanks!" an especially cute blonde called out.

"You got it!" Fred smiled as she started mixing shots for the young women. She smiled even bigger as a gentleman in a suit grabbed the tab and dropped a crisp fifty in her tip jar.

The guy was a regular. He smiled and wiggled his eyebrows at Fred. She just laughed and wiped the bar clean. He was a good guy. Came in every week with his work pals. She watched him turn his attentions back to the flirtatious young woman who ordered the drinks.

Good luck, buddy! She could hardly remember when she was that young and optimistic about love. What was it they said? *Once bitten, twice shy.* Well, that was, Winifred. No. New. Men. Period. *Not even on Valentine's Day!*

CHAPTER

TWO

Fred filled order after order of cutesy named Valentine's Day drinks. She would never admit it, but she wished, *for just one moment*, that she was one of the girls on the receiving end of one of these *Shotz-Thru-the-Heart or Kiss-Me-Nows*. Those were the days, when she could just have some fun. Not worry about what came next. Back when she still believed in true love and happily-ever-afters.

Not anymore.

She was still reeling from her latest relationship disaster. Her live-in boyfriend, Josh, literally skipped out on her. No note, no phone call, not even a text. He was just gone. Poof. Like magic. Only it wasn't magic. It was a con. One she should have seen coming.

You should have known better, Fred.

Not only did he disappear without a trace, but he also stole every cent she'd saved the last few years. He emptied their joint bank account, packed up, and took off. He even took her new memory foam pillows.

The jerk.

Then, as if that wasn't bad enough, her new landlord paid her a

25

visit. And not a friendly one. Turns out her rat bastard of an ex hadn't paid their rent in three months! It was a good thing the full moon was two weeks away, otherwise her Wolf would've hunted down Josh and tore him to shreds. She still might.

This would have never happened if she hadn't been so desperate for a normal life. She let herself be persuaded by his not-so-subtle hints that he move-in with her. He was a smooth talker, she'd give him that! But it was all a lie.

"Hey baby, my lease is up and I'm always at your place anyway, why don't I move in? I love waking up to you. It'll be great! Making love every night and we could even ride into town to work together."

Except he never did. While she worked two jobs, he had none. He convinced her it was temporary. When weeks turned into months, he told her not to worry, he would take care of the house while he looked for a job.

He'd shop, cook, clean, do the laundry. So, it made sense to open a new checking account with him. She could transfer her paychecks and he'd sort out everything. He'd pay the rent and the bills. She wouldn't have to worry about it.

Yeah. Right. She should have gotten the hint that everything wasn't hunky-dory when she found herself doing laundry at two o'clock in the morning most nights while he was nowhere to be seen. *Ugh, Fred you are so dumb!*

If Mr. Ingles, her former landlord, was still alive he would have understood why she was late with the rent. As it was, her late landlord's distant nephew inherited the property and took control immediately. He wasn't interested in listening to anything she had to say. He wanted her back rent and he wanted her out. Period.

Of course, Fred figured, his end goal was to sell the old building for a mint. It was, after all, prime beach-front property. Her time working in a realtor's office taught her the land alone was worth millions.

The home itself had character and style, though it was a little weather worn. The paint was peeling, and the shutters were broken in places. The roof needed repairs if not replacing, and some of the windows were rusted shut from the salt in the air.

It would take a fortune to get the building back in shape. But what she wouldn't give to see it the way it looked back in its hay day. Mr. Ingles had framed pictures of the place back in the early sixties all over his section of the house. It was glorious. Fred wished she could afford it. The house was perfect!

She loved waking up to the sound of the waves crashing on the shore. The smells of the beach and the sea tantalized her enhanced senses. It was beautiful. Even in winter. There was nothing quite like snow falling on the ocean. She begged her new landlord, Mr. Kaepernick, to reconsider, but his answer was a big, fat, resounding, *"No!"*

"Pack up and get out or I'll have the Sheriff's department pay you a visit. And you better pay me what you owe before you go moving any furniture."

To think she sent the creep a condolence basket when his uncle passed. She even baked the cookies herself. And she hated to cook! Now, he was going to kick her out without a leg to stand on and hardly any warning. *And* he was threatening to go to the cops! *Just great!*

"I'm so going to kill Josh!" she kept her voice low, but her boss still heard her. She felt him move towards her and knew she was in for a mild scolding. *Ugh. Werewolves!*

"Stop talking to yourself, Fred, and get the lead out! The bar is crowded with thirsty customers. Kill Josh on your own time," Mike stalked towards her and grabbed a case of cold longnecks from the top of the pile she had forgotten about behind her.

He slammed it down on the counter with just enough force to startle her out of her stupor. *So dramatic!* She shook her head as he pushed bottle after bottle of craft IPAs, Pale Ales, and Porters into the ice filled stainless-steel coolers behind the bar. Freezing cold water dripped over the sides as he shoved in the beer. Fred used a rag to dry them off.

The only problem with the newest additions to *The Thirsty Dog* was keeping them stocked. She liked the look of the trendy open-top coolers. It certainly made her job easier. Bending down constantly to figure out which beer they had, and which bottles were cold was time consuming. Especially for impatient customers. Like the ones there tonight. Holidays were always crowded at The Thirsty Dog.

The coolers displayed the beer bottles, kept them cold, and within easy reach. Tonight, it was her job to keep them filled and, so far, she failed miserably. She let the coolers go down to empty not once, but twice. *Yikes. Get your head on straight, girl.*

"Sorry, boss, I was making *Bite-Bombs* for that group over there. Mason's newest flavor, *Cinnamon Fire*, is his best yet."

"That it is," Mike looked at the crowd. She was glad to see him here tonight. Her boss lost his mate and their baby three years ago. Childbirth was difficult for Wolves, and in some cases fatal. Fred bit her lip. He was a good guy and she wished him all the happiness in the world. As if he felt her thoughts, he nodded his head in her direction and continued to watch the bar.

The small acknowledgement felt right. They weren't exactly close. Mike knew where to draw the line between employer and employee, but their Pack bonds sometimes allowed feelings and flashes of memories to come through.

Jordan, the other bartender on duty, shot her a thumbs-up. He was probably listening in too. He was a member of the Pack too, so he had no trouble hearing her conversation with Mike even as he took orders.

Jordan was cute as hell, with thick, dark hair and piercing brown eyes. He was lean and muscular with long legs and a fantastic build, but he was a little too cocky. Bottom line, guys that were conceited were not to Fred's tastes.

Jordan flirted shamelessly with anyone of the opposite sex who was within the vicinity. As if he read her mind, he turned around and gave her an exaggerated wink and blew her a kiss before setting up a round of tequila shots.

Fred laughed and shook her head. *Dope!* She stopped dating

Wolves when she was around twenty. She wanted to improve her odds at finding true love and figured she'd never get anywhere with any of her kind. They were such dogs anyway! Pun intended. Not that dating normals turned out to be so great either.

Maybe she should try dating women? She looked back at Jordan and took a sec to admire his firm backside. *Uh uh.* His ass was perfectly outlined in the tight black jeans he wore as part of his uniform. *Nope, no way,* she shook her head and sighed.

It was guys for her. All the way. *Damn it!* But cute ass or not, Jordan didn't really do anything for her. They were buddies, Pack-mates, co-workers and nothing more. The first night he worked there he hit on her, but she made it clear she was only interested in being friends with Pack. He understood and backed off immediately.

That was one thing she loved about her Pack, the *Macconwood Pack*. Respect and loyalty above all else. That was the unspoken motto. Right now, she just wished she got that little tingling feeling in the pit of her stomach when she looked at Jordan's ass or *anyone* for that matter.

Was Josh right about her? Did she attract misery and loneliness? Was she dried up on the inside? *Ugh,* maybe she was broken or something?

She read an article online about women whose libido diminished after they reached their late twenties. Maybe it was true? Or maybe she just wasn't good at sex? *Aaahh!* Maybe she just wasn't sexy? Or attractive to the opposite sex? OMG! Josh hadn't touched her in weeks before he left town!

Fred looked down at herself in the barely there uniform and shook her head. She was not conceited herself, but she knew damn well, she had all the right parts, and they weren't half bad. But something killed whatever attraction Josh had felt for her in the beginning.

She closed her eyes for a second and admitted to herself that, yes, they had other problems. He thought she was lying when she stayed out all night during the full moon. And she knew he was lying when he said he was trying to find a job.

In one particularly memorable fight, he accused her of cheating on him with her boss. Yeah, like she and Mike were getting busy in between taking orders at the bar. *As if!*

She could not believe she ever considered revealing her true nature to him. After one difficult night of lying there next to him, she decided to tell him the truth. It was after another failed attempt at making love. She was tired from working two jobs, it was in-between moons, and she was feeling alone and scared.

She still couldn't believe she almost blurted out her secret. Fred wondered if it might bring them closer together. Especially after he told her he just couldn't touch her not knowing where she spent her nights. At the very least, she thought if she told him, maybe he'd shut up about her supposed cheating!

Thank goodness, she had the foresight to keep her mouth shut. Too bad she didn't have enough intuition to keep her bank account and credit card information to herself as well. *Idiot.*

"Hey, can I get a beer, here?" Fred looked up with a plastic smile and filled the order.

Enough, girl, forget Josh and get your head on straight. Maybe she should just have some *straight-up-dirty-against-the-bathroom-wall* sex with a stranger. Just to wash the taste of betrayal out of her mouth. She could call it an experiment. *A Valentine's Day Sexperiment!*

OMG! That was truly cringe-worthy. Possibly the worst thing she had ever thought of! She mock gagged as she imagined the re-tweets that would get! LOL!

"No, you keep the change, cutie! Happy Valentine's day!" Fred smiled at the customer, he was short, about five-foot one, but his smile was friendly and his tip was large!

She shook her head as she tossed it in the tip jar. Who was she kidding? *A Sexperiment?!* That just wasn't her style. Winifred was greedy. She wanted it all. *Romance, love, trust, friendship, passion.* She wanted the whole damn thing, and she wasn't going to settle for less.

Since there seemed to be a shortage of reliable, trustworthy, honest men, she'd have to do the next best thing. Steer clear of all men. No harm, no foul that way!

She smiled and straightened her shoulders content with her new attitude. No more guys! This was going to be a historic Valentine's Day for Winifred Castillo!

She even ignored a couple of male customers while she focused on her new mantra. *Men are evil. I don't need them!* Mike cleared his throat loudly and glared in her direction then at the waiting customers. Fred narrowed her eyes and went back to work with a vengeance. *Work, concentrate, make some cash, pay the evil landlord. This will be the best Valentine's Day yet, Fred my girl!*

"Oooohhh!" Fred squealed just as Mike snuck up behind her and dropped an ice cube down the back of her black tank top. She yanked it out of her miniscule clothing as quickly as she could.

"Lighten up, Fred, it's Valentine's Day!"

"Oh, that's just great, Mike! I did just break up with my boyfriend, you know! All these hearts and flowers and people looking for love are giving me the willies."

"So, you got dumped, so what? That normal was nothing but a bum anyway. He didn't deserve you, Freddie. Now get to work. And smile! Maybe Cupid will be kind," her normally taciturn boss joked.

"Geez, Mike! Now I'm cold!" She didn't tell Mike about the money. That was her problem.

"Well, duh, Fred, it's ice! Now, hustle, before Jordan alienates all the male clientele! Tell him to start stocking the back bar while you wait on those suits over there, and where are your uniform pants?"

Fred rolled her eyes and kept working. She was wearing black jeans today instead of her complete "uniform". If you could even call it that! The thing consisted of short shorts with ripped stockings, stiletto-heeled boots, and a black tank top strategically cut along the sides and torso that read *The Thirsty Dog* in bright red letters with a tongue rolling out of the letter "g".

Oh, yeah. Classy. But Fred knew the drill, the more she showed, the more tips she made. *Sexist?* Yes. But it was also true.

She was more than comfortable with her toned and athletic body. Most Werewolves were. And it didn't matter that it was February and her tank top left little more than a few inches of skin covered. Werewolves ran a little hotter than normals.

But still. Ice was ice. She squirmed uncomfortably. *Great!* Now she'd have to deal with a cold, wet bra strap for the next few hours. *Boys!*

Fred stuck her tongue out at Mike. Her boss raised a salt and pepper eyebrow and tossed another ice cube in the air.

"No, no, I'm working, I'm working," she raised her hands in surrender and laughed.

It was good to smile. Just minutes ago, she doubted she would ever do that again. She turned around as quickly as the thick rubber mats that lined the bar floor would allow her and finished her task before taking over for Jordan.

She grabbed and folded the thick pieces of cardboard left over from the cases of beer they had just stocked. She exhaled a breath. The activity gave her a second to take in the scene.

The place was getting more crowded as the seconds ticked by. A few patrons were seated at the bar waiting for her to notice them. One guy looked kind of pissed. *Hope that doesn't affect my tips.* She smiled widely and mouthed "one second" before tossing the cardboard under the trash can.

"Hey Jordan, Mike says get more *Bite* from the cellar," she called out to her co-bartender. He winked at her as he waved bye to the group of young women who were all but swooning at his heels. *Ugh, this is why you don't date Wolves. Whatever.*

Fred poured a heavy dose of scotch and soda for the formerly annoyed customer and smiled as he handed her a twenty. She never flirted with the customers, but she was friendly and knew when to listen and when to talk.

"Keep the change, doll." Of course, his eyes never seemed to rise higher than the dip of her tank top.

"Yeah. Thanks! Enjoy your drink," she automatically rang up the tab and tossed the change in the tip jar.

Maybe tonight wasn't going to be so bad after all. This plus her paycheck from *Maccon City Estates* might allow her to put a dent in what she owed Mr. Kaepernick. All she had to do was not eat for the next six months. *I hate you, Josh!*

She didn't really hate him. She couldn't. he was what he was. She'd just gotten lazy.

What Fred really hated, was the idea of having to move. That was much worse than Josh himself. And under these conditions! Her meager belongings wouldn't even fill a small storage cube, but she'd have no choice. She'd need to rent one to hold her things because the only other place she could afford to live was the little roach motel right off the highway. *Yuck.*

What was that again about life and lemons? Fred had no idea how she would make lemonade out of this mess. She had no choice. All she wanted to do was finish her shift, go home, and figure out plan.

THREE

The minutes felt like hours as she mixed drinks for customers and cringed at one lame Valentine proposal after another.

"I'm good." "No thanks."

"No, I can't sit on your lap while you drink that."

"No, I don't want to see your Cupid's arrow."

"I bet I can change your mind! Come here, sugar, I got a long, hard Valentine just for you!"

Fred looked over at *Prince Charming*. The two hundred eighty-pound stranger was barely able to hold his head up. She inhaled. Hmm, a drunken normal. Just what she needed.

She focused all her attention on the stranger. Her eyes looked into his without flinching. Most normals didn't like to be confronted by supernaturals even though they had no idea what they were. It was a sixth sense of sorts. They recognized danger even if they didn't know why they were afraid.

She turned her steel gray eyes on him and gave him a hard look. No teasing smile or light banter. A cold look was usually enough to scare normals straight.

"You a fucking tease or what?"

"Listen up, buddy, you are cut off. Walk out of the bar now before I call the bouncer," Fred had no patience for that kind of behavior. In the mood she was in, it was all she could do not to let her Wolf out a little to scare the crap out of him.

"I got what you need, baby, right here. A little pushin' and you'll be good as new," *short, fat, and sweaty* reached over and grabbed Fred's arm.

"Move your hand, before you lose it," Fred's voice had just a hint of a growl in it.

The guy seemed to get the message. *Grrr.* There was always one in the crowd. Can't handle his liquor. Got all grabby and stuff. She dealt with customers like him every now and again.

The sound of a pleasant masculine laugh filled her ears. Fred turned her head to the right, her blonde ponytail swung behind her. A pair of eyes that shimmered like gold in the dimly lit bar stared at her. Her pulse tripled and Fred felt her mouth hang open. *Whoa.*

"You handle yourself admirably," the man stood up from his seat and walked over to her.

He looked formidable. Hard as he was handsome. His smiling face like something out of a book on ancient heroes or demi-gods. Her stomach clenched and Fred sucked in a breath. *Holy crap.*

"Hey, uh, excuse me I forgot my drink," the guy with the hands tried to reach in front of the stranger with the golden eyes, but he was stopped with a hard look from Fred's new friend.

"No, I believe you have had enough. Leave. Now," one look at the stranger and the drunk guy left without another word.

"Thanks, but you really didn't need to do that. I had it under control," Fred leaned forward to get a better look at her would be knight-in-shining-armor. *Damn, but he did look like a knight.*

The man was drop-dead gorgeous. More attractive than anyone she had ever seen, and that was saying something. She was used to men with larger-than-life personalities and amazing looks. After all, she was living in the heart of Werewolf country. And boy, were they a good-looking bunch. But this guy. He looked as if he was carved from marble.

She wasn't exactly a fan of the classics, but the only thought she had when staring at this man, was that he had the face of Adonis. *Beautiful. Perfection.* Masculine, *yes*, but beautiful, nonetheless. She wanted to reach out and touch him. To see if he was real.

He had impossibly dark hair. The color of midnight or what she pictured midnight would be in the darkest part of the universe. *So dark*, Fred imagined she could get lost in it.

It was cut short on his neck but hung well over his perfect forehead. Thick, straight locks reached all the way down to his chin in the front. It was glossy, and slightly windblown. She itched to reach out and touch it.

He had a strong, straight nose. *Never been broken*. Full, dusky colored lips that complemented his olive-toned skin. Maybe he had Spanish blood? He could just as easily be Italian or Greek. It didn't matter to her other than the fact that she was curious about him.

He stood up and moved to a stool closer to her. *Oh my!* Were those black leather pants? He wore them with a black button-down shirt that was open at his throat. She watched his pulse throb steadily at the base of his neck and was shocked at the strong urge to put her lips just there.

She shook her head and pasted on her friendly bartender smile. Fred appreciated the whole pirate meets rocker look. It was seriously hot. Not to mention the rippling muscles and long limbs. He was a feast for the eyes. *Panty-dropping gorgeous.*

She wouldn't mind getting lost with him for a few hours. She realized she was staring and cleared her throat. He smiled at her, seeming to notice and maybe even enjoy her temporary embarrassment.

Damn, he is seriously gorgeous. She liked the way his lower lip jutted out slightly farther than the top one when he smiled. And *ooh* that smile.

His lips parted to reveal bright white teeth. She appreciated good dental hygiene. It was a Werewolf thing. But it was his eyes that struck her the most. They were unlike anything she'd ever seen.

Ambers and golds swirling around like something out of the cosmos. He had entire galaxies swimming in his eyes. Her heart raced inside her chest.

Fred was dazzled.

"Well, are you here as a special Valentine's Day gift from the Fates or am I just lucky?" She decided to go with humor.

It's not like she was going to trust her instincts. Not after Josh. Fred was simply unlucky at love. And didn't, she just swear off men for good? She was going to ignore that nagging little voice inside her head telling her to go for it. *Quiet, you are off men, but that doesn't mean you can't tend bar and maybe get a tip out of the guy.*

"I'm sorry?" The handsome stranger didn't seem to get her humor, so she tossed some heart shaped glitter in the air.

"It's Valentine's Day! You know? The hearts, Cupid, anyway it was a lame joke. I am staying Valentine-less this year. So, what can I get you?"

"Valentine-less? That seems a shame for one as lovely as you are, but if I may have a moment please, if you will?" His voice was nothing more than a rumble in the noisy bar.

It struck a chord deep inside of her. Her stomach muscles clenched. Were her palms getting sweaty? *Oh, no you don't! No butter-flies brought on by good-looking men.*

"A moment? How about a drink instead?" She tried a bit of harmless flirtation as a distraction, but all she wanted to do was reach across the bar and touch her lips to his. *Whoa girl! Slow down now.*

"Well, I have this ale, but I am afraid it is not to my liking."

She eyed the mug of beer in his hand. It was nothing special. An over-produced brand that the country as a whole enjoyed, but a real connoisseur avoided. He struck her as someone with finer tastes than that.

"Maybe you'd like a stronger drink? We happen to have some

really good local whiskey, ever heard of *Bite*?" She ignored the urge to touch him and started prepping her workstation for his drink instead. *Idle hands and all that.*

"No, I have not. Would you pour some for me?" his voice was deep and pleasant.

The small smile that played at the corner of his mouth was sexy and inviting. Fred wondered if that smile was for her. She noticed a few other women slide up to the bar, hoping he'd notice them. When he didn't, Fred let go of the breath she didn't know she was holding. *Uh oh. He's just a customer. You have no claim on him.*

"That's my job. I pour the drinks! So, how do you want it?" Fred bit her lip and eyed him from behind the bar. That came out all wrong. *Or* maybe not. *More lemons, life?*

"I will leave the choice to you, sweet lady," he seemed intrigued by the way she bit her lip.

His gold eyes followed the movement. Fred turned abruptly, breaking the sudden tension between them. She needed to keep it light and simple, ignore the little sensation in the back of her mind that was telling her this man was different. Special somehow.

"Well, we, uh, have a few different flavors. Vanilla, cherry, and their latest, cinnamon, but that one is a bit spicy."

"I like spicy."

"Do you? Well, then, how about I mix you something special?" Okay fine. Now, she was flirting.

"Again, the choice is up to you." He seemed to be studying her as she moved.

There was the subtlest smile on his mouth, but none of the shameless flirting she'd witnessed from other customers. *He was different.* Everything about him seemed to set her nerves on fire. She was aware of him in ways she'd never imagined she could be with anyone. Especially a stranger. *It is just a fluke. A Valentine-induced misconception. There is nothing special here, Fred. Just make the drink.*

"So, you like it spicy, let's see if you can handle this. I made this little concoction during our *Spicy New Year's Eve Party*. I call it *Dragon Bite*," Fred took the bottle of *Cinnamon Fire Bite* down from the shelf.

"That is an interesting and fortuitous name for a drink," the gorgeous stranger smiled and leaned his elbows on the bar. There was nothing subtle about his grin now, this was a thousand-watt grin that threatened to knock her off her feet.

"Yeah, I always liked dragons when I was a kid so, anyway," her voice trailed off as his smile grew even brighter, if possible.

Just get the drink, Fred. She wasn't bad for a part-time mixologist. The drink had gone over well with those who dared to try it. She gathered some of the fresh ingredients she stored behind the bar and got to work.

She quickly measured three shots of *Bite,* poured in half a bottle of ginger beer, one slice of lemon, one slice of lime, one slice of fresh jalapeño, some freshly grated ginger, then for the finale, she donned a pair of rubber gloves and got out a black glass vial.

"What is that there, in the vial?"

"This? It's ghost pepper oil, just a tiny drop mind you, I wouldn't want to kill you!"

"Ha! That would be difficult indeed for such a dainty flower as you."

She eyed him over the dropper and added an extra-long squeeze.

Dainty flower? Take that you conceited—! Oh shit.

Before she could take back the drink, he had the glass raised to his lips. Fred froze. Her insides tightened. What did she just do? Mike would kill her!

"Hey look, I think I put too much! Let me make another," she turned but it was too late, he had the drink in his hand, "Oh, my God! Are you okay?"

The stranger tossed back the entire glass in one gulp. He bowed his head and slammed the glass upside down on the table. There wasn't a drop left.

Oh shit. Fred's concern only grew as he remained in that position for a full thirty-seconds, during which Fred suffered several minor heart attacks. *Would Mike fire her if she killed a customer?*

His hand gripped the bar as he continued his perfect imitation of a statue. Fred tried to wait it out, but she just couldn't. She reached out a hand and touched his. Sparks of electricity raced up her arm at the contact, but she was too concerned to pay it any mind.

"Hey, you need some water or something? Buddy? Pal? You okay?"

Bright gold eyes met hers and she almost jumped out of her skin. Those were not human eyes! She inhaled, but whatever this guy was she had never encountered anything like him before. *Magic. Beast. Man.*

"My lady, my name is Callius Falk and that was the best refreshment I've ever had the pleasure of imbibing and that really is saying something." His voice was deep and pleasant. There was a sexy rumble to it, an intensely masculine quality that made her want to just crawl in his lap and beg him to talk to her.

She pulled her hand back and ignored her need to go to him, to touch him. Instead, she went into concerned bartender mode. She needed to find out just what was going on with this guy.

He was not just a customer. Definitely not a normal. His eyes glowed gold and something non-human had peeked out at her for the briefest of flashes. Whatever he was, he was powerful and new to her. Maybe he was using some kind of magic on her? She needed to be careful.

"You're okay! Want some water?"

"I shall have another!"

"Another?"

"Yes, please, another, what did you call it, ah yes, *Dragon Bite.*"

"Oookay," Fred mixed another drink and placed it before him. As she turned to move his long fingers brushed against hers sending a thousand little nerve endings into a frenzy. She pulled her hand back quickly.

"Come, lady, talk with me. Will you? Now?"

"Uh, I'm working right now, but can you wait here a moment?"

"As you command."

A thousand different thoughts entered Fred's mind at once. But every single one of them left her brain when he touched her hand and asked her to go talk to him. Her skin burned where he touched her. In a good way, but first things, first. Fred needed to find out who, or rather, what, this man really was!

FOUR

Callius was mesmerized by this female. Her entire aura seemed to light up the dim establishment, beckoning to him like a siren. He felt the pull like it was something physical. As if he were a fish on a hook. When he finally laid eyes on her, she stole the breath from his body.

He wanted to go to her, to pick her up in his arms and take her far from this place. From the prying eyes of all, especially the men who frequented this establishment. He could sense most of their intentions and they were not at all honest.

He'd tear the heart out of any who did more than just approach her for more than just a drink. Even then, it took an enormous amount of restraint not to act on his instincts. He managed it though. *Barely.*

He used the time to study her. She tended the bar with quick efficiency. Her banter with the patrons was easy and honest. She was no stranger to hard work. He admired that in her. The last time he was free to pursue a female, things were much different. Noble maidens did little but preen the day away. He'd never met one who made his heart thunder the way this female did.

Callius waited over an hour for an opening to speak with her. When she poured his drink, she did not try and use her femininity to seduce him. Much to his dismay. He doubted she was even aware of the invitation in her eyes or the seductive way her hips swayed as she walked away from him. It only made his desire for her grow more intense.

Her curvaceous backside was perfectly outlined in her form-fitting pants, another new one for him. Maidens wore dresses and bustles the last time he was out and about, but it was not the pants that did him in.

It was her long blonde hair that had his full attention. It hung down her back in a long, wavy ponytail. Yellow topaz, citrines, golds, ambers, and silver threads all flowed together in an array of softly curling waves. *A Dragon's treasure trove.*

Callius wanted to stretch out his hand and run his fingers through the shiny locks. Her hair reminded him of the strands of golden thread Dragon artisans, like his brother Alexsander, used to make tapestries. His kind prized the unique pieces as they took dozens of years, sometimes hundreds, to create just one of the prizes.

He had no patience for the task, but he witnessed his brother at work. The first step was to take dozens of precious metals and to carefully mold and make them into long strands of glittering, delicate thread. Just like the female's hair. *All unique. All beautiful. Sacred to Dragons.*

As she is sacred to me. She was beautiful. Striking and alluring. He watched her long before he talked to her. Her silver-gray eyes had flashed from across the room drawing his attention. *Silver, gold, bronze,* she was captivating.

"Lady? That word if I may?"

"Just a sec," she turned around and his heart thudded in his chest.

Her heart shaped bottom was completely outlined in her fitted clothing. Someone to the right of him was unfortunate enough to make a similar remark aloud. Callius growled and stood to his full height glaring at the offender.

"Oh dude, is that your girl? Sorry man!" the human retreated quickly.

Callius rubbed a hand over his face. *Fool. You are acting like she is in your possession already.*

It was not completely the boy's fault. His lady's attire was entirely too revealing. It excited him as much as it enraged him that other males were gawking at what he now considered to be his. He would have to talk to his chosen mate about this. *And soon.*

He sipped from his second tumbler of *Dragon Bite,* his new favorite drink, and rolled his shoulders. He was quite tired from his flight. The amber liquid warmed his stomach.

It made him think of *other things* he'd like to have to warm him in the night. He shifted in his seat uncomfortably, his leather pants were a little too restrictive for such thoughts. It was neither the time nor the place.

While his lady was busy, he took a moment to view his surroundings. Strange styles of dress surrounded him and even stranger methods of communication. Yes, he had a cellular phone, but the box remained in his pocket. These patrons were simply glued to the things.

He knew about the latest technology, but he'd never seen it in use in such a large group. *Fascinating.* His younger brothers were part of a group Dragomir sent into the world to explore and learn new technology every couple of decades or so.

Callius and Edric were seldom freed and when they were, it was mainly to fight in battles and wage wars. He'd killed and maimed many a foe in five-hundred years. Blackthorne Castle had seen a serious increase in Demon activity the last hundred years or so.

He'd been called upon to kill them and defend the Castle by his former keeper. That was the most noble battle he'd fought these last five-hundred years. More often he'd fought to fatten Dragomir's coffers. *Yes, he'd killed for land, for money, to avenge some insult or other, for greed, for power.*

Dragons could be so very petty. When you lived as long as they did, priorities got blurred at times. At any rate, hanging up his sword was not difficult at all. Sometimes, it was difficult to believe he survived the last five centuries at all. But he never gave up. That was what counted.

So much time had gone by since he'd last spread his wings. Thank goodness for Nikolai and Alexsander, otherwise he'd have no idea what these people were up to with their flashing little screens and constant talking to rectangular shaped boxes.

The world always seemed to turn whether he was rotting in his cell or not. It amazed Callius, humanity's ability to create and expand without benefit of shapeshifting or magical prowess. *Ever curious, ever hopeful, such a delightful though delicate species.* Dragons and humans rarely interacted in the past, but things were different.

He did not wish to retreat to some cold rock in the middle of nowhere. He wanted to live. He wanted to be free. He wanted to stake claim to Castle and mate as soon as possible. *Speaking of which.*

Back to the task at hand. Claiming his mate. Callius needed to devise a strategy. He thought about what he knew of her. The lady worked with nimble hands. Speed and efficiency her allies. Callius liked the way she moved. Each action made with the fluidity of practiced ease and confidence. Open and friendly, but slightly guarded. *Smart. Cautious.* He approved of both.

She greeted her customers with a quick wit, charm, and grace that intrigued him. The man in charge treated her with respect and kindness, but nothing untoward. The patrons of the establishment responded with smiles and tips to her natural warmth and charisma. Everyone seemed drawn to her. He was no exception. She was like a bright beacon in the dark night.

It pleased him that she reacted positively to his physical appearance. It was good that she found him attractive. He'd been told during the rare times he took a lover that he was quite something to look at. Though he couldn't say his appearance was of any great importance to him. Only in that his mate might approve of his looks.

His mate. Callius finally found her. He knew it the moment he laid eyes on her from across the crowded room. She was resplendent in her beauty. Silvers, coppers, and golds harmoniously blended to create a palate of precious metals and gems in her hair and her eyes.

Ruby red lips that tilted at the corners as she spoke to the patrons. Her smooth skin, pale as ivory, was exposed in various degrees across her miniscule clothing. Aye, she was a veritable feast for his eyes. The other women in the bar did not even compare.

When she poured him his aptly named drink, he wanted to beat his fists on his chest. She was providing him sustenance. Caring for him. Callius' Dragon stirred beneath his skin. He wanted to claim her. *Now.* This woman was his destiny. *Es meus.*

He only needed wait for the right moment to ask. He tried to sit still while she completed whatever task it was that stole her away from the bar, but seconds felt like hours. Patience was not one of his virtues.

Just a while longer, then they could talk. And he could ask his question. When she agreed to be his, he'd give her the *diamond rose.* Only then would she be his. *Forever bound.*

He tapped his knuckles on the bar. The sound of the rapping allowed him to tune out the other noises all around him. Callius focused his attentions inside of himself. He needed to look into his Dragon's heart. A low, deep grumble erupted from his chest as the words sank into his consciousness.

Es meus. Carpe Domina.

Mine. Seize the maiden. Claim her. Mate. Bond.

He opened his eyes and felt the rightness of his choice settle around him like a cloak or mantle.

To think he chose this establishment on a whim. He shook his dark head. Perhaps the Fates were finally being kind? Or was it that his heart had simply led him to she who was his destiny. He inhaled deeply, trying to discern her exact scent, but there were too many foreign smells in the crowded tavern for him to single her out without having breathed her in first-hand.

His Dragon stirred restlessly. He was unhappy with uncertainties. He wanted to claim her here and now. Callius clenched his jaw to stop himself from acting on his instincts. He needed to remain in charge of his beast. *Soon. I will claim her, but patience is necessary.*

He looked to where she had disappeared a few minutes ago but saw no trace of her. That only caused greater anxiety. He closed his eyes to get himself under control.

Once I mark her, all will change. I will know her heart and mind and she will know mine. There will be no need for this worry or anxiety. Peace now.

He'd heard all the stories since he was a child. There was only one true mate for every shifter. He found his female through the unbreakable bond a Dragon shared with his Maiden. A bond of such strength it defied nature.

The Dragon then claimed her and gifted his female with a part of himself. Enabling longevity and sometimes telepathy between mates. Not even death dared to break the sacred matebond. Though a Dragon could choose to give up his immortality to pass into eternity with his mate.

Without the bonds of a true mate, without a clan, or a castle, a Dragon would grow weak in his mind as well as physically. The older the Dragon the quicker the slide into madness. It would poison his brain, and jealousy would take hold of his heart. Callius was at an age where he could feel his emptiness begin to consume him. It was not a pleasant feeling, more like an impending doom settled around his heart the last hundred years. He'd seen what emptiness could do. Such horrors he'd witnessed first-hand. *In Dragomir's Castle.*

He could never want such a half-life. Like the one his former jailer lived. Consumed by greed, lust, and insatiable in his desires. The Chief was empty no matter how many pastry cremes he stuffed into his mouth or how full his coffers grew.

Callius would not grow to be like him. Not ever. He would not have to. The golden-haired beauty was his true mate. *His diamond rose.* He had no doubt.

To think, he landed not far from this tavern only hours before. It was not the shoreline or the lights that intrigued him from the heavens. No, it was the spirit of the city. It was different. It was special. Like a supernatural pharos.

A light in the dark that pulsed with energy calling to all those who were, like him, of the other side of the world. Humans and Shifters lived here side by side whether the normals knew it or not. Within the crowded room he smelled traces of Vampire and a whole lot of Wolf. He smiled to himself.

Callius had fought many a Wolf Pack in his day. They were worthy of doing battle with a Dragon. Fierce warriors, and loyal to boot. He hoped they were friendly as he had no present wish to fight. His years of subjugation to Chief Blackthorne had left him wanting naught, but peace and freedom.

He wished only to look upon his mate. To pull her supple body close and breathe her in. To mark her so that no man, normal or not, dared look at her again. To fill her completely and wholly as he desperately needed to. Callius waited impatiently for her return.

Red glitter heart confetti stuck to his hand as he continued tapping the bar with his fingertips. *What strange decorations*, he thought to himself and tried twice before succeeding in shaking the frills off his skin.

He turned his mind to his journey. He'd almost forgotten how exhilarating flying could be. With each shift to Dragon, his body was replenished with strength and power. That was why Dragomir had not allowed them to shift at will. The bastard had no more claims on Callius and his brothers, but still the memory was sharp in his mind.

He wished his brothers had stayed with him. As eldest his need to keep them safe and to secure them a home was intense. But he understood their desire to spread their wings and explore the world. A world that they had only glimpsed at the past five-hundred years.

Not Callius. He saw enough of the world while waging war for

Dragomir, Chief of the Blackthorne Clan. He'd not waste another moment of his time. After his long imprisonment, he understood the value of time more than most. His first order of business was to find his true mate. *Done.*

Next, he needed to find a castle. *A home.* He liked the look of this land as he circled from the heavens above. Of course, it was never as easy as all that, but he never looked for the easy way. Not Callius. *The Falk Clan will claim this place*, he thought to himself.

This land, this New Jersey had everything. Lakes, mountains, cities, suburbs, farmland, forests, and of course, the ocean. A perfect place for a Dragon Clan to settle. And unclaimed by any Clan he knew of.

In the few times over the last five-hundred years that Callius had been in contact with Dragons from other Clans, he had never heard of one settling in America. Most of those Dragons had decided the country was vile and filthy. Full of ingrates, criminals, and vermin.

He shook his head. For all their long lifetimes, his fellow Dragons tended to be old-fashioned and unwilling to change. No, there would be no other Clans to fight for dominion here. This New World would belong to him and his family. Theirs for the taking. The Falk brothers waited long enough for a place to call their own. *Home.*

Callius was finished waiting. He stood up. He'd make his claim here and now. First his mate, then his castle.

"Hi, this is Winifred Castillo at *The Thirsty Dog*. I think you need to come here and check someone out...He's different...Not a normal...No, I don't know *what* he is, that's the problem. Okay, bye," Fred put the cell phone back in the old black leather hobo bag she carried around with her. She snapped it shut and tossed the bag back into her employee locker.

Fuck. What did she just do? Was it the right thing?

Fred didn't usually doubt herself like this, but something was very strange about the guy. And not just the way looking at him made her stomach do somersaults.

Maybe you're just antsy cause you've got the hots for him...

Shut up.

She growled working hard to keep her humiliating inner thoughts to herself. Gosh, she could be such a jerk sometimes. She rolled her eyes and peeked out from the backroom towards the bar stool where she left her mystery man sitting just a few minutes ago. Only now, he was gone.

Dammit. Maybe I should have waited before calling the Pack.

"*Milady*, I really must speak with you."

Fred jumped at the sound of his deep voice near her ear. Her heart pounded in her chest and she had to stop herself from swinging out with her fist.

How the heck did he manage that? She couldn't recall a time after her Change that anyone was able to sneak up on her. Maybe she needed her ears checked or something?

"Ooh! You scared me!"

"Forgive me, sweet, I wasn't trying to startle you," the dark-haired giant tilted his head. Fred followed him with her eyes, hypnotized by the pulsating warmth that shone in his.

His irises were translucent. Like hot caramel sauce. The kind Fred ordered on top of her ice cream. But they weren't all sweet, there was fire there too. They burned along the edges with a lightning-like glow.

She could see herself falling in those depths and never finding her way out. *No, wait.* She tried backing up a step. He was just so big. He took up most of the space in the room. But he didn't crowd her. Not at all. In fact, she liked it.

She wanted to lean into him, to brush her body against his. Was he as solid as he looked? Did those muscles go everywhere? And what was the deal with those crazy gold eyes? A woman could fall in love with eyes like that. Especially the way he was looking at her, like he could eat her whole.

Holy hotness. He was practically oozing sex, and her Wolf was panting, *er*, that is she was really paying attention to the tall, delicious stranger. Totally eatable one in a sexy fun way. But she didn't believe in love, anymore. Did she?

He reached out with his right hand and traced a path from her hairline to her jaw. Little jolts of electricity seemed to sizzle along her skin where he touched, distracting her from her wandering thoughts. She felt herself leaning into him. The way she imagined only seconds before.

Heat seeped through her clothing from his large body. His hands continued to trace her face, her neck, her shoulders. She should stop him, she really should, but it felt so damn good.

"Beautiful," his voice was soothing, mesmerizing even.

His fingertips seemed to get warmer as he traced little patterns all over her body. She was sure his body temperature was well over hundred degrees. She ran a little hotter than normals which was typical for a Werewolf. Maybe three degrees' higher tops, but this guy, well, heat seemed to *radiate* off him.

Fred swayed a little closer, unable to stop herself. *Mmmm.* His warmth was so enticing, so inviting, especially when she thought about the cold outside. It was a rough winter. Cold and bitter. But there was nothing cold about him. Slightly callused hands continued their exploration. She stood perfectly still. Unwilling to break the fragile spell between them.

He gently traced lines from her jaw to her brow then back down again. Her eyelids dipped low, though she fought to keep them open. She wanted to watch him as he touched her. His fascination evident in his own heavy-lidded stare.

Even breathing seemed intrusive. Fred slowed down her breathing as much as she could. Not an easy feat when her heart felt as if it was going to burst through her chest. She didn't want him to stop.

The noise from the bar, the problems with her landlord, and Josh the rat, all faded away in the space of a few seconds. She existed in that moment for one reason. To feel his touch. His warm fingers tenderly caressing her skin. *Harder*, she thought, *more*.

"I don't want to hurt you, love," he whispered against her temple. He kissed her head and his lips seemed to sizzle on her skin.

Did she say that aloud? She needed to get a hold of herself, *for fuck's sake*! She was acting like she was in high school. Letting some guy paw all over her! She didn't even know him! *Slow down there, Fred.*

"Okay, look, I'm sorry, I don't even know you-" she almost lost her balance as his hand fell away and he backed up half a step. She immediately felt cold. *And empty.*

"Did I frighten you, love? I apologize, I simply had to touch your skin. You're pale as freshly whipped cream and just as soft-" his gold eyes seemed to glow as he reached for her again, but Fred evaded his hand. She needed to think clearly and that was not going to happen if he touched her again.

"No, you didn't frighten me, I- I just don't *know* you."

"But you *do* know me," his words were nothing more than a growl as he stared into her eyes.

Fred's stomach tightened. *Yes, I do know you.* She bit her lip to keep from answering aloud. The lie tasted foul in her mouth, but what was she supposed to do? She had no idea who or what he was. What if this was some kind of trap?

"What's your name?"

"Callius Falk. And yours, milady?"

"My name is Winifred, but people call me Fred."

"My sweet Winifred, you are beautiful as your name," he leaned close again. Fred's eyes rolled back. Heat seeped into her.

Wait, did he say her name was beautiful? Seriously? Mmm, when did he start rubbing her shoulders? Mmm, feels wonderful!

"My name's a joke, definitely not beautiful."

"I am sorry to disagree with you, but, love, you could not be more wrong," he placed a whisper of a kiss on her brow, and she swayed closer to him. The soft material of his shirt felt good against the places where her skin was bare.

She'd never been so turned on in her life. *Certainly not by Josh.* She wanted to trust him, but how could she? Even if everything about him said he was telling the truth. *Okay, so maybe he liked old-fashioned names.* She took a deep breath.

Werewolves could often smell a lie. *Mmm.* He smelled good. Pure and honest. Not one trace of deceit as far as she could discern. *Yes,* he was telling the truth.

His scent was like cinnamon spice with a hint of Applewood smoke. *Wow.* She hadn't breathed in that particular fragrance in years. It was like being in a time machine. The past caught up to her. Suddenly, she was thinking about her life before she came to Maccon City.

Fred travelled across the country with her older brother in an old, beat-up RV. They often stayed in the woods and slept outside near the campfire. They told each other stories while breathing in the pleasant smoke. She recalled making cobbler in an old cast iron pot outside on the open flames.

She burnt her lip after stealing a bite of too-hot apple cobbler on their very last trip together. The flaming-hot cinnamon sugar left an angry red mark, but it tasted so good. She remembered what she told him afterwards. *It was worth it.*

Her mouth watered a little as she stared at the man in front of her. *Cobbler? Maybe. Just maybe.* She wondered if he would taste as hot and sweet. One thing she was willing to bet on was that he'd be worth the burn.

"I wonder, milady, if I may?" his voice was a rumble in the darkness. It pulsated right through her, making her tremble. *This was getting dangerous.*

"If you may *what?*"

"If I may *this*," he pushed her gently against the exposed brick wall and placed his hands on either side of her head.

Fred was used to being stronger than most of the guys around her, even the Wolves. This man was easily twice her width and a good ten inches taller than she was. *Would she be able to move him if she wanted to?*

The question was valid, but the thing was, she didn't want to. She tilted her head back to meet his golden eyes. Her Wolf generally did not like it when she was outsized, but for some reason she was not bothered by him at all. In fact, she seemed to encourage Fred as she pulled him closer.

He felt solid and deliciously warm against her scantily clad body.

She readied herself for what she assumed was going to be a passionate assault on her mouth, but he leaned in the top of her head and sucked in deep breath of her hair.

She narrowed her eyes at him. That was a Werewolf thing to do, but she already knew that he wasn't one. *What was he? And why was he smiling like that?*

"You are a Wolf?" his voice was laced with pure delight.

"How did you know that?" her voice was higher than normal in her panic. Now she wanted to step back, but she was trapped between him and the wall behind her.

Fred waited a moment for the panic to come, the fear that she'd been outed. But it didn't. She was not scared. She felt *excited*, not anxious. And she liked it.

"This is very good! Excellent! Fortune is smiling at me at long last, my love! *Ha! Gaudium et veritate!*"

"What?"

"There is joy in the truth, sweet Fred!"

"Why do you say that?"

"For many reasons, love."

"Name one."

"It will be easier on you, for one thing," he dropped a kiss on her temple and held her face gently while he breathed in her scent.

His smile was contagious, but she needed to keep her head on right. How did he know what she was? She was determined to find out, but what did he mean by that last remark?

"What will be easier on me?" she asked.

"This," Callius pressed the hard length of his body into hers.

He pushed his hips into hers as his mouth inched closer. Her lips parted, stunned by the thick length of his arousal. It strained against his tight leather pants and pressed against her stomach. Fred could hardly think as he flexed his hips into hers, a growl escaping his lips. *Mm, so good.* She opened her legs a little wider. She wanted to *feel* him.

Their bodies fit like puzzle pieces. Locked in his embrace all she wanted was to feel his lips on hers. To taste that smoky-cinnamon flavor that was all his. As if he read her mind, his tongue snaked into her mouth and she opened for him, welcoming the fiery heat that came with his kiss.

Fred couldn't think. She didn't want to. All she could do was feel. His lips were masterful. He kissed, licked, sucked, and even bit as if he could read her every want.

His hands were the same. Just as proficient. They were everywhere all at once. *Searching, fondling, caressing, gripping, squeezing.* Fred held onto him for all she was worth. All the while, his lips locked onto hers and the world around them simply fell away.

"I must ask a question," he said coming up for air when all Fred wanted was to drown in his kiss. He panted with the effort it took to speak. That pleased Fred. She'd hate it if this were all one-sided.

"Ask already," she nodded following his lips with her eyes. *Just hurry up and kiss me.*

"*Milady*, sweet Winifred, I need to know. Can I have you?"

"I'm sorry, what?"

Yes! Of course! Her brain was screaming at her to take him somewhere they could be alone. Where they could finish this explosive interlude. But wait he was talking again. *What was the question?*

She could hardly focus. She couldn't believe how much she wanted him. Heck, she was about to jump him right where anyone could walk by without a single care, what other confirmation did he need? His question echoed in her mind, *Can I have you?*

Yes, you can have me! Her mind screamed. *As long as you never stop doing that with your hands!* Her nipples hardened under his touch. His clever fingers pulled and squeezed. Finally, he closed his mouth over one then the other, right over her thin shirt. She hissed out a slow breath.

It had been months since she felt the touch of a man. Josh had lost interest long before he emptied her bank account. If she was being honest with herself, she'd admit she stopped trying too. He wasn't the man for her. She'd known it all along.

Now this man, well, he teased her body into such a frenzied state of passion, she thought she'd burst right there. She felt alive. His hands travelled up her spine and down again. He cupped her ass and squeezed in a way that hurt so good.

"Oh, don't stop, Callius!"

"Say my name again," he grazed her throat with his teeth and ground his body into hers.

"*Callius.*" Fred felt his pleasure at the sound of his name on her lips and she smiled with her head thrown back. She held onto his face as he kissed her and moaned when he lowered his head.

He licked a hot trail from her collarbone to her mouth and touched his lips to hers. *Oh, my God!* Fred drove her tongue inside of his spicy hot mouth. Holding him there with her hands while she explored the sweet cavern of his mouth. She couldn't get enough of the taste of him.

Electricity sizzled between them. Like little bolts of lightning dancing along her nerve endings. The world stopped and spun round again. She thought she even heard her Wolf howl.

His lips were spicy and sweet, like a bite of 70% chocolate and a sip of Bordeaux. A dark sort of delicious that went straight to her head.

His hands roamed over her body with free reign. She allowed him access to her secrets without any reservations. His tongue and teeth teased her mouth until she was almost mindless with need. She wanted him, craved him. Fred couldn't hold back any longer, she wrapped one leg around his hips and pulled him close.

If he could, then so could she. She steered him deeper into the small backroom. He squeezed her thighs and lifted her fully onto him, carrying her the rest of the way. She allowed him to do just that.

Her hands had better things to do. Like running up and down his heavily muscled back, down to his hips, and finally, to his firm ass. He felt *soooo good* in his tight black leather. She bit his lower lip. *Grrr.*

He seemed to growl in response. Fred's hands moved to the front of the soft leather that encased his manhood. His cock was long and hard under her curious fingers. She groaned again as he throbbed in her hands. Up and down, she traced and squeezed, again and again.

If the way his entire body vibrated under her touch was any indication of how he felt, he definitely liked it. She couldn't get enough. Fred wished they were in a bed somewhere where she could peel off every barrier between them and explore.

"I need your answer, please, I beg you. You must tell me," he lifted his head, eyes glowing, "Can I have you?"

The question. There it was again. She thought he would have gotten the answer by now. But maybe he needed the words.

"*Yes,*" Fred moaned the word and squeezed her thighs around him.

"It's done then," he took her hands and put them around his neck, pressing as close as he could get to her with their clothes still on.

He put his hands under her ass and lifted her up so that she was practically riding him. She moved and bucked, pressing into him as close as she could get. So close, but still so far. A sweeter torture, Fred had never felt.

He bent his head to her neck and first his lips were kissing her, then his tongue, and finally she felt teeth. She groaned and clung to him as he sucked. His teeth grazed her neck again.

Shivers travelled down her spine. Fred wanted something, she needed something more. She didn't know what it was, but she held onto him and exposed her throat fully to him. Longing for something she didn't quite understand. Then, her body tensed and before she could name what it was, she wanted, he bit down. *Hard.*

Fred gasped aloud as pure pleasure shot throughout her body from the place where he bit her on her neck to every nerve receptor. The brief pain of his bite was immediately forgotten, lost in the most intense orgasm she had ever felt. Then he was licking and sucking again, and Fred felt a delicious heat seep into her.

"My sweet, sweet Fred," he penetrated her mouth with his tongue and kissed her again more thoroughly than she had ever been kissed before.

His hands moved up and over her firm breasts. He flicked her nipples with his left hand while his right hand snaked down her tight jeans. *Thank God for jeggings!*

He parted her hot, wet lips with just the tips of his long fingers. Circling the swollen skin, teasing and tempting her, but not quite filling her. Fred bucked against him. She wanted him. Now.

"Oh, my God, don't you dare stop, Callius," Fred said into his mouth. She bit his lower lip and swore she felt him smile against her.

His hand dipped down further into her jeans. Fred grabbed a fistful of his dark hair and groaned as he inserted two large fingers inside her throbbing heat. With a third finger, he found the place where she ached the most and applied just the right amount of pressure.

"*Yes, oh, yes,*" she moaned into his mouth, loving the smoky taste of his kiss.

With fast, even strokes he played her body as if she was an instrument and he its master. No one had ever come close to being as attuned to her every desire as this man, this stranger, who was like something out of one of those *telenovelas* her great-aunt used to watch. She let go of all her inhibitions and gave herself over to the pleasure of his touch. She kissed him hard, clinging to his lips to stop herself from screaming out as he rocked her into the sweetest orgasm she'd experienced.

"*Oh God, oh damn, oh damn, Callius,*" she growled his name as he continued to stroke and kiss and soothe.

"*Es meus,*" he growled and slid his hand out of her damp panties.

His golden gaze locked with her as he licked each of his fingers. One. At. A. Time. It was almost enough to make her cum again.

"What does that mean?" she asked as she tried to regain some semblance of control over her trembling body.

"It means *you are mine.*"

"*Yours,* huh?"

"Yes. My mate. For life."

"Wow, I mean, really, that was great, amazing even. I mean, mind-blowing, but it was really just a kiss."

"Just a kiss? I still taste your woman's honey on my tongue, and I can't tell you how much I want to indulge in it for the rest of the evening."

"I'd like that too, but-"

"No buts. Let us leave here now, I've already marked you, love, our bond is made."

"What bond? What mark?" Inside her heart she knew exactly what he was talking about. Her hand flew to the place on her neck where she'd felt his searing kiss just minutes ago.

Fred ran over to the small mirror on the wall of the employee locker room. She turned her head and lifted her hand. When she saw the raised puncture marks, her face fell. *He bit her! Like actually bit her!*

"You did say 'yes', my love. I've given you the most precious gift I have to give, the *diamond rose,*" Callius talked to her reflection in the mirror, but all Fred could see was the bite mark on her neck.

It wasn't two little holes, like a vampire bite or anything like that. This was a full-on bite. It looked a little rounded, wait? *What was happening?!*

"What is going on?"

As Fred looked in the mirror, the mark began to grow. It turned, and swirled. First a bright angry looking red, then a glowing, ethereal white, until finally, it stopped moving. The remaining pattern was an intricate bluish gold. Like a very detailed tattoo of a, what was it? *A rose.* It was a rose.

"It is there on your neck and here, in this stone. The *diamond rose.* It is my heart, my soul, my pledge to you, my most prized possession, it is my oath to our bond, and it is yours," he removed a ring from his leather pants. *Those things had pockets?*

Fred gasped. She was in serious danger of going into sensory overload! First, the amazing connection, then the mind-blowing orgasm, now she was marked! She didn't know if she could process everything that had happened in the last half-hour.

One thing for sure, that ring was the most gorgeous thing she had ever seen. Layers of gold molded into the shape of a blooming rose with dozens of small blue diamonds surrounding one larger center stone.

She looked from the mirror to the ring and back again. The small mark on her neck resembled the pattern identically. *Beautiful.* The *diamond rose* pulsated on her neck in time with the one in her hand. The two of them magically linked. Both pulling her towards the man standing right behind her.

Fred wanted nothing more than to take it and put it on. But it was too soon. Logic warred with instinct and she felt the niggling sensation of doubt creep in. Could she trust her heart again so soon after her latest disaster?

"My sweet Winifred, we sealed our bond with a kiss. How did you put it, a *Valentine's Day gift from the Fates*, remember?"

"Yes, but I was joking!"

"We often reveal truths in jests. You are my mate, and I am yours."

"I don't even know you!"

"I am Callius Falk, and I swear this day that I will forever treasure you and protect you with my life's blood."

"This is not funny, okay?"

"This is no joke. You are my heart's desire. The diamond rose is yours alone."

"But I-" Fred started.

"Hey Fred! Someone's here for you!" Jordan yelled from the front bar.

"One sec," Fred almost made it out of his embrace, but Callius stepped in front of her barring her exit. His stance was protective and where she normally would have been annoyed a such macho tactics, she was kind of flattered. *Hmm, never had a protector before.* She watched him inhale. So much like a Wolf, yet different. He was majestic in his battle stance, almost regal. What was he?

"More Werewolves. *An Alpha Werewolf.*"

"Okay. Let's start from the beginning, shall we? Seff, back off. Let's go with formal introductions first, yes? Alright then, I'm Rafe Maccon, Alpha of the Macconwood Pack, my territory includes most of the continent of North America. This is Maccon City, my hometown and base of operations. You seem to know what we are and now you know my name, so, you are?"

Rafe Maccon sat at a table in a dark room at the back of *The Thirsty Dog*. Some place where they wouldn't be disturbed. With him were Seff, his Beta, and Randall, his Third and another of his Wolf Guard. These were the highest-ranking Wolves in Fred's Pack.

The Macconwood Pack was well known and highly respected in the supernatural community. She had little dealings with the Alpha and his Wolf Guard, but as promised, they came when she called. Tears threatened to roll down her cheeks as she realized the implication. She had a home. She had family. As long as she had Pack.

"Thank you, for the introduction, I take it Winifred contacted you when I made her acquaintance earlier this evening. Do not fret, I am pleased that she acted so wisely, and even more pleased to see you answer her call. Many a Pack that I've witnessed fail over the centuries did so because they lacked that which I see you have in abundance, loyalty and mutual respect."

"Thank you for the compliment, but you didn't answer my question."

"Ah, yes, I am Callius Falk. I shall speak plainly. It is my desire to settle in this place with my Clan. We are four brothers, by birth and in arms, and we have waited a very long time and come a very long way to live in peace and freedom."

"I see. So, you have all left your former Clan?"

"Yes. We have completed our servitude under Chief Black-thorne," Callius answered the questions asked.

Fred could tell that he was being free with his answers, meaning he was speaking openly, and he was not accustomed to it. She wondered what he was hiding. More than that, she wondered if she didn't grossly violate his privacy by calling her Pack here. But what was she to do?

"Why were you in servitude and for how long exactly, if I may inquire?" Rafe leaned forward, his Wolf Guard flanked him on both sides.

He was a good Alpha. He personally welcomed Fred to the Pack when she made the decision to stay. It was not something other Alphas did. The fact that he cut a striking figure was another boon in his favor. Nearly as tall and even wider than Callius. He was impressive. His black hair and ice blue eyes were legendary traits of the Maccon family.

Like many of the Pack, Fred was glad he had finally settled down and got married. She whole-heartedly approved his choice. Charley Maccon was amazing. She was an advocate for Pack families. Like Rafe's own sister, Cat, who with her husband, Tate, opened a new youth center in town that was quite the success.

Fred volunteered there at least once a month. It was what made her want to get a degree in counseling. Troubled young Werewolves needed all the help they could get. The loss of her own brother taught her that.

Callius' deep voice interrupted her wandering thoughts. Did she just hear that? He had been bound in servitude. To whom? For what? She was startled at his admission and at once wanted to destroy the person responsible. *Possessive much?*

"My brothers and I were bound for five-hundred years to serve at Castle Blackthorne," he stated matter-of-factly.

"That is a long time for a, what are you exactly?" Rafe asked the question without subtlety.

"*Ha, ha!* It seems I have forgotten to mention that. I must be the first of my kind that you've seen hereabouts for quite some time," Callius turned his golden eyes to Fred and smiled, a heart-stopping grin that made her melt.

He returned his attention to Rafe. *Not a minute too soon.* She didn't want to make a fool out of herself in front of her Alpha by drooling all over the damned place. He seemed to be enjoying the mystery and grinned wickedly.

"Will no one hazard a guess?" he laughed and stood up from his chair. "I am a Dragon."

Silence followed Callius' revelation. Thirty long seconds of it before anyone spoke. The Wolves in the room looked at each other. Disbelief marring their features.

"A what?"

"A what?" Fred echoed her Alpha.

"A *Dragon.*"

"No way! How is it possible?" Seff, Rafe's second, spoke up only to get a look from his Alpha. Rafe nodded for Callius to continue.

"This room is not big enough for me to fully transform, but shall I show you a little?"

"Yes, please do," ever the diplomat Rafe smiled and lifted a hand in invitation.

Fred's heart thudded in her chest. Her eyes grew large as she watched Callius remove his shirt and stand in the center of the room.

Her eyes were riveted to a spot above his heart where a familiar looking rose was branded. Everyone seemed to hold their breath. Everything inside of her told her he was for real. But a Dragon? They only existed in fairytales. Didn't they?

Yeah, right, Winifred, just like Werewolves.

Callius stood and waited while Seff, closed the door. He nodded his approval. They would need complete and total privacy for this.

He was pleased his mate seemed to accept his statement as truth. He sensed her wonder and wanted to beat his chest with pride. It was a primitive feeling, but he relished it. His *diamond rose* was a treasure indeed.

It would be difficult for the others to believe him. Dragons were an exclusive bunch. Choosing to step back from both the normal and supernatural worlds for ages at a time. The fact that no Dragon Clan had ever settled in the New World before now probably added to their doubt.

There's no time like the present, he thought, and turned his attention back to the task at hand. Transforming was a natural thing for Shifters, but it had been a long time since he *half-changed.*

He called upon his inner beast and felt his perception of the world suddenly intensify. Callius growled as he felt the air around him shimmer with familiar magic. Light and shadow played across his features.

The searing pain that was the half-change was gone but not quickly enough. He felt his mate's nerves heighten. He knew she could read his feelings and tried to shield her from the struggle between dragon and man. *Soon, it will be over soon, love.*

And it was. Within seconds. Callius faced the stunned room with even sharper vision than he had before. He zeroed in his mate. Every fiber of his being demanded he claim her and finish their bonding. It took more control than he thought he had to remain still.

The taste of her lingered on his lips and on his tongue. Honey and fire, the memory of his mate's kiss while in his half-change with all his heightened Dragon senses threatened his sanity. But it was not the time or place for him to stake his claim.

Instead, he focused on what his audience saw. Long, black horns protruded from either side of his head. They spiraled towards the heavens, close to three feet in length. They were as sharp as they looked.

He swished his long, black tail back and forth across the hardwood floor. It was over six feet long, heavily muscled, and lined with razor sharp spikes along the back. A low rumble reverberated from his chest. It took him a moment to stifle the sound.

Though he was in control of his beast, his Dragon objected to the small space and the scent of strange Werewolves in the room. Especially so close to his mate. His instinct was to destroy every male near her, to rip their flesh from their bones and roast them over with his own flames. His golden eyes glowed brilliantly in the dark room. *Es meus.*

Gleaming black and gold scales covered much of his torso, arms, legs, and face in a pattern much like the armor of a medieval knight. His teeth were longer and sharper too, though hidden behind his lips. His fingernails grew thicker and longer as well. Much like talons, obsidian in color and deadly in battle. Every inch of him was weaponized. *The perfect warrior.* As had been his role for centuries.

He felt an increase in energy flow through his semi-changed body. Power and strength coursed through his veins. *Fight. Defend. Challenge. Claim.* The voice of his Dragon pulsed through him, but Callius remained vigilant and in charge.

He flexed his enormous wings in the small room. They grew out of his spine and were an inky black color on the back. The inner membrane; however, was lined with veins of brilliant gold. Like living marble.

The Wolves in the room were drawn to them as he knew they would be. *Okay.* So, he was preening a bit, but he couldn't help it. The sound of his mate's increased heartbeat was tantalizing.

He caught her gaze and puffed a stream of white smoke out of his nostrils. He would not risk breathing fire in such a small space, but he could not resist a little show. *For his mate.*

The way her silver-gray eyes widened with amazement left Callius satisfied that he had made a favorable impression. The Wolves would see strength and know he was more than capable of defending their Packmate. But he had no wish to threaten them and kept himself calm.

He was a FireDragon. Feared and coveted throughout the ages. Loyal and honest. He'd been without a home for too long. But no longer. He found his *diamond rose* and he meant to stay. Callius felt Winifred's eyes on him and read the amazement in them.

Just you wait, my love.

He was menacingly beautiful. Unlike anything Winifred had ever seen. Power, energy, and raw, primal magic seemed too radiate from him.

Her heart began to pound. The room they stood in felt cramped. She felt exposed in front of their audience. Werewolves were good at reading emotions and she might as well be wearing a sign.

She wanted him. The strange, beautiful creature that stood before her. An intense attraction began in the pit of her stomach and spread throughout her body. She felt as if she was being pulled toward him, like they were connected somehow by some invisible rope or thread. She was hungry for him. Her heart thudded in her chest as her hands itched to trace his shimmering scales and exposed skin. She stepped forward without thinking. Callius seemed to watch her with curious eyes as she moved towards him.

Oblivious to their audience he turned and faced her. The heated look in his eyes melted whatever hurt had caused her to lock her heart in ice these last few months. Nothing mattered in that moment, just him.

The old building creaked aloud as the cold February wind blew outside. The sound stopped her in her tracks. *What was she doing? Was she nuts?* She looked over at the other Werewolves and noted a few raised eyebrows. She felt her blush and wanted to kick herself. Anger and embarrassment threatened to overcome her.

Callius flexed his wings. The movement was subtle, but it drew her Packmates' eyes away from her. Was that his intention? She knew it was, he must have sensed her anxiety. She inhaled and almost swooned when she caught his scent. *Cinnamon and Applewood.*

"*Mmmm,*" she meant to do that in her head, but the sound escaped her lips.

Rafe cleared his throat, his ice-blue eyes were wide as he took in the semi-changed Dragon. His Wolf Guard seemed too stunned to speak. They just stared. Fred couldn't blame them.

He looked like a warrior out of a fairytale. She wondered how impressive he'd be as his full Dragon! *Would he breathe fire? Could he fly with those wings?*

"Yes, to both your questions, love. I can in fact fly right now. And breathing fire is my specialty."

Fred licked her lips. She had excellent hearing as a Werewolf, but she couldn't read minds. His Dragon senses must be extremely heightened in that state. *Maybe Dragons were telepathic?* As soon as she thought it, he turned his head towards her and his golden eyes glowed.

"Yes. I can sometimes see into the minds of others. More so with you, love," he narrowed his eyes and tilted his head, *listening*, "I can hear your Wolf, Winifred. I can hear all of your Wolves. They seem trapped in a way my Dragon and I cannot comprehend?"

"Yes. It is our curse," Rafe spoke up, His voice tinged with sadness, "We remain separated from our Wolf-selves until the night of the full moon, but that is our concern. And we have someone working on that."

Callius tilted his head. Fred heard the guarded answer from Rafe and was sure he had picked up on it too. She stilled, her nerves getting the best of her.

"I assure you, Alpha, that I am your friend, you have nothing to fear from me or mine," Callius' voice was even deeper in his semi-changed state.

He was obviously the stronger here and now, but he did not exert his strength in any way. He was respectful. *And gentle.* As if he knew how much it meant to her to have her Alpha and her Pack so close.

It only illuminated his strength to see him so humble in front of her Pack. He demanded nothing. He did not press his advantage in any way. For that alone, Fred's heart melted in his favor just a tad more. *Damn, that was so hot!*

I can see your Wolf, my love, she is beautiful as you are now. Pure white fur with eyes as gray as a winter morning before a storm. She waits for you.

"Did you hear that? Is it true?"

"We didn't hear anything," Rafe answered, one black eyebrow raised in question. But she turned her attention to Callius.

"Callius? Can you really see her?" Her heart thundered in her chest. She could almost feel the warm communion between her soul and her other self, her Wolf, howling in her mind. A tear rolled down her cheek.

"Yes," he answered with one simple affirmation.

In the blink of an eye, he shifted back to his human form. He was every bit as delicious as before, but this time it was more than Fred's body that reacted to him. It was her heart.

"Sit down, please, Callius, let's talk," Rafe tapped the table. Fred stood where she was and tried to listen, but they were talking so low it was difficult.

After a brief discussion about territory and politics to which Callius made little demands, Fred gathered that he was welcome to stay in Maccon City. Relief coursed throughout her body. *Now, why was that?*

The men shook hands and Fred noticed a very strange smile on her Alpha's face. Who was he smiling at? Not her! In fact, he was avoiding making eye contact with her!

"You must come to the wedding," Callius spoke aloud as he stood with Rafe.

"Wait, what? What wedding?"

"Ours, of course!"

"But I just met you! I just met him!" Fred pointed at Callius while shaking her head. Did he just tell her Alpha they were getting hitched? *No way!*

"Love, you agreed. You made a bond with me, remember?" Callius' voice seemed to drop an octave and she watched horrified as he licked the middle finger of his right hand. She immediately felt heat rise to her cheeks. *He wouldn't!*

"Callius!" She wasn't sure if the others noticed, but if she were being honest, they probably did. *Ugh, Werewolves!* Her Alpha smiled and put on his coat as his Guard continued to flank him.

"Well, Callius, I tell you what, if Fred here says yes, then I would be honored to attend. My wife loves weddings, especially now, in her condition."

"Oh yeah! I heard about that! Congratulations, to both of you," Fred smiled at him and offered her heartfelt congratulations, momentarily forgetting her own impending nuptials.

"Thank you. I'll pass it on to Carlotta and, uh, I'll let her know she might need some formal maternity wear in the near future?"

"Oh yeah, I mean, no! I am not getting married!"

"My sweet Fred, our bond is made. Marriage is the next step,"

"Cal, may I make a small suggestion?" Rafe interrupted.

"Certainly," Callius answered though he never took his eyes off Fred.

"Get her to say 'yes' before making any wedding plans. And by the way, about that *castle* you're looking for, I believe you are closer than you think."

"That's right," Seff spoke up with a grin on his boyish face, "Wouldn't you agree, Ms. *Castillo*?"

"Your name is *Castillo*?" Callius grinned broadly at her.

"Really?! Why did you tell *him* that?" Fred screeched.

"Ha! I think you are correct, Rafe, I have found my *Castle*!"

CHAPTER

SEVEN

"Well, I think it's been an interesting night. I'll be off now," Fred shook her head when the giant Dragon Shifter followed her outside, "Where are *you* going?" Fred walked out of *The Thirsty Dog* slamming the back door behind her.

It was after three AM and she just surrendered more than half of her tips to Jordan! *And all because of this guy!* Was a little fooling around really worth it? *Ugh.* She wanted to kick herself when her little inner voice practically jumped up and down shouting, *duh, Fred, yes it was,* inside her head.

Apparently, Pack loyalty didn't extend as far as bartending! Jordan completely ratted her out to Mike! He told her boss that she abandoned him for the back room for half the night; therefore, she didn't really earn more than quarter of their tips.

If she were being completely honest, she was gone a lot longer. That is, if she counted her time alone with Callius. Heat rushed to her face as she thought of the way he had rocked her body into the best orgasm she had had in months within minutes of meeting him.

75

Oh, well. Who was she kidding anyway? That little rendezvous was totally worth losing all her tips for the next month! *Oooh la la.*

"You are my mate, Winifred, I go with you," his voice struck a chord inside of her whenever he spoke. As if her body was hearing things her ears were not.

Her Wolf stood on attention at just the sound of him. She could almost see her long pink tongue hanging out of her snowy lupine head waiting for a pat on the head! *Geez. Really?!*

Fred rolled her eyes and pulled her thin coat closer around her body. She usually didn't mind the cold. But February in New Jersey was bitterly cold, especially in her little seaside town. *Would it be hers much longer?*

"Great, I almost forgot, soon I won't have a home! And now I have you telling everyone we're mates and what am I supposed to do? Ugh!" She covered her eyes with her palms and breathed in deep.

The events of the last few days were catching up with her, exhaustion and hopelessness were rearing their ugly heads and she immediately felt guilty for snapping at Callius. *Oh Fred, what are you going to do?*

"I'm sorry, I just-"

"Hush now, sweet," strong arms pulled her into a loose embrace and Callius lifted her chin, so she looked up into his golden eyes as he spoke.

"What do you mean? Why will you lose your home?" The concern on Callius' face only added more to his already handsome features.

"My old landlord passed away and now his greedy son-of-a-bitch nephew is kicking me out!"

"Why would he do that? That seems the opposite of what a land-lord should do."

"He wants money, and, uh my *ex* kind of stole the money from our joint bank account and took off without paying the last couple of months' rent. And before you say anything, believe me, I know it was stupid!"

"Look at me, love, you are many things, but stupid isn't one of them. I am very sorry this happened to you. If it pleases you, I will gladly hunt the traitorous bastard down and roast him to ashes," Fred swore she heard a quiet sort of fury in his voice. It was kind of a turn on, even if a little bloodthirsty.

"That's alright, though I do appreciate the thought, he isn't worth it. The truth is I'm kind of relieved he is out of my life. It just cost me a little more than I thought it would.," she shrugged out of his arms and immediately felt the cold. *Suck it up, buttercup. Stand on your own two feet. As always.*

"Are you sure? Roasting him to char and ash is rather tempting," he fell in place beside her, smiling as another gust of wind blew. The chill didn't bother him in the least.

"I'm sure."

"Tell me, do you like this place? This home of yours?"

Fred stopped walking and thought about it, a small smile played at the corner of her mouth. He watched her as though he wanted to kiss her just there, but he didn't make any moves. She appreciated that. He didn't use her obvious attraction to him to pressure her. He listened to her. *Whoa. When's the last time a guy did that? Uh oh.*

"I mean, it's beautiful! There's really no place like it. The sand and the ocean are my backyard. It's the first place I ever really felt I belonged."

"What about the place you were born?" He moved a dirty cardboard box that blocked their path out of their way and gently steered her by the elbow around a pile of blackened snow and slush that sat on the ground.

His movements were careful and genuine. His eyes searched the dark street as if looking for danger. She recognized the reconnaissance, after all she was a Wolf. But she was never on the receiving end of such treatment. Fred felt her heart stir at the idea of him caring for her. *Keep talking, Fred, it's just the holiday that's making you whimsical.*

"Nah, after my parents passed away when I was very young, me and my brother wandered around. We lived in a little RV that we drove from town to town. When Jeff died, I was pretty much alone. This was the first place I found that I felt like I belonged."

"I am sorry for your loss, love."

"It's okay. I mean, not that it's okay, but I made peace with it. Jeff just couldn't deal with the depression anymore. Missing his Wolf was too hard on him," she felt tears burn her eyes, but she fought them. She stopped crying for Jeff a long time ago.

"Come here, my love, it's okay to mourn your brother."

"I know, I, uh, just, it's been a long time. I miss him still-"

"It's alright, Winifred, you can cry all you want, but you will not mourn alone," Callius pulled Fred into his arms and she sank into him. He made her feel safe, secure, *and loved*.

"Thank you, I'm okay now." She pulled away from him and shoved her hands in her pockets. Afraid she'd reach for him again. It was a weakness she couldn't afford, after all, what did she really know about him?

"So, what are your plans? I mean, I heard you what you told the guys in there, about being a prisoner and all."

"Ah yes, well, my one goal upon obtaining my freedom was to find my mate and Castle. I have found you. I like this place, this Maccon City, now I just need to find a Castle. How long have you lived here?"

"Uh, Callius about this whole mate thing, I mean how can you be sure?"

"Don't you feel it, here?" He tapped her chest above her heart, and she had to admit there was something there. Something warm and strong. It unnerved her. *Just keep talking.*

"Uh, I've been here about six years. The main house, where I live, is kinda run down. Most of it is closed off, but it has such potential. The property is huge, a realtor's dream, my old boss has been after me for years to get my landlord to sell it. Looks like she'll get her wish now."

"Tell me more about it."

"Well, it's right on the beach. Private entrance and everything. It's on the end of a strip so there is a lot of privacy. You can hear that great, big Atlantic Ocean crash onto the shore every single night. It's amazing," her voice trembled as she realized this was probably one of the last nights she had there. Kaepernick was coming back Monday. *Wow.* It really did break her heart to leave.

Fred hated to think about it, but there was just no fixing this. Even if she had the rent money, Kaepernick wanted to sell. Callius placed warm hands on her neck and kneaded the muscles there. Fred exhaled and leaned into him. He was working magic with his fingers. *No, no, you need to stop this,* she thought to herself, but her traitorous body begged him to continue.

"I swear this is all us, not Dragon magic, Winifred. You are my destiny."

"What do you want from me, Callius? What could I possibly give you?" Her voice was a mere whisper, but she heard the childlike question it. *Am I worthy of love?* She hated that she revealed that much weakness to him. It was a Werewolf thing.

"Do you not know I would do anything, give anything, just to get to you? Now, I am asking you, Winifred, please take me home with you," his breath tickled her neck. She felt herself nodding in agreement, "Thank the Gods. Let's go, *now.*"

"Um, you know what? It's probably not a good idea," Fred felt herself softening towards him. *How could this be happening? She only met him hours ago!*

Her neck tingled and she reached up only to find herself touching the place where he marked her. It pulsed under her hand spreading warmth and something else throughout her body. *Was it love?*

"Winifred, I know you can feel my love for you. Dragons bond quickly when they are decided. My Dragon and I have decided on you. I am yours, as you are mine. *Mates.* For life."

"Callius, you don't know me, really. You have no idea who I am," Fred turned away from him.

What would he think if he knew she let her brother die? Whatever this intense attraction was between them he would never want someone who could do something like that.

"Then tell me who you are," Callius lifted her face by the chin with a gentle, yet firm finger.

"I have secrets, Callius, dark ones, you wouldn't understand."

"I am six hundred and thirty-eight years old, my sweet Fred, do you think I am free of secrets or sin? Come, let's go."

"I want to. Really, I do. I appreciate the whole *Dragon*-bonding thing. Werewolves do something similar. You seem really sincere, and I want to be honest with you," she bit her lip, this was harder than she thought, "I think things will look different to you in the daylight."

"*You are mine.*"

"I am not-"

"*Es meus.* I have given you the diamond rose. I cannot take it back."

"The ring? But you still have it! I didn't take it."

"No, the ring is only part of it. Come, we will discuss this in private."

Oh boy. Fred wished she could say that this macho display was so not her thing, but who was she kidding? She allowed him to steer her to a private corner of the street.

Her Wolf, though weeks away from speaking to her, seemed nearer ever since he walked in the door. *And boy,* was she taking notice! The Wolf inside of her would follow this Dragon anywhere. She felt it in her heart.

"Callius, look, I just want my bed."

"So, do I, Fred, so do I," Callius' eyes glowed with a heat that made Fred shiver.

The wind blew right through her, she turned and backed up a step only to collide with his broad chest. He wrapped his big arms around her and immediately she was warm. Fred couldn't help it, she leaned into him. Her ass settled right into his hips and she bit back a moan. They really were built for each other.

"Where is your car?" His breath tickled her ear.

"I don't have a car."

"How do you get places?"

"I usually walk or take a bus."

"*Hm.* I've been travelling for days. I don't think I can wait any longer. I apologize, I've had no time to see to things properly. Come here, love."

"Why?" Fred's body obeyed even as she asked the question. *Stupid legs!*

"Close your eyes and think of your residence," his speech pattern was odd at times. *Old fashioned, but sweet.*

The timbre and tone of his voice were almost hypnotic. She closed her eyes and did as he asked. She thought of her house and suddenly it was like he was there. Inside her mind.

"I see it. Now, hold on, love."

Fred opened her eyes just in time to see the air surrounding Callius' body shimmer. Instantly, she found herself wrapped around the muscular leg of a forty-foot-long black Dragon with golden scales on his chest and belly.

His long serpentine neck wound around till he faced her. Like something out of a fairytale, spiral horns protruded from his head, a long, forked tongue licked his scaly lips, huge nostrils puffed out a stream of smoke, Fred gasped. Then large, familiar golden eyes turned to stare at her and she felt calm again. She could hardly breathe. *He was incredible.*

Are you ready, love? Callius' voice echoed in her mind, a soft, warm whisper. Familiar and soothing. *She trusted him.* The acknowledgement made her dizzy, but still Fred nodded. She wrapped herself around one of his legs just as he flapped his wings. Suddenly, they were airborne.

Her whole body tensed as he took off. She expected to meet the frigid air head-on, but the heat from his body kept her warm. She felt the muscles in her arms and legs relax as he soared to extreme heights, hiding among the shadows and clouds. It was amazing! He was amazing!

Fred sat perched on his clawed foot. She ran her hands down the scales of his muscular leg. They were almond-shaped. Hard as metal, but smooth as glass. Iridescent in the subtle moonlight that passed through the scattered clouds as they flew over Maccon City. *Beautiful*, she thought again.

His scent seemed to multiply when he was in this form. *Applewood smoke and cinnamon spice.* There was a majestic beauty to him that struck her right in her heart. She wanted to lose herself to this man, this Dragon. *Was it possible? Was she really in love with him so quickly?*

She squealed with excitement as he did a spiral in the sky just above the ocean. She thought for sure she was going to get soaked when he reached one magnificent claw into the waves and brought up a spray of water, but he angled it so that she remained dry.

"Callius! That was amazing!"

Just you wait, his promise echoed in her mind and Fred felt her stomach tighten in anticipation. She hoped he was going to keep his promise.

Whatever the future had in store for them, she could give him tonight. The thought left her breathless.

CHAPTER

EIGHT

They arrived at her home in record time. She stepped onto the solid ground on wobbly feet. Fred knew she was grinning like a fool, but she didn't care. Her eyes widened with wonder as he stood before her, allowing her to look her fill.

"You're beautiful, Callius," Fred couldn't help herself. He was remarkable. Probably the most amazing thing she had ever seen.

She reached out a hand tentatively. She didn't know whether she should touch him or not. He lowered his head and winked at her with one golden eye. The small gesture her the courage she needed to reach out and touch him. She ran her fingertips over the large rectangular scales that protected his chest. His heartbeat was strong and steady beneath her palm.

He leaned his serpentine head down and licked her hand where it rested with a long, black tongue. She felt the pounding beneath his scales increase. Fred couldn't believe her eyes. A soft ethereal light began to glow under her palm.

It was bluish-gold and it travelled up her arm slowly. It pulsed once at the rose-like mark on her neck then continued to where her own heartbeat inside her. Heat and energy filled her. *Callius,* she felt

83

him inside of her. *Love. Mine.* Her Wolf howled inside her mind's eye. Fred staggered as an intense array of emotions flowed into her mind and body.

Something was happening to her, something strange and magical. She was awestruck. She opened her eyes, and the world was slightly askew. She was seeing through her Wolf eyes, even though the moon was weeks away!

She blinked and her gaze returned to normal. Callius stood before her, again as a man. *Still remarkable.* She felt his smoldering gaze reach her very soul.

"That was-" Fred couldn't find the words. Her mind raced with questions. *Was this love? Was this a matebond?* Whatever it was, it left her breathless. A second later and the dragon was gone, replaced by the man. He was just as striking in his black clothes, with his dark hair, and glowing golden eyes.

"*That was* what?" White smoke streamed from his mouth as he spoke to her.

"This is insane," chills raced up and down her spine as she tried to get control over her body, "I want you so badly. With every single piece of me, even my Wolf is howling in my mind closer than she's ever been without the full moon."

"I know, my Dragon senses her and calls out. He has found his mate in her. Just as I have found mine, in you."

"But it's so fast-"

"A lifetime can be lived in a single moment. I've lived for nigh on six centuries and I swear I've never felt alive until I met you."

"Callius, I-"

"I want to go inside with you, Winifred," he stepped closer to her, almost close enough to touch, but not quite, "I can feel your desire, my love. It's making me ache with need. Let me love you. Let me show you how it will be between the two of us. Will you make me wait much longer?"

"I want to. I really do, but I'm afraid."

"I swear on my life I would never harm a single hair on your beautiful head."

"No, not afraid that you'll hurt me, but, what if I'm not enough for you?"

"You are my everything, Winifred, my all. *Es meus. In aeternum.*"

Every nerve ending in her body stood on edge. She stepped closer to him, her body swaying with the movement. *Callius.* He reached a handout and brushed back a wisp of hair from her face.

The touch was light and so full of feeling it made her head spin. He exhaled slowly and his smoky scent floated into her nostrils. Fred willingly breathed him in. *Mmm. Applewood and cinnamon whiskey.*

"Can I have you?" He tugged her gently to him, allowing her to feel the heat of his body without being overly possessive.

He brushed her forehead with soft, warm lips. Fred closed her eyes and held her breath. Desire was one thing, but tenderness, well that was something else entirely. She answered his question before, but she felt he deserved to hear it again.

"*Yes, Callius, oh yes, you can have me.*"

"*Thank the Gods,*" he seemed to whisper to no one in particular.

He trailed kisses down her face until he finally reached her lips. Fred swore she felt the world itself turning. In and out, round and round, gravity and momentum all that held her in place. Her heart thudded in her chest as entire galaxies of feelings seemed to be created and destroyed in the seconds they were connected.

He was like the tide sweeping her away in this all-consuming wave of need and passion. *Callius.* His name played over and over again in her mind as she wound herself around him. Arms and legs and entwined, Fred held on to him and kissed him back with every-thing she had. She felt herself fall deeper and deeper under his spell with every stroke of his masterful tongue.

Nothing had ever felt so right. She reached up and held his face right where she wanted him. A small smile played at his lips then vanished while their kiss grew from sweet flirtation to intense desire. *Grrr. Mine.* Fred gasped for air as he broke their kiss.

"I hear your Wolf howling. She cries out for me to claim you, for our bond to be sealed, don't you hear her? Can't you feel how *right* this is?"

"It's so strange, Callius. I can hear her, in a muffled sort of way. The moon is too far though, I shouldn't be able to hear her at all."

"The *Curse of Natalis*, yes, I have heard of it."

"It's been so long. I am not sure there are any living Were-wolves who remember what it was like before he cursed us to live separately from our Wolves. Only to become one during the full moon."

"I am sorry, I cannot imagine being apart from my Dragon."

"Thank you, but it is not your fault."

"I cannot change the past, but I can promise to be here for you, Winifred, from now until the eternity," he trailed kisses down her throat and neck.

Fred trembled under his careful ministrations, and he was so very careful. He didn't rush or overwhelm her with his obvious skill. He was patient. Kissing and stroking, teasing her senses. He held her loosely as if he was waiting for her to wrap her mind around the idea that she was his.

My mate. My only. Together we are stronger, better. Mine. Fred's snow-white Wolf seemed to whisper in her mind. All the things she was feeling. Every doubt suddenly vanished under the strength of her emotions. The diamond rose on her neck tingled with each passing moment, as if it too felt their bond growing stronger with every passing second.

Fred knew that she should step back, calculate all the possibilities. *Wait, don't rush, you've been burned before.* But logic and reason had no place in her mind right then. She moaned as his lips found a sensitive spot just below her earlobe.

He kissed and licked and nibbled. Anticipating her every desire. It was like he knew her better than she knew herself. In a span of just a few hours. Fred's heart pounded. A sudden panic filled her.

He was doing things to her mind and body she was not ready for.

Maybe she would never be ready. Maybe she was meant to be alone. How could she trust herself after Josh?

Then she saw her Wolf in her mind's eyes. She was strong. She ran on instinct and faith. Fred's heart pounded as that fierce strength filled her. *I am here.*

"Did you do this? Why can I hear her?" Tears escaped Fred's eyes.

"My sweet Fred, it is the strength of our bond that brings you closer to her."

"I'm sorry I'm always emotional when I talk about my Wolf out of time with the Full Moon. It's hard on all Werewolves to be separated from their other selves, and I get that, but for me, well it's worse."

"How do you mean?"

"Um, well some find the separation too difficult to carry on with their lives."

"Hush. Don't speak like that. I will do everything I can to help you, Winifred."

"No, not me, but my brother," her thoughts momentarily turned dark, and Callius stopped kissing her immediately.

He turned her face up as he held her in his arms and traced a line from her temple to her chin. His gold eyes stared at her as if she were something precious to behold. Fred wondered if anyone had ever looked at her like that before.

"I am so sorry, my love. I can't imagine being separated from my Dragon even for an instant and the hurt that I would suffer if one of my brothers were slain, I cannot fathom. Your pain is understandable, but still, I would do anything to stop it."

"It's not something I enjoy discussing, but it's a fact of life for me and so many others."

"Then it is a fact that I vow to change."

Fred believed him. The depth of his sincerity and the verity of his vow touched her in a way she hadn't expected. A deep rumbling sound vibrated in his chest as he kissed her lips, sealing his promise.

Could he really be her mate? She wanted to believe it, she wanted to belong to someone. But what if he was wrong? What if he changed his mind?

"There is a rumor about a young girl, a Wolf, who's trying to break the curse. But it seems like a fairytale," Fred kept talking, trying to break the spell he was weaving with his kisses.

"Ah, you mean like Werewolves and Dragons," Callius smiled against her neck.

"I guess," she grinned.

"Well, *we* are very real, Winifred. *This* is very real. I am yours, completely, as you are mine."

One moment she was standing in his arms, the next he lifted her right off the ground. Fred gasped as he pressed her against his body. All her doubts vanished. All she could do was feel. *Hunger, desire, passion.*

Fred lived for so long with loneliness as her constant companion. Ever since her brother took his own life. She attempted to fill the gap with shallow relationships like the one she had with Josh, but who was she kidding? How could Josh ever *really* know her?

He couldn't. Not like this. The short hours she spent with Callius were more honest than the months she'd been with Josh. She saw that now.

"I need you, my love. Let us seal our bond completely," his whispered plea tickled the hair at the base of her neck.

Fred's head fell back as he kissed her throat. She didn't want to think, she only wanted to feel, but a decision needed to be made. Had she really let her own insecurities blind her to Josh's faults? *She didn't love him. She couldn't have.* Not when her heart was pounding the way it was inside of her chest while Callius' arms held her.

Sure, Josh took off. He made her feel insecure. Unsure if she could trust herself. He left her broke. *But not broken.* She was far from it. She felt alive for the first time in her life.

She looked at the face of the man, *the Dragon*, who wanted to claim her as his mate, *for always.*

"I need you too, Callius. Come with me."

Callius lifted his mate in his arms. She was lighter than he expected for a Werewolf. And so very beautiful. He'd never seen anything as hypnotizing as the silver in her eyes and the gold in her hair. She was precious as any horde of treasure he'd ever seen, more so. It sent a rush of fierce pride through Callius' veins.

Es meus.

He wanted to shout it across the universe. Five hundred years he waited to find her. His one true mate. She who was worthy of his diamond rose. Five centuries of imagining, picturing her. And yet she superseded all expectation.

She was breathtaking. Beautiful, smart, honest and fierce as only a Wolf could be. Everything he ever wanted and so much more. His arms tightened for a minute as he opened the front door to her home.

The house was a little worse for wear, but yes, he agreed it had potential. He smelled the salty sea air and smiled. He'd grown up with that smell. It had often been his solace. The street was private and secluded. There were no other houses for nigh on a mile or more.

Potential. The place definitely had potential. Tomorrow he would get a better look. He had something much more important to do at the moment.

His Dragon growled in his mind. He demanded Callius eradicate every trace of sadness he felt emanating from his mate just moments ago. He would not have her feel unhappy for all the world.

No, he would see her smile in ecstasy before this night was through. That was a promise. The thought of her spread out before him made his heart race. He could not wait another moment to delve into her sweet body.

Go slowly with her. Gently. He told himself harshly. She deserved every bit of restraint he could muster. He did not wish to frighten her in his ardor. He would worship her with his body this night.

"Which way?" he rumbled. His voice nearly unrecognizable in his desire.

He looked at her face. He was afraid he may have frightened her with his gravelly voice, but it would seem to have had the opposite effect. His Fred's eyes were heavy-lidded with desire as she pointed to a narrow staircase. He took the steps three at a time and opened the door to her bedroom with a bang.

What she called an apartment was no more than one large room. His eyes had no trouble finding the bed in the darkness and he headed straight for it with his sweet burden. He landed on top of the plush blankets with her neatly tucked underneath him.

"Now, I have been waiting to do this since I laid eyes on you," he licked a slow trail from her lips over her exposed skin to her navel. *Pepper and honey. So good.* He needed more.

His mate responded to his attentions with enthusiasm and more passion than he'd prepared for. Her moans of pleasure excited him. Callius wondered what other noises he could pull from her, and he intended to find out.

She gripped his head and tugged his lips down to hers jogging him from his musings. Her tongue was slick and wet with her desire, soft and warm like sinking into a hot spring. She sucked and nipped, licked and tangled with his, she held nothing back. Swirling around and around in the deep cavern of her mouth, Callius kissed his mate with everything he had.

Her silver eyes bore into his as their lips met again and again. *Beautiful. Captivating. And mine.* He growled and undulated his hips against hers, cursing the clothing that separated them. As if she read his mind, her nimble fingers began to unbutton his shirt.

He hissed out a breath as she skimmed her cool fingertips over his heated skin. He had little hair on his chest and belly. His skin was a golden bronze color, much darker than her milky white pigment. When she could no longer reach the buttons, Fred grabbed the material in both hands and ripped his shirt in two.

It'd been years, decades even, since Callius felt the softness of a woman beneath him. His jailer preferred to keep him hungry and isolated with no relief save a Dragon's long memory. Callius marveled as she continued her exploration of his body. Her clever hands made him burn with desire and every single one of those memories fled his mind. None of his encounters could compare to the stunning sight that was his mate aroused.

He licked the side of her throat and felt the pulse of her heartbeat there. It pleased him to feel it speed up under his careful ministrations. Callius' chest rumbled with pleasure. It was as if his heart and soul had finally become whole after living a half-life for eons.

He almost lost himself as Winifred dipped her hands further down to the waistband of his pants. *Not yet, my sweet.* No, it was his turn to touch, to explore. He needed to see her. He was desperate to feel, to taste every inch of her and, most of all, he needed to be inside of her. *Now.*

The hours since he marked her with his bite had ticked away slowly. The fact that he still hadn't consummated their vow was making him tremble with need. As they kissed and touched and rubbed Callius panted with the need to claim her.

He felt as though he would explode right then and there if he did not have her. His Dragon roared in his mind as he brought her to as frenzied a state of arousal as he was in. *Seal the bond. Es meus.* It was all but consuming him. His Dragon demanded he do it. *Now.*

"Winifred Castillo, I mean to make you mine, here and now," he growled in her ear.

"Yes." Her soft reply was all he needed.

The diamond rose. The most precious gift he had to give. It was hers. She was the one. His other half. His soulmate. His castle. *Mine.* Her bar uniform barely covered her, but it was still too much. He needed her, bare and beneath him.

"This, off, now," he nuzzled her stomach while his hands made short work of her top.

"Yes, please," Fred moaned and helped him free her breasts from her lacy, black bra.

Callius growled again as his eyes feasted on her bare skin. His cock hardened painfully in his tight leather pants. His eyes hardly knew where to look. His mate was gloriously nude, all full of peaks and valleys, miles of soft, smooth skin stretched out before him. And he meant to taste every inch. She was pale in the moonlight coming from the open window. She was stunning. Toned and tight, soft and round, in *all* the right places.

Her breasts were high and firm, topped with rosy nipples that pebbled under his tongue as he took first one then the other into his mouth. She groaned as he licked, sucked, and scraped each one gently with his teeth.

"Beautiful, *mi Castillo*," he growled and did what he'd been dying to since he first laid eyes on her. He reached up with his hands, his mouth never leaving her breasts, and took the ribbon out of her long blonde hair. He fanned it out behind her head while he continued to suckle her sweet body.

This was how he had pictured her, with her long platinum waves flowing around her beautifully flushed face as he claimed her. He stood up reluctantly, a smile teased his lips at her groan of disappointment. Silver eyes watched him as he undid the fastenings of his pants.

Callius slowly removed every inch of his clothing. He knew he was well-built, years as a warrior left every inch of his frame covered in muscle. Her eyes ate him up, she obviously approved of his physique for which he was ever grateful. He felt his cock jut out proudly under her intense stare, finally free of that blasted confining material.

He throbbed under her scrutiny and nearly came right as he watched her bite down on her plump bottom lip. *She shines like treasure.* Her eyes glowed a brilliant silver in the semi-darkness.

Callius groaned when she reached out with her long fingers and traced a long line slowly up his swollen cock. She stopped at the head, swirling her thumb over the sensitive tip before slowly making her way down again. She repeated the movement, increasing speed and pressure. Again, and again, until he was panting just to get some air.

She knelt on the bed and leaned forward, the slight creek in the mattress the only noise in the room. He froze in position, afraid to break the tentative contact. He watched the sway of her full breasts and throbbed in response.

And here he thought he'd have to seduce her into bed. She dipped her head down without any warning at all and took the tip of his shaft into her hot mouth.

"Winifred," Callius growled her name and threw his head back.

She teased him with her tongue. Sucking gently, then backing off, working him into a stupor. Her hand traced the rest of his length and ended at the very bottom of his manhood. He watched with wide, gold eyes.

His eyes taking in every gesture, every movement. She was a goddess on her knees. Her mouth a thing of magic, made just for him. She cupped him and he hissed. All the while, she continued to lick and suck, slowly building pressure as she took him more fully into her mouth. Callius needed to pace himself or it would all be over before he even started.

"No, let me, my mate," he gently lifted her head up, kissing her full on the mouth before easing her back down on the bed.

Callius exhaled the breath he'd been holding. Her eyes were heavy lidded with desire as she opened her legs wide for him. *His mate.* He purred deep in is throat as he spread her even farther and licked a trail from the exposed skin of stomach to her hard-tipped breasts and then back, to her sweet mouth.

He sucked her lip and bit down, swallowing her moan as she writhed beneath him. She tasted like honey and cayenne. His two favorite things. But, *damn it*, her pants were still on, and Callius needed them off. *Now.*

He flicked his tongue over the throbbing pulse on the side of her neck as his hands made quick work of her pants. He instinctively ground himself against the apex of her thighs, allowing her to feel his long, hard length against her.

Soon, yes, now. He spread her legs apart and ran his hands over her sex. She was hot and wet with need. He lay down on top of her and thrust his hips letting out a frustrated growl at the lace barrier that kept him from penetrating her sweet womanhood.

Callius hovered over his female and looked into her eyes as he grabbed the top of that pesky swatch of lace. He growled. At her nod, he tore the piece of lingerie in two.

"Finally, love. *Es meus,*" with one hard thrust Callius buried himself inside of her.

He growled as he pushed himself deeper. She was warm and ready, slick and tight. She seemed to cover his swollen length like a glove. As if she were created just for him.

He pulled nearly all the way out and pushed back in again, going all the way up to the hilt, reveling in the moan that escaped her lips. *Gods*, she was sweet, the shock of pleasure in her wide, silver eyes. Callius used one hand to anchor her hips and the other to pull her mouth closer to his. He needed to taste her, to complete the feeling of perfect completion as he drove into her.

It was like coming home. *Five-hundred years, he waited to feel this.* He lived in isolation, fear, and pain for too much of his life. Restless and listless. Without any place of his own. Now, finally, he was home, with her.

She rocked her hips into his thrusts with equal fervor. The perfect foil for him. No cowering miss, she met him every step of the way. He moved faster and harder with every grunt, and groan, and sigh. A hard, pounding rhythm that they both seemed to crave.

"Don't. Ever. Stop." The words seemed torn from her throat.

He wanted to mark every inch of her. To cover her in his scent. He felt his fingers bite into her flesh as he continued to pound into her. He intended to go slow, to be gentle, but he could not help himself. He plundered her body with an almost mindless need, blind to everything but the sensations shooting through his every nerve ending with each movement.

He growled as she bit her lip. Fred answered with a guttural moan and slapped her hands down on his hips. Her sharp nails dug into his skin, pulling him down harder and faster. She wrapped her long legs around his waist and thrust up, matching him every step of the way.

"Callius, oh, I think I love you, Callius," she screamed his name.

"Say it again."

"What?"

"Say it again, sweet Winifred," he stopped moving despite the need driving him to fill her with his seed.

"Oh, no, no, don't stop, please," she was mindless with need. She thrust forward, trying to coax him into continuing, but he remained still.

"Please, I'd hear you say it again, my love."

"Callius! I, I love you, Cal-li-us!" with each syllable he thrust into her, loving the tightening of her walls around him. She was slick and hot, and he needed her more than ever.

"Es meus! Sweet Winifred, my love, my life, my bond. Tell me you are mine!"

"I am yours!"

"Yes! Mine as I am yours."

Her breasts bounced up and down as he drove into her. The sweat of their bodies made her skin shiny and slick. Her eyes glowed in the darkness, silver to his gold. Callius ran his hand over her body from her neck to her hips as he thrust harder and harder.

He ran a hand over her neck and breasts, pinching her taut nipples and growling when he felt her tighten and quiver in response. The pleasure built up until he feared he could no longer contain himself. Her walls tightened around him and he felt his Dragon fangs descend, he tasted smoke on his breath and growled in anticipation.

Then he bit down on the same place he marked her earlier that night. Callius sucked on her neck as she screamed her completion and then, he let himself go. She arched against him. Her tight body wrapped around him as close as she could get.

He covered her in his smoky cinnamon scent as he gave her everything he had to give. *His full weight, his full sex, his full heart, everything.* He tossed his head back and roared her name as his body got caught in the most powerful release he ever experienced.

A spark of fire escaped his lips and he vowed in his native *Dracan* to love and treasure her. His true mate. His diamond rose. Far more precious than any treasure. His alone. *Es meus.*

"What does that mean?" she asked breathlessly.

"You are mine, *my diamond rose*, my mate, until the end of time," his voice was deep and gravelly as he pushed up on his elbows. He took her hand and placed it on his heart.

"And are you mine as well?"

"Of course. I am yours alone, Winifred Castillo. Until the end of all things."

Fred's eyes filled with tears as she felt a warmth spread beneath her palm. That same bluish-gold light from before shone beneath her hand and pulsed up her arm to her neck where he marked her.

When she lifted her hand Callius' grin grew even wider. Right there on his chest, where she had seen a mark earlier, was a rose just like hers. Only it was larger. A blue gold rose the size of her hand just above his heart.

TEN

Fred rose with the sound of the ocean crashing against the shore. It was like any other morning, only it wasn't. She turned her head to find herself staring into the golden eyes of the man who claimed her heart and soul only hours before.

"Good morning," he reached for her and kissed her softly on her lips.

She couldn't help her smile. Especially when she thought about where those lips had been only hours before. Her Callius was insatiable. *Mmm. Her Callius.* She liked that.

"What worries you so this morning, my sweet?"

"I was just thinking, this is like a fairytale. Not all fairytales have happy endings."

"Ah, yes, I see, but, my love, fairytales were created by normals to scare them into behaving a certain way. We are not bound by the false moral codes of normals, we make our own happy ever after. I am a Dragon, and you are a Wolf and together we are the first couple of the Falk Clan."

"The Falk Clan?"

"Yes. My brothers and I, and now you of course, are to have our own Clan. Here, in this place you have made your home."

"Is that why you told Rafe you intend to make a Castle here?"

"There are many layers to things we said. You, *mi Castillo*, are my Castle, my Mate. But yes, in the literal sense we need a place of our own."

Sadness threatened to surface its ugly head and Fred turned away to get her emotions under control. If only that lowlife ex of hers didn't steel her cash! They could have stayed right where they were.

Change was difficult for her. She didn't like the idea of having to leave the place she called home the last few years. But she'd be with Callius and that was definitely worth something. *My mate.*

"So, where were you thinking? I could access the database of my old job at the real estate office for you-"

"I've already found a place."

"Really? Where?" She was curious. He never mentioned that. Then again, they were too busy to talk last night. She felt her cheeks heat up and knew she was blushing. *Oh boy.*

"Here of course."

"But what do you mean? I told you, Mr. Kaepernick is kicking me out."

His eyes narrowed and Fred was shocked at the rage she saw in them. His scent grew strong, and he placed a possessive arm around over her stomach.

"No one is kicking my mate anywhere!"

"No! I just meant I had to leave because of Josh-"

"Do you like it here?"

"Uh, yes, of course."

"Do you want to stay?"

"Um, yes?"

"Then it is settled. We stay."

"But how-" she started to ask questions, but then he was hovering over her. He traced a path along her neck and tugged the sheet off her body, exposing her to his eyes. Every thought left her mind.

"Callius," she moaned as he began to touch her.

He seemed to know what she wanted before she knew herself. Anticipating her every desire with each tender caress. Fred had never experienced this kind of love.

And it was love. Of that, she had no doubts. She trusted in her Wolf's instincts and she loved the Dragon as Fred loved the man. She was bound to him, not just by the diamond rose, but inside her heart. Her soul recognized something in his. As if they were two halves, only now becoming whole.

This time their lovemaking was slow and careful. His eyes bore into hers the entire time. He never broke contact. Fred's heart ached with the tenderness he showed her. He was amazing. Wonderful. *And hers.*

"I love you," she whispered in his ear as he slowly pushed inside of her welcoming heat.

She felt tears sting her eyes as he lowered his head and kissed her lips. She'd never belonged. Never had anyone of her own. Not after her brother had taken his own life. It was new and frightening, but she wanted it, wanted him, so very much.

He brought her to heights she'd never experienced before. He rolled onto his side and brought her with him. Never losing contact, he used his hand to lift one of her legs up high on his waist. Then, his fingers found her as his long, hard length continued to pump in and out.

Fred saw stars explode behind her eyes as Callius threw his head back and groaned out her name. She barely felt the tears on her face before she heard him whispering to her. She felt his warm erection still inside of her as he kissed her on the eyelids and temple. *Soothingly. Lovingly.*

"Shhh, my love, do not cry. I could not bear it if I caused you any pain," his confusion made her smile.

"I'm not crying because you hurt me, I am crying because I believe you."

"You believe me?"

"Yes, when you say you and I are mates."

"I don't understand. Of course, you are my mate, Fred."

"I know!" She laughed through her tears and ran a hand along the side of his gorgeous face.

"I am still confused, my love."

"It's just, after Jeff took his own life, I felt guilty. Unworthy of love. You see, he had to watch me, raise me, really, and I guess I was too much for him. I was always getting into trouble. I never left him any time to be with his friends. I, I killed him," the last was a whisper and she turned her head. Unable to look at him. to see the disgust that would be there. She'd murdered her own brother. She didn't deserve Callius' love.

Strong fingers turned her head, and she was forced to look at Callius. His gold eyes glowed in the dim light of the chilly February morning.

"I am so very sorry for your loss. Death is a sad thing, it is true. But *you* are no more responsible for your brother's death than I am for my father's."

"What do you mean?"

"Didn't you wonder why I was held prisoner for five-hundred years?"

"Um, yes, but I figured it was some Dragon Shifter secret or something."

"I have no secrets from you," he eased off Winifred and pulled her close to his chest.

His strong arms wrapped around her in a tight embrace. She was sad to lose the connection they had when they made love, but clearly, they needed to talk. She listened to his heartbeat as he spoke. Her eyes half-closed as she concentrated on his words.

"First, I should tell you Dragons are immortal."

"You can't die?"

"No, we can die. We can be wounded and even killed in battle, but unless we choose death, we can live many, many lifetimes."

"Who would choose death?" Winifred felt his body stiffen as she asked her question.

She was curious. She never heard of Dragon Shifters before. This was all very new to her and she wanted to know more about the man she gave her heart to.

"My father."

"Oh, Callius, I am so sorry. You don't have to talk about it if you don't want to."

"I will have no secrets from you, my love," he exhaled and kissed the top of her head before continuing, "Dragons live by a code. *Service. Honor. Loyalty.* My father pledged himself and, therefore, all his kin to the Chief of the Blackthorne Clan after my mother was killed in an attack on our home."

"You see, back then, not all Dragons had Castles of their own. Some would choose to serve one chief in a grand castle while others, like my father, chose to live as normals do in small village."

"Was your mother a Dragon too?"

"No, of course not. All Dragons are males. We must mate with females of other kinds, though mostly mates are normals. I admit I am grateful for having a Werewolf as a mate is most fortuitous."

"Is it now?"

"Of course, you are, how should I put it, sturdier than most."

"Gee, thanks a lot!" She swatted playfully at him and he laughed and tickled her belly. When the laughter and kisses subsided, he continued.

"When the Chief to whom my father pledged his loyalty died in battle, the throne was handed to his son, and with him all pledges handed down as well," he hissed when he said the word son and Fred understood. She rubbed his chest in soothing circles until he settled down enough to continue his tale.

"Chief Dragomir is a tyrant. A dangerous one. Lazy, spoiled, and unjust. Shortly after becoming Chief, he brought several concubines to court. One in particular, was beyond the rest in beauty and value. He had one of his Dragons steal her after we'd won a battle for him."

"Steal her? Sexist pig!"

"Yes, well, that was not uncommon in that day. Spoils of war and all that. Anyway, *the Chief* does not fight himself. My father was a very mighty warrior. He taught me everything I know. He was the one who captured the maid for Dragomir, but he made a mistake. He fell in love with her. Our own mother's passing left him hollow, and he found solace in her."

"What were their names?"

"My father was called Castor and she was Igraine."

"What happened next?"

"They were discovered. Their affair made public. Dragomir was humiliated. He had her beheaded unbeknownst to my father who was out waging another war for him at the time. When he returned to discover her dead, he fell on his sword. Choosing death over life without love."

"That's terrible! But how did you and your brother's come into all this?"

"Dragomir is a vile, petty sort of man and a much worse Dragon. He was not appeased by the death of my father. Deprived of his ability to punish Castor, he decided that his kin should bear the weight of his wrath. So, my brothers and I were bound to serve him. Five-hundred years of servitude. We were not allowed many freedoms. I am glad it is over."

"I bet you are! But that's so unfair!" Fred sprung up in the bed, startling Callius into sitting up, "The jerk! The creep! How could he do that? That isn't justice!"

"Don't fret, love, it is done with. Please, sit," he smiled at her vehemence on his behalf and Fred felt foolish.

"No, please, do not be embarrassed. I am pleased you would fight for me, for I would surely kill for you."

"Callius, seriously though, I am so sorry for all that you've been through."

"It doesn't matter now. I've found you and nothing else matters. My brothers and I are free. Your Alpha has agreed to have us build on his territory. All is well."

"But you've been a prisoner for centuries? How do you plan to make a home? I mean, shouldn't you look for a job first, save up, you know, be practical?"

Fred hated to bring it up, but she was a realist. Even if she was a Werewolf in love with a Dragon. *Her Dragon. Mmm.* But where would they make a home? How would they pay rent? She was already broke. She had virtually no money and was about to be kicked out onto the street. It seemed impossible.

"Do you doubt my ability to take care of you?" He frowned and Fred rolled her yes. *Men!* She guessed Dragons were a lot like Wolves when it came to their egos.

"I am not insinuating that you can't take care of me, but I imagine the world has changed since you've been an active part of it. Money is king. I don't make much, but whatever I have is yours, Callius. I love you."

Fred felt the truth in her words down to her toes. Her Wolf was strong in her mind and she knew it was because of the intense bond they shared. He was her mate in every sense of the word and she'd give him anything she had. She wasn't afraid of hard work.

His silence worried her. His golden eyes were downcast, and she wondered if maybe she insulted him. then he looked up, a dazzling smile on his face. He walked over to where she sat perched on a chair next to the bed, unashamed of his nudity. He knelt at her feet and dropped a soft kiss on her lips.

"My sweet, Fred. I can't tell you how it warms my heart to know you are as fierce and loyal as you are beautiful. My mate, you would give me your all and I would offer you nothing less from myself. But I should tell you my brother's and I have amassed a small treasure trove over the years."

"Yes, but Callius," she began just as he laughed aloud and stood up in his full naked glory. Fred was rendered speechless for a moment.

"Come, let's dress and I shall show you the financial portfolio Nikolai, my brother, has provided me with to make my way hereabouts. Do you have WIFI?"

Fred followed him into the small corner of her apartment that was both the kitchen and the office space. She was a little stunned to hear him talk about WIFI and even more when he grabbed her laptop and expertly clicked away on the keys.

That was nothing compared to her face when she saw Callius' bank statements and stock portfolio. He was loaded. Like *rich* rich.

"Holy shit!"

"Will this suffice?"

Fred had never seen so many zeroes. Especially not any preceded by a dollar sign. He narrowed his eyes and crossed the space between them just as Fred's legs buckled.

"Winifred!"

They landed in a heap on the floor with Callius frantically whispering her name and caressing her face. She started giggling uncontrollably. He exhaled and kissed her head while she wrapped her arms around his neck.

"My love, you scared me. Are you okay?"

"Am I okay? Callius! You have more money in that account than I have ever seen!"

"Oh, that, well, Dragons do like their treasure, my love. But it is ours now, mine and yours."

"Oh Callius, I couldn't, I mean, that is *your money.*"

"Winifred, you are my true mate. I share everything with you. My heart, my mind, my body, my diamond rose, and of course, my treasure."

"You know the money doesn't really matter to me, right? I mean I would choose you if we had to live in a cardboard box."

"I know, my sweet Fred, that is part of the reason I chose you as well."

She smiled and sighed when he leaned down and kissed her. This time their lovemaking was slow. Fred exhaled as he caressed and worshipped her with his mouth and hands. She didn't mind the hardwood floor one bit. Not when he loomed over her with his big, warm body, and especially not when he pushed inside of her.

He touched more than just her body when they were like that. He touched her heart. *Her Dragon Valentine.*

EPILOGUE

Oone week after Valentine's Day at *The Thirsty Dog.*

"Are you certain you want it this way?"

"Yes."

"Alright then," Callius picked up a large piece of the nine layered, white-chocolate wedding cake with habanero-raspberry filling in his hand and mushed it right into the face of his beloved wife as he fed her a bite.

He grinned widely as his bride laughed and lovingly did the same to him. Callius licked the sweet and spicy confection from her cheek as the small crowd of friends and well-wishers that filled *The Thirsty Dog* applauded and toasted them.

"Is it everything you wished for?"

"Oh yes, Cal, I love it," Fred had never been so happy in her entire life. She wished her brother could be there but knew in her heart he was there in spirit. It warmed her that he would approve of her mate, *her husband now.*

"Shall we sit?"

"Um, you go on, I need to be excused."

"Oh, okay, I will be here."

"Okay, I'll be right back," Fred excused herself to the ladies' room.

She could hardly believe this was all real. Days ago, she was dumped, almost homeless, with no real prospects, but look at her now! Dressed in a marvelously expensive white dress made from the finest silk and lace, with a diamond on her finger. *Married.* To a Dragon!

She stared at her smiling face in the mirror and gasped. Was that really her? She was so happy it seemed to radiate from her skin. It was like a beautiful dream. She jumped a little when the restroom door opened.

"Congratulations, Fred!" Charley Maccon, Alpha female and Rafe's wife, entered the bathroom with one hand resting on her barely visible baby-bump.

"I am so happy for you two! So, a Dragon, huh?"

"Yes, thank you! He is a Dragon, did Rafe tell you everything?"

"Oh yeah! And I for one would love to see him, you know, Changed and all! So, ooh, excuse me, I have to pee," she ran into a stall and continued talking as Fred washed her hands in the sink, "So how did you know he was the one?"

"He's my mate and I'm his. That's all there is to it," she couldn't stop smiling, saying it aloud gave her a rush like none she had ever felt.

"I know how that is," Charley laughed and exited the stall. Her pretty, blue dress swirled around her legs when she walked. She smiled radiantly at the new bride as she dried her hands.

"I just wanted to say thank you for inviting us. I really love weddings! It's so important to celebrate the good things with every-thing else that is going on, you know what I mean?"

"Absolutely! And of course, you are invited, you are my Pack, thank you for coming," Fred smiled and hugged the shorter woman.

"Now that's enough, I swear I'm like a leaky faucet these days. You'll make me cry out my new mascara!"

"Oh, I know! Me too! I swear I never knew I could be so happy."

"That's married life, though there are downsides too. Not that I can think of any, ha! Anyway, Rafe told me Callius bought the place you were renting and is planning on fixing it up?"

"Oh yeah! You should have seen Barbie, you know the realtor, when he pulled an emerald the size of his fist out of his pocket to pay for the property. She almost died!"

"No way!"

"Oh yeah. Dragons really do love their treasure!"

"Wow! Well, I am so happy for you especially when I heard you'll be getting your degree and working at the Youth Center on a full-time basis once you have it!"

"Yes, it's my wedding gift from Callius."

"That's awesome! Ooops, excuse me, I have to *go again*, this little one is resting right on my bladder!"

"Oh, no worries! Thanks again, Charley!"

A few moments later.

A slow rock ballad played over the speakers as Callius spun his bride in circles on the small dance floor.

"Callius?"

"Yes?"

"You know, you have never actually told me you love me."

"No? Well, I've given you my diamond rose. It is my lifeblood, Winifred, my heart and soul, as it beats and breathes inside of me, it rests in you as well. Is that not enough?"

"Well, that's incredible, but still, I'd like the words."

"Very well then, Winifred Falk, *mea Castillo*, I love you."

"You do?"

"Yes, my sweet Fred, I love you from the silver gold strands of your hair to your blood painted toes. I love the way you moan when I touch you and the way you cling to me when we sleep at night. I love all of you. Your snow-white Wolf and your amazing heart. You are my diamond rose and I intend to love you and keep you, to treasure you, forever. *Es meus.*"

· · ·

 *he end.*

If you enjoyed The Dragon's Valentine, try the rest of the Falk Clan Tale Series here.

Go on and lose yourself in these dragon shifter romances, take the plunge, and escape into the Falk Clan Tales today.

Thank you for reading don't forget to spread the word by leaving a short review.

Did you know the Dire Wolf Mates series is getting a new look? It's true!

The Dire Wolf MC are parking their bikes for good on the outskirts of Blue Valley. Can these sexy prehistoric Shifters find their mates and settle down for good?

Begin the series with Shake That Sass. Now available in ebook and paperback.

DIRE WOLF
MATES
SHAKE THAT
Sass
USA TODAY BESTSELLING AUTHOR
C.D. GORRI

C. D. GORRI

THE DRAGON'S CHRISTMAS GIFT

A FALK CLAN TALE

BLURB

His heart is frozen. Can she change his mind about love?

Alexsander Falk is content to let his heart grow as cold as the ice he breathes in Dragon form. When his newlywed brother calls him home to Castle-sit during the holiday season, he reluctantly agrees. Unaware that he's to host a Christmas party for the local teen outreach program.

Noelle Gifford is the new owner-operator of Present Tastes. She's been contracted to cater the party at the newly remodeled home on Beach Drive, aptly named Castle Falk.

She is determined to be bright and cheerful for her client! But what's a girl to do with a Sexy Scrooge who refuses to listen to any of her ideas?

PROLOGUE

White clouds, heavy with unfallen snow, pressed in on Alexsander as he sped forward through the winter sky. He had one destination, a place he'd been avoiding ever since they were freed, *home.*

"Brother," Sander replayed the familiar voice of Callius in his head. His eldest brother had called to him through the telepathic link they shared just a few hours ago.

"Winifred and I must go away. We go to announce our dominion over these lands to the High Chiefs and, well, my bride requires a vacation. Besides brother, after months of building, Castle Falk is complete. Come home, Alexsander."

Without any hesitation, Alexsander took to the skies. The air was frigid at such heights, but the bitter wind bounced off his translucent white scales. His Dragon was fast and strong. He reveled in the speed with which he flew towards his new home.

Power pulsed through his veins as he raced towards the place his brother had built for the four of them. To think that the Falk brothers were now freed and had a home of their own was almost too much to wrap his mind around.

Years of abuse had almost killed any hope he'd had of ever seeing the day when he'd be free to live his own life. He'd never imagined they'd have a castle of their own too. *Leave it to Callius*, he thought. His brother had found both mate and home within hours of leaving the icy island that had been their prison.

Sander held out no such hope. He was destined to be alone. Seeing Callius settled with Fred only added to his pain. Despair and anger warred within him as he flapped his mighty wings against the cold air, gaining altitude.

Still, he continued his journey. Sander knew that he could not ignore his brother's request. It was his duty. He owed Callius that much. *For you brother, I will come home.*

Icicles formed on his snout as he broke records soaring through the skies, but he didn't mind it. He was an IceDragon after all.

Sander loved the cold. His unique coloring allowed him to hide in the blinding December sky. A useful tool, shielding him from the spying eyes of normals.

They travelled in enormous commercial airliners by the thousands during this time of year. It was the busiest of all seasons. *The holidays here again! Bah!*

He blew out a stream of crystalized ice from his nostrils as he pictured them, poor slobs, crammed together like sardines in great big tin cans. Normals were like pests.

They crowded and polluted the heavens that were once the domain of his kind alone. This time of year, it was almost unbearable! *Christmas*, he growled the word in his mind's eye.

The season had been celebrated by normals and supernaturals alike since before he was born! Whether it be the Winter Solstice or a virgin-birthed Messiah that caused you to hang your lights and wrap your gifts, winter was a time for celebration. Yet, he felt nothing of the kind.

Sander snarled in his mind's eye at the hypocrisy of it all. Greed was the motivation behind these so-called *holidays*. It was neither religion nor faith that brought normals to intrude on his rightful domain at such a frenzied pace.

No. It was self-gratification. Money was the bottom line. He who received the most, the newest, the biggest, and the baddest was deemed winner of the season.

Bah, he thought to himself again. What was it that fictitious misanthrope said, *ah yes! Bah humbug!* Sander couldn't agree more. If Dragon's could snort, his did as he pictured the famous anti-hero.

Distracted by that bit of whimsy Sander almost missed the huge jetliner that came hurtling forward through a dense cloud. The thing nearly took his right wing off. He growled ferociously but managed to veer left just in time.

When exactly did airplanes start taking off within seconds of each other, he wondered as he ducked to avoid yet another one of the damned contraptions. His knowledge of current events was somewhat limited. While Dragons in other Clans were growing with the modern world, enjoying the freedom to learn and observe normals, Alexsander had been kept behind stone walls.

A prisoner, held in servitude for a crime he didn't commit, along with his brothers, Callius, Edric, and Nikolai. Five-hundred years, they'd served and scraped to get by under the torturing claws of Chief Dragomir of the Blackthorne Clan. *The Bastard.*

Just thinking about his soft-bodied, cruelty-inclined captor made Sander want to throw his head back and let loose a roar loud enough to shake the heavens. *Do not got there, Sander. It is over.*

He was free now, and there was nothing more to rage against. The past was done. He could not change it. No good came from dwelling on what had once been. He should accept it and move on, but he couldn't no matter how hard he tried.

He'd been irrevocably changed. He'd always carry around physical proof of the horrors he'd endured. There was no escaping his past. *No future either for a half-handed Dragon.*

Sander had tried to make peace with that a long time ago. He knew his time on this Earth would soon be up. His heart was growing cold as the ice he breathed.

His inner GPS alerted him that he'd reached his destination. Pushing his morbid thoughts aside, he closed his great Dragon wings and caught the wind hurtling himself down towards the tiny speck of land that grew larger with each passing second.

He'd arrived at the place his brother called their home. *Castle Falk.*

He landed on the large runway Callius had installed on the roof. An empty helicopter sat there new and unused. *Probably so as not to draw attention*, he imagined.

He glanced around approving of the location. *Private, protected, easy access to the water, the air, and the forest.* He'd found the place without any problem.

He'd memorized the latitude and longitude before taking off from the deserted island where he'd spent the last few months swimming in the deep and trying hard to bury his past. *He should have stayed there*, he thought for the hundredth time since he'd set out. *Alone.*

He smirked as he looked at the towering structure his brother had conceived. It had all the beauty and intricacies of any castle of old, along with modern tech and convenience. Clearly, Callius had spared no expense.

Each brother had chipped in a quarter of the total costs. They could afford it. Dragons did love their treasure after all. Even captive Dragons were allowed some of their plunder and with access to the internet and stock markets, increasing their assets in the past twenty years had been easy enough.

Castle Falk. He started down the stairs to one of the secured entrances to the common living quarters. After placing his hand on the scanner and entering a passcode that only someone fluent in *Dracan*, the ancient language of Dragons, would understand, he entered.

His brother ensured that all four brothers spoke the language fluently, something modern Dragons did not undertake. He smirked at the memory of the tedious hours of study. Callius was a good brother, if a little serious at times.

He still couldn't believe it was true. His brother had succeeded in finding both mate and Castle in record time. It took a while, but it was finished.

A formidable presence on the Eastern seaboard. The Castle was made of the finest brick and mortar as far as Sander could tell. It was, indeed, grand. Enough private wings for all four brothers. Outfitted with the highest technological advances and comforts.

Shame filled him as he descended the stairs, he was the last to see the place. He should have at least honored his brother's efforts by showing up sooner. Truth be told, he didn't feel as if he belonged there. Not with his ruined hand and his cold heart. He had not wanted to see his brothers' worry.

There were no happy endings in store for him. He would die alone. *And soon.* Without a mate, his *sapphire rose* would turn to ice and his body would follow. That was his fate.

CHAPTER
ONE

Noelle Gifford parked her small, *new to her*, metallic teal SUV at the top of the long, winding driveway that led to *Castle Falk*. She'd loved the color of the surprisingly powerful machine and couldn't stop herself from signing the deal to purchase it on the stop.

She'd gone looking for a bigger car to help cart around her purchases from her daily market trips. Owning and operating a catering business meant she'd had to make a lot of changes in her life just lately. Upgrading from her tiny yellow smart car was just one of them.

Noelle had yet to regret a single change she'd made in her efforts to increase her business. The SUV was kind of a perk. It gave her confidence, especially when driving in the snow. *Okay Noelle, it's show time.*

She exhaled a long, nervous breath that came out as a long, white stream from her naturally pink lips. *You got this!* She thought to herself as the butterflies in her stomach went full on mosh-pit!

This job could mean the difference between having an exclusive catering business or providing school lunches forever. *Cringe!*

Not that anything was wrong with hormone-free cold cut sandwiches on white bread, *crusts cut off*, with sides like mandarin oranges and baby carrots. After all, that was where she'd gotten her start.

Providing wholesome lunches and snacks for a half dozen of the local preschools and another handful of the private schools in the area were all well and good, but the chef inside of Noelle longed to create foods for the more discerning palate!

She wanted to cater exclusive affairs! Events like engagement parties, bridal showers, weddings, christenings, conferences, holiday parties, fundraisers, that type of thing.

Noelle was a professional now! Sure, she'd begun her journey way back in high school by making brown bag lunches for the nursery school nearest her home.

She'd actually gone there as a child. In fact, her mother still worked there as an aid. She used to wake up at five in the morning to hand pack and then deliver the food every single day.

It began with a few requests from kids she babysat for, but soon others were asking about the homemade meals and treats. By senior year, she'd had more orders than she could fill all by herself and she'd had to hire some help.

Zoom in to present day, Noelle still shivered with excitement when she told someone she was the very proud owner and operator of her own catering business. It was early days yet for *Present Tastes*, but she vowed to work very hard to make it a success!

She'd listened patiently to all the naysayers who'd told her the food industry was cutthroat and didn't suffer fools. But in the end, she'd listened to her dreams and went ahead and invested the little money she'd saved.

It's now or never, she thought checking the time on the dashboard radio. Noelle squared her jaw and set about getting herself prepared for this meeting. She needed to come off as experienced, confident, and capable.

She took off her fuzzy, pink gloves and rubbed her cold hands together. She'd worked too hard to start her own company to blow it all now. She closed her eyes and hummed a Christmas carol to soothe her anxiety.

She'd always felt close to Christmas. *Probably because of my name,* she thought and smiled. Ever since she was a child she'd loved the holiday season. She even listened to Christmas music year round. It always calmed her nerves.

She checked the time again. *Early, as usual.* She looked at her reflection and ran her fingers through her straight-brown hair. Despite her efforts, the wispy strands that hung around her forehead and cheeks went right back to where they were only moments before. There was just no hope for it. She blew her bangs out of her face and sighed.

Noelle often cursed her pin-straight, baby-fine hair. She tried chopping it off once and cringed at the memory. She'd showed the stylist a picture of a model with a cute little pixie cut. To make a long story short, it was an epic failure.

She'd looked like one of those nerdy little kids from every 70s movie made. You know the ones with those awful, unforgiveable soup-bowl haircuts. *Yup.* That was Noelle for one entire summer. *Super sexy.*

She shook her head to stop her runaway thoughts and sighed. *Ugh.* This wasn't doing anything for her. She was still nervous. She hummed the carol louder and went to grab a breath mint from her purse.

She nearly hit the ceiling when her cell phone rang. Noelle fumbled with the zipper on the inside pocket in her purse before she found the blasted thing. She smiled when she looked at the caller ID. It was Joss, *her bestie.*

"Hey Noe, you're like fifteen minutes early, *chica!*"

"Hello Joselyn, I know I'm early! I'm just nervous."

"Yeah, but you don't wanna seem too eager. Just chill! Did you get any sleep last night or were you too busy making Christmas wishes?"

"Sleep? Me? You know better than that! I was too busy drawing up the final plans and making sure everything is perfect for today! You know how much this means to me, Joss," she did her best to sound exasperated. *Okay, maybe she did make a couple of Christmas wishes too. Joss didn't need to know everything.*

"I know. Look you worked so hard, Noe, and I know it'll be great. Just chill already, come on, deep breaths," Joss said.

"I've hummed three carols already-"

"Uh huh. And how is that working so far?"

"Not great, my hands are starting to sweat."

"Noelle, relax, you'll be fine. Now, tell me the truth, you did ask Santa to bring you your *Christmas wish* again this year, didn't you?"

Noelle rolled her eyes at the laughter coming from the other end of her cell. Joss was great, but she could be a terrible tease sometimes. Sometimes she was more like a big sister than a best friend, But Noelle loved her all the same.

She wasn't lying though. No matter how annoying her teasing was, Joss was accurate as ever. Noelle had visited Santa at the local mall last night. Just like she did every year. And, *yes*, she did wish for that same special someone that she asked for every single time. She'd been doing that since she was fifteen years old.

"Well, maybe he will bring me my wish one day, so there," she pouted as she said the words, feeling like the world's biggest baby.

"Yeah, or, maybe it's time you let someone besides yourself see you in those sexy little bra and panty sets you spend all your cash on! For real, girl, I am sensing serious sexual tension coming from you! Why don't you unbutton whatever it is you're wearing and let some cleavage spill out, and then, hike up that skirt a little and show some leg, and who knows, maybe your wish will come true," Joss said in sing-song voice.

Noelle rolled her eyes as her friend's booming laughter soon followed her verbal teasing. It was old news that her BFF was a phone psychic, but seriously, the woman did have amazing intuition. Noelle often wondered if maybe she truly was clairvoyant.

Maybe she was onto something here, Noelle quickly shook off the thought.

"Joss! Like, *ew*, a *married* couple live here! They want me to cook for them, not to see me in my undies, I'm sure!"

"Yeah, but I have a feeling, Noelle, in all seriousness, something big is about to happen to you. Be careful, okay?"

"Yeah, yeah. By the way, Joss, you are coming to the party, right?"

"Of course, I am! The *Macconwood-Nighthawk Teen Outreach Program* is an important addition to our community. I am proud to support them. Ooh, I'll call you later, my *other line* is ringing."

Noelle laughed as she hung up. Joss had quite the demanding clientele with her psychic hotline, but she was far from a fraud. She never gave out bad or fake advice. She was the most honest and trustworthy person that Noelle knew.

Ten minutes to go, she frowned. Why did time drag when it was something important? She shook her head and dialed Paul and Rick next. The two young men were *Present Tastes* most recent hires. The two newlyweds just finished getting their Culinary Arts and Hospitality degrees when they'd contacted her after she'd placed an advertisement in the local paper.

After inviting her to their home and cooking her a wonderful brunch, she hired them on the spot. When she started this venture as a teen, she'd been the only chef in the kitchen. But now, with her steady clientele growing and her expansion to event catering, she needed help.

It was one of the many things she'd agonized over in the beginning. Needing help in the kitchen and elsewhere was something of a problem for her since she liked to be in control, but she trusted Paul and Rick. Delegating wasn't exactly a strong point of hers, but she was learning.

"Hey, Rick? Yes, the vegetable market has the order. Great, thanks!"

Both of her new employees were efficient and dependable. They'd even found her some people to do the decorating required for this party. The three of them spent hours going over what was needed for this event and now, Noelle was there to make sure everything would go according to plan.

"Yes Rick, tell Paul I hear him," she laughed as he shouted reminders about the chaffing dishes they were going to use.

The two of them chatted loudly to her over the phone and she smiled. They were always finishing each other's sentences. Such a cute couple and completely devoted to each other. *Sigh.*

Noelle tried not to be, but she couldn't help it, she was just a little bit jealous. She hadn't had a date in a year. *Okay, never mind your love-life or lack thereof, it's go time.*

She got out of the car and shivered as a strong wind whipped right through her thin coat. *Brrr.* She smiled despite the cold and started walking to the large carved, mahogany door. Temperatures were in the low thirties, but she didn't mind. It was Christmas! *Her favorite holiday!*

She clutched her leather-bound tablet to her chest and readjusted her purse. *Here we go!* Noelle put on her best professional smile and rang the doorbell.

While she waited, she looked at the castle grounds. The place was certainly beautiful. From the cobblestone pathway to the various evergreens that stood guard along the front of the castle, it was like stepping into a fairytale.

She could see it now. Her decorating crew would be there shortly to hang thousands of fairy lights from every limb before nightfall! With the promise of a few flurries, it would be like a winter wonderland. *Perfect!*

She still couldn't wrap her mind around the fact that the owners had made the old beach house into a real-life castle! Four turrets, brick walls, and a mini-portcullis mail slot. She could just picture the postal worker raising the tiny chain to slip the mail inside! *So cool!*

Castle Falk was the last property on this stretch of beach in Maccon City. It sat right on the border of their little town and Macconwood, the property owned by Rafe Maccon.

Rafe, along with his sister, Cat, were descendants of the founding father of Maccon City, Eoghan Maccon. He was the governor or something a couple of hundred years ago when this part of the world was just settled by Europeans. Of course, Noelle knew that Rafe Maccon was more than that.

Rich and powerful, he was well known in the business world. He was also the Alpha Werewolf of the largest Pack in North America, the Macconwood Pack.

Noelle was aware of the supernatural community that lived and breathed among them because her father had been a Werewolf. He died when she was just five-years old and, though she didn't inherit his gift, she'd been raised with some knowledge of that world.

Rafe had taken over the Pack from his father who was something of a backwards tyrant from what she knew. The changes Rafe made since his ascension to Alpha were amazing. He even made sure her mother collected from a life insurance policy that the Pack had on all their members. It was a nice amount, but of course, it couldn't replace her dad.

Still, being able to pay off the mortgage and get their bills current was amazing. Her mother even invested some cash in *Present Tastes*.

This party was her big chance to show the elite of Maccon City what she could do! She exhaled and looked at her phone. She wasn't early for her appointment anymore, nope, now she was five minutes late! *Crap!*

She waited a few minutes before she rang the bell again. Noelle rubbed her damp palms on the back of her black leggings, nervousness was not a friend of hers! She'd been planning this event for months! She could do this! *Okay, Santa, for Christmas, just let this be a success!*

She wondered what could be taking Callius and Winifred so long? Surely, they were expecting her. She decided to risk looking desperate and rang the bell again.

TWO

Alexsander groaned in his sleep. *What the heck is that noise?* The shrill sound had him sitting up in bed and wiping the sleep from his eyes. *Fuck.* He'd only gone to bed a couple of hours ago. *No way.* He rolled over and buried his head under the fluffy warm pillow, willing that awful ringing noise to just go away.

Ah, finally. Just when his eyes closed, the blasted thing went off again! He sat up in a tangle of sheets and growled. Who dared disrupt his sleep? Seething, his Dragon close to the surface, Sander puffed out a cold breath that left tiny icicles hanging from the huge silver-edged mirror that hung in his room.

He threw off the heavy brocade blanket and leapt from his bead. He stormed off down the stairs that led from his sleeping quarters to the main part of the castle.

Whoever was ringing that absurdly loud bell was about to see what happened when you roused a sleeping Dragon. *Grrr.* After travelling all day yesterday, he felt a bit hungry after all. *Some fairytales got it right.*

What time was it anyway? His stomach growled, his head pounded, he was, all in all, a very cranky Dragon. After his flight, he'd stripped his clothes off, took a steaming hot shower, and fell onto the soft heather-gray bed that his new sister-in-law had picked out for his bedroom.

Just one more mark against him. *I am sorry Callius. If only I could give you more.* Shame swept over him as he recalled his thoughtlessness. He hadn't been interested in choosing furniture or color schemes for his decor. He'd given *Fred* full reign over his quarter of the castle. He still had a difficult time thinking of his brother's wife in terms of her preferred nickname, but *Fred* insisted.

He tried to shake off his shame at disrespecting his brother's efforts by showing their home the least possible amount of attentiveness. The only thing Sander had been interested in was having a workroom with natural lighting and enough wall space to hang his art. In fact, it was the first and only thing he checked when he got in last night.

He'd been pleasantly surprised to see the remarkable job Callius' wife had done. The muted grays and silvers complemented the tapestries he'd sent on ahead to *Castle Falk*. He smiled involuntarily. *If only he'd be around long enough to get used to the sound of their name on a castle,* he shook his head at the melancholic thought.

Sander rubbed a hand across his face. What was he doing anyway? *Maybe he could simply ignore the bell ringer and go back to his bed.* He turned and started back to his room when the interloper began pounding on the door.

Boom. Boom. BOOM! That was it. Clearly, this person couldn't take a hint! He'd just have to deal with it himself. *I wonder if Callius has any ketchup in the fridge.* He preferred the tangy condiment atop freshly charred meat most days. To prove the point his stomach growled.

He stalked down the hall and pulled open the front door. Sander was ready to tear into the fool who dared wake a Dragon from his bed, only to find the air stolen from his lungs! A pair of sparkling eyes the color of blue sapphires opened wide as the dainty waif who owned them took in his nude form from head to toe.

Snow was falling around her in huge, white flakes and the tiny thing shivered in the doorway. Beautiful was too mundane a word to describe her. Sander could hardly think of one appropriate for such loveliness.

The fairy gasped, her mouth opened and closed as if she wanted to speak, but words seemed to fail her as well. Sander knew he should do something, but he remained immobile. Stunned by the vision before him. He felt his Dragon surge and he stilled the beast with a command.

He should have dressed, he realized belatedly. He should say something. Anything. He shook his head to clear it of the fog that seemed to surround his brain. *Wait, why should I do anything?* This woman wasn't welcome. She was a trespasser. But that thought didn't stop shame from staining his cheeks pink, but still, he didn't move. He stood tall and proud and naked as the day he hatched.

"Well? What do you want?"

His voice was gravelly and stern. He barely recognized it. *Cruel of the Fates to bring this creature to his door when his heart was almost frozen through.* He narrowed his eyes in anger. The fairy continued to stare at him. Her soft bow of a mouth opened and closed several more times.

Sander's lips closed in a hard line. He couldn't help the turn of his thoughts when he looked at her pretty mouth. Full pink lips without any paint or glitter. Begging to be kissed. *Were they as soft as they seemed?*

He could certainly find better uses for them than to simply open and shut like a fish out of water. In fact, they'd look heavenly wrapped around his firm cock. A thought that made said member stand at attention. Unfamiliar heat flared inside of him and Sander hissed at the strength of it.

He preferred the cold. He was used to it. The flaming heat of his arousal was as unwelcomed as it was unfamiliar. This woman was dangerous. He held himself rigid and ignored the stirring that was awakening deep in his loins. Nudity didn't bother him. He was a

Dragon. Proud, regal, strong. He did not even blink as his body betrayed his interest.

The fairy; however, was most definitely embarrassed by it. *Normals and their hang-ups.* He'd have loved the opportunity to wipe her free of those silly notions, only one thing stopped him. He looked down at his mangled hand in disgust. He was not fit for fairies.

Just when he thought to close the door and pretend none of their strange meeting ever happened, the vision spoke. Her voice was stronger than he imagined it would be. Clear and businesslike, it still sounded sweet as honey to his ears. *Bloody hell.*

"Um, I'm sorry, that is, I beg your pardon, but can I come in? I'm freezing out here, and Mr. Falk is expecting me," she met his eyes as she spoke.

"It's normally cold in winter, and I'm sorry to say I am not expecting you."

"I said Mr. Falk was-"

"I am Mr. Falk."

"No, you're not Mr. Falk. I met him at the *castle-warming* a few months ago-"

Sander felt guilt flare up at the mention of the party. Callius and Fred had invited him, but he'd declined. As he had all of the invitations he'd received from them. In fact, he'd completely withdrawn from his brothers after they were freed. Unlike them, he had no hopes for the future.

"Look, even though I have no idea who you are, I doubt very much that Mr. and Mrs. Falk would approve of you answering the door in your birthday suit! Now, excuse me, I'll wait in here if you don't mind," she pushed past him, her pert little nose high in the air.

Sander grinned as she swept by, careful not to let an inch of her touch his nude frame. *Pity.* He hadn't wanted to come when his brother called, but maybe he should be grateful to him. Though he was resigned to his fate, he found himself intrigued by the woman. Even more so now that she proved she was no fairy, but more like a minx!

"Look, *miss*, I'm Alexsander Falk and you can't just barge into my house uninvited-"

"Oh, no! Are you one of the brothers? I'm so sorry, I'm Ms. Gifford," she held out her hand, and then withdrew it when her eyes wandered a little south. She blushed furiously but met his gaze head on. The minx was clearly fighting not to look down again.

"I'm sorry, but, you see, I was, *I am*, invited. Invited, hired and paid for," she thrust a piece of paper into his mangled hand, and Sander held himself still.

He waited for the usual disgust and judgement to mar her perfect features. When neither came, and the hand that held out the paper remained firm, he lifted an eyebrow. She'd certainly seen the thing that made him more outcast to Dragons than being a prisoner had.

Still, she showed no signs of either pity or horror. She simply waited for him to take the parchment. He looked at it and after reading it briefly, he recognized it was a receipt of sorts.

"Now, my catering company, *Present Tastes*, was hired by Callius and Fred Falk to host their Christmas party. It's tonight."

"What? No! Absolutely not. Cancel it immediately!"

"I can't do that! They've already invited everyone! Besides it's for charity!"

"What the devil are you talking about? Have it when they come home."

"But I can't do that! Tonight, is Christmas Eve!"

"What do I care? Look, if it's money you want, I'll write you a check-"

"*Ew!* Who are you? Scrooge's long-lost brother or something? No, you can't buy me off. The guests aren't just people from town with money, some of them are the actual kids who go to the *Macconwood-Nighthawk Teen Outreach Program*. Not to mention their counselors and the philanthropists who are funding the program. Some of these kids have nowhere else to go! Their families either can't afford to celebrate the holidays, or they don't even have families," she said, her voice growing angrier as she went on.

"And I care because?"

"Um, because you're a human being?"

"That's debatable. Now, please, *leave*," he hated his curt manner, but he had no choice. Sander simply hated Christmas and he found being around *her* almost painful. She made him *want*. A feeling he hadn't experienced in an age or more. It was most unwelcome.

"Well, I'm not leaving! You get Mr. Falk, *the nice one*, on the phone, please, and he'll tell you I belong here."

It was the way she said that last bit that made Sander narrow his eyes. It felt right somehow. *She belongs here. With me.* His Dragon perked up inside his mind's eye, and Sander had to fight to not let him out. He growled, but the minx simply folded her arms and raised an eyebrow.

"Seriously, dude, I've delivered lunch to preschoolers who have more attitude than that. Now, look, if you could go put on some clothes maybe we can talk about this like adults?"

Sander stood there. He alternately wanted to toss her out on her bum and to scoop her up and carry her to his room, caveman-style. He'd never felt such a warring inside of him. She infuriated him, intrigued him, heck, she even woke his beast! *The little minx!*

"Well? Get some clothes on and then get on the phone. *Shoo!*" She said and waved her tiny hands towards the hallway.

He had never been *shooed* before in his life! Sander didn't know whether to growl or laugh! One thing he did know for certain, was that she was losing the battle not to take-a-peek at his nudity.

The idea both aroused his curiosity and amused him. He turned his body a fraction of an inch so that he was standing directly in front of her own rather pleasing form and waited. *Aha! Success.* The small movement caused her gaze to drop, just for a second. *So, she is not all business after all!*

Sander grinned wickedly. He won that round. Her sparkling, blue eyes widened as she took in his size and girth. She gasped and closed her eyes just as he felt himself harden even more under her intense gaze.

Heat flashed through him for the second time since he'd laid eyes on her. What would it be like if she reached down with her soft feminine hands and wrapped them around his now fully erect cock? Sander hissed out a breath.

Shock made his own gaze widen. What started out as a bit of fun, left him practically crazed with desire for the dark-haired beauty. Her eyes wandered a little more boldly down his body, Sander felt them as if they were hands on his skin. He sucked in a breath, listening as her heart pounded inside her chest.

He frowned as his own heart sped up. He'd only been having a bit of sport, but he hadn't expected to feel this way. Desire and longing welled up inside of him.

The minx's cheeks turned a dusky shade of pink, and her blue eyes darted up to his. He was shocked by the heat he saw in them. She was bold and so incredibly beautiful.

Too much beauty and innocence for the likes of me. She deserved someone whole who could worship her. Someone capable of giving her his heart.

He turned away first, breaking contact. *Not all things are fair game.* His Dragon was a predator, and he recognized prey. This pert little human was off-limits.

That's the only reason your loins are stirring. She is prey, for the taking, but you will not indulge, he told himself sternly.

His heart was too deeply encased in ice to ever be free to love.

THREE

Noelle released the breath she was holding when he finally left the room. *Alexsander Falk.* She recalled Fred telling her about her three brothers-in-law. They were her husband's younger siblings.

She'd even met two of them at the castle warming. Edric and Nikolai, if she remembered their names correctly. Both had been huge and handsome, much like Callius, but none had taken her breath away like *him. Alexsander Falk.*

He must be the youngest. Anyway, the family resemblance was uncanny. The man was every bit as delicious looking as the rest of them, maybe even more so.

He was long and lean with rippling muscles and an awesome six-pack. His dark hair was cut short, but that didn't stop it from being lush and thick. His eyes stood out the most, they were gorgeous.

Their color was almost teal. *My favorite.* Every now and then they looked so light, she thought they were white. *Hypnotic.* They seemed to follow her every move with such intensity she trembled just thinking about it. It was as if he was recording her.

He was the most beautiful man she'd ever seen. His skin was pale as snow with thick ropes of muscle cording both his arms and legs. *And his ass. Ooh, la la.* She tried not to think about that, about *him.* She was there for work!

Still, Noelle had never seen a naked man before. Even in a flaccid state, he was something to behold. Not that he remained soft for long. She didn't think she'd ever forget the way he grew under her stare.

She gave herself a mental slap and wandered into the kitchen. She didn't exactly have a lot of time to prepare for the hundred or so guests that would be arriving later that night. She'd been in the castle before, but a quick recap would be just the thing to get her focused.

Her stomach rumbled, and she bit her lip. It was already late in the morning, and she hadn't eaten anything all day. *Hmm.* An idea took shape.

After running to her car and bringing in a few boxes of supplies, she took off her jacket and rolled up her sleeves. Her mama always said the way to a man's heart was through his stomach. Not that she was after his heart. Just his cooperation.

Anyway, maybe her host would be a little more amiable after some food. She hummed more Christmas carols as she dug through the cabinets of the pristine, restaurant quality kitchen. Imagine being able to cook in here all the time!

She'd love to have so much space and so many handy appliances for herself. Still, her mother also told her a good chef only needs a knife and some fire to whip up an incredible meal!

With that thought in her head she grabbed some food and got to work, murmuring the words to *Let it Snow* as she washed and chopped some veggies.

Noelle had always a had a knack for creating the perfect meal for people she'd just met. Her natural affinity for cooking somehow combined with her innate friendliness and before she knew it she was introducing someone to their next favorite meal!

She thought of the handsome man who'd left her breathless after barely ten minutes in his company and bit her lower lip. Something about him was almost wild, untamed, but she had an idea how to soothe his savage beast.

This was going to be a meal her host wouldn't soon forget!

Sander left the foyer as soon as he could without emasculating himself. What the fuck had just happened to him?

He frowned as he got into the shower. His reaction to the lusty little vixen was most inappropriate. He had already resigned himself to living out the rest of his life alone. As an unmated Dragon, he did not have much longer.

It had been centuries since the mere sight of a woman could reduce his mind to nothing but desire and need. In fact, he'd never felt anything quite like it. His entire body seemed to hum with energy at the thought of his little minx.

Easy, Sander. She was hired by his brother to do a job. That meant she was a guest to be protected and treated with respect. *Fuck.* Not that he would mistreat her. No, he was pretty sure she would like what he'd been thinking about doing to her delectable body. However, as a *guest*, he could not simply ravish her and then toss her out.

His mind totally comprehended this, but his randy body, not so much. The raging hard-on that plagued him the second he set eyes on her hadn't diminished in the slightest. Not even after he'd walked away from her. *Sexy little minx.*

Oh, crap. Sander had it bad. Well, he had only one recourse left. Since his cock wouldn't abate, he needed to give it his immediate attention. It wasn't that difficult to get in the right mindset. All he had to do was picture the blue-eyed vixen.

Her scent had wafted into his nostrils the second he opened the door. He inhaled and could practically taste it. It was as if her fragrance was imprinted in his mind. He wanted to rub himself all over her, mix their scents so all others would know she was his. *Mine. Es Meus.*

What the fuck was he thinking? Sander shook his head and

turned the water on the hottest setting. He rolled his shoulders. His mind a mess. One thing that knew exactly what it wanted was that damn piece of meat between his legs. His cock stood out long and hard. He groaned as he pictured that perfect little mouth wrapped tight around him.

Fuck! Sander was in serious trouble. He moved under the water and gasped aloud. His skin highly sensitized because of his ferocious desire. He felt naughty as hell, but still his right hand moved down his body.

He hadn't indulged in anything like this since he was a boy. How the hell was he going to get the woman out of his house when his body reacted this way? He closed his eyes and took himself firmly in hand.

Sander groaned as he began stroking himself. He pictured her soft, elegant hands holding him, working him, under the sweltering spray of the showerhead. *Yes.*

Would she be shy with him? Or would his little minx turn into a wild cat in the throes of passion? She was so fucking perfect. Her inky dark hair and milky white skin were the perfect setting for those gorgeous blue eyes and bow shaped mouth. He pictured her hair spread across his bed like silk as he moved over her, licking, sucking, tasting.

He groaned again, picturing her spread beneath him, pink lips calling his name as he took her to heights she never dreamed existed. Sander tightened his fist around his cock, he pumped harder, seeking oblivion no matter how brief. Finally, he groaned his completion.

Spent, but not satisfied, he exhaled. *Fuck.* He sagged against the wall. *Why do this? Why not just take her?* His eyes fell to his ruined hand.

Nay, he'd never know that female nor any other. Not under any circumstance. He was a broken thing. Damaged and unworthy.

Sander washed himself hurriedly and turned off the shower. His eyes fell to his reflection in the mirror as he towel-dried his otherwise unblemished body. *Damn her for making him want.*

He scowled and threw on a pair of jeans. He searched his drawers for a t-shirt. He'd brought nothing with him, but Callius had assured him he'd seen to his needs ahead of time.

Sure enough, his favorite brand of blue jeans, t-shirts, even his choice of boots lined the closets. He sniffed the black cotton shirt as he pulled it over his head. *Pre-washed too.*

A Dragon liked his comforts and who better to know that than his big brother? He stuck his feet into a pair of socks and was just pulling on his boots when the scent of food struck his nostrils. His stomach growled in response. When was the last time he ate?

Sander headed down the stairs to the kitchen two at a time. His stomach growled loudly when he found *her* with an apron tied around her trim waist. What a picture she made, bent over the oven, smiling softly to herself. She seemed genuinely pleased with whatever it was she'd made.

He could hardly contain himself. He wanted to rush to her side. Sniff the back of her neck, maybe give it a kiss or a lick too. *Mmm. Shit. No.* Her presence was proving something of a challenge to him.

His Dragon stirred beneath his skin. He looked down at his ruined hand, the one with two and a half fingers remaining, and he scowled. His eyes found her again. She was perfection and he, well, he was unworthy of her. He shook his head. *She is not for you.*

The Dragon inside of him roared, but Sander stilled the beast with a firm command. He had no hope of ever finding a mate. Ruined things did not mate in his world. No, and without a mate a Dragon's fire withered and died. He knew this, and he'd accepted it.

Besides, he was only feeling lust for this stranger. He might have given up on a mate, but he'd had sex before. Sander was no monk.

Granted, his sexual appetites were something he had infrequently indulged in over the years as was necessary. Perhaps it was simply time to sate his beast again? One more bang before he left this world. *But not with her,* he told himself firmly.

Warning bells sounded in his head. His Dragon seemed to scoff at his command. Sander had never liked being told what to do. Even by himself.

Rules were made to be broken, weren't they? And he'd always found it difficult to toe the line. He didn't need to look at his hand to remember how it got that way.

"You're cooking?" His question seemed inane as it was obvious she was doing just that.

"Oh! You scared me," she flushed prettily as she arranged pastries and cooked meats on a plate. A small smile played at the corner of her mouth as she handed the plate to him.

He expected her to be shy with her offerings. It wasn't the first time a woman tried to soothe his beast. But his little vixen was not bashful. Not here at any rate.

No, here she exuded confidence in a way she hadn't before. She stood tall and proud as she proceeded to hand him utensils and a napkin as well. Her inner joy at what she'd produced made her practically glow with pride. Sander took notice. If anything, it made her even more attractive to him.

"I thought I'd give you a preview of tonight. This round one is a mini ham and cheese quiche, this one is spinach and herb, these are hash brown bites filled with cheddar cheese, scallions, and bacon, here we have salmon croquettes, those are mini blueberry scones, and here we have savory turnovers stuffed with ground turkey sausage and sage leaves."

"You brought your own ingredients?"

"Some of them, *yes*. I had them in my car in that little cooler there, when I heard the shower turn on I figured you'd be awhile. The others, I admit, I took from the fridge. I hope that was okay?"

"Uh-" his stomach grumbled, and he knew it was more than okay. She smiled as if she understood his hunger and handed him a napkin.

If only he could tell her why his shower had taken so long. Would she blush prettily if he told her how he'd stroked himself to thoughts of making love with her?

Whoa! Back up. Where the hell did that word come from? Sander didn't do love. He liked to fuck, but love was not in his vocabulary. *She is not for you,* he told himself firmly. *And yet...*

"I said, how do you like your coffee?"

Her smile was infectious as she held a mug in one hand and a pot of the steaming brew in the other. She seemed to glow, a warm and brilliant light that came right from the center of her being.

That sweet smile called to him. It made him *want.* He was used to taking what he wanted. Dragons rarely asked permission. They simply took. *He could take her...*

No, he stopped his wandering thoughts. *Her joy is her own. Her smiles are not for me. She looks that way because she loves her craft.*

That he could understand. As a master of his craft, Alexsander often got caught up in his art. But still, he wondered if he looked that way when he was weaving. As if all the moments that came before had culminated to create that perfect instant when everything turned out just right. *Hmm. Probably not.* He'd lost the brightness that came with being unburdened many, many years ago.

"Um, I take it black, thank you," he answered.

He watched as she poured the strong, hot coffee into a thick mug and handed it to him. He sat awkwardly until she filled another plate and joined him. He approved. Sander liked a woman with a healthy appetite.

"I hope you don't mind, I haven't eaten today, and I thought it was better to chat on a full stomach," she smiled as she took a bite out of one of the pastries.

"Of course, you should join me, *you cooked,*" he said a little more gruffly than he meant to.

"Well, dig in," she said and took another bite.

Sander watched her chew and practically salivated at the small moan of pleasure she made when she swallowed. He noticed a small crumb right at the corner of her pretty pink mouth, and before he knew what he was doing, he reached out and brushed it away.

His hand lingered on her cheek. Smooth and soft to the touch. She was beautiful. *Perfect.*

Energy sizzled from the place where his skin traced hers. Neither of them moved for a moment. *You will ignore that little zap of electricity, this one is not for you.* Again, he heard his Dragon snort.

"You, uh, had a crumb," he mumbled. Still, no matter how much force he put into telling his Dragon to back down, he could see the great white beast moving underneath his skin.

His fingers lingered long after he should have moved away. Heat scorched his veins and thunder pounded in his ears. Sander couldn't turn his gaze from her as he heard the deep, rumbling roar in his mind's eye. His entire body felt electrified in that moment. He felt his eyes flash as he growled.

Es meus.

FOUR

"I can do the dishes," Noelle protested after they'd finished the rest of the food in silence. Sander ignored her and stood. He started loading the dishwasher with ease and confidence of a man who'd done it before.

"It's a fair division of duties. The food was well-cooked," he grumbled.

"You know, your speech is a little odd sometimes, like your brother's. Where are you guys from?"

"Oh, we're from the North. *Far North.*"

"That's what he said, but I was wondering, like *where-*"

"Now, I know you can cook," Sander cut her off before her questions became too personal. He wasn't about to announce that he was a Dragon shifter banished from his first home, the place that had been his prison on the Isle of Pain these last five hundred years.

"Yes, and I promise this party is going to be great! Everything is prepped-"

"I applaud your culinary skills, they are all fine and good, but I simply can't pretend to be host to 100 people I don't know for a holiday I don't believe in."

That announcement seemed to stop her dead in her tracks. And he thought nothing could dampen her natural enthusiasm and energy. *Good job, Sander. One afternoon with you and you've disillusioned the poor girl. You dolt.*

"You don't celebrate Christmas?" She looked like he just told her he kicked puppies, for Pete's sake!

"No, I don't," for some reason that was totally beyond him, Sander searched for an excuse. All he could come up with was a vague, "We aren't Christian."

"Well, even people who aren't Christians celebrate Christmas nowadays, you know, as a commercial holiday?" There it was. That positive outlook was back and in full force.

"Not me," he said and grew more uncomfortable by the second.

"Okay, I can try to accept that," she said.

"Well, gee, thank you for respecting my right to choose not to celebrate a Christian or commercial holiday," he murmured back.

"But you still need to let me throw this party."

"What? No!"

"Look, Alexsander, I'm not trying to convert you or anything, but I think everyone should celebrate Christmas."

"Why?"

"Well, it's a time for joy, kindness, and *love*."

"I thought it was about a baby born in a barn because no one would let his parents in their house."

"Okay, first off it was a *stable* and the inn was already full."

"Really? That sounds, *er*, nice, and how's it about *love*?" He couldn't keep the sarcasm out of his voice even if he tried. *Love, ha,* he didn't believe in such things anymore.

"Well, people are nicer this time of year. It's the Christmas magic, you see. They forget old grudges, get back in touch with past family members or friends, smile a little easier at strangers, hold doors open, believe a little bit more in things like happiness and love, you know, that *kind of thing*," Noelle looked down and bit her lip.

"I'm afraid I simply don't believe in any of it. I'm sorry, but there will be no party."

"Oh, yes there will."

Sander's eyebrows flew up an inch on his forehead at the tone she'd used. Did she just scold him? like a school teacher does to a wayward child?

Ooh. He could so picture her in a bun with a ruler in her hand. He'd never had a thing for roleplaying, but he could so imagine a teacher-student fantasy with his feisty little vixen. Dammit, there goes his cock again.

He needed to get her out of here. Fast.

"Excuse me?" His voice was deep and growly. For some reason it sent shivers up Noelle's spine.

"I said, there will most certainly be a party, Mr. Falk. Look, I believe in Christmas, whether you do or not is your choice, but I won't let all those people down because you are acting like a Scrooge. Whether you think so or not, you need this."

She sounded like a foolish kid, but she couldn't help it. It was her favorite holiday. Maybe the big man standing next to her could use a little kindness too. Something to banish the pain from behind his brilliant teal eyes. Those eyes that sometimes glowed like magic.

He must be a Werewolf, she thought to herself. Living in Maccon City, she was bound to know about the supernatural creatures who seemed to love this section of the Jersey shore. That and her own familial connection to the Macconwood Pack made it all the more likely that she'd recognize other supernaturals.

Still, she couldn't help but feel for the man, Especially, since he seemed to have no idea at all about the joy the season could bring.

Maybe he'd just had a hard time of it, as Wolf families often did? *The Curse and all.* But that was all in the past if she understood Fred correctly. Someone was changing things. The future looked brighter for all Werewolves.

Maybe he didn't know that yet? Noelle wasn't a therapist or

social worker, but she had buckets of empathy for the suffering of others. Seeing Alexsander's pain, hurt her for some reason.

"What did you just say?" He asked.

"I said there will be a party here. Don't you want some joy and love in your life?"

She tried to shake off the feelings that threatened to drown her. He was so big, so handsome, she'd never felt so instantly attracted to a man this way before, but more than that, she wanted to help him. To soothe his troubled soul. The same way she wanted to help the teenagers in the area who were alone this time of year. *Well, maybe not the same way...*

Still, she knew the Werewolf teens, those who used the services provided by the *Macconwood-Nighthawk Teen Outreach Program,* often had no family life to speak of. Holidays were lonely times for kids like that.

They needed something to show them that Christmas was about making family where you can, forging lasting friendships, and spreading joy and love. As a volunteer there, she'd thought this party was a wonderful idea.

She looked at her reluctant host and saw something behind the gruff exterior. *Maybe he was in need too? Maybe he could use a little Christmas in his life?* She almost thought she saw a longing there in his teal eyes. Something honest and hopeful, *then he opened his mouth.*

"So, are you proposing some sort of mad orgy in my house tomorrow night? Cause I could get behind that!"

"What? Oh, my-! You know, just when I thought I liked you!"

Sander laughed aloud at the shocked look on her face and even more so when she slapped his shoulder and laughed with him. It felt warm and welcoming, this comradery with a stranger, but what else could she do. Things were straying into the slightly uncomfortable.

"So, you like me? Uh, you know, I'm sorry, but I don't know your first name?"

"Oh my! Really? Geez, I'm sorry! It's Noelle. *Noelle Gifford.*"

"Ah, now it makes sense. Your love for this holiday, your name means-"

"*Christmas gift.* My birthday is tomorrow, so my parents thought it was appropriate! I have a cat named *Holly* and a fish named *Ninny-mungins.*"

"What?"

"Never mind. Look, Mr. Falk, I um. I know about you know, *your kind*-"

"Call me Sander, please, and I sincerely doubt you know anything about *my kind*," she was sitting so close to him he couldn't help himself, he leaned over and inhaled.

She smelled sweet and spicy like the ginger cookies his *Ama* used to make. He hardly remembered his mother anymore. She was fragmented in his mind, but those cookies, those he'd never forget. Thin slivers of almonds and flour mixed with butter and candied bits of ginger throughout. They were his favorite.

He looked at the woman in front of him and his mouth watered. He clenched and unclenched his fists. *Fool. You are maimed. Unfit. A monster.*

His bitterness burned inside of him and he missed nearly everything she'd said. He did catch the part about her employees coming over in less than an hour to set up.

CHAPTER

FIVE

"No, I'm sorry, but it's impossible."

"Mr. Falk-"

"Call me Sander."

"Okay, Sander then, please. It's Christmas, and these kids have nowhere else to go. Besides I have a signed contract."

"It was signed by my brother. Not me."

"But it's for this address!" Noelle couldn't believe her ears.

Just when she thought they were getting along! He'd even made a few jokes, and then, *bam, Mr. Wannabe-Grinch* was back in gear. *What happened to make him this way?*

"You have to go, I just want to be left alone," his anger seemed to come out of nowhere. *No, not anger exactly, more like frustration.*

"No," she narrowed her eyes at him.

"No?" His look of astonishment amused her further.

"You heard me, *no.*"

"I think maybe I heard you wrong," he glowered at her, but Noelle didn't back down.

"Nope, you heard me just fine. Excuse me," she turned her back

155

to him and jotted notes on her tablet before shooting off a message to her assistants.

She walked into the ballroom where the party was to be held ignoring the tall man who practically oozed energy as he stalked behind her.

She felt his teal eyes burning holes through her, and she wanted to tremble. Instead, she turned to face him. He glared some more. Noelle lifted an eyebrow and yawned, barely covering her mouth with her free hand. She turned her back to him again. Dismissing him, as it were.

She lifted the tablet again and sent off another message. They were going to need several small tables to fill the area so people could mingle and fill the space. Food brought people together and rather than serving from one central spot, having several small stations would create movement and encourage conversation.

It was going to be perfect!

Sander was reeling. The little vixen yawned at him! At what he knew was his most scathing glower. Where did she think she was going with this anyway? It was his house, dammit!

She turned her back to him and kept right along taking notes and sending messages. His sensitive ears heard the little whoosh noise every time she clicked send. Jealousy reared its ugly head as he wondered who it was she was messaging. A boyfriend perhaps? *Grrr. No fucking way. Es meus!*

Startled at the turn of his thoughts Sander closed his eyes and ran a hand over his face. *Who was this little ginger perfumed minx anyway? Why did he want her so damn badly?*

His Dragon growled in his mind's eye, and Sander stiffened. He needed to get more fully in control. He couldn't think straight with her so close to him. He walked over to a window and threw it open. He inhaled the fresh, cold air, allowing it to wash over him and soothe his beast.

She is not mine! He was destined to be alone. His heart safely locked away. His sapphire rose would never go to another. He would go *cold*. And he welcomed it.

There was a reason he was an IceDragon. The white lightning that shot from his mouth was colder and could burn faster than any flame, save his brother's.

He was an outcast in his world. Any hopes he had as a youth to find a mate was destroyed when Chief Dragomir cut his hand in half. He could still feel the searing pain of his torture during his enslavement. Fury flashed through his blood only to be replaced by the familiar emptiness of his current state.

The dull thud of his heartbeat was a constant companion. A reminder that he was still alive, though he had resigned himself to a solitary existence. One that was all too fleeting.

Ever since he opened the door that morning, he'd felt different somehow. A strange stirring in his blood. An awakening in his Dragon that he never thought to feel. The beast moved under his skin, prowling, hunting, as if he sensed something close by. Something the human side of Sander was fighting tooth and nail.

No. I am broken. Maimed. Not long for this world. But we could have pleasure with her, completion. She is ours. Mine. Es Meus. His dual natures warred within him. The sweet sound of her laughter rang in his ears, piercing the cold ice surrounding his heart. He wanted to roar his frustration.

This was far too dangerous. He could not allow himself to form an attachment to this woman. This gorgeous, sweet, and surprisingly tough as nails, woman. *She was not for him.*

He snorted aloud. He couldn't believe she was carrying on with her plans. Completely ignoring him! It was outrageous! Sander fumed.

"Excuse me, it's getting a bit drafty," she side-stepped him and closed the window.

"I said there will be no party here tonight!"

"No."

"No?"

"Oh, you heard me! You, big bully! The answer is *no*. I will cater this event, and it will rock, despite your Scroogey attitude! Now, excuse me, I need to make some calls," she grabbed her cell with slightly trembling hands.

Sander couldn't help the smile that curled his lip. So, she wasn't as unaffected by him as she seemed. *Good*. He'd hate to think he was losing his touch, but still, he felt ashamed.

All he had to offer her was an afternoon tryst. It was a pretty shitty thing to do to someone as bright and full of optimism as she.

No. He must resist temptation. She was not responsible for his acceptance of his fate. She was not the reason for any of it. *Fuck*. He had no right to drag her into his fucked-up world.

Sander needed to remain strong. It was best if she left the castle grounds and he simply forgot about her. Before he asked her to go, he'd best apologize for his rudeness.

"Noelle?"

He turned down the long hallway that led to yet another section of the castle he had yet to explore. The place was huge. He'd have to remember to tell Callius what a fine job he did of it. He almost called out her name again, when he heard her trembling voice.

"Yeah, I'm okay. No, he's, he's not that! Oh, Fred, I am so sorry to bug you! But why didn't you tell him I was coming? You forgot? Saying he was shocked is putting it mildly...No it's not that, he just hates the holidays...No, of course, he didn't come on to me...Oh, well, no I mean, Fred! Of course, he's attractive! He's freaking gorgeous! No, no he doesn't strike me as being the type of guy to, well, you know, be interested in someone like me... I don't know, but that's not the issue...I won't let those kids down. You got it... Okay, have a great trip. Bye."

His teeth ground together. He had no idea what he was about to do, but he couldn't just stand there. Sander caught up with Noelle in three long strides. Her eyes flashed up at him as he turned her to face him.

"Sorry, that was-"

"My nosy sister-in-law."

"Well, it was Fred, but-"

"Did she hire you to seduce me?"

"Seduce you? No! I'm a caterer! I mean, do I look like a seductress? I mean, how could you think that I-" She sputtered and looked down at herself shrugging as if to say, *not in a million years*, but Sander interrupted her reply.

"Because if she did, I have absolutely no objection."

For one instant, Sander stopped fighting the intense attraction he had to this woman the second he'd laid eyes on her. He pulled her flush against his hard body noting the flash of desire in her blue eyes.

All rational thought left his head. Every single reason he'd given himself for why he should refrain from touching her, was gone. Just. Like. That.

His body was being taken over. More beast than man, and he had only one master. *Noelle.*

The soft fullness of her womanly curves made him harden instantly. He didn't wait or pretend. No clever wordplay or shallow flirtations.

Why should he bother with all that trifle? He was Dragon. Dragon's took what they wanted. And he wanted her. *His Noelle.* He felt his teeth elongate and he bit down hard against them.

Not forever. I will not doom her to life with a malformed beast. No marking! I will borrow her, just for the now, he told himself firmly.

He could have *now*. But that was all. His teeth retracted, and he growled, pressing his lips firmly against hers.

Sander swallowed her moan, dipping his tongue into her sweet mouth and losing himself in the oblivion of pleasure that was her kiss. She tasted as good as she smelled, like ginger. A hot, spicy flavor that was almost enough to melt his resolve. *Es Meus.*

CHAPTER

SIX

Noelle wasn't sure if she was dreaming or not. She was a twenty-seven years old business owner with an agreeable disposition and she worked very hard.

Love was something she never thought she'd have. As for sex, well, she'd always been open to the idea, but let's face it, she was mousy. Not just her looks, but her personality as well.

She wasn't particularly tall. Her body had some padding, but it wasn't enough to be called curvy like her best friend, Joss. Her hair was brown, her skin pale, well, she had nice blue eyes. But nothing like the teal of Sander's eyes.

Sander who was owning her mouth like he'd die if he didn't have a taste of her. *Holy crap!* This was the most intense kiss of Noelle's life. She clung to his broad shoulders like some whimpering maiden in a fairytale, but damn it if, if she let go, she just might slide to the floor in a puddle of lust.

He growled against her lips, his tongue probing the inside of her mouth, sending shivers of desire through her body. Noelle almost groaned in frustration when he broke the kiss and started tugging on her top.

161

"I guess my panty and bra sets aren't a total waste of money after all," she murmured as he pulled her sweater over her head.

"What?" Sander's head cocked to the side as if he was trying to make sense of her words.

"Nothing," she wrapped her arms around his neck and brought his head back down to her. he was so tall, and incredibly sexy.

She kissed him without restraint. Noelle didn't know enough about sex to play coy games or sophisticated flirtations. She only knew she wanted him and hoped he wanted her enough to overlook any clumsiness. The thought of her red and white striped bikini briefs with her white lace demi bra gave her confidence.

Her hair might be flat, but Noelle had no such problem in the chest department. His growl of appreciation as his hands found her full breasts sent zaps of pleasure straight through her core.

No, no more thoughts or second-guessing. He was the only thing that existed in that moment. Chills shot through her body as he squeezed and tugged. Their kisses grew hotter and deeper with each passing second.

His big body seemed to swallow hers as he enveloped her with his warmth. His skilled lips and tongue were positively sinful as he stroked and tasted her slightly damp skin. She was putty in his arms.

Noelle had been kissed before, but never like this. Electric currents sparked from his fingertips as they circled the base of her spine, down over her hips, and around her full buttocks. He ground his hips against her soft belly and groaned into her mouth, a sound she echoed.

Her heart pounded in her chest like a freight train. Noelle's skin seemed to scream out for his touch, and when he did trace the fingertips of his right hand over her body, *oh*, sheer pleasure hummed through her from the center of her being to every nerve-ending.

He held her against him with his left hand, the one that was missing a few fingers. Not that she cared, he was perfect in her eyes.

It was the way he held her tight against him that gave her pause. As if he feared she would run away given the chance.

I'm not going anywhere, she thought. She chose this, chose to be there with him. *Yes*, she thought, *I am staying here with you.*

She reached up with her hands, forgetting all her clumsy shyness. She wrapped them firmly around his neck and pressed herself fully against his chest kissing him back with everything she had.

It was true, she didn't know anything about him. Only that he was probably a Werewolf and that she had never felt so alive as when he was kissing her. More than that, an overwhelming sense of rightness filled her. As if she belonged there, with him. *Yes.*

All her life she wished for a happily ever after. She'd thought she was blessed being born on Christmas Day, and yet she'd always felt so alone. *Till now.*

Sander made her feel alive. True, he had a sort of sadness about him. She didn't quite understand it. After all, how could someone so beautiful be sad? *Maybe if she kept kissing him, that look would vanish.*

Noelle ran her hands through his thick, wavy hair, down his muscled back and, finally to his perfectly formed ass. Before she knew it, she was the aggressor. Kissing and tasting, putting his hands where she wanted them and ignoring his flinch when she brushed against the left one. She held his wrist firm when he would have pulled away and opened her eyes.

"Maybe we should stop," his whisper was more grunt than words.

"No, Sander, I don't want to stop."

Noelle felt his hesitation. She took his left hand and brought it to her lips, never breaking eye contact. She kissed his fingertips and the scar where the rest of his fingers should be.

Then, she lifted it to her lace-covered breast. He hissed out a breath as Noelle's head sagged backwards. She sighed and fit herself more fully into his hand. Using his long fingers to caress her exposed flesh and, finally, after tugging one breast free, she held him tight against her, using his fingertips to tease her sensitive nipple. She groaned at the sensation.

"Noelle," he breathed her name, making it sound more like a wish than a statement, "Noelle," once more against her throat and she shuddered under his lips and tongue as he kissed his way from her neck to her mouth.

Before she knew it, they were both almost nude. Clothing littered the floor, hers and his both. He reached down and picked her up as if she weighed nothing. She swallowed his grunt of approval as she wrapped her legs around his waist and continued to kiss him.

When she opened her eyes again, they were in a bedroom decorated in soft grays. She leaned back as he placed her on the massive bed and loomed over her with his big body. His body tensed as he took her in with his eyes.

She appreciated his beauty in that moment. His muscular frame was perfection itself. Never having done this before, she exhaled as anxiety threatened to take over.

Before she had time to freak out, he kissed her. His lips travelled down her neck, exposing the soft side of her throat to his tongue and teeth. Next, he found the tops of her breasts. She nearly leapt out of her skin when his hot mouth closed over one lace covered nipple. She groaned out his name as he tugged on her tight little bud with his teeth. Her eyes flew open at the tide of pleasure and landed on the most beautiful piece of artwork she'd ever seen hanging on his wall.

"That's beautiful," she gasped, and he looked up to see what she was staring at.

A tapestry, she thought, but it was entirely unique. It glistened and glittered in the white light coming from the enormous window. It was a scene of a snow-covered field with huge, snow-frosted trees and a frozen creek running down the middle.

A perfect picture of winter beauty, *still and serene.* The one bit of color came from a single red cardinal that sat perched on a silvery branch. The only bit of warmth in that glittery gray world. Noelle loved it.

"Like it?"

"Oh, yes. Where did you *get* it? It's beautiful," she whispered.

"I made it."

"Really?"

"Yes. I weave tapestries, it's how I process my life's experiences, I guess. I just feel the desire in me to create and I must," he talked for a moment more about his art while she listened underneath him, clad in nothing but her panties and yet it seemed right. She realized these were things he'd never shared with anyone, and it warmed her.

"Well, you should never stop, it's so beautiful, Sander."

"Not as beautiful as you," he seemed to ask a question with his eyes, and she nodded.

He closed his eyes and touched his forehead to hers, then he gently and reverently relieved her of her underthings. All the while, he kissed and nipped her skin, leaving trails of fire in his wake.

Noelle wasn't uncomfortable with her body, but this was the first time she'd been entirely naked with someone else in the room as an adult. She sucked in air, but still she couldn't seem to breathe.

Her heart hammered in her chest. Sander's eyes seemed to glow as his mouth latched onto hers. Desperation, desire, and so much more burned into her soul from that single kiss.

Her body hummed, and she grasped his hair, his shoulders, the smooth lines of his back as pressed her down into the mattress. She was mindless with need.

Noelle bucked under his touch as he slid his hands up her legs to the insides of her thighs. He took a moment to caress the soft skin there before pressing her legs open. She sucked in a breath, his eyes delving into her as he reached up and touched her, where no man ever had. She gasped as he parted her lips, and pressed one long finger into the hot, wetness there.

"You are untouched," he looked shocked and pleased at the same time. Heat flared in his teal eyes.

"Does that bother you?" She was grateful for some reason that she'd saved herself for now, *for him.*

"Bother me? No, quite the opposite. Your first time is a gift, are you certain you want me? I'm *maimed*," he said the word as if he hated it.

"You mean your hand?" Noelle was angry. Not at him, but for him. At whoever made him feel less than what he was, *magnificent*.

"Aye. *Yes*. My burden."

"You listen to me, Sander Falk, that doesn't make one bit of difference to me. It doesn't change the man you are."

"You don't know me, Noelle."

"Look at me, I know it's fast, and it seems impossible, but I swear to you this feels more right than anything else in the world to me. *I know you, Sander*," and she believed her words.

He was her very own Christmas wish, finally coming true.

CHAPTER

SEVEN

Sander closed his eyes, testing the sincerity of her words. *Yes, she spoke the truth. She was more than willing to give herself to him.*

Him. Unworthy of her perfection. Disfigured beast destined to roam alone.

He sighed, the struggle not to give in to his doubts was great. *Es Meus.* He felt his Dragon vying for control. The great white beast demanded he claim her. *Es Meus,* the growl grew louder in his head.

"Noelle, if I, if we do this, I do not think I-"

"Shh, Sander, I want this, here and now, with you."

She flexed her hips against his hand and loved the way his eyes closed on his groan of pleasure. She reached down the length of his body boldly with warm, gentle hands.

He watched as she tugged his briefs down and used her foot to push the material all the way down. When he was bare to her, she gasped with eyes wide and bright. She bit her lower lip and ran her hands over the swell of his cock.

Sander hissed as she stroked him tentatively. She opened her legs wide and wrapped her feet around his calves pulling him closer. Her lips touched his chest and moved upwards, traveling until they met his. Her woman's warmth spread open and willing beneath him. All rational thought left his head.

The scent of her arousal wafted into his nostrils, the cinnamon and ginger spice seemed to roll off her in waves. Sander wondered if she'd taste of it. He bent his head and sucked on her lips, gentleness gave way to passion and soon they were both panting.

Her fingers found his chest. She traced the slightly raised, blue mark that sat there. Normals likened it to a tattoo. It was so much more, and it sat there in the shape of a rose, though small and closed, like a bud. Her hands caressed it, and to his shock, the thing stirred.

He watched her eyes widen, she felt it too! Sander knew if asked, he'd be forced to tell her the truth of it. He wasn't ready for that yet.

His Dragon roared in his head as he opened her legs wide and pushed his hardness into her soft, untried body. She gasped with the pain of her first time, and Sander swallowed it with his kiss. He hated having to hurt her.

"I am so sorry, love, but it will be better now," he kissed her softly and held her in his arms. Then he moved ever so slowly, so carefully, inside of her. He eased himself inside of her. Stretching her slowly to take all of him.

"That's it, *mi bellus*, open for me," he gasped and rocked his hips. She was so tight, his little minx, so slick and wet with her desire for him. The feel of her hot channel as it squeezed and stroked his shaft brought him to heights he'd only ever dreamt of.

She felt like heaven. Even his Dragon roared his pleasure inside his mind's eye, the beast demanded he mark her, claim her now. *Give her the sapphire rose. Es meus.*

"Sander!" An excited little scream left her lips, and he knew she was close, so close to fulfillment. Pride filled him as he held her tightly and pumped his hips. He thrusted in and out, seating himself balls dip into her hot core, reveling in the sweet, honest innocence that was all her.

She scraped her nails down his back and arched pushing her

breasts up. He licked one and the other, sucking on the tips, taking and giving pleasure as he never thought he could. But that was all he could think about, making her cum, giving her all he could to ensure her satisfaction. *Grrr. Es Meus,* the beast roared in his mind's eye.

Her body seemed to sing for him. She was so beautiful, so attuned to him, moving with him, not against, opening for his touch. As if she was created for him alone.

Sander lost himself to her scent, her touch, the warm, wet feel of her as she squeezed his shaft, milking him for all he was worth in the heat of her pleasure.

"Es Meus," he growled aloud at the same time she tensed and called his name. His body throbbed as he erupted inside of her. His teeth elongated, fangs sharp, but he stopped himself before he could bite down and mark her. *No.*

His Dragon roared in his mind's eye and though Sander's body was sated the frustration he felt was enormous. He had no right to claim the sweet little minx. She didn't know what he was.

Noelle moaned under him and looked up with her lovely blue eyes. That sweet expression was like an arrow to his chest. He felt himself harden again but removed himself from her body before she could react. He wrapped her up in the soft, heather-gray blanket and pulled her against him.

"I'm not cold," she said and took his face in her hands. She was sweet and soft and tired. Her blue eyes sparkled when she drew his face down and kissed him. Sander broke the kiss. Shame and anger welling inside of him.

"I, uh, I'm sorry, Noelle, I shouldn't have done that."

"What do you mean?"

"I shouldn't have seduced you-"

"You didn't. I mean, I wanted you, didn't you want me too?" Hurt and confusion marred her beautiful face, and Sander's guilt doubled.

"I didn't mean it like that. I wanted you, hell, I want you now, but I'm not what you think-" He frowned when she interrupted him with a giggle and a wide smile. That smile made his heart squeeze. *You are a cad, Sander Falk.*

"Oh, that! But I know what you are, Sander, it's okay really."

"What is it you think I am, little one?" He smiled and brushed a strand of hair away from her cheek. She couldn't possibly understand what he was. *Dragon. Broken. Maimed. Untouchable. Unable to mate.*

"A Werewolf," she gave him a knowing look, but Sander sat straight up in bed. He didn't know whether to laugh or be insulted. The little minx!

"It's okay, my father was a Werewolf. I know all about you-"

"Noelle-"

"It's okay. I know Rafe Maccon, the Alpha of the Macconwood Pack. And he knows I know about you guys-"

"Noelle! Stop-"

"But really, Sander, it's fine. I can keep your secret. You don't have to be afraid of that with me."

"Noelle, I'm not a Werewolf!"

"You're not?"

"No, you amazing little minx," he kissed her and laughed though his heart was surely breaking, "I'm something else."

"What else could you be?"

"I'm a Dragon."

Stunned silence was an expression he never truly understood till now. Noelle sat up, beautifully mussed and stared at him. Her eyes roamed over his body as she tried to come to grips with what he'd said.

"A Dragon?"

"An IceDragon to be exact."

"What does that mean?"

"Get dressed."

CHAPTER

EIGHT

Noelle stood on the rooftop of Castle Falk. It was Christmas Eve, her favorite time of year. She'd just given her virginity to a man that she fully believed she was in love with, even though she knew him for a total of about ninety minutes. Said man just confessed that he was a five-hundred and ten-year old Dragon. *An IceDragon to be exact.*

"Are you warm enough?" Sander called above the wind. Snowflakes were falling heavily from the white sky and Noelle nodded as she snuggled down deeper into her borrowed parka.

He closed his brilliant teal eyes, and Noelle felt her heart pound. *Holy crap.* It was like every Christmas wish she'd ever made *times ten* was about to come true. *Dragons? Real Dragons? Holy Christmas Wishes!*

She watched as the air that surrounded Alexsander seemed to hum and shimmer. Like a thousand little fairy lights switching on and off at incredible speed. *Magic.* She knew about things like Pack bonds, but the transformation from human to Wolf was an unpleasant one, or so she had been told. She could only imagine what it would mean to turn into a Dragon!

171

Those little fairy lights blurred around in a fury of movement and she gasped as, an instant later, no more than a blinking of an eye, there was a forty-foot long, white Dragon standing before her!

He was, in a word, *magnificent*. Three horns spiraled out of his large, long head. Large, oval nostrils stood out at the tip of his long snout. Smoke puffed through them as he breathed. Familiar teal eyes gazed out at her and Noelle shivered at the look of pure possession in them. *Did he just wink?*

He spun around on his perch and she took in his huge wings that came out of his back. They were large and powerful looking with something that resembled spikes along the top ridge. He also had a long, spiked tail that swirled to and fro behind him. *Like an excited puppy*. She giggled at the thought, certain her Dragon would not be amused by the comparison.

Sander's diamond shaped scales glittered under the bright sunlight making him hard to see among the clouds. In fact, if she turned her head a certain way he vanished right before her eyes! Like camouflage!

His chest was a bluish-white to her eyes, and she scanned every inch of him, unsure what it was she was looking for. He was so enormous and beautiful to her eyes. She stopped searching when she found the same rose-shaped tattoo that marked his skin when he was a man.

Not a tattoo exactly, it was something *more*. She felt drawn to the blue image. It was glowing, and the bud seemed larger, almost as if it was opening. Heat warmed the spot above her chest. The place mirrored the spot where Sander's tattoo sat. *Odd.*

Noelle took a step back. Her heart was pounding at a furious rate. Then he caught her with his eyes. She felt hypnotized by him, but she knew this was no trick. *Sander.*

Her first and only lover, and if she was being honest, her first *love*, was a Dragon. She stepped forward slowly, amazed at the majesty and the beauty of Sander's *IceDragon*.

"You're beautiful," magic and wonder filled her as she reached out with a trembling hand. He lowered his head. To her surprise, he wasn't cold. His scales were cool and hard, but beneath them, he felt very warm.

He snorted, and Noelle giggled as a spray of soft snowflakes floated over her. He moved suddenly, and she stepped back, loving the way he stood tall with his wings open and lifted his head to the sky.

The Dragon rumbled, and from his mouth, he shot out a line of what looked like white fire, like lightning. It was beautiful. Noelle clapped her hands and laughed out loud.

More snow fell, and she spun round and round like a child. She threw her head back and caught some snow on her tongue. A moment later, she was caught in his arms as he reached out to her. He was a man once more. *Her man*, and he held onto her before she could stumble. She was dizzy and breathless and yes, so very much in love with him.

"That was amazing, oh Sander! Best Christmas gift ever!" She felt his hesitation and pushed further into his arms. Whatever this man, this Dragon was, he was her destiny. She felt it.

"What does that mean?" His crooked smile was perfection, and Noelle reached up and kissed him.

"I forgot. You never had a Christmas gift."

"Okay, my guys arrive in a half-hour to start stringing the lights out front, the tree is coming fifteen minutes after that, and my two *sous chefs* will be here at three to start prepping the food. It's finger-foods, so nothing complicated. Then we have gifts for the kids. Oh, and I was wondering if you wanted that is, if you didn't have plans, maybe you'd like to have Christmas dinner with me and my family, no pressure-"

Noelle's mouth was moving a mile a minute, but she didn't care. After he'd shown her his Dragon, Sander had dragged her back to bed and made love to her again. To say it was fantastic would be a gross understatement.

They'd been lucky her employees ran late at the market, otherwise they'd have been caught in several compromising situations. They'd only just picked up the clothes they'd left strewn about.

She was so happy. She could hardly contain herself. She hummed Christmas carols as she started decorating and making notes for her staff. She almost didn't hear Sander call her name.

"Noelle? Noelle, look, I said you could throw the party here, but you should know. I'm leaving in the morning."

She stopped her preparations and turned to face him. The kitchen was crowded with cookie sheets and ingredients for canapes and hors d'oeuvres. She had all her "to-do" lists ready for her employees.

After a few dozen more kisses, she nearly lost it when he told her the time. He even helped her set up some indoor decorations in the ballroom for the night's festivities.

Christmas Eve was her favorite day during the holiday season. She loved the preparation and anticipation for the coming day. For years, she wished for something, someone, special to share it with and for the first time ever, she felt this was it. She didn't have to wait any longer.

It was really here. Her favorite day, and she was not sitting home with her mom waiting for a Christmas miracle. She was living one!

Looking at her like she was about to break was the man who, in one day, had stolen her heart. And now, he said he was leaving. *Her Christmas wish up in flames.* She dried her hands on her apron and turned to face him.

"Okay," she said.

"Noelle, I-"

"Let's not worry about tomorrow. Look, I hear a truck pulling in, please tell the guys to come inside to get their lists?"

"Okay. Noelle?"

"Yes?"

"I'm sorry," he sounded terribly sad, and it was all she could do not to tell him it was okay. She swallowed the tears that threatened to spill.

"If that's Paul and Rick just send them in here, okay? Thank you," Noelle kept working. What else could she do?

She closed her eyes as she listened to his receding footsteps. She knew she was foolish and naïve for building whatever this was, up in her head, but she could feel her heart breaking at the thought of him leaving. *Not when she'd just found him.*

Anger and confusion threatened to overpower her as she stepped into one of the several guest bathrooms. She took a look in the mirror and sighed as she bit back tears. She'd never been one to wallow or indulge in self-pity.

Her mother had been made a widow young in life, but she'd never been bitter. On the contrary, she'd shown Noelle nothing but love and contentment. One thing she'd always said to her daughter was that you had to go out and take you're shot at happiness when it came your way. *You only get one life, honey, so you better live it.*

She wiped her tears and took a good long look at herself. It was Christmas Eve. A time for miracles. Noelle was nothing if not a believer. And she believed with all her heart that she was in love with Sander. Her heart squeezed, and she hiccupped at the admission.

So, what? You love him. You love that big, scaly, sexy IceDragon. And this is what you are going to do, Noelle, you are gonna pull yourself together and show him that Christmas is a time for love and magic.

He may not believe in the things she did, but she knew how he felt. Even if he didn't. She wasn't giving up yet.

Hope warmed her from the inside out. She straightened her shoulders and headed out to the ballroom. She had an event to host!

TEN

"I can't believe you did all this in three hours!" Sander's exclamation rang throughout the whole of Castle Falk.

Several strangers wearing black shirts with the *Present Tastes* logo on the back looked at him with raised eyebrows. A few shrugged and simply continued to go about their work. Sander didn't mind. He was still taking it all in.

Boughs of holly and mistletoe covered the doorway, wrapped with red velvet bows and dozens of twinkle lights. The entire place smelled like cinnamon and pine trees. His Dragon growled at the reminder of Noelle's spicy fragrance.

His beast was not the only impatient one. Despite being taken aback by the holiday splendor she'd managed to create, Sander still longed for a glimpse of his little vixen. The time without her had dragged on almost unbearably. *Where is she anyway?*

He'd left his home earlier after trying several times to talk to her about the bomb he'd dropped. *I'm leaving in the morning.* What an idiot he'd been! He'd realized his mistake immediately, but Noelle had work to do and couldn't spare him a moment.

At first, he huffed and followed her, expecting her to give in.

When she showed no signs of relenting he found himself at a loss. He'd never experienced anything like it.

He was happy, frustrated, exalted, upset, forlorn and delighted all at once. He didn't know what to make of the jumble of emotions, so he did the only thing he could think of. He called his big brother.

"Sander? This is a surprise!"

"I need your help, Callius."

"Of course, what's wrong? Is it a battle-"

"No, no battle, brother, calm yourself. I, I met a woman-"

"Ah, the lovely Ms. Gifford, I take it. Well, that's wonderful man! What is the problem?"

"You know the problem, Cal! I'm maimed! No good for her. I had already accepted my solitude and impending death years ago, but now-"

"You love her, Alexsander."

"But I do not deserve her. I do not want to feel like this!"

"You know, Sander, the one thing I have learned since I've found my mate is that what we want and what we need are sometimes two very different things. Have you asked yourself what it is that she wants?"

"She wants me."

"Then why deny it. It is fate. Be happy, brother."

After that brief and unsatisfying call, Sander left the castle. He'd run out on Noelle, and on his feelings. Leaving her alone with her team to perform their jobs while he tried to sort out the jumbled mess of emotions he'd been dealing with since the second he looked into her striking blue eyes.

She was the most perfect woman he'd ever seen. And he didn't just mean the curve of her inner thigh as it led to heaven, the swell of her sumptuous breasts as they filled his mouth, or the spicy scent of ginger and cinnamon that seemed to ooze off her silky skin. *Fuck.* If he kept thinking like that he'd need to excuse find himself another cold shower.

It was more than her physical perfection that drew Sander to her. Noelle was the most giving and optimistic person he'd ever met. Like a ray of sunshine, her smile held promises for a future he'd never thought possible. She made him *want*. He craved her like a starving man craved food.

More than that, he wanted to make her happy, to see her pleasured until her limbs were useless, and her mind eased from worry. He wanted to keep her safe and protected, cherished and loved. Yes, *loved*. Fuck, when did that happen? When did Sander begin to think in those terms? It was more than this sad excuse for a Dragon had felt in a long time.

Shame washed over him again. He'd treated her too roughly. Had since the second he opened the door that morning, naked as the day he was born. He hadn't been able to control a single instance of their time together to his utter embarrassment. She'd turned him into a horny teenager again.

You are a fool, Sander. She is too good for the likes of you. Nothing more than a carnal beast at first glance. Driven by desire, he had taken her precious innocence.

Not that she'd complained or anything, but still. He had no right to her. That privilege was for the one meant to be her husband. Someone whole, pure, worthy of her.

His Dragon reared back and loosed a deafening roar inside of him at the very thought of another man's hands on his Noelle. *Rip. Break. Kill. Mine. Es Meus.*

Fuck. He was in trouble. Walking outside in the cold had done nothing to clear his head. But while he was out inspiration had hit him. Sander felt practically giddy with purpose.

He'd needed to do something for Noelle. After all, she'd given him so much of herself. *So selfless and gracious. Pure and innocent. Her emotions were like a beacon leading him home.*

Now that he was back inside of his home, he realized his paltry offering paled in comparison to the amazing job she'd done in his absence. She was no damsel or maiden waiting for a Dragon or Knight to save her. She was like nothing in any of the tales he'd read from his prison on the Isle of Pain.

Noelle was a woman, fully at home in the modern world. And

yet, she was pure and honest, warm and caring, like every dream of a mate he'd ever had. Before Dragomir had maimed him. Before he'd thought his world was over.

Sander exhaled and took slow steps into the place his brother had made their home. Warm and inviting, Castle Falk had never felt that way to Sander before. She was the reason. His heart swelled with the realization.

Noelle had turned his castle into a home just by being there. She'd taken one Christmas party and created a certifiable winter wonderland in the middle of the castle!

Sander's heart thudded inside of his chest. He felt a thrilling sort of pain right there, where his heart was beating so furiously. He recognized the fierce swell of pride as he looked around. He was proud, *of Noelle*, of her accomplishments. Proud, and something more.

ELEVEN

He shook the snow off his leather shoes and wandered the hall until he reached the ballroom. Piles of mouth-watering food were beautifully arranged on long silver trays. Mini quiches, croquettes, sliced fruit, a wide variety of cheeses and crackers, cocktail sausages, tiny little finger sandwiches, and so much more. His mouth watered, but he bypassed the trays looking for something else to satisfy him.

A crystal bowl full of sparkling cranberry punch sat on a cheerfully decorated table with dozens of little crystal glasses surrounding it. It looked tempting and sweet. Sander smiled as he automatically associated it with Noelle. She was sweet alright, and he longed to taste her again. There were smaller tables set with comfortable looking chairs surrounding a space that had been cleared for a dance floor.

Playing cards and board games were arranged on small shelves for easy access around the room, as well as ornament and cookie decorating stations. The teens from the outreach program were going to love it. She'd really thought of everything.

If he didn't know anything at all about Christmas, that room with all its beautiful décor was enough to get him and anyone else in the holiday spirit. Christmas music played softly in the background, and twinkle lights glittered everywhere. But what struck him from the second he came into the room was the enormous Christmas tree.

It sat opposite the marble fireplace that was glowing with soft flames. She'd used a single-color theme on the enormous fir tree, big and beautiful enough to rival any department store version. Dozens of white ornaments graced the branches. There were snowflakes, feathered birds, balls, sprigs of holly, presents, bows, and strings of silver and white beads with tiny crystal stars hanging from every limb.

His eyes stopped and went wide when they reached the top. He sucked in a breath. Sander couldn't look away. Atop the twelve-foot, blue spruce sat something he never imagined he'd see on a Christmas tree. His face broke out in a wide smile. *That little minx!*

He turned suddenly and looked for Noelle, but she was nowhere to be found. He went from room to room calling out her name, but she managed to evade him. *Some Dragon you are!* People began to arrive, a mix of adults and teens. The crowd grew thicker as did his frustration.

Thankfully employees from *Present Tastes* were there to greet them and take their coats, because Sander had no time for such niceties. He ignored them in his search. Where the devil was she? It was as if she'd simply disappeared!

He returned to the beautifully decorated tree and stood there. His eyes were riveted to the white Dragon who sat atop the boughs. He stuck his hands in the pockets of his black slacks and frowned.

He'd dressed up for the occasion. *For her.* It felt right and proper as he donned the expensive suit that was perfectly tailored to his body. He hoped Noelle would approve.

Sander growled deep in his throat as he thought of her. *Noelle, where are you?* One corner of his mouth lifted, and he shook his head. It was hopeless. He was a goner. She was incredible. *Sigh.* Only his little minx would put a Dragon on top of a Christmas tree!

"Do you like it?" A soft, familiar voice tickled his ear. Sander tensed then exhaled, relief making his shoulders drop as he turned to face her. *Thank the gods! She is still here.*

His eyes widened as he took in the sight before him. *Holy Shit!* For the second time that day, Sander's breath was stolen from him.

Noelle was wearing a blood red dress with long, sheer sleeves. The fabric clung tightly to her shapely curves and the bodice dipped slightly in front. Just enough to make him want to pull it all the way down to free those magnificent breasts of hers. His mouth went dry and his cock twitched as he took in every inch of her, devouring her with his eyes.

Her long, dark locks floated around her shoulders. Like a sheet of silk, one he wouldn't mind seeing spread across his bed. Her blue eyes sparkled like sapphires as he continued his thorough perusal. Noelle's lips were painted the same blood red color of her dress, the contrast against her ivory skin stark and stunning. *Beautiful.*

"I asked if you liked it?" She nodded her head towards the tree, but Sander couldn't look away from her.

"Yes," his voice came out deep and growly. He liked it alright. He'd never liked anything more.

"I had Paul run into town, there's a shop there with all sorts of treasures, I saw it there before and, well, after today it made me think of you."

"Noelle, I-" Sander took a step towards her, but she backed up. He frowned, disliking her retreat. He moved again, but before he could speak a short, dark whirlwind interrupted them.

"Hi, Noe! Kisses! So, who is this?" The woman with the dark, curly hair was obviously a friend of hers.

The stranger wore loud, vibrant colors over her curvaceous frame that oddly enough didn't clash with her dark olive skin tone and tightly curled hair. She had a certain charisma about her that was hard to ignore, though Sander would have preferred doing just that. However, ignoring the woman was not an option as she headed straight towards them and embraced Noelle.

"Joselyn! Hi! I am so glad you made it. This is Sander Falk. He's, um, Callius' brother. This is my friend, Joselyn."

"A pleasure to meet you, Joselyn," he said.

"Yeah, well, just so you know, you hurt her, you deal with me," the shorter woman glared at him, a warning flashing in her eyes. Sander inhaled as he took in the obvious threat. *Ah. A Witch in our midst.* He smiled and arched an eyebrow.

"I have no intention of hurting anyone, *augura* Joselyn," he added the common term for her kind in his language wondering if she'd notice. The sudden flare of her nostrils told him that she did. Her eyes darted to Noelle's puzzled ones and she forced a smile.

"Listen Noe, you sure you're okay?"

"Yes, Joss, sheesh. Will you please greet the guests while Sander and I talk a moment?"

"Yeah, sure," she walked away, but not before she returned Sander's smile with one of her own. Any other time, he'd enjoy the challenge, but not right then.

His heart was pounding, and his head was roaring. Every time he tried to speak to Noelle, they were interrupted by another guest. Patience was not one of his strong suits, especially not when he was so close.

"Noelle, may I have a moment?"

"Yeah, sure, just let me check on things. Okay, everyone seems okay."

They almost made it out of the room when a pleasant looking, brown-haired man with a wicked grin walked up to Sander with his hand outstretched. *Werewolf.* Sander wanted to roar, but he understood from his brother he was in Werewolf territory and needed to remain cordial.

"Hello! You must be another Falk brother? My name is Seff McAllister, I uh, work for Rafe Maccon. He wanted to tell you he was sorry he couldn't be here, new baby and all that. Anyway, thank you for hosting this event it means a lot to us. The *Macconwood-Nighthawk Teen Outreach Program* really appreciate the gesture. Ah, Noelle, darling, you look gorgeous," he leaned in and kissed her cheek and, that time, Sander did growl. The Werewolf looked up. The slightly amused grin on his affable face did not warm him to Sander in any way, shape or form.

"What a wonderful job you've done here! Your father would be proud."

"Thank you, that means a lot to me," she smiled at the Werewolf and it was all Sander could do not to shift and swallow the man whole! *Merry Christmas indeed!*

As if sensing he was on the menu, the Wolf said his goodbyes and moved through the crowd. Sander didn't stop watching him until he sided up to a woman with a mane of wild red hair and eyes that kept changing colors. *Another Witch.* The town seemed full of them!

"Oh my God, that's Seff McAllister, he's the Beta for the Macconwood Pack. He's taller than I expected, cuter too-" before she could finish her sentence Sander was dragging her into the hallway.

"Sander?!"

"Did you just call that dog cute?"

"Sander! Where are you dragging me?"

"I've been waiting to tell you this, Noelle. I know I lack the tact, but about what I said before," he pulled her up the staircase that led to his quarters and locked the door with a swipe of his hand.

"Sander, let's just-"

"Please, hear me out, love."

He turned her to face him and grasped both her hands in his. Nothing had ever been as important as that moment.

"Noelle, I'm a fool."

kaaayy. Not exactly the declaration of love she was looking for, but what did Noelle expect? Her Dragon was not the average guy. *Her Dragon. Yes. Mine.*

The flash of possessiveness caught her off guard. She knew it wasn't logical, okay, it wasn't even near the realm of logic, but she loved him. From the second she laid eyes on him, she'd lost all claim to her heart, her soul, *heck*, every single inch of her body. Sander was it for her. *The one.*

Sure, it hurt when he told her he was leaving in the morning. *Heck.* The quiet statement he'd made practically ripped her heart out of her chest. As it was, the wound still gaped open.

She'd wished for someone to love her entire life. Every birthday and Christmas wish, since it was the same day for her, was spent on the same thing. *Send me someone of my own, someone to love, who will love me back. A love like mom and dad had.*

Well, she'd found it alright. Only to lose it just as quickly. Her body trembled as he stepped nearer to her. She wasn't sure she could handle being this close and not touching him. Her fingers itched for his skin.

She'd never known desire or pleasure like she'd found in his arms. His beautiful, strong embrace that had taken her to heights she'd never dreamed about. She took a step back, knowing that if he came any closer nothing would stop her form throwing herself at him. *Be strong. Don't make a fool of yourself, Noelle.* But was it too late for that?

"I don't know if it's Christmas or if it's you," Sander said closing in on her, "but I swear on everything I am that what I am about to say I mean with every part of me."

"Sander, please, you don't have to do this."

"Yes, I do," he smiled at her, his eyes glowing teal in the dark room, he reached out with his good hand and took one of hers, holding it tightly in his warm grip.

"I love you, Noelle," she swayed as the word reached her ears, but he wasn't finished, "I truly do love you, and I need you, my sweet little minx. I want you, now, and always."

"Oh Sander!" She gasped and walked into his embrace, confused when he pulled back and looked into her eyes once more.

"I must know if you can love me, maimed hand and all?"

"Sander, how can you ask me that? Of course, I love you! You are perfect to me," she cradled his imperfect hand and kissed the digits there, holding it to her chest. She felt him tremble and her heart swelled even more.

"I have a question, love."

"What question?" Noelle gulped, tears brimming in her big, blue eyes.

"Can I have you?" His whispered plea was more growl than anything.

The words he uttered sent ripples of emotion through her frame. The question echoed in her ears and made her heart pound. Could this really be happening? She gasped and laughed as tears fell from her eyes.

"Can I have you? My little minx, please say yes," he begged.

Noelle could only respond in one way. She jumped into his arms and locked her mouth against his in a kiss that sizzled through them both.

"Noelle, I must have an answer," he groaned into her mouth. She hated breaking that kiss, but Sander trembled under her hands and she loved him for all his vulnerability. She reached down and ran her hand along the long, hard length of him moaning in anticipation as he grew under her searching fingers.

"Sander, you've got me. *I'm yours,*" she breathed the words into his mouth, her tongue swirling around his as her heart threatened to explode.

"I must mark you, love, now, *es meus,*" he growled against her lips.

Noelle could practically read his thoughts and her body practically begged to be marked by his. She panted and moaned as they rubbed against each other. She reached up and moved her hair to one side, pulling down the front of her dress to reveal the long lines of her throat and the ripe swell of her breast.

"Here, I will make you mine," his gravelly voice was deep. The vibrations sent waves of pleasure down her body to the slick heat between her thighs. She looked up at him.

His gorgeous face hovered just above hers, his beast shining through his eyes. They glowed an intense teal color as he growled and without warning, bit down on the soft flesh just above her right breast. Noelle groaned out loud. The sound echoing in the confines of his bedroom. It quickly turned into a sigh as the pain rapidly exceeded to white, hot pleasure.

In seconds, he had her skirt hiked up around her waist, his fingers gripping her hips. He tore the panties off her body with a harsh sound and found her wet and ready for him. Noelle moaned and flung open the buttons of his tailored shirt. She needed to touch his skin.

Her fingers skimmed over the smooth muscles there. Stopping at the *sapphire rose* on his chest. Under her fingers the marking hummed and vibrated, heat so strong it burned underneath her fingers. She bit her lip as she watched in wonder at the magic that caused his rose to open and bloom. Sander gasped with the pain of it.

"Ah, Noelle, yes, my mate, my true mate," he growled and flung his head back as the mark grew and sizzled on his perfect skin.

It was as if his heart had been frozen for the last five-hundred years and was thawing out all at once. Noelle bit back a moan as the place where he bit her began to grow warm and tingly.

"That's it, love, *es meus*," he growled and thrust inside of her.

She tensed as her pleasure came riding over her in great waves, rocking them both to ecstasy. He tensed and groaned his completion, pouring his seed into her welcoming heat.

"Es meus," he said at her ear.

THIRTEEN

When they were utterly spent, Sander lifted his mate and carried her to the bed righting her clothing as he did. He watched as Noelle's pleasure glazed eyes found his mating mark on her body. The identical, though smaller, marking on her chest was the same teal blue color.

She ran her hands over the delicate blue rose and sighed, "Oh Sander, it's beautiful."

"You are beautiful, my love. And I do love you, Noelle, you're my one true mate. My first Christmas gift. *My sapphire rose is yours.*"

"I love you too."

"I've another, more traditional gift for you, my Noelle," he helped her stand and straighten her dress, dropping soft kisses on her neck and lips. He reached in to his pocket and pulled out a velvet box.

"We're not like *normals*, you've been raised by Werewolves, and I'm a Dragon. I don't need to tell you that I've marked you, my love and that you're mine forever as I am yours. This symbol of our bond is for you. *Es meus,* we say in our language," he opened the box.

Inside was a beautiful ring. A platinum band that resembled rose vines. It opened into beautiful petals with a deep blue sapphire in the middle.

"Sander, it's beautiful."

"I want you forever, Noelle. This as with my marking, is a symbol that we are one, for eternity."

"I like the sound of that."

"I am a Dragon, darling, forever is a very long time for us."

"But I'm not a shifter?"

"True, but when I opened my gift to you and gave you my rose I also gave you access to some of my gifts, longevity is one of them."

"Really?"

"Yes. My Dragon has chosen you as well, Noelle, and he will not let you go any more than I will. I need you, sweet little minx."

He could not get enough of her. *This woman. His mate.* He took her beautiful face in his hands, ruined and whole alike, and kissed her with everything he had inside of him.

He still could not believe the miracle that he held in his arms. In the span of one magical Christmas Eve he'd gone from being alone and defeated to having everything. And she was his everything.

He'd spend every single day from then until eternity showing her just how much she meant to him. her blue eyes smiled at him as she held out her hand and took his maimed one in it. Together they walked down the stairs to their guests. An overwhelming sensation of contentment hit him. He tugged his mate to him and kissed her one more time before they joined the others.

Later that evening, surrounded by dozens of guests, Sander stood with his arm around his mate and looked up at the three-foot white dragon that sat curled on the top of *their* Christmas tree.

The inanimate beast was almost identical to his own Dragon, with three horns spiraling at the top and translucent white scales covering its skin. It even had thin membrane like white wings sprouting from its back. *Beautiful, like her.*

"You never told me if you liked your gift?" Noelle nodded at the tree and smiled up at him. She was breathtaking when she smiled.

Sander's gaze dropped to her lips and he pulled her to him gently. He growled as he leaned down and fixed his mouth over hers, kissing the breath out of her in front of everyone there. He ignored the giggles and wolf whistles, his every focus on his mate and her alone.

When he finished the sensual assault on her mouth he placed a finger under her chin and lifted until her eyes met his. She was so open and trusting, so in love with him it took his breath away, humbling him and completing him all at the same time.

"You are my true gift, Noelle Gifford. *I love you.*"

EPILOGUE

Christmas Day was a big day at the Gifford house. Sander looked skeptical as he pulled up to the two-story colonial that sat on a cul de sac off Broadway.

"Come on, Sander, they don't bite," Noelle teased as she unlocked her door.

Sander was out of the car and helping her from her seat before she had the chance to do so for herself. Not that she minded, he was such a gentleman with her.

Spending the night with him had been scandalous enough, but after a long phone call home and explaining to her mom that she'd found her true mate, her romantically inclined mother insisted she bring him over immediately.

Sander walked slowly beside her, stopping only to pick up the rare bottle of wine and the carefully wrapped tapestry, one of his own, that he'd brought as gifts for Mrs. Gifford.

"Hello Alexsander, I'm Crystal, Noelle's mother," the small, cheerful woman who'd opened the door had embraced Sander in a fierce hug and then Noelle.

He entered the small abode to the delightful smells of roast turkey and all the fixings. A handful of other people were there. An uncle, a cousin, and of course her friend, Joselyn.

"So, when are you going to make an honest woman of my friend there, *fly boy*?"

The entire room stilled, and Joss' words seemed to echo throughout the house. Noelle paled, and Sander wanted to growl at her obvious distress.

"Well, *augura*, how does Valentine's Day suit everyone here?"

Noelle's face broke out into a huge grin and her mother clasped a hand to her heart. His mate stood up and walked around the table only to jump in his lap and hug him tightly to her chest.

"Well done, *fly boy*, well done," Joselyn said.

"Are you sure?" Noelle whispered in his ear.

"I've never been surer of anything, my love. Happy Birthday and Merry Christmas, my darling little minx."

"Merry Christmas, Sander."

"*Es meus*," he murmured and took her lips with his.

She was his. Now. Forever. His first and best Christmas gift. His Noelle.

T*he end.*

Thank you for reading *The Dragon's Christmas Gift*! I hope you enjoyed it!

For more of The Falk Clan Tales CLICK HERE!

USA TODAY BESTSELLING AUTHOR

C.D. GORRI

THE DRAGON'S HEART

A FALK CLAN TALE

BLURB

Some wounds run deep, can a Dragon's heart be unbroken?

Edric Falk vowed long ago to never fall in love again. With two of his brother's having fallen into that trap, he's more determined than ever to remain alone.

When he's asked to be best man at his youngest brother's Valentine's Day wedding, the Dragon shifter has no choice. He is all set to go through the motions until he meets his partner for the event! Sparks fly, and this Dragon isn't sure he can control himself!

Joselyn Coracao is the maid-of-honor for her best friend's wedding. She also happens to be a clairvoyant Witch! When the universe sends her a message that she's about to meet her destiny, what else can she do but fight tooth and nail?

Edric and Joss both agree the Fates have messed up! They make a deal to put aside their differences for the sake of the wedding, but some things are beyond their control!

PROLOGUE

Edric Falk tossed his cell phone onto the glass-topped, wrought-iron, side table that sat next to his bed. The clinging sound rang through his head. It had been an exceedingly long drive in.

He'd been in upstate New York picking up the latest model, supercharged Range Rover that he'd purchased as a wedding gift for his new sister-in-law. The luxury SUV was the best in its class with all the perks and bonuses.

He'd had it custom painted in a metallic white with silver accents that was reminiscent of his brother's *IceDragon*. Tailor made teal colored leather seats graced the interior of the vehicle. It was gorgeous, not to mention safe and sturdy. Overall, he approved of the quality of the vehicle.

Sander was not his closest brother, but he was a favorite of the other three as he was the youngest. The baby, his mother had called him. He could still recall his sweet *Ama's* face the day she introduced them to the youngest Falk.

Sander was always a stubborn one, but now he was getting married to his one true mate. A Dragon could not hope for a more blissful state or, so he'd been told by both Sander and Callius, his oldest and closest brother.

The two of them mated. It was almost impossible for Edric to conceive of the notion. He stretched his muscles, stiff from the six-hour drive. He shook his head and sat down heavily. He wished he could have flown, but he didn't trust the car to anyone else. Besides, he wanted to test it in the wintry conditions they were experiencing this February in South Jersey.

The SUV handled well in the extreme weather. He was satisfied. He parked it in the garage and fastened an enormous bright teal colored bow on the top of it. Noelle would love it if what he knew about the woman was true. For Sander, he had only one gift, and that was a wish for him to be genuinely happy as Edric himself would never experience.

Fuck it, he exhaled. He wasn't going to sit around all day. After the long drive, he needed to expel some energy. Edric grabbed his sneakers and headed downstairs. He spent the next three hours punishing himself in the state-of-the-art gym and dojo that they'd built inside of Castle Falk.

He was a warrior, and although he'd tired of the fighting, he enjoyed the release he usually felt after a hard workout. He lifted weights, ran on the treadmill, free climbed the rock wall, and did deadlifts until he thought he couldn't stand anymore, but even after all that he still felt on edge.

He returned to his room and sat down hard on the edge of his bed. He peeled off his sneakers and tossed them in the small trash can. He'd ripped the damn things again. Thank the Gods he had a dozen more pairs in his closet.

The bed was monstrous in size. Extravagant with its dozen or more pillows and thick velvet coverlet. After five hundred years of sleeping on cold stone floors, he figured he was entitled to a little luxury. He stripped off his clothes and stretched his sore muscles, catching a glimpse of his body in the mirror.

He was not vain, but he kept in shape. Being a Dragon shifter didn't mean you were guaranteed to have an athletic physique. As with anything, it took work. He had an enormous appetite and spent hours every day in training or in the air to spend the extra calories. He'd learned long ago to keep his body perfectly honed and ready for battle. *Just in case.*

He'd spent most of his servitude waging war for a tyrant to atone for a crime that was not his. He'd learned early not to lapse in his training, mental focus and physical prowess were his best weapons. He'd survived hundreds of battles and yet, only one scar marred his bronzed skin.

The small puncture wound was barely visible inside of the dark red rose that sat over his heart. *His ruby rose.* The mystical symbol of the bond that would connect him to his maiden. A Dragon needed a mate, else he would die. It was really that simple.

It was a ragged looking thing. Thin and shriveled among all the bulging muscles of his arms, chest, and abdomen. It had once been on the verge of blooming, only to be struck down. The pain had been like a knife to his heart. *Never again.*

His lips formed a thin line as he headed to his bathroom. He slammed the door shut and vowed once again that he would never be taken in by the opposite sex again. *I will die first.* His vow echoed inside his mind's eye, and he closed his eyes at the roar of his beast inside him. He was angry and wounded.

Edric could feel the furious pounding of his heart. The heart he and his Dragon shared. It was hard and hollow. The air outside echoed that sound and Callius threw his head back and growled. He was a *ThunderDragon.* Rare and unique, he could call upon the weather to hurt his enemies.

The connection, however, also meant the weather sometimes reflected his moods. Storms seemed to follow him around. Betrayal did that to a Dragon. He frowned and turned his head.

He would not dwell on the past anymore. After all, he was home now to celebrate his brother. Edric blew out a breath and looked at his room. Except for the bed, the room was sparsely furnished. In fact, his entire wing was rather empty.

Clean and functional, he told himself. The warrior in him didn't have any fond memories that he cared to recollect. His soon to be sister-in-law, Noelle, had asked his youngest brother, Sander, to make him one of the prize tapestries he was renowned for in their world. He'd been honored by so valuable a gift.

It was the only piece of art to grace his walls. The tapestry depicted Edric in Dragon form. The glittering red scales winked at him in the light from the sun that streamed in through the large glass window. They had no neighbors in sight, so he hadn't bothered with curtains or drapes.

Edric had lived behind stone walls too long. He liked the sense of freedom he got from the uninhibited view. He thoroughly approved of Callius' choice to build *Castle Falk* on the sea. The view was breathtaking. He never imagined he'd see the New World, much less live in it.

From what he'd heard, he expected New Jersey to be an unfinished, smog infested wasteland of degenerates. However, much to the contrary, he found it to be surprisingly beautiful. He was fond of the aptly named Garden State.

His bathroom was enormous, like the rest of the castle. Green marble tiles ran across the floor, the shower stall was large enough to fit four of him inside, and with a single voice command he turned on all six shower heads. His preferred temperature and water pressure already programmed into the main controls.

His brother Nikolai was the resident genius. Edric did not necessarily like technology, but he was getting used to it. He increased the room temperature and ordered a little mood music while he soaped himself up. The smell of clementines and lemons filled the room. *Yes,* he thought, he did like modern times and conveniences.

Then again, anything was better than where he'd spent the last five-hundred years as a prisoner on the Isle of Pain. The name was perfect. It was a cold, dark, and desolate place. His memories of it even darker. Especially, when he thought of his once almost betrothed. *No, Edric, do not think of her.* He tried to turn his thoughts to something else, but it was too late.

His mind raced back to a time when he was younger, more foolish. When all he dreamt about was tasting freedom again. He'd planned to break his bonds through his prowess on the battlefield. His goal was to claim the wench who'd captivated him. She who had served at his former Chief's beck and call.

Theodosia's platinum hair hung down in glowing pools around her hips as she climbed on top of him. Her pale skin was marred with the dirt of her toils for the day, but he didn't mind. Edric was dusty and bloody after his latest battle, but she liked him that way, or so she said. She rode him long and hard, groaning loudly as she fondled her own breasts and flung her head back.

She smelled of rose oil and lye as always. Prime ingredients for the soap she crafted for the Chief himself. She toiled away daily in a small, dark room in the basement of Castle Blackthorne. Edric had once been called on to deliver the sharp smelling lye to her workroom, and that was where he'd met her.

He enjoyed the feel of her soft, warm body as he thrust in and out of her womanhood. After the day's battle, he was tired and spent, but he could never get enough of the pretty thing who moaned astride him. She slowed her pace just as he was about to explode inside of her and he gripped the hay bale he sat on in frustration, but she grinned haughtily and stopped her movement altogether.

"What have you brought me, Edric, my brave one, come now, give it, or I shall sit here and not move a muscle," she raised her hands and caressed his slick chest while he gasped and tried to move. She was as strong as she was stubborn, his Theodosia, and she sat straight up, sending shivers of delight up his shaft, but not moving a muscle more.

"My gift, Edric, now," she said and brought her fingers to her nipples and squeezed and pulled, tempting and teasing him with the sight.

He knew she wouldn't continue their tryst without a trinket. She'd stop cold, she'd done so before. He understood that now. He pulled a strand of silk from his dirty and worn pocket. From the middle of the red ribbon hung a large black pearl. It was rare and precious, as was his time with her.

"Tis lovely, Edric, but I want more," she pinched one flat, male nipple as she lifted herself almost all the way off him, but Edric would have none of that. Not when he felt so near to bursting. He reached into his pocket again, this time pulling out a small sack of gold coins.

Theodosia's eyes lit with pleasure, and she slammed back down on his thick cock making him growl with pleasure. He plunged in and out of her a few times more, desperate for his completion. The brief oblivion that came when his cock was spent was worth the game and toil, he'd told himself. Afterwards, he'd scurried back to his confinement.

"Soon, Thea, you will be mine," he'd often told her. As usual, she seemed not to hear him because she was wrapped up in admiration of the pearl, he'd given her. It was just her way, he'd told himself, she'd never spoken soft words to him. It did not matter. He was ready to mate.

Sure, stealing from the plunder of Chief Blackthorne was unwise, but he had to have her. His ruby rose for certain. Why else would his body lust so for hers? Each minute he'd spent in that hole, she'd been his light in all the darkness. His heart, his true mate, just like his mother had once said to him.

A week or so after that, the Chief had summoned Edric to his quarters. It was an unusual request, but he was nothing to refuse. Edric had entered the opulently decorated quarters when he was bid to do so. The sight that had greeted him still haunted him.

His Theodosia had been bent over on all fours among the pile of furs and silks. She'd been grinning and moaning like a wildcat as his jailer, Chief Dragomir Blackthorne, had thrust into her from behind. Edric could still hear her moans, still see her push her body back into the soft, flabby, white flesh of his then Chief. Edric's heart had turned to stone that night.

"You see how she howls like a dog, Edric, does she do this for you?" The Chief had laughed and laughed. His guards held him and forced him to watch as he'd fucked the woman Edric had thought to mate. When he was finished, he lifted his long, braided hair to show off his black pearl choker.

"What thinks you of this trinket from my bitch here? Ha ha ha, tasty is it not?"

Later he'd gone straight down to his cell, lifted his sharpest dagger and drove it into his heart, but Dragons were never easy to kill and Callius, his brother and fellow warrior, would not see him dead yet.

Edric was roused from his past by the sound of his cell phone's alarm. *Fuck.* He had only thirty-minutes to dress for dinner. Then he had to try and remain pleasant and sociable. After all, it was his brother's wedding weekend. For the first time, the four brothers would be in residence at Castle Falk at the same time.

It was momentous indeed.

ONE

Joselyn looked down at her cell phone and cringed. It was her business line. The one she used for her psychic website. Customers could phone in their questions for a fee as opposed to filling out the online form and buying a package.

She offered tarot card readings, dream interpretations, clairvoyant readings, scrying and more. A lot of people thought this kind of thing was uber scammy, you know, run by con artists and criminals. But every now and then, someone was, in fact, the *real deal*. Joselyn Coracao *was* that *real deal*. She was a Witch. An actual, magic-wielding Witch.

All Witches have talents or gifts, and for Joselyn, that meant her psychic capabilities. Most Witches don't receive their gifts until after they've reached puberty, but not her. Nope, she was reading other people's minds and getting visions since she could speak.

Not an easy thing for a child to understand. Especially, given the number of inappropriate thoughts that went through people's minds every second. Nowadays, Joselyn specialized in precognition and scrying. She had a gift for reading the future and locating lost or stolen items and sometimes, even lost people.

Mind reading was much more difficult for her nowadays. She assumed it had something to do with getting older and more jaded. However, Joselyn never questioned her gifts. She used them responsibly and did everything she could to maintain balance in her craft.

The thing about Witches that not everyone knew was that there was only a finite supply of magic in the universe. Each Witch had their own store of magic that they were either born with or that was left to them by someone. However, talent ran much differently. Some talents could be inherited, for example, a certain Witch family might be renowned for their potions or spellcasting, and some could come out of nowhere.

Joselyn's talent was the latter. She was the only born psychic in her family, and she had only a small supply of magic. She always thought that was funny. The psychic Witch didn't know where she got her gifts! *Ha ha.*

Ugh. Her phone rang again. It was *him.* Her business line had caller ID. Still, no matter what number he called from, she always knew when *he* was on the other line. She cursed under her breath and wished for the millionth time that she could've read his mind when she met him.

Then she could have avoided this whole mess. That creep was the entire reason she was back to begging for a handout from the local coven. It was also why she'd stopped dating.

Joselyn didn't do covens. She had little to offer and wasn't into the whole "greater good" philosophy they had. Yes, she used her powers for good, but she wasn't about to devote every waking moment to tending the woods and gifting her limited powers to the entire coven. She'd be at their beck and call. *Ugh, not again.*

She clicked the end button and turned to look at her best friend and her almost sister-in-law as they took turns trying on their dresses for this weekend's celebration. Noelle was getting married, and Joselyn couldn't be happier for her. If only her creep of an ex would stop calling her. But that was the price she paid for being foolish and ignoring the warning bells that she'd gotten when the smooth-talking reporter discovered her psychic abilities.

Now he wouldn't leave her alone, and she was getting worried. Normals tended to get addicted to magic. That was one of the reasons why she'd kept her talents secret. She avoided telling the normals in her life that she was anything more than a run-of-the-mill phone psychic.

Luke, her ex, knew the truth. Joselyn was a Witch, and she was clairvoyant. She was not a powerful caster, and she didn't make the best potions, but she had magic. She often got strong psychic vibes that led to accurate and sometimes helpful visions.

Noelle interrupted her musings with a loud squeal as she lifted the confection of white silk and lace from the gift bag Joselyn had given her. Her best friend had a thing for matching lingerie which was why Joselyn had bought her the ridiculously expensive garter. It went with the rest of the underthings Noelle had ordered for her wedding night. The garter was beautiful! It was the finest silk and lace and had tiny, blue roses sewn all around it.

"Joselyn, this is beautiful! Thank you!" She hugged her friend and watched as she unzipped the dress bag to reveal the gown Joselyn would be wearing.

"*Tada!* You are going to look gorgeous in this color! Won't she, Fred? It's positively divine! And yours is going to go great with your new baby bump. I am so excited! I get to be a bride and an aunt in just a few days!" Noelle jumped up and down like a kid in a candy store as she showed her best friend and her soon to be sister-in-law the gowns she chose for her bridal party.

"Oh Noe, I've got months to go yet! But yes, I agree, they are perfect, I love that the colors are different!" Fred smiled at Noelle and held her navy blue gown up to her body, she was all sleek and toned except for the small, perfectly round bump where she carried hers and Callius' first child. Joselyn looked down dubiously at the ruby red gown in her hands.

Joselyn looked back over at the pregnant bridesmaid. Winifred, or Fred, as she was known locally, was absolutely, drop-dead gorgeous. She was about the same height as Joselyn, but with multifaceted blonde hair and silver eyes. She was athletically built, as Werewolves tended to be, and had flawless, fair skin.

Her pregnancy only seemed to enhance her beauty. Joselyn knew carrying a child was difficult for Werewolves, but Fred seemed perfectly fine and as lovely as ever. She subconsciously rested a hand on her belly while Noelle went on and on about the materials and cut of the gown. *Matte silk crepe, snug bodice, acres of material in the skirt, side slit...*

Joselyn simply smiled. Noelle might as well have been speaking ancient Sumerian for all Joselyn knew what she was talking about. Her thoughts wandered as Noelle talked.

Her best friend was beautiful too. She was lean with fair skin, blue eyes, and long, thick brown hair. Joselyn was the exact opposite of the two of them. Not that she was unattractive to a certain guy, but there was a huge difference.

They'll look great in their gowns, and I will look like a damn heifer in a silk sheet. She shook her head and exhaled as she stared at the perfectly smooth length of the silk.

Joselyn could be a little anxious about her size sometimes. She was blessed or cursed depending on what mood she was in, with full, rounded hips, a double-D cup size, and some mighty powerful thighs. She in no way resembled the women who made up the rest of the small bridal party.

Not that she wanted to. She wasn't jealous of them. She loved Noelle and Fred. She just hated the idea of everyone else judging her when she stood next to them. With her curvy body, dark, tightly curled hair, and tanned skin, she most definitely stood out.

The dress *was* amazing though. She had to admit it. The fabric was gorgeous. Soft and smooth, yet rich and heavy, it felt warm in her hands. In truth, it was the most beautiful thing Joselyn had ever seen. Tears threatened to spill from her eyes as she stared at the maid of honor's gown.

The cut was only slightly different from the bridesmaid's dress. The bodice was fitted and cut low enough to be modest and still sexy. The most notable difference was the color. Her gown was a deep, vibrant, ruby red. Noelle had chosen it without her. Joselyn didn't mind, she wasn't a clothes horse and didn't really care about fashion all that much.

She wondered if she'd need to buy some Spanx or if she could manage with what she always wore. As she caressed the dress in her arms, she forgot all her worries. She somehow knew deep down in her bones that it was going to be perfect on her.

"Nice job, Noe, thanks. I'll see you later Joselyn too, I'm uh, going to rest a bit and then I'll get changed for dinner," Fred waved goodbye and left the room.

"Yeah, uh huh, *get changed?* You know that was Callius texting her! She's probably meeting him upstairs! Gosh, I hope Sander still wants me like crazy after we're married," Noelle went on, but Joselyn didn't hear a word she said. Her focus was on the dress.

The color was hauntingly beautiful. It would look great with the olive tone of her skin and her hazel eyes, but there was something else that was drawing her to it.

Suddenly, Joselyn felt light as air. She could feel herself smiling as the dress grew even warmer in her arms. Something somewhere was calling to her. Her fingers caressed the soft fabric and then, *whoosh.*

Joselyn closed her eyes and allowed herself to be swept away by the vision. She recognized the pull of her powers. She didn't fight them, that would be counterproductive. She ignored the yell of her friend as she eagerly fell into her sight and allowed the vision to fill her mind.

It was a tad bit hazy, but she could see herself there, in the ballroom of Castle Falk. There were flowers and candles and soft music playing. She couldn't make out the other people in the room, but there she was. She was wearing the ruby colored gown, and she was swaying. No, not swaying, *wait for it, ah!* She was dancing.

Large, muscular arms surrounded her. The owner of those arms caressed her back and hips as they swayed to the softly playing music. He was laughing, a deep rumble in his chest and she laughed too. She felt safe and deeply satisfied. Wanted. Sexy. She could almost feel him holding her now. She rested her head against his large chest and felt the beating of his heart, a strong and steady beat.

He was warm and smelled pleasantly of smoke and pine trees. Joselyn loved the combination. She was not alone anymore. Her heart squeezed inside her chest. He was important. Unique. She couldn't see a face, but she could sense him. Powerful and true. Oh, my! Dragon.

Her heart squeezed inside her chest again. She gasped and felt her heart swell, though whether it was in the vision or in the present, she couldn't tell. She only knew she felt happy and full of, of- Oh Goddess, no! She was in love!

"No way!" She yelled aloud.

There was no way Joselyn Coracao was falling in love at her best friend's wedding! Not with everything she'd just set into motion for herself. She shook herself out of the vision that threatened to change her life. Noelle was waving a hand in front of her face, and she smiled and apologized.

"My bad, I was just, um, thinking."

"Was that a vision? Did I just witness your witchy powers at work?" Noelle whispered excitedly.

Joselyn laughed. It wasn't an easy adjustment for her, living out in the open, but Alexsander, Noelle's fiancé, had outed her to his intended. She couldn't blame the guy. He wouldn't keep secrets from his soon-to-be wife, and that meant she had to come clean. She was grateful he'd given her the chance to do it herself.

"Um, yes. Remember I told you about my talent. I'm telepathic, well, clairvoyant really. Mostly, I get these visions-"

"OMG! Was it about me? The wedding? Sander? Ooh, the coven?" Noelle whispered the last word, even though they were alone.

"No, Noelle, it was not about you," Joselyn had to laugh at her friend's enthusiasm.

That didn't always happen. Most people, even Witches, got freaked out when she told them she could see their future or hear their thoughts. Her talents were rare and kind of scary at times. No one wanted to hear when their dog was going to die or, that their girlfriend was sleeping with their best friend or, that they were going to get fired that day. At any rate, she grew up without many friends.

Joselyn had learned to hide her visions from people if she wanted to keep them as friends. It had worked. She and Noelle had been friends since high school. Noelle zipped the dress bag closed and handed it to her. Joss smiled, she still couldn't believe Noelle and Fred just accepted her the way they did, but she was grateful for it.

She didn't have to keep her powers secret anymore. Even better, she had someone to sort of talk to about what she was going through. A Witch without a coven was a target. Especially a psychic one. She needed protection.

It took her a whole month to get enough courage to petition the local coven again for a meeting. She'd done so once before to notify them of her presence when she'd moved there as a teenager. They wanted her to join them then, and she'd politely declined. She only hoped they didn't rub it in her face now.

She walked over to the spare bedroom where she would be spending the weekend and hung up the tempting gown. She didn't have time for an affair. She had to make certain she had proper protection so that she could live and work in peace.

"Are you sure you're okay?"

"Yes, I am sure. Go get ready for dinner."

"Okay, then, I'm here if you need me," Noelle squeezed her hand and left the room.

Joselyn went to the adjoining bathroom and ran cool water over her face. She gazed into the mirror and took a good, long look at herself. *What the heck just happened?*

Her hazel eyes flashed red, then gold, then green as she watched herself. In her lifetime, she'd been deeply impressed that the only guarantees were maybes. She'd have glimpses of futures that could be, not that would be.

There were only two constants in her life. Joselyn would always be a Witch, and she would always be alone. She didn't want or need anything else. It was time to teach the Fates to stop meddling!

CHAPTER

TWO

Joselyn had been fidgeting with her napkin ever since he'd walked into the dining room. She recognized him immediately and judging from the looks he'd been giving her from across the table, he sensed something too.

Frigging Dragons! It had to be Dragons! Why couldn't Noelle fall in love with a banker, or a teacher, or hell, even a Werewolf? This was Maccon City after all, and the damn beasts were everywhere! But a *Dragon!*

Now that was something different. Ancient and powerful, why, she could feel the magic pulsating through his veins from across the table. The rhythm was hypnotic. A deep throbbing ache welled up in the pit of her stomach. *Was this what she had been waiting for all her life?*

"Joss?"

"Huh?" She looked up into the startled blue eyes of her best friend and sat up straight. Her dark, curly hair was pulled back in a ponytail, but still, she smoothed the sides as if righting some imaginary out of place strand.

"Sorry, Noe, what did you say?"

219

"I said let me introduce you to the best man and *your partner* for the weekend," Noelle nodded her head towards the man with the intense eyes and Joselyn felt the urge to run from the table. Noelle spoke his name, and Joss knew before the last syllable left her tongue that she was a goner.

"Edric Falk, this is my best friend and maid of honor, Joselyn Coracao. Joss, this is my soon to be brother-in-law and your partner for this weekends' festivities."

Joselyn gave a half smile as the man seemed to measure her up. His dark jewel toned eyes glowed brightly as he inhaled. Recognition flared in the depths of his eyes and curiosity too. She knew he'd scented her *anima magicae*, the heart of her powers, so to speak.

Supernaturals could usually tell one from another, though not always. She'd encountered his brother Sander a few months ago, right there in the castle, during a Christmas event, Noelle had catered. Joselyn hadn't recognized his scent. Now she knew it as soon as she inhaled the smoky pine scent of her partner for the wedding festivities. She felt her own powers stir in response. *Dragon.*

Each brother's scent was different of course, as it pertained to their gifts. Callius' scent had a deep, Applewood smoke quality to it. Sander's, the groom-to-be, smelled like winter frost and snow. The one with the flaming red hair reminded Joselyn of books for some reason. *Nikolai,* she recalled since she'd been introduced to him earlier. It was a pleasant odor, familiar, but nothing like this brother's scent. It reached her nostrils and sent shivers through her entire body, pine and smoke yes, but there was more. His scent was like lightning if such a thing had an odor.

She wondered which fragrance he attributed to her. His nostrils flared, and his eyes seemed to consume her from across the table. Joselyn *saw* the growl build up in his chest. It was a bright, glowing thing, a magical force, as it were. She knew what it would say though she'd never heard the language of Dragons spoken before. Her senses were confirmed as she heard the strange words echo from his mind's eye to hers. *Es meus.*

His lips hadn't moved, but Joselyn suddenly knew what they meant. Furthermore, she knew that *he knew*. Goosebumps popped out all over her bare arms. She felt naked under his stare. Noelle said something to break the tension, but Joselyn couldn't concentrate on her friend's words.

Her mind was racing. Why the hell did she wear a sleeveless shirt anyway? It was twenty degrees outside! Joselyn usually felt warm indoors, but suddenly she was shivering. She felt too exposed under his weighted stare.

There was simply too much of her visible in the sleeveless black cocktail dress she wore. The skirt flared out around her hips in a fun and flirty way that made her feel feminine despite being larger than was deemed popular these days. She wore her favorite knee-high, black velvet, high-heeled boots with it.

They usually made her feel confident, but not while he watched her so closely. Joselyn was a woman with a healthy appetite, and she'd make no apologies for her size. The way he seemed to growl at her as if he disapproved of her very existence put her back up.

In fact, he seemed barely in control of himself. His eyes roamed all over every bit of her that was visible from behind the table. Noelle tried again to make a joke, but neither she nor the Dragon responded. *Oh no*, she thought, *he wouldn't say something disparaging in front of everyone, would he?* Her last boyfriend had no problem teasing her about her body and telling her to slow down when they'd gone out to eat with friends of his.

She'd been embarrassed and humiliated beyond words. This was Noelle's and Sander's dinner party. Surely, he wouldn't cause a scene here. He stood up suddenly, startling her out of her thoughts.

"We need to talk, now, *minha bruxa*."

THREE

Edric could not believe it. *Here? Now?* His heart thundered in his chest to the point where it was almost painful. What tricks were the Fates up to this time? Did they not have enough entertainment at his expense?

Well, he would have none of it. No more games with his heart. He'd live and die alone. In solitude. He was a Dragon shifter, and he would not be trifled with.

He was not in the mood for games. No matter what the crimson beast inside of him wanted! He felt more than heard the deep, rumbling growl of his Dragon penetrate his mind's eye. *Es meus.*

Edric gritted his teeth. He'd do anything to stop the madness that was certain to follow if he listened to his Dragon. He couldn't risk it. He'd die if he were betrayed again.

Heck, he'd die without his maiden too, but at least that was his choice. The one thing a Dragon of a certain age needed more than air, food, and water, even more than treasure, was his one true mate, his *maiden*. He shook his head. It was better to die on his own terms.

He heard her step behind him as he walked into one of the spare rooms on the ground floor of *Castle Falk*. This one was decorated in soft beiges and ivories. It was perfunctory, but not especially beautiful. Not until *she* stood before him.

Edric inhaled, and her scent hit him again. Like nutmeg and saffron, a dark and spicy flavor that made his mouth water. Her eyes were hazel and seemed to change right in front of him from green, to brown, to gold, then to a darkish, purple color. *Hypnotic. Beautiful.*

She wore a modern dress, but Edric applauded her modesty. The bodice was high, to her long, smooth neck, and the skirt fell softly just above her knees. He didn't particularly like the way, so many normals wore clothing that resembled little more than underwear.

No, she was dressed perfectly. The belt at her waist showed off its small size in comparison to her bountiful breasts and perfectly rounded hips. He had to force himself to look away. She was *perfection.*

He wondered when she would make her play. When would the temptress begin her dance to enslave him? Would she bat her long eyelashes and beg him to take her? Would she promise him power, pleasure, or wealth? He felt sure he could resist her. Well, maybe not sure, but he was determined to at any rate.

He stood straight to his full six-foot-four-inch frame and waited. The air felt warm to him. His Dragon stirred beneath his skin, and he closed his eyes to calm the beast within. He'd never felt so nervous in battle as he did standing in front of her. He waited.

Edric was stumped when she made no move. He exhaled and narrowed his eyes. *She toys with me. The better to entrap me.*

The shine of her long, curly, dark tresses hanging down her back made him think of the onyx mines he held deeds to in South America. She was voluptuous and alluring as a woman should be, but there was danger there behind her full lips. More danger than there was in the fact that she was a Witch.

There was a time when Witches hunted Dragons for their magic. Not that it ever did them any good. Witch Magic was a finite thing in the universe, and those who practiced casting could hardly be expected to harvest and manage the magic of a Dragon. He crossed his arms and decided their staring contest had gone on long enough.

"I don't want you," he said.

He watched her expression. She seemed more amused than angry. Still, Edric thought he detected a hint of outrage. *Sassy. Good.* He had no interest in a scene that involved tears or begging. He'd simply let her down easy.

They'd just have to get through this weekend then never see each other again. *Brilliant!* Before he could vocalize his amazing idea, she opened her full, red lips and spoke. Her voice hit him in the gut. Alluringly steady, Edric forgot how to breathe the precise moment her voice reached his ears, much less talk.

"Well, that's good, because I don't want you either,"

FOUR

J oselyn could not believe that man! He was the tallest man she'd ever seen with shoulders larger than the doorway and an ego about twice the size!

Just because his eyes were the color of emeralds with hints of red around the rims and pupils, and dominated his gorgeous, angular face, didn't mean a damn thing! *Forget his hair while you're at it*, she told herself. Joselyn had a weakness for nice hair. His was thick and dark as espresso beans. It hung down to his chin in softly mussed waves. She was shocked at the flash of jealousy that shot through her as she imagined some woman running her fingers through it to get it that way.

"Look, before I respond to your ridiculous statement, let me say congratulations on your perfect Portuguese. I don't hear it anymore, not since my grandmother passed," she raised a hand to stop him, "Now, yes, I heard the *call* too, and I agree with you. There is no way on this Earth that I will *ever* be with you. Nothing personal, I just have a lot to deal with right now."

She waited for him to acknowledge her, but it was a long time coming. She guessed Dragons weren't used to hurrying since they lived notoriously long lives, but still, the way he was staring was simply rude.

She fidgeted under his watchful gaze. His eyes had a haunted look about them. Joselyn couldn't help but be drawn to him. *Curse the Fates. Damn tricksters.*

She needed to find something else to look at. Anything, anywhere other than those deep multi-faceted pools. Joselyn knew if she looked at them too long, she'd dive in regardless of her own safety. *No, not today. Not any day. I will not be love's pawn.*

She turned her eyes down only to run into his delectable body. *Warrior.* She'd picked that out of his mind earlier and cringed when she pictured him in battle. He'd been fierce, she knew it without asking. Fierce and brave, maybe even foolish once or twice on the battlefield and off.

"Then we are agreed, Witch," he looked down at her from his great height.

Joselyn narrowed her eyes as she tried to decide if he was insulting her or not. *Hmm. Not.*

"We will resist this *thing* and get through the nuptials this weekend for the sake of Alexsander and Noelle," he continued.

"Okay."

"Okay?"

"Yes, it sounds good to me," she said crossing her arms against the ache that suddenly flared up inside her chest.

"Aye, me too."

Joselyn was the first to move to leave the room. She paused for only a second. She wasn't sure why. She forced one foot in front of the other and left the room, only to head straight to the hallway bathroom.

What was the matter with her? She had too much on her plate right now to worry about some freakishly handsome Dragon's love life. He didn't need her to warm his sheets. The man was gorgeous!

She exhaled and closed her eyes. *Focus.* She had a conference call after dinner with a Council member from the *Coven Silva*. Her petition was being heard by their Council. *Finally.*

She tended to need protection since her powers did not include casting spells. Yes, she could make potions in a pinch, but they were hardly powerful. Anyway, the idea was they needed a reason to want to include her. She had to bring something to the table per se.

Joselyn had nothing. The grandmother who'd raised her was gone now. Josefina Coracao had very little in her lifetime. No property, no money, no powers of her own. All she had was her talents and a good work ethic. Her small collection of orchids helped her keep the balance between her powers and nature, but she was no great gardener or horticulturalist.

She ran a psychic hotline and sometimes phoned in anonymous tips to the local Sheriff's Department to help solve crimes. The Coven Silva was a small, tightly knit group who tended the pine barrens and focused their energies on keeping the lands free from development.

They were environmentalists. Not really her cup of tea, but they had strength and she believed she needed that. Word was getting around about her psychic hotline and website. She knew what this meant of course. Endless readings and being at the coven's beck and call.

She was getting better at focusing her talent, but as was true with any powers, there were those who sought to use her for their own personal gain. She needed them to protect her from people like that. People like her ex.

She couldn't believe she fell for it too. He only pretended to care about her for her powers. She dated off and on but always managed to keep things light. Luke was unlike anyone she'd ever met. He was an investigative reporter for a local paper. He'd made it his mission to get her to go out with him after they'd met on a missing person's case where she advised the police.

He got wind of her psychic abilities and was hooked. She was shocked at his easy acceptance and flattered by his belief in her. She shook her head now, *fool.*

The person who'd been missing was a woman from the hospice center Joselyn's grandmother had been living in after her last surgery. The old woman was all alone in the world and had wandered off the hospice premises one afternoon without anyone noticing.

Well, Joselyn had noticed. When the cops were about to give up, she'd summoned a vision. They found the woman thirty-hours later in the pine barrens. She was bruised, but alive. Joselyn had visited her every week until she passed from the malignant brain tumor that had sent her to hospice, to begin with. She still brought flowers to her grave.

After her success, the local police took her tips more seriously. Luke, well, he seemed to get more serious as well. He started asking her for tips on crimes and things so he could get ahead in his writing career. To her utter shame, she fell for it.

Until one day when they met for dinner. Joselyn had had a lousy day. Normally, Luke was attentive. He'd ask about her feelings, listen to her, but not that day. He'd been impatient. There was a ring of car thefts, and he wanted to unveil the crooks behind it, but the cops had no leads.

"I'm sorry, Luke, I don't think I can help you."

"What? You ungrateful bitch! After all the time I've spent hanging out with your fat ass, listening to you whine and complain, and you won't help me!"

He'd made a move towards her, to grab or smack she didn't know. But Joselyn had sensed something foul about him that night. She'd seen his anger before he expressed it. She knew better than to ignore her feelings. Before he could grab her, she was already up and running to the bathroom. She used every ounce of magic she had that night to hold the lock closed.

Oh, he beat on it for an hour or so, but the neighbors had called the police, and he'd fled before the sirens had gotten too close. Joselyn hadn't gone out on a date since. Luke started calling her a few days later. He'd done some other things too. Like leave her rotting flowers in front of her apartment, and she couldn't prove it, but she suspected he'd poisoned her neighbor's cat too. All because Joselyn fed the poor thing.

That was why she needed the Coven Silva. To petition them for membership or at the very least, sanctuary. Joss had no time for Dragons. No matter how gorgeous he was or how pent up inside she felt. She counted to ten, smoothed out her dress and walked back to the dining room.

"Everything okay?" Noelle whispered as she took her seat. Joselyn nodded and noted that Edric had not come back to the table.

She tried to ignore the regret that welled up inside of her, but there it was. She wondered if he was okay. Before, she knew what she was doing she reached out with her mind and found him. He was on the roof.

Castle Falk had been designed with a special landing area for the brothers. To normals, it looked like a helipad, but she knew better. She watched from her mind's eye as he transformed instantaneously into a huge red Dragon. His oval scales were dazzling in the moonlight.

She felt his turmoil and his anger. She gasped and was briefly aware of Noelle touching her shoulder. Edric opened his enormous wings and flapped them upwards, touching the tips together. At that very moment, lightning touched the sky and seemed to shoot through him.

She heard his roar before anyone else did. Saw the shock on his brothers' faces, but that was nothing compared to the pain she felt. His pain. *Heartbreak. Anguish. Betrayal. Death.* Tears stung her eyes, and she bit her lip to keep them from falling.

She ignored them as all three brothers, Nikolai, Alexsander, and

Callius, watched her. They turned in unison to the window where a nasty hailstorm just began to punish the grounds. They whispered to each other in their language, *Dracan*. She did not understand the words, but she *knew* that they whispered about Edric.

He'd brought the storm.

FIVE

Edric wrapped the thick towel around his waist and ran his fingers through his hair. It was longer than normal. The wet, dark brown locks grazed his neck as he took in his reflection. Not quite as dark as the long, curly hair of that *woman*. The one who'd invaded his mind since he'd laid eyes on her.

His cheeks flamed red at the thought of the spectacle he'd made of himself. He'd been so out of control, he even missed dinner! Of course, now he was paying the price. His stomach rumbled loudly in the quiet room, he needed food. *Now.*

A hungry, not to mention sexually frustrated, Dragon was no good for anyone. He threw on a pair of sweatpants and headed downstairs. At least he could fill his stomach, if not his heart. *Haven't you already paid the price for believing in love?*

He shook his head trying to rid himself of the temptation that was her. *Gods, Edric, get hold of yourself.* It'd been decades since he'd indulged. Maybe he just needed a woman? *No*, sex without love did not appeal to him in the least.

He opened the heavy wooden door that led to the industrial-sized kitchen. Dragons had huge appetites. Castle Falk's kitchen would make even the haughtiest chef drool with envy. There were two enormous refrigerators, a walk-in freezer, a roots and vegetable pantry, miles of marble counters, two six-burner stoves, a triple-wide stainless-steel sink with restaurant style faucet and pasta arm and more.

The décor was clean and classic, much to Edric's own tastes. Dozens of solid wood cabinets topped with golden-hued marble lined the walls. There was a glass tile mosaic backsplash, stainless-steel appliances, a line of stools surrounded an enormous kitchen island like soldiers, straight and tall. The hardwood floors gleamed in the dim light. Edric approved of the room in every way.

He was looking forward to rummaging for leftovers. He caught *her* scent before his eyes found her. Edric stopped in the middle of the room his mouth wide open. There she was, leaning over and giving him a perfect view of her assets as she searched one of the refrigerators.

She was wearing a thin t-shirt and a pair of tiny shorts. Her shapely legs were on full display. Edric followed them with his eyes all the way down to her pink painted toes. Her hair was loose and hung down her back in a wild display of tight, dark curls. He wanted to run his fingers through it and test its softness.

Edric hissed out a breath as a certain part of him sprang to life. The sound was loud in the empty kitchen, and Joselyn turned abruptly. The half-gallon carton of organic milk slipped from her hand, but Edric was in front of her in a flash. He steadied both her and the milk.

"My apologies, I uh-"

"No, it's my fault, sorry," she laughed softly and looked down.

Her warm breath teased his neck. He reveled in the feel of her heavenly body as he held her tightly in his arms. Her soft, womanly curves were pressed up against him in a delicious accord that was almost too good to be true.

Edric was in no hurry to release her. No hurry at all. She turned her body slightly to better stabilize herself, and the slight movement caused more of her scent to waft into his nostrils. *Saffron and spice.* He wanted to bury his nose in her every nook and cranny, just to see if she smelled like that everywhere.

"Don't be silly, Joselyn, I should have announced myself," it was the first time he'd ever used her name. He felt the weight of it on his tongue keenly. It felt good.

"Are you hungry?" His voice was a deep rumble. *Gods* was he hungry, and not for food.

"Well, I couldn't sleep. I had a call that didn't go so well, so I thought I'd heat up some milk," she eased out of his embrace, and Edric felt her absence immediately. He frowned.

"Ah, I'm sorry to hear that. Wanna talk about it?" He watched the play of emotions cross her face. Something was wrong, and he bristled with the knowledge, though why he should feel so protective of her was a mystery to him.

"So, my ex-boyfriend is a normal and a bit of a douche, he won't leave me alone, and I was getting worried, so I petitioned the local coven for sanctuary, but they won't go for it unless I am willing to dedicate my powers to them. I use my talents to survive. It's how I pay the bills, but they won't have that, and there is literally nothing else I could do. My visions take up a lot of my time and energy. Can't hold a regular job with that kind of constant interruption, ugh, I'm sorry, you were probably just being polite, I shouldn't have rambled," she pressed her palm to her forehead while she gripped her waist with the other. She was clearly tense.

Edric listened intently. She did seem to have a problem. He hated the idea of her having to ask anyone for help other than him, foolish as that sounded. His Dragon roared inside of him at the thought of her ex-boyfriend. It took him a moment to quiet his beast before he trusted himself to speak.

"I know we don't know each other well, Joselyn, but I swear I am here for you, uh, that is we are at your disposal, my brothers and I."

"Thank you, you don't have to say that, and I'm sorry I burdened you with all that," he saw through her embarrassment to her worry and gritted his teeth.

"So, you're not getting any food," he thought distracting her might get her mind off her troubles. It worked because she smiled, and his heart stopped. *Breathtaking.*

"Did you need help?"

"I can make my own plate, but I, uh, could use some company. I don't like eating alone," Edric held his breath as he waited for her answer.

Foolish. He didn't know if he could remain sane being so close to *her.* He should just leave. The room, the castle, the whole damn state. Yet, he couldn't bear the thought of it. Especially if she was in danger.

He felt his Dragon's intense disapproval at the very idea of walking out on his Joselyn. *Es meus.* The beast's growl was deep and threatening. Edric felt the possessive side of his nature roll through his entire body. He closed his eyes for a second to calm himself.

"Um, sure," she moved to heat her milk then sat down.

Edric prepared his plate and moved beside her. His dish was loaded with a variety of roasted meats and fresh vegetables. His future sister-in-law owned and operated the catering company that had prepared the meal for that night. He savored each morsel as it passed his lips. *Delicious.*

He moaned as he bit into the perfectly roasted prime rib. It was pink and tender and went exceedingly well with the horseradish sauce it was served with. It was unusual for a Dragon to eat his meat rare. Charred was the norm, but Edric had always liked it that way.

"This is good," he said to break the ice.

"Yeah, it's one of Noelle's signature dishes. May I?"

Edric nodded and nearly swallowed his tongue when she took a long, grilled asparagus spear from his plate with her nimble fingers. She lifted the vegetable and bit the tip off with her brilliant white teeth. *How could the act of eating a vegetable be so damn erotic,* he wondered as he watched her? He damn near fell off his stool when she opened her full, pink lips to take another nibble. *Grrr.*

"Signature dishes?" He forced himself to speak. He couldn't trust himself not to lean over and finish the food she held in her strong hand. He'd lick the remnants of the delicately salted vegetable from her fingertips. *One. At. A. Time. Grrrr.*

"*Present Tastes* has come a long way in the six weeks since the Christmas party," she chatted away oblivious to the tension rising in him. *Thank the Gods, she doesn't see me near to bursting in my sweats for fuck's sake*, he thought, *or maybe she just isn't interested.* He frowned at that latter thought.

"That's the one that brought our bride and groom together?"

"Yeah, though a little birdie told me that Callius and Fred may have had something to do with it."

"A little birdie or your visions?" He noticed right away the rigidity in her posture, and he could've kicked himself.

"Joselyn, look at me, I meant no insult."

"Yes, I know, but I've never had so many people *know* about me before. Fred, Noelle, and all you Falk brothers and, uh, I don't know. It feels strange."

"I know what you mean, I'm a Dragon, and *you* know about *me*," he raised an eyebrow and waited till she chuckled in reply.

"Ha ha, like you care what I think," she said.

"I do care, Joselyn," he meant it.

"I believe you," she said. He saw the truth shining there in her eyes.

Edric wanted to beat on his chest at the thought of this gorgeous creature's belief in him. He couldn't say why, but those three words meant a lot. She looked down again, and the momentary connection was gone. He missed it.

"Yes, well, I think Noelle and Sander are perfect together. They complement each other, both being artists of a sort," he was rambling to prolong their encounter.

"*Mmhm.* Noelle's culinary expertise certainly require some

artistic capabilities, and as for your brother, well, his tapestries are just beautiful. Is everyone in your family gifted?"

Edric closed his mouth for a moment. He'd never felt jealous of one of his brothers before, but right then he wished he had one iota of artistic ability. What could he tell her? That the way he sliced open a throat or tore out the bowels of some dying filth was art? That running onto a battlefield in his half-formed state caused his enemies to shit themselves in terror. *No.* He was a warrior. A killer. That was all.

"Well?" She asked her full lips tilted up in a sort of half-smile. He wished he had something else to tell her, but he wouldn't lie.

"No, I'm afraid art is not genetic. I've no gift for it. All I know is how to kill."

"I am sure that's not true," her whispered words barely registered as his mind threatened to be overcome by the past. Luckily, the sound of her sweet voice brought him back.

They sat quietly for a few minutes. The air between them seemed to sizzle in the dimly lit kitchen. Her scent invaded his nostrils. He wanted to breathe her in. To bask in the solace of her scent, her warmth.

It was as if she brought a kind of peace to him. Something he'd sought for a long time after all his years fighting for that bastard, Chief Blackthorne. Did he deserve it? That was another question, probably best left unanswered.

"What is it, Edric?"

"Huh? Oh nothing, I uh, was thinking of the past."

"I guess Dragons have a long past. You must have a lot to remember, don't you?"

"Yes, but there is also a lot I'd like to forget."

"I know we don't know each other well, but you can talk to me, Edric. I'll listen to you, and I won't judge."

He felt funny at her words, warm and sort of proud. *Claim her. Es Meus.* His Dragon's roar thundered in his head as he looked at her.

Edric fought the urge to take her for his own. If the rumble in his throat was anything to go by, he was losing the fight. *Damn him.*

"Are you okay?" Her soft voice interrupted his inner dialogue.

Was he okay? Hell no. Not when he considered her eyes. They seemed a bit purple just then, like sweet, berry jam. Edric's favorite.

She was so beautiful sitting there. Her aura was vibrant and powerful. *Witch, beautiful,* that much he knew, but that was all.

What did she do with her powers? What were her desires? He wanted to know her. He licked his lips before he spoke, trying to ignore the demands of his body. It was not an easy battle.

"Look, I want to apologize for being rude earlier. It's not you, Joselyn, I mean, it's not that you aren't attractive. I like a woman with a healthy appetite-" Edric wished he could take back the words before they left his mouth. *Idiot.*

"Well, gee thanks, *Ed.* Just for a second, I thought maybe you're not that bad, but I'm quite sure you just called me fat. You egotistical jerk."

A flash of magic flew from her hand to his. Edric yelped as he shook his wrist to stop the sensation.

Magic could sting. They both knew that. Joselyn stood up and refused to take any note of the pain she just inflicted on him. He deserved it, *the jerk*!

She was painfully aware of how tiny her pajamas were! She knew just how much of her body was on display thanks to her "healthy appetite," and like always, she was totally humiliated! She felt her cheeks burn with embarrassment as she rinsed her cup and placed it in the dishwasher.

Healthy appetite! Puhhhleeeease, that was code for fat, and she knew it! She'd been overweight most of her life. In a world where models were a size negative zero and anyone without thigh-gap was considered obese, it wasn't easy. And no, she couldn't magic herself skinny.

Being a Witch couldn't stop her from eating bread, or rice, or pasta, or *rojoes a moda do minho*, a Portuguese pork dish that was served with stewed potatoes and was her absolute favorite. Joselyn liked food. She liked to eat.

She was almost thirty years old, and she was finally comfortable with her size. *Or at least she was before he walked into her life!* Some Witches had the gift of glamour, but not Joselyn.

She wore anywhere from a size twelve to a fourteen on any given day. Yes, she was overweight for her five-foot-six-inch frame, but there was nothing she could do about it. She tried starving herself once, and it was so not worth it.

She ate healthily. *It wasn't all chocolate!* She enjoyed vegetables and smoothies as much as the next person. She even exercised a few times a week. She just couldn't seem to get down past a size twelve.

"You know, I've heard this song before, Edric. I don't need to hear it from you too. In case you don't recall, I said I wasn't interested in you either, *cabrao*."

Before she could turn around and leave the room, she felt him close in just behind her. *Damn*, he moved fast! Even for a Dragon.

Joselyn turned to meet him head-on. She felt the beast within him stir, but she felt no fear. He wouldn't hurt her. Even when his temper had been roused, and his eyes burned at her like emerald and ruby fire. A treasure trove of feelings untold.

The fates must have been drunk when they decided the two of them would suit! She looked up at him. She had to. He was well over six-feet tall, and his body was covered in rippling muscles. He was the very embodiment of athleticism. Even more so than his older brother Callius.

If they were a couple, they'd be beauty and the beast alright. Except she'd be the beast! Shorter, rounder, with brown hair and olive skin, she was hardly a beauty! She blew her curly hair out of her face and put her hands on her ample hips. She had enough of this already.

"Alright, lizard boy, move it or lose it."

"No. Not until you let me explain! Wait a second, did you just call me *lizard boy*?" He looked as if he swallowed a bug when he repeated the phrase and Joselyn bit her lip to keep from laughing.

"Explain what? Yes, I'm fat. I get it, okay, I know I'm overweight! Now, move aside, or I swear I will zap you again."

"Damn it, woman, that's not what I meant! The very sight of you has been driving me out of my mind since the second I laid eyes on you-"

"Well, if you'd just move, I won't be in your sight anymore!"

"You want me to move?" He raised his voice to match hers, but she sensed no real anger behind it. Still, she should have backed off. All her senses were tingling, the same way they did when she was going to have a vision. Only they seemed stronger.

"Yes! I want you to move!" She yelled back at him, unable to control herself.

Her chest was heaving, she could only imagine how she looked, braless with her thin nightshirt on, but she didn't care. Joselyn was trembling all over. She wanted, oh, *she wanted something*, but she couldn't name what.

"Fine! I'll move," he growled the last word just as his arms whipped out and encircled her.

He pulled her up against him and hissed when his skin touched hers. Before she could protest, he claimed her mouth. His strong lips fastened themselves to hers. Joselyn moaned. It was like no kiss she'd ever experienced. Maybe the Fates had hand-picked him for her?

She arched into him, wrapping her hands around his thick neck and giving as good as she got. She threw her head back as he licked his way from her mouth to her throat and back up again. Joselyn's mind went blank as his hands and mouth and tongue teased her senses. She wanted them all, everywhere at once.

So good, so hot, burning, everywhere, more, harder, touch meeeeeeee...

As if he read her mind, she felt him move. *Touching, feeling, groping, kissing, licking...* Everywhere she wanted him to. When she thought she couldn't stand anymore, he picked her up with strong hands fastened firmly to her ass. He slammed her down firmly onto his engorged manhood, and he hissed her name as he rubbed against her core through the thin cotton fabric of her shorts and his sweatpants.

"Mmm, you taste like heaven, *minha bruxa, my little Witch,*" he said as he locked his mouth over one plump breast over her thin cotton shirt.

"Joselyn? I need-"

He was asking her permission, and she knew she should refuse, but it had been so long since anyone had wanted her this way. So long since she'd felt passion. How could she refuse? Not when she wanted him just as much.

"My room is down the hall."

CHAPTER

SEVEN

Edric met her eyes and nodded. His Witch was sexy as hell, and she tasted divine. He couldn't wait to get the full experience of her without barriers.

He kicked the door shut behind them, carrying her the entire way to her bed. She weighed next to nothing compared to him. Edric was near three-hundred pounds of rock-hard muscle. *Big as a damn house.*

Joselyn was perfection in his arms. He could've kicked himself for making her think she was fat. She was full and round, soft and firm, everything a woman, *his woman*, should be. Edric had been a warrior most of his life, but all of that went out of his head when he looked at her. This was why he'd been born. *To love her.*

Her olive toned skin matched his own, though in truth he was a shade darker. Her long hair curled softly over her shoulders, almost black in color he wanted to bury his nose in her soft tresses and breathe her in. But that was for later.

He had other things to see to first. His heart damn near stopped beating in his chest as he peeled off her shirt. Her breasts were even more perfect than he imagined as he freed them from their flimsy confines.

245

"You are a vision, Joselyn," he growled reverently as he gazed at her. Her naked breasts were large and firm, tipped with dusky, dark nipples. Heat sizzled through him.

"Oh, Edric," she moaned as he gripped her by the backs of her knees and pulled her to him. He pushed her back down on the bed as he suckled her. She tasted of her magic, a spicy flavor that was like ambrosia on his tongue.

Edric removed his own clothing while he kissed and licked his way down her soft belly to the apex of her supple thighs. He was desperate for contact, but he held himself back, allowing only his hands and mouth to touch her body.

He wanted to go slow. He wanted to memorize every curve every freckle, but his Witch would have none of that. Just as his mouth was this close to tasting her sweet woman's honey, she slipped out from under him and took control.

He growled as his Joselyn knelt on the bed. She was no longer self-conscious of her nudity, no, now she was proud. She beckoned her almost lover forward, and he obeyed. *Fuck*, he'd crawl over shards of glass to get to her.

As it were, Edric moved across the bed and nuzzled her head with his. He kissed her hard on the lips, but only when she allowed it. She turned her head, and he followed, licking a trail down her long neck to the hollowed space between her clavicle and her breasts. Once again, she stopped him, and he obeyed. He'd do anything she asked. *Anything*.

He'd never wanted to be vulnerable again. He'd never wanted to feel desire or lust after Theodosia's betrayal, but this was different. He was no longer interested in controlling his feelings. Not when his Dragon was right there too, in his mind's eye, urging him onward. His ruby rose itched and burned as he touched the dazzling Witch in front of him.

He felt the rumbling growl of his Dragon, and it reverberated through his body. His Witch must have heard because she smiled and ran her hands over his chest and stomach. The desire to take her, to claim her was strong, but Edric let her set the pace.

She grabbed his face and brought her full lips down on his. Her tongue tangled with his as she dipped her hands lower still until she reached the long, hard length of him. He hissed and sucked in air through clenched teeth as she gently traced and cupped him.

"Joselyn, if you've a mind to stop, you best do so now. In another second the matter will be beyond us both," he growled as she held him firmly in her grip. She laughed then squeezed and pumped.

"I don't want to stop, Edric."

She looked up at him with eyes that changed from green to gold, to purple, to a deep, deep red. Lust glazed and beautiful, Edric allowed her to push him down on the bed so that his legs were splayed, but his torso remained upright.

She stood on the mattress and then over him. He ran his hands up her and down her calves while he used his lips, tongue, and teeth on the soft skin of her inner thighs. Finally, she allowed his long tongue to sink into her sweet, hot womanhood. Edric growled as he feasted on her sweet honey. He explored her with his mouth until he found the tiny little nub of flesh that controlled her pleasure. He closed his mouth over her and sucked.

Joselyn cried out just as her knees went weak, but he held her firm. She was ripe and deliciously decadent. He growled softly as he lapped at her. She pulled on his hair as pleasure found her. When their eyes met, she smiled and stood tall, exhaling and stretching like a cat. Edric thought he'd burst right there just from the taste of her on his lips, then she grabbed his face, locked lips with him, and sank down.

They cried out in unison as she slammed her supple body onto his thick, swollen cock. She was hot, and wet, and oh, so ready for him. Edric dug his fingers into her hips as she rode him. He met her thrust for thrust, delving deeper each time. Pleasure shot through his every nerve cell as her body sheathed him.

Edric growled as he filled her. Each thrust, each moan, brought him closer to completion. Finally, he felt himself touch heaven as white-hot pleasure coursed through his body,

Es meus.

EIGHT

Joselyn basked in the afterglow of the most mind-blowing sex she'd ever had. Edric had kissed and sucked and licked her from head to toe. She thought to set the pace by taking charge of him as she had at first, but now she realized he'd simply wanted her to initiate they're coming together. After that first time, he slowly took back the controls, and she'd been gasping and moaning ever since.

He'd had her on every surface of that room. And when he could find no satisfaction there, he picked her up as if she weighed nothing and carried her in his arms all the way to his quarter of Castle Falk. On the way, he explained that from the outside the castle looked like one large home, but on the inside, it was much more complicated.

Each of the four quarters was separated by soundproof walls, long corridors, stairs, and even four elevators, with enough space in between to feel like four separate residences. Only the common rooms like the enormous kitchen, the ballroom, the formal dining room, and so on, unified them.

"We lived too close for five hundred years to want to part ways, but we each crave freedom and privacy. Two things we were not allowed in the time of our imprisonment."

"What were you held for?" She'd asked him as he climbed the stairs to his bedroom.

"We were punished for a crime on our house committed by our father. It was a long time ago, *minha bruxa*, do not fret."

"I'm sorry, Edric."

"Don't be. All my trials have brought me to you, and I can think of nothing I wouldn't do to be by your side."

After that announcement, Joselyn didn't need any more words. She readily admitted right then that the extra-long, king-size bed was much better than the one in the spare room. They could fully explore each other without fear of falling off. Although they had ended up on the floor a time or two.

She ran her hands down the silky sheets and smiled. The entire castle was furnished with the best quality everything. From the flooring to the furniture, even the paint on the walls. Not that she cared about such things. Each quarter held several bedrooms, bath-rooms, living rooms, private theatres, and even their own kitch-enettes. The place was like something out of a fantasy and Edric's bedroom had the best view of the ocean Joselyn had ever seen.

They'd stared at it together for a while, and Joselyn had felt a peace like none she'd ever experienced before. A calming sort of sensation, one of security and love. Then he lowered his head and encircled her ear with his delectable tongue, and all her peaceful thoughts turned into something more carnal. His lips were gentle as a whisper. Nervous chills ran up and down her spine despite having spent half the night naked in his arms. When he turned her face to his, she was blown away by the sheer desire in his glowing red tinted eyes.

She knew then, without a doubt, that this was the man from her vision. He was the one the Fates had chosen for her. Her heart pounded as if she'd run a marathon, she could hardly breathe. How? Why? *Because he is my other half. My fated lover.* She felt tears sting her eyes as he took her face in his large hands and moved his lips insistently on her.

With the utmost care, he guided her backwards to his bed. Joselyn trembled at his touch. She was falling in love. The realization struck her as he tasted her with his tongue, licking his way ever so slowly down her sensitized body.

He parted her legs and rubbed his cheek against the soft skin of her inner thighs. She could almost feel his need and wondered at it. He used his fingers to part her as he trailed kisses closer and closer still to where she throbbed the most. Every touch, every kiss, a perfectly planned seduction. He used his hands to anchor her to the bed, and he dove in, lapping at her with his tongue as if she were a feast for him alone.

She whimpered and groaned. She wanted to move freely, but he held her firm, restricting her to his pace. He growled in satisfaction when she pulled on his hair. The sound trembled through her taut body. He didn't stop then either.

Nor did he stop when she lost all self-control and begged him. He continued the slow torture, probing just outside the perimeter until finally, he thrust first one then two fingers inside as he swirled his long tongue up and down her most sensitive flesh.

He parted her legs further, putting her on display for his eyes and mouth and whatever else he wanted. She felt deliciously exposed and wanton. Magic, passion, and *love*, yes, love, pulsated through her. Joselyn was like a bomb ready to detonate by the time he rose from the ground and entered her in one swift movement.

He stood at the edge of the bed and brought her legs up to his shoulders as he thrust himself deeper still. Stars exploded behind her eyes, and she felt her body squeeze and tug at him, a crazed animalistic instinct had her lifting to meet him. He bared his teeth, eyes glowing, hips flexing, hands caressing.

Joselyn saw his fangs lengthen and before he could protest, she pulled him down to her. She knew it was her destiny. The Fates were right, she'd have to thank them. He was the man in her visions, and she wanted it all, more than ever. To belong to this man, this *Dragon.*

She kissed his lips, avoiding his teeth and nodded her head, offering her neck to him. He growled and looked at her a question in his glowing fiery eyes. She understood. It was his need to mate that was bringing his teeth down. And she wanted them on her, breaking her skin, marking her body as his. *Forever.* What was the phrase she heard from inside his mind's eye? *Es meus.*

"Can I have you?" His voice was barely human, but to her, it was the most beautiful sound in the world.

"Yes, oh yes, Edric, as long as I can have you," she answered.

"This cannot be undone, Joselyn."

"Do you want me, Edric? As yours?"

"Aye, more than I want to breathe, *minha bruxa,*" he grunted.

"Then please, mark me, now," she begged, and he struck like the lightning that fed his magic.

It hummed through the air as he continued to pump his hips, she gasped and moaned as he closed his mouth around her skin. With the pain of his bite came a pleasure so intense Joselyn cried out and held on to him for dear life. Pure, undiluted ecstasy seemed to fill every cell of her being. She opened her eyes and saw only stars. They were red and gold, like fairy dust, and they filled the air.

Joselyn felt his ruby rose spread through her, the wonder and beauty of it causing tears to spill down her face. He caught them on his finger and lifted them to his lips.

"I would have you as my only sustenance, *minha bruxa,* for all my days on this Earth."

"And I you, my Dragon lover," she replied.

Magic, hers and his, filled the room. They forged an unbreakable bond, a sacred promise, right then with the combination of their vows, their blood, sweat, tears, and of course, their sex. The magic then surged through them both, and they cried out in unison as they reached untold pleasure.

Nothing had ever felt so right.

Edric really needed to stock his private kitchen, he thought as he waited for the coffee to brew. He came down to what he thought would be an empty kitchen. It was early enough, but to his dismay, first one, then all three of his brothers entered the room. Callius spoke first.

"So, are you going to share your news with us, brother?"

"Yes, tell us about her, Edric," Sander joined in.

Edric was private by nature. Ever since Theodosia, he'd not taken a lover for the entire night, choosing to satisfy his physical needs in fast, impersonal places. But this was different. He gritted his teeth. He had no wish to talk about his mate. The bond was too new. He felt his control might slip.

"So, your Witch, bespelled you then, has she?" It was Nikolai's words that broke his resolve. He turned and lifted his younger brother clear off the floor by the collar of his shirt.

"Easy, Ed, he meant nothing by it," Callius was always the voice of reason when the brothers quibbled.

"I am sorry, Nik," Edric dropped him and turned to face all three. They wore identical smiles, and he realized they were simply excited for him as brothers were meant to be when one of them found his true mate.

"It is true, I have found my mate, and she has accepted my ruby rose. I did not mean to get physical with you, it is just-"

"You don't need to explain, brother, I understand," he saw from the flash in Callius' golden eyes that his older brother and former comrade in arms did understand perfectly.

"And so do I," Sander put his ruined hand on Edric's shoulder and squeezed with his good fingers. It was a testament to his love for Noelle and the positive effect she had on him that he did not try to hide his injury. Edric smiled.

A buzzing sounded from the counter, and the four of them turned towards the sound at the same time. It was Joselyn's cell phone. She must have left it there. Edric growled as he recalled just what had been happening in her personal life.

"Just a second," he said to his brothers and reached for the cell. Being protective was in his nature. He weighed the outcome of answering the cell phone or leaving the pest on the other side to harm his mate, and the answer was obvious.

He clicked accept and waited. The voice that greeted him was demanding as it was sniveling. He growled into the phone.

"Listen up, dick, if you want to remain in one piece you will forget this number, you will forget Joselyn, do I make myself clear?"

"Who the fuck are you, buddy?"

Edric roared into the phone, so loud and menacing a sound that he and his brothers actually heard the man cringe through the phone.

"I said forget this number."

"Okay, okay, sorry."

Edric clicked end and willed himself to release the tension that had built up inside of him.

"Well, that was easy enough. Why so grim then, brothers? The three of you mated, and I've never seen a sorrier bunch of Dragons! Ha!" Nikolai reached for the coffee, but Edric swatted his hand away.

"That is for my mate, runt, wait your turn."

They laughed and teased each other until Edric had his tray set and made his way back to his quarters. Sander had suggested the fresh squeezed orange juice, the selection of jams with the toasted croissants. The poached eggs and slices of bacon he'd cooked for his mate himself.

Edric guessed Noelle was behind his brother's sudden interest in food and plate arrangement. He laughed and entered his bedroom to see the bed empty. He practically threw the tray on the side table and was about to run from the room when he heard her.

She was humming a soft, pleasant melody and Edric moved towards it. She was in the bathroom. He knocked first then opened the door to see his Joselyn sitting back in the enormous bathtub. Steam rose up from the clear water, and he was treated to a tantalizing view of her naked form.

"What's wrong? You look upset," she moved to stand, but he stopped her.

"No, no, I just thought, um, never mind. Dear gods, Joselyn, you look ravishing," all thought of food vanished from his mind as he watched her smile at him.

"Why don't you join me then?"

As if he needed to think about it! Edric dropped his pants and sank into the tub behind her. He used the citrus-scented body wash to soap up her back and arms. His fingers lovingly traced the mark he'd left on her olive skin.

"Do you mind the rose?" He hadn't brought it up before for fear she'd hate it. The truth was, seeing his ruby rose boldly displayed across her right breast, vines circling up her shoulder and neck filled him with a fierce pride. His own rose was now blooming and more than twice the size it had been before.

"Oh Edric, it's beautiful, like you," she whispered and leaned back into him like a cat waiting to be petted.

"You think I'm beautiful? You're sublime, *minha bruxa*," he said and continued to trail his hands up and down her delectable body.

A couple of hours later, they were finally dressed and headed downstairs. Edric held her hand as they entered the dining room. The wedding guests were gathered for the rehearsal lunch, and both bride and groom were grinning like fools.

Only now Edric understood. He wanted to pound his chest and announce to the world that the woman next to him was his. He'd never felt such a strong array of emotions. Love, tenderness, the need to protect, desire, happiness, it was all so much at once. *Es meus.* His Dragon growled, and he knew she heard it too.

His Joselyn looked at him and smiled that slow, wide grin that he loved so much. She linked hands with him and leaned her head on his shoulder just as the party began to bundle up to move outdoors.

"So, where are we going?"

"Ah, Noelle is kind of a nature nut, and even though it is twenty degrees outside, she has planned a hike around the property followed by an outdoor rehearsal luncheon. Don't worry it's in a tent with lots of firepits!"

"The cold doesn't bother me, but what about you?" His concern was real. Joselyn was a Witch, but as far as he knew she still felt cold. Dragons survived and even thrived in arctic conditions, after all, they made their own heat.

"Oh, I'll be fine, baby, I'll just hold on to you if I get cold."

"Of course," he grinned and kissed her neck.

They spent the day talking and joking as they followed the wedding guests through the planned two-mile hike around the castle grounds. The woods were sparsely covered with snow, but someone had cleared the path. He imagined his brother had a hand in that. Sander had a way with snow and ice.

As a matter of fact, he'd placed carved ice statues every fifty feet or so. There were hearts, wedding bells, doves, a dragon, and lastly an exact replica of the bride and groom in ice that brought tears to Noelle's eyes. Her mother snapped pictures while all the guests raved over Sander's artistic abilities.

Edric felt himself tense. He could never do things like that. He did not have the gift or the skill. He was good with his hands and with knives, but not much else. What if she grew bored of him? As if she could tell what he was thinking Joselyn squeezed his arm. Then he realized she probably could tell.

"Of course, I can tell, *psychic Witch,* remember?" She smiled at him, and he felt warm inside.

"Edric, I don't need you to make me ice statues or tapestries. I don't need the fanfare."

"Then what do you need, Joselyn, I will give you anything I have."

"Just you. I only want you."

He didn't think it was possible, but right then, Edric fell even more in love with her. His Witch who wanted nothing, but his heart. He'd never thought it was possible.

"You've got me, *minha bruxa,* for all eternity. I love you."

"Well, that's good, Edric, because I love you too."

EPILOGUE

"Did you enjoy the wedding?"

"It was beautiful."

"Are you upset at all that we didn't have a traditional one? We still could you know."

"Edric, I told you already, I don't need all this, the dresses and flowers and bells. I just need you. Besides, I don't have any family except for you. And the entire Falk Clan. Well then, I guess we are all here. This is perfect."

"But no one knows-"

"Even more perfect! It's our secret for now. Let's cherish it."

Edric leaned forward and kissed his wife on the tip of her nose. He'd needed to make their mating official in the eyes of all that walked the Earth. Dragons were funny that way.

After they'd watched Sander and Noelle at the rehearsal lunch the day before, he'd gotten the craziest idea. He took his mate to the rooftop of the castle in the middle of the night and in one moment of magic and mystery, he'd turned into his Dragon.

She'd gasped at the forty-foot-long ThunderDragon with his

shining ruby scales and enormous wingspan, but when he connected to her mind, she'd smiled and agreed. It was simply a matter of her climbing onto his back on the soft blanket he'd had her carry up from the bedroom and like that, he whisked her away to a local justice of the peace, who also happened to be a Werewolf and wouldn't be alarmed at a Dragon landing in his yard with a Witch.

The Falk Clan had a treaty with the local Macconwood Pack, and all Wolves had been alerted to their presence. So far, they'd been a friendly lot. The old Wolf who married them was no different.

It took all of thirty minutes, then Edric and Joselyn flew back to the castle and spent the evening wrapped in each other's arms. The next day they watched as his brother, and Noelle spoke their vows with identical, secret smiles on their faces. They wore the same expressions as Sander and Noe shared their first dance as man and wife.

No one seemed to notice the two of them, and that was good. Edric had no wish to steal their moment away from them. He looked down at his own wife and smiled. He felt his ruby rose throb with life and love. It was a sensation like no other as he twirled the matching ring around Joselyn's finger. Edric watched as she looked down at it, a curious smile on her face.

"I think Noelle was right, my love," she said.

"How's that?" he asked.

"Red really is my color."

He laughed at that and wrapped her up in his arms. The spicy scent of her magic filled his nostrils, and he let his thoughts wander to the ways he'd revel in it later that evening. *Es meus.*

When the band leader invited all the guests to join the happy couple, Edric whispered in her ear as he led her to the dance floor. She looked absolutely beautiful in the ruby gown she wore, but not as amazing as she would when he peeled it off her. *Later. Grrr.*

"You are my heart, Joselyn Coracao Falk, my life, and my love for always. *Es meus. Minha bruxa.* My sweet Witch."

• • •

The end.

Thank you for reading *The Dragon's Heart*! I hope you enjoyed it!

For more of The Falk Clan Tales CLICK HERE!

C.D. GORRI

THE DRAGON'S SECRET

A FALK CLAN TALE

BLURB

She just wants a little fun, he's looking for a lifetime.

Melody Casper is all work and no play! She spends eighty-hours a week crunching numbers for Merlin Banking Solutions, the most secure supernaturally run bank in the world. Talk about boring!

One failed marriage behind her, this Coyote Shifter is more than ready for a little fun! What better place to let her hair down than the annual World Banks Charity Ball?

Nikolai Falk needs a break from the pressure of finding a mate! With three brothers wed and mated, Niko is the last single Dragon in his Clan. Called away to the city to represent the family's interests, he attends a charity ball where he discovers the one the Fates designed just for him.

Can Nikolai convince his sexy Coyote that she is his one true mate?

PROLOGUE

Nikolai Falk looked up from his laptop and cursed soundly. How the fuck was it three o'clock already?

He groaned and quickly stretched, standing up in the process. All those lines of code had a way of sucking him in for hours on end until he lost track of space and time. *Shit.* His EnergyDragon growled at him.

The beast needed to fly, to stretch his wings against the cooling skies. His ability to exercise control over technology was something unique to him. Energy came in many forms, and he simply excelled at this one.

He'd discovered December was an unusual month in their new hometown of Maccon City, New Jersey. It was milder than fall on some days, then colder than a witch's tit on others. *Er.* He'd best not repeat that colorful colloquialism in front of his brother, Edric.

Dragons and Witches had some history together. Mainly an antagonistic one seeing as how those who followed the Dark had a nasty habit of killing Dragons to get their bits and pieces for spells. *Fucking monsters.* But all Witches were not evil. IN fact, he knew quite a few that followed the White and practiced their craft honorably.

Either way, his brother, Edric, was more than a bit touchy about the whole *Witches* thing, and he did not appreciate any negative remarks about their kind. The *ThunderDragon* was mated to a Witch, and he didn't take kindly to any perceived slurs against her.

As if Nikolai would ever disrespect his newest sister-in-law. Joselyn was just great and perfect for his older sibling. Her psychic powers were benevolent far as he could tell, and she chose to remain outside the local coven. Choosing to look to her mate for protection and security. *As it should be. Lucky bastard that Edric was.*

Another one mated. And he alone. Nikolai rolled his eyes as he looked back down at his laptop for a second. *Hmm, just one more adjustment.*

His cell chirped annoyingly with the alarm he'd set for himself. *Fuck.* Good thing though. He'd never hear the end of it if he was late for his niece's naming day.

The ceremony was going to start in half an hour and he still had a shit ton of work to do. *But not today.* Being responsible for their small Clan's finances was one hell of a job. Especially when his brothers had no concept of managing money, only spending it.

He smirked and shook his head. Arrogance was not only a human fault. But he had a right to be overly confident. Nikolai was damned brilliant at making money. The Falk Clan's worth was currently in the hundreds of millions. Not too shabby indeed considering where they'd been a little over a year ago.

He jumped into the shower and hurried to dress. Nikolai had no time to revel in the hot spray of water. He washed quickly and chose a pair of navy-blue Armani slacks with a simple white silk shirt.

Like his brothers, his tastes were expensive. *Dragons loved treasure of all sorts*, he mused as he tucked a strand of hair behind his ear. Besides, after five-hundred years of servitude to a tyrant, he figured they were entitled to a little luxury.

With his newest endeavor, they could have all the luxury they'd possibly want! He'd managed to secure the future of their newly founded Clan in a year! *Booyah!* He mentally fist-bumped himself, proud of his pending success. The four brothers would be able to provide for their mates and children for many generations to come.

Generations that were coming upon them sooner rather than later. He frowned. His siblings had all been blessed with their fated mates within a year of settling in the supernaturally inclined town of Maccon City.

They'd found their little slice of heaven in New Jersey of all places. He'd been none too happy when his elder brother, and their leader by unanimous decision, Callius, had told them where they were going to build their castle and live.

Quite frankly, he'd always thought New Jersey sounded like a shithole. At least, it did according to the internet. Nikolai had flown around the world a few times before visiting. He'd tested his wings and tasted the freedom they'd all craved. Duty had forced them to serve out their sentence without much resistance.

He'd always wondered why Callius hadn't fought to get out. He'd asked his brother about that once and the *FireDragon's* reply had been one word. *Honor.* Nikolai was young and didn't understand, but he'd done his part. Because of that, he had always had more freedom than his brothers. For that, he'd always felt guilty.

Nikolai had used his talents and brains for his captor for centuries. The technological advancements the last hundred years had made it easier and necessary for him to interact with the outside world.

He'd travelled outside of his old cell every time he opened a book, and later, when he'd turned on the computer. His two eldest brothers were Clan Warriors, fierce Dragons of worth and honor, his youngest an artist highly valued amongst their kind, but Nikolai was the odd man out.

A geek. A money maker. Sure, he had value, but the Blackthorn Clan followed the old ways. He'd been mocked and ridiculed, but he'd added to their jailor's coffers. So much so, his excursions, virtual and real, had been tolerated.

He fucking hated thinking about his old cell. His *tomb of informa-*

tion where he'd thought to die under the weight of all the scrolls and books. Most of all, he hated when his mind strayed to that prick who'd kept them under lock and key for the past five-hundred years. Dragomir deserved no more of his time.

The second he left that compound on the Isle of Pain, he'd sworn to never look back. He'd gone positively wild in the months since. Making a name for himself, converting the fund they'd been allowed to keep into stocks that multiplied with the slightest bit of concentration.

He excelled at increasing their holdings, but lately he'd developed other interests. *Software development.* He'd started a small firm to get his toe in the market. He now found himself firmly grounded in technological advancement specifically designed towards supernaturals. Unheard of really, but totally obtainable.

This *New World,* he smirked as he recalled his brother's archaic name for the country, they now called home, was a wondrous place indeed. Supernaturals of all types intermingled with each other. *Wolves and Bears, Goblins, Faeries, Witches, Vampires, Dhampirs, and now Dragons too.*

They conducted business just like the normals, who lived oblivious to the powerful creatures that surrounded them. From giant corporations to small independent consultants, they all used computers to operate. They were at the mercy of technologically inefficient firewalls created by normals to keep them safe.

Not anymore. He'd just solved all their fucking problems! And he should be psyched and ready to party, but instead he was dreading going downstairs.

Nikolai was the last single Dragon in his Clan. All three brothers found their mates, gave them their *roses,* and were fully mated. All but him. He tried not to think about it. Choosing instead to bury himself in work.

Anything to stop him from dwelling on that one all-important question. *Would he ever find his one true and fated mate? Would he find his emerald rose?*

He'd been hiding behind the old line that he would rather hang himself then be chained to some maiden, but the truth was, he'd simply given up. He'd circled the globe and had not felt the pull in any town or country. *Better not think on it till after the party.*

The idea he was doomed to die alone was too damn depressing. That and the way he'd been fielding unwanted attentions for the last century had led rise to certain ugly rumors he'd rather not think on. Nikolai had a secret. A deep, dark one, he did not want advertised to the entire damn universe.

He hid the truth behind his good looks and charm, using his work, books, and computers as an excuse. Genius had its prices after all. He told himself he was too busy for such trifles as affairs. It was true to a point, he had plenty of pressing work to concentrate on.

With several patents pending on groundbreaking new software, he was an extremely busy Dragon. Nikolai had been thoroughly involved with the technological age since its infancy. Being over five-hundred years old had its advantages.

Right after they'd been granted their freedom, he flew solo for a few months. Stretching the wings of his emerald-green Dragon and breathing freely for the first time in his long life. He'd met up with other supernaturals he'd done business with for the Blackthorn, attempting to reconnect under his new Clan.

It had worked to a point, until he turned down the offer to spend the night in a certain skinny, blonde Witch's bed. He'd pleasured her, there was no doubt, but he'd hated the taste of her on his tongue.

She was a hard one, but she had many connections. *Valuable ones.* The excuse he gave as to why he didn't seek pleasure for himself was the usual, lack of time, urgent business, etc... She'd accepted it at the time.

He hated that he gave in to her seductions even a little bit, but she'd repeated the dreadful rumor and he'd had no choice but to stifle her tongue. *So, he did. With his.* It would have been funny if the woman wasn't at the party tonight. *Fuck.*

Afterwards, he'd flown to the mountains and stayed alone for a few days until he'd returned to the castle his eldest brother had built them feeling refreshed and ready to work.

He'd partnered up with local guru, Randall Graves. He was the creator of the online gaming universe called *Wolf Moon* and an overall computer genius.

They'd just finished the last round of testing on his secret project. An extremely sophisticated firewall system that had been recently purchased by *Merlin Banking Solutions*. The largest international bank covertly owned and operated by supernaturals in the world.

Nikolai had worked on the finer details of the program using his incredibly unique ability to imbue software with Dragon magic. *Merlin Banking* was just the kind of corporation to benefit from his expertise. They required a *special* system.

When he'd approached Randall, a Werewolf in the Macconwood Pack who were both allies and friends of the Falk Clan, he'd been very excited to partner up with Nikolai. Being isolated as a result of his incarceration had left him at a distinct disadvantage when it came to networking and Randall had used his contacts to make the project happen.

The Falk brothers had only been out from under the Blackthorn Chief for a little over a year. It was under Dragomir that Nikolai discovered his aptitude for technology. After making money for that cretin for centuries, he was finally allowed to reap the fruit of his efforts. *And they were sweet as honey.* The only kind of honey he was getting his hands on these days. *Stupid stubborn Dragon!*

Nikolai shook off his anxiety. It was always difficult to keep his secret when confronted with a crowd of women as this party was sure to have. They were an important up and coming Clan. Their business connections alone afforded them a long guest list at any of their social events.

Necessary for business, he reminded himself. He took in his appearance one last time in front of the large black framed mirror that sat against his bedroom wall. He nodded at himself. Taller and leaner than all three of his brothers, Nikolai had the same rugged good looks.

His pale green eyes glowed with the presence of his Dragon and he worked to soothe the magical beast inside of him. He smoothed his hands over his dark hair and readied himself. *You got this.*

He'd played the carefree playboy several times over the past year, and he'd do it again to save his reputation. *Draco Fortis* meant everything, and its CEO could not be perceived as weak in any way. Nik would get through the party just fine.

He grabbed the small blue box from his dresser and headed to the first floor of *Castle Falk* where the naming day ceremony would begin.

CHAPTER

ONE

Nikolai went through the motions of greeting guests and smiling politely as well-wishers came forward with gifts and praise for his adorable little niece.

It was somehow fitting that Callius, his oldest and most powerful brother, a rare *FireDragon*, and his Werewolf mate, Winifred, were the first to bear children. The dimpled beauty wore a pink silk gown and grinned at him from her father's arms.

He smiled as he approached his healthy and beautiful little niece. A shame she would not inherit the Dragon gene, as Dragon Shifters were all male, but still, she'd be a Werewolf and that was nothing to scoff at. He watched as Callius laid the child down with such tenderness Nikolai's breath caught in his throat.

The babe was precious, as all young were. She had fine blonde hair and big blue eyes, cheeks round as a cherub's, and a small cleft in her tiny chin. He leaned down to brush a soft kiss over her head as she slept in the small, elegant bassinet his other brother, Sander, had made for her.

Sander had a profound talent for art, usually tapestry weaving. He'd put his talents to great use here. The unique crib was made of

275

aged redwood, He'd carved an enormous Dragon, wings elevated to the skies next to a howling wolf with an enormous rose encompassing them like an umbrella on the tiny headboard.

Three more Dragons circled the bottom of the bassinet, along with other bits of fancy, a magic wand, a Christmas tree, bows, flowers, and some stars here and there. The detail was amazing. He'd stained and polished the wood until it gleamed.

A thing of exquisite beauty. It was perfection itself, as was his sleeping niece. His heart squeezed painfully. He was happy for his brother and his mate, but he secretly longed for what they had. *A mate. Love. A family.*

"Brother! You've joined us at last," Callius and Fred greeted him with fiery embraces. Nik couldn't help but return them enthusiastically even as his own emptiness threatened to consume him.

It always did when he observed any of his brothers with their mates. The bond between them beautiful and solid, thriving as if it were an independent living thing. Nikolai was ashamed of the jealousy he felt, but he did his best to keep it under wraps. He thrust the small blue box into Fred's hand and laughed as she exclaimed over what he considered a trifle.

"Oh my! Look at this! Two tennis bracelets for a child! Nik, it's too much!"

"Nonsense, this little one deserves the best, besides it's only a total of about five carats, hardly worth mentioning."

"Are you nuts?"

He laughed again, always shocked at his American sister-in-law's outspoken ways. She was definitely something alright! Blonde and lovely, a perfect foil for his darker and formally brooding brother.

Callius was admiring the emerald tennis bracelets, smiling as he did so. *Yes, Dragons certainly loved treasure.*

The gift was designed to please and honor both his niece and her parents. He'd called the world-famous jewelers known by their special blue boxes, with express instructions to have one bauble made to fit a child and, to make an exact replica suitable for when she was an adult.

Emeralds to remind her of him. He always wanted her to remember her Uncle Nik on her name day. What better way than with jewels almost as precious as she was? He'd had them shipped raw from their mines in South America and cut and designed by the jewelers at his behest. *A fine choice.*

Callius kissed his wife indulgently and practically beamed with pride at his newest treasure. He brushed a large hand gently over his precious baby's head and beckoned Nikolai to follow him as he sought out their brothers.

"Can you believe it, gentlemen? I am a father!"

A round of congrats passed amongst the brothers as they toasted him and his family. Sander smiled blissfully, his own Noelle was pregnant with their first child, and he was soon to join the ranks of fatherhood.

"While we are all here, I want to share the news with all of you," Edric began.

Nikolai plastered a smile on his face as yet another of his brothers announced his impending fatherhood. *I am alone*, the panicked thought had his breath struggling to get out. Yet through it all he remained passive on the outside.

"Nik? I said aren't you going to congratulate me?" Edric held out his hand and Nikolai grabbed it briefly.

"Indeed, but don't get too close, it might be contagious," he barked out a false laugh, but the others ate it up.

They rejoined the crowds, each of his brothers joining their mates while he stood to the outside. Crowds of people, some friends, other business acquaintances milled about the ballroom. Enjoying the food prepared by his sister-in-law's event planning and catering company, *Present Tastes.* Noelle was radiant in a flowing blue dress that lit up her eyes. The small baby bump did nothing to detract from her beauty as she and Joselyn spoke to guests, their husbands at their sides.

Local Whiskey tycoon Mason Lane and his wife, Abigail were there. So was, Rafe Maccon, Alpha of the Macconwood Pack, and his wife, Charley. His beta, Seff was in attendance with his mate, a renowned White Witch, Sherry Morgan. They all laughed and chatted pleasantly.

Everyone seemed to have a mate. Except him. *Always on the outside.* He supposed he could mingle with the business contacts who'd been invited, but he was not feeling up to it.

His hiding behind work was like second nature. Fortunately, he had a small office in the main part of Castle Falk. It was nothing like his sanctum upstairs in his own private wing of the castle, but it was fully functional and allowed him to get info down whenever the inspiration hit.

Unfortunately, a certain Witch that he'd been hoping to avoid took it upon herself to follow him in there. *Fuck.* He smelled the heavily perfumed woman and growled his distaste.

"Hiya, handsome," she said, pressing her artificially enhanced breasts against his back and curling her hand around his stomach.

He wanted to snap and snarl and fling her across the room, but that would not do. She was a powerful businessperson and he had to keep that part of his life professional. His lip curled in disgust.

Nikolai halted the progress of her wandering, red tipped hands, but he did not push her away. Impeccable manners wouldn't allow. Plus, it was partly his fault.

She'd obviously misread the bit of oral pleasure he'd given her some months back, for an open invitation. He'd acted the playboy for so long, his reputation was bound to make the rounds. Even at an afternoon family friendly gathering as this was.

"Hello, Ms. White," he chose to call her by her surname, hoping the formality would speak for itself, "I'm sorry but you caught me at a bad time."

He hoped to bluff his way out of this without the obligatory performance. As a matter of fact, he was damned determine to avoid it at all costs. She was not his type at all. *No one was.* But especially not her with her too much make-up wearing, bathed in perfume, and bespelled body. His Dragon snarled in revulsion.

"Oh, I don't think that's true, *Nicky-boy*, you see, I've heard some fascinating things about you since we last met," she said and ran her red tipped fingers up and down his silk shirt.

Nik had to fight to keep himself from pushing her off. His Dragon was repulsed. The Beast wanted no part of any female who was not his mate. Ms. Angie White was certainly not his anything. She held controlling interests in several corporations. In fact, he'd learned that her tiny Coven was devoted to her desires for power in the business world.

Interesting, but not his business. He simply did not want to start anything with the woman. She could find ways of retaliating he was sure to dislike. His Dragon agreed. The beast would rather spend his time searching for his other half.

The obsession with finding his one true mate had started centuries ago, but Nik had been able to hide his obvious lack of interest in the females who threw themselves at him in other ways.

He used to be able to simply fuck them and leave well enough alone. A quick little lay and a pat on the head as it were. He knew it was wrong, but his conquests had all understood. Women simply threw themselves at him. And he hadn't really wanted a single one of them. Not. One.

A fact that was increasingly obvious to the Witch in front of him. Her pouty blood red lips frowned as she pressed herself more firmly against him, trying to grind her hips into eliciting a response from him.

"Is it possible I heard wrong? And after we had such fun last time?" she narrowed her greedy eyes, and he could see the wheels turning. *Oh shit.*

"My dear, you wound me! On any other day, I'd be happy to take you for a spin, but my dear, it is my niece's name day," Nikolai forced a chuckle and casually distanced himself from her.

Fuck. She knows! She smirked and plastered her lips to his in a skillful tease that did absolutely nothing to garner his interest. Luckily, the gong his brother had installed in the ball room sounded and he was able to extricate himself once again.

"I am sorry, Angie dear, but I cannot miss this. Another time," he inclined his head and looked at her over-used body with what he hoped she'd think was lust shining in his eyes.

His acting skills were better than he thought he mused as she preened in front of him and turned around like the cat that ate the canary.

"Later, lover," she purred and slunk away on her too high heels.

Nikolai exhaled and moved to the sink in the corner. It wasn't that he disliked sex. He liked it very much. The fact was his body had other ideas when it came to coitus. As in, if it did not involve his mate, he wasn't having any.

Shit. He dried his hands and strode out through one of the many secret corridors in the castle to the ballroom. He arrived in time to hear his brother announce the name of his beautiful little niece.

"We would like to introduce you all to *Rosanna Juliet Falk*, our daughter," Callius' voice boomed across the ballroom with pride and love as cheers broke out all around.

Niko raised his glass and cheered right along with them, accepting congratulations and brimming with love for his brother's family. But at the same time, he couldn't ignore the hollow feeling in the pit of his stomach.

Will I ever have this for myself?

CHAPTER

TWO

"Ms. Casper! How nice to see you, honey! Isn't it exciting?"

"What's that, Mrs. Grayson?" Melody Casper looked up from her oversized purse and smiled at the shorter woman. Mrs. Grayson was a fixture at the company watering hole! Well, it was actually an exclusive, organic coffee and pastry shop.

"Well, now that we have addressed all external threats to our accounts with this improved firewall from *Draco Fortis* and *Graves Enterprises*, I expect you are sleeping better these days! Oooh, are those cranberry scones, dear?" Mrs. Grayson, a softly rounded woman in her mid-sixties smiled with her sharp little teeth showing as she spoke to Melody.

"yes, ma'am, I think they are," a management accountant for *Merlin Banking Solutions*, Melody Casper was responsible for verifying whether or not certain projects were worth the risk to her company.

They'd recently been hacked by a magically enhanced virus that had been downloaded by a fellow management accountant in their

281

Dallas cooperate offices and everyone was shaking in their boots expecting to be fired.

Merlin Banking Solutions was based out of New York City, but they had offices all over the world. They handled professional and personal banking needs for millions of people, mainly those in the supernatural community.

"Yes, Mrs. Grayson, I am very excited about the new firewall and I believe those are cranberry currant scones with cream cheese frosting!"

"Oh my, I think I'll have to get me some of those!" Half-Sugarplum Fairy, Mrs. Grayson had a bit of a sweet tooth. Melody shared the affliction, though she was a Coyote Shifter herself.

The two had become office friends a year ago when they'd both almost fought over the last salted-caramel brownie in the shop after a particularly trying week. Melody had offered to split it, and they'd hit it off.

"You know, I'd never have believed anyone could pull it off, if I hadn't seen the improvement in network performance myself," Melody sighed and inhaled the sweet fragrances coming from the shop. The line was a mile long, but she was not getting off before she had a steaming peppermint latte in her hand!

"Really, dear, well I am glad to hear it! It came at a substantial cost."

"All good things do, Mrs. Grayson. Even the magical element is a vast improvement than what we had in place before."

"Yes, well of course it is. Melody dear, you do know the owner of *Draco Fortis* is an exceedingly rare, very powerful, and I hear very handsome, *Dragon Shifter*."

The older woman's eyes practically glowed in glee at the secret she'd revealed to Melody.

"Really?" She smiled at the older woman with wide-eyed interest. As a Coyote Shifter, Melody knew when others were lying or faking. Thank goodness Mrs. Grayson was not a Shifter of any kind.

It was rumored the older woman, while one-half Sugarplum

Fairy, was also half-Sprite, a tricky, gossipy bunch if *supes* if ever there was one. But it didn't matter to Melody. Mrs. Grayson was a sweet woman and Melody enjoyed having coffee with her.

"Yes! A real Dragon! Can you believe it? And I hear he is a bit of a hound, if you know what I mean, you know if I were your age, *ooh la la*," she practically purred.

Of course, Melody was very aware the owner of *Draco Fortis* was, in fact, a Dragon. Having heard the whispers and rumors about the formidable and quite brilliant, Nikolai Falk, she was both impressed by his genius as she was in awe of his beast.

Dragon Shifters were rare and uniquely gifted with more magic than any of the other Shifter groups. Melody was a Coyote Shifter herself and relished the ability to change shape into her cunning little animal.

When she was in her human form, she still had many of her supernatural senses like fast healing, heightened senses, and the usual. Coyotes were sort of like Wolf Shifters, or Werewolves as they were commonly called. They lived in smaller Packs or Bands and adhered to a hierarchy based on dominance. Her family was not in the inner circle, but the ruling Alpha of her small band back home was fair enough.

She was too dominant enough to gain notice, but she was no pushover. She couldn't afford to be. Unlike many of her kind, Melody sported a rounded figure with large breasts, wide hips, and big legs. Chubby as a child she was used to taunts and the meanness of other *pups*.

Nowadays, she stood five and a half feet tall and had long brown hair with large, natural, honey-colored chunks that fell framing her face. Her hair had always been multi-colored and where she hated it as a child, she loved it now. Not that many believed it was her real hair.

She wondered what they'd say if they knew her hair was honey-colored down below too! Not that she cared what others thought. They could suit themselves or not. Melody liked her body and her hair!

Her best feature, of course, were her fiery amber eyes. Sometimes they gleamed like liquid gold. A true Coyote trait inherited from her father. Of course, he was all muscle and good looks. Like her mom. Both of them still thin and muscular in their late fifties.

Melody sighed. *Oh well.* She was still pretty, if a little plump, and more so, she was happy. Her size was what it was. She ate healthy and exercised, but yes, she had a sweet tooth, and she did not deny it.

It in no way affected her happiness with her shape. Something her ex-husband could not understand. Thomas had tried in so many ways to change her, to her utter mortification and eventual heartbreak. But she was at peace with it now.

Their marriage had ended three years ago, and she was better off without him. Still, that didn't mean she was an option for the Dragon playboy. But she smiled and listened to the rumors Mrs. Grayson had gathered all week about the elusive techie millionaire.

Melody knew a lot about Nikolai Falk, including his amazing portfolio. Apparently, the wiz didn't just develop software, he was also a genius at investments. He'd been in charge of his brothers' portfolios for a long time. She'd been able to trace his work back to about two hundred years or so.

Records got tricky any further back than that. He even kept some of his money with *Merlin Banking*. And from what her boss had told her that morning, they wanted more.

She'd been put to work assessing the risks and benefits of using the *Draco Fortis* firewall weeks ago and had voted in favor of the change much to her boss' approval. He'd wanted to do business with the Dragon very badly.

"Dear, did you hear me?" The lilting voice of her companion brought her back to reality.

"I apologize, Mrs. Grayson, what did you say? My mind just wandered a bit there," she smiled apologetically.

"That's alright, Melody dear, I said I ordered your latte."

"Thank you."

"Oh, you were far away in thought I gather. You know you do remind me of myself when I was younger," the older woman smiled, and Melody returned it.

"Nah, I'm much too shy to be like you!"

"Nonsense! I know what you need, a nice shopping trip! Go on and get yourself something sexy and new for the *World Banks Charity Ball!*"

"What do you mean?"

"Well, he'll be there. He's the VIP, you know."

"Oh, Mrs. Grayson, I doubt someone like Nikolai Falk will even notice I'm there," she began.

"He sure won't if you don't make an effort. Melody dear, life is passing you by. You work eighty hours a week-"

"How did you know that?"

"Honey, I'm in human *and supernaturals* resources, it is my job to know! Now, everyone there will be vying for the man's attentions! You have to stick out, dear! My daughter-in-law runs an up-and-coming little boutique down on West 37th Street, just tell Carol I sent you!"

Melody didn't have the heart to tell her that the boutique was unlikely to offer anything that would flatter her fuller figure, but she listened silently. After a lengthy monologue by her colleague and some nudging, she eventually promised to go and check it out herself before taking what would amount to two buses and a train ride back to the small apartment she rented in Hoboken, New Jersey.

Damn my commute! She said her goodbyes, promising to stop by Mrs. Grayson's daughter-in-law's shop, *Skin Deep*, before she headed home that night. She stood and threw away her used cup and napkin before heading back to her desk. *What have I gotten myself into?* She groaned.

Melody had genuinely loved working in the city at first, but she'd hated living there immediately. She'd frequented the one-square-mile town of Hoboken to partake of its restaurants and bars, as well as the frequent festivals the place offered. It had small-town charm, with the convenience of being close to her place of employment. Of course, after ten years the shine had worn off.

She longed to just slow down. Work had become her life when all she really wanted was a family of her own. She had no one left here. No siblings or cousins. Her parents had moved down to Florida the second she was old enough to move out. Melody visited once a year, but even that was strained and awkward. Close, they were not!

Life was supposed to turn out differently, she growled. She'd married the first man who'd asked her out of sheer joy that someone had wanted her. Her parents and peers had told her often enough she'd never find a mate. *Ugh.*

Thomas was handsome and funny at first. A Coyote Shifter like her, but unlike her he had a gambling habit and no ability to hold down a job. *Yeah.* He was a real winner.

His teasing had quickly turned ugly. The comments about her weight grew frequent and nastier over time. Thomas Newton had battered her fragile ego until she couldn't stand to be in the same room with him.

He'd wanted her to lose about forty pounds and wasn't shy about saying it loudly and in public. She stuck by him for five years, trying every fad diet she heard of to make him happy. All that time together and with truly little to show for it, she'd finally had enough, and said goodbye.

That was three years ago, and she hadn't looked back. The thing was, she hadn't looked forward either. *Mrs. Grayson is right, Melody, you need to start living.* Working eighteen hours a day was hardly that.

If she were being honest, she'd admit what she really wanted was a real home. *Children.* But at thirty-five years old how likely was that to happen? Anger threatened to cloud her vision as she felt herself slide into old patterns.

No! I don't need a man to make me happy ever after! Fuck that! That was true enough, but Mrs. Grayson hadn't suggested she needed a member of the opposite sex to find happiness. She'd said a night of wild sex and fun. *Hmmm.* The idea had merit after all.

Maybe a new dress was called for. *Hell, maybe after I splurge on something sexy for this godforsaken party, I will have me some wild sex with a hot as hell Dragon too!* Hell, to the yeah. Melody Casper was single and free. She could do anything she damn well pleased.

Melody straightened her shoulders and went back to her office, her new plan in tow! *Operation Get Me Some* was under way!

THREE

*W*hat the fuck is with all the emails and voicemails this *morning?* Nikolai fumed as he went down the huge list of contact information his inbox was streaming with.

True, they were potential clients, but really? Was all this necessary? I mean, give a guy a day to get back to you. Some of them were repeats. One particularly insistent firm, which after a little digging, he found was run by that bothersome Witch, Angie White, was located on the west coast. They called themselves *Viridi Lux* or Green Light Coven.

He rolled his eyes. He'd dealt with their kind before. Witches had access to a finite amount of power and often held the upper hand in dealing with Shifters. This particular Witch seemed upset at his turning her down.

Well, Dragons were not like typical Shifters. She'd find out soon enough if she persisted in antagonizing him. *Virdi Lux* was spreading rumors that his firewall was less than what it was described as. He'd fix that very quickly.

Dragon Shifters had stepped out of the world at large some centuries back, preferring to deal with their own kind. Perhaps the

Witches simply forgot that he had access to magic of his own. Phenomenal powers with unlimited access, unlike Witches.

He'd get back to *Viridi Lux* when he was damn well ready. He disliked liars and bullies in general, those traits in a Coven of Witches were a serious *no-no*. He sent a quick email to Callius, as head of the Falk Clan, he was to be kept abreast of all potential threats and this was a threat. However slight.

When he'd announced that *Draco Fortis* was building a firewall for *Merlin Banking Solutions*, he had no idea how many other companies would be interested in his product. Both in obtaining it and in destroying it.

Well, that wasn't exactly true. He'd had some idea, of course. But this? No. He was not prepared for this bombardment. How was he supposed to code and work on growing their treasure horde if he had to answer all these inquests?

He'd need to take on more help if he were to continue. Creating something as complex as this firewall project with Graves Enterprises wasn't like playing the stock market. This was something else. He needed an assistant. Someone to manage the business end of things.

He'd ask Randall for suggestions. In the meanwhile, he needed to pack a bag. He was headed out for the World Banks Charity Ball and to meet with the Merlin Banking Solutions president about the last upgrade to their system. Everything had gone beautifully, and he had the report to prove it.

So, why was he so fucking restless? Hmm, you know why, damn you. He was a lone Dragon Shifter in a castle surrounded by his three mated brothers and their families. He was not jealous per se, but he was feeling his age and his circumstances grievously.

It was wreaking havoc on his inner beast. His Dragon roared and slunk off in the deepest most cavern of his mind's eye. The beast was still pissed off after his last failed encounter.

After that brief and somewhat embarrassing scene with Ms.

White, he'd attempted to try again. He'd convinced himself it was okay to try and let off some steam with the opposite sex.

For fuck's sake, I am a Dragon! Unfortunately for him, Nikolai found he was still unable to, um, *rise to the occasion.*

His Dragon roared and huffed out a breath of green smoke at the memory. *Only our mate will do*, he growled at Nikolai. *None other.*

Fucking bloody bastard. His body had failed him, and he was beyond furious. No sex for a century could do that to a male!

His Dragon's scales glowed like emeralds in his mind's eye as the beast opened his massive jaws to let loose a roar. The deafening sound was enough to send Nikolai to his knees.

He glanced at his chest to the place where his emerald rose sat as he undressed and went to shower. His frown was deep as he gazed upon the sacred marking. It was closed and pitiful looking. A tight, wrinkled bud, where a powerful blossom should be.

Fuck. He was running out of time. Alexsander had told him how he felt at Death's door before he'd met his mate. *The legend is true, Nik, without Noelle I'd have died.*

Fuck. Nikolai did everything he could to find the one the universe had created for him, to no avail. So, he'd occupied his time with as much activity as possible. Trying to fill the void inside of him.

This new firewall he'd developed was a great accomplishment. Something he was immensely proud of. And yet, without finding his maiden, *his one true and fated mate*, it was all for nothing.

Soon, his beast would do one of two things. Either he would wither and die, or he would go stark raving mad. Nikolai already had an inkling which way things were headed.

His *EnergyDragon* was growing increasingly hard to control. Anger rolled off the beast in waves, he was restless and furious with his human half for failing to find his lifelong companion. His lack of libido was just one small symptom. There had been others lately.

Quick rise to fury. Lack of focus. Why just this week he'd almost decked two normals at the local sushi place, *Roll Over*, that he frequented. He couldn't even think of a reason why he should be so angry at them. Only they'd rubbed him the wrong way somehow.

He shrugged as he stood under the hard spray of hot water. Even the *normals* had enough sense to avoid him. They knew better than to approach a predator in his state. Humans had some self-preservation skills at least, all evidence to the contrary aside.

He bathed himself in quick steady movements. Efficiently washing over his *no longer working* bits. *FML.* He growled and rinsed off his shoulder length dark hair, scrubbing his face roughly before stepping out onto the thick bathmat.

Nikolai stared at his reflection. His eyes glowed a pale green as his Dragon came forward. *Yes,* he was too thin, his rose shriveled, and his mood foul. But he had to push it all aside for now.

He had work to do. First thing on the list was to pack his bag and head out to New York City. He'd be driving himself in his sleek silver Phantom Rolls Royce. The luxury vehicle dominated the road the way his Dragon did the skies.

Though he could fly into the city unnoticed, Callius frowned upon such theatrics. So, Nik opted for second best. He hurried out of the castle without running into any of his brothers or their wives and exhaled a breath of relief.

Soon, he promised his Dragon, *we will search for our mate again and we will find her. Or die trying.*

FOUR

Melody spun around in front of the full-length mirror in her bedroom. She could not believe the transformation in herself.

When she'd walked into *Skin Deep*, she didn't know what to expect. Finding exquisite couture gowns for plus-size women was like stepping into a dream! They'd even had some gowns that fit her curvaceous frame without alterations. *Talk about a bonus!*

Melody could have stayed there for hours just trying things on. The place was that good! She was thrilled to meet Amelia Grayson, Mrs. Grayson's daughter-in-law. The woman was an absolute gem!

After a few minutes of looking around, Amelia had gotten a twinkle in her deep purple eyes. She'd darted to the back room only to return with the most gorgeous dress Melody had ever seen!

It was a long, strappy gown, a deep green color, made of the softest fabric imaginable. It looked amazing with Melody's honey-kissed hair and lightly tanned skin. She simply had to try it on. *Thank goodness she did!*

She never wore sleeveless anymore. After listening to her husband rant about her fat arms and too large breasts, she'd given up wearing anything without a high neckline and at least three-quarter sleeves. *Funny how she hadn't started wearing them again even after the divorce.*

The gown was cut as if it were made for her. The silky material clung to her curves, flattering her fuller frame. Her large breasts were beautifully displayed without being vulgar. The built-in bra made it possible for her to wear only a pair of sheer seamless panties underneath. She bit her lip as she stared at her reflection.

She looked sexy. Hell, she felt sexy too. Melody turned to check out her butt. All women did! She ignored the blush of her cheeks as she took in the way her heart-shaped ass was outlined in the fabric. *Day-um. Baby got back alright.* She cringed then allowed her gaze to travel upward.

The gown dipped way low in the back, the material stopping just over the swell of her ass. Four thin, beaded straps, loosely criss-crossed the span of smooth skin, revealing the tip of a tiny wing from the tattoo she'd gotten years ago just over her left hip.

She'd chosen the dragon tattoo to spite her parents who'd often scoffed at the idea of her decorating her buxom shape in anything other than work clothes or sweats. Whenever she'd tried to wear something even the slightest bit flirtatious, she'd been told that wasn't made for someone like her.

The second she was old enough and had earned enough from her first job, she'd gone to a Shifter run tattoo shop. She'd chosen an emerald-green Dragon, for some reason the fierce beastie had called to her and green was her favorite color.

The tattoo wrapped around her hip, the tail curving under her left buttock and the wings spanning from her back to her soft belly. The design was executed perfectly, the Hawk Shifter who'd applied it had been the first boy she'd ever kissed.

Just a sweet meeting of the lips. He'd been a little too mature and wild for a seventeen-year-old virgin. Ultimately, he was not for her, but she loved that tattoo.

Needless to say, she'd gotten it before Thomas, back when she was young and wanted to take on the world. She liked that hint of something wild the low back revealed. *Yes.* It was perfect for tonight!

Not that she had any reason to get all worked up. In her humble opinion, sex wasn't all it was cracked up to be. *No. Not going there.* Even if she was tempted to fall into bed with someone.

Melody refused to go down that dark and dangerous road. She bit her lip and did a quick turn-around. *Focus on having fun!* It had been too long since she let her hair down.

She looked curvy and sexy as hell. Melody had piled her long hair on top of her head, leaving curly tendrils to frame her lightly made-up face and neck.

She'd always hated artificial things and make-up was up there on the list. She had great skin and full lips and used only the barest minimum of powder to dust her cheeks, nose, and forehead. She chose a shimmery, gold shadow for over her eyelids, dark brown mascara to enhance her already long lashes, and a shiny mauve lip gloss to finish. She was more than ready to have a good time.

Melody's stomach muscles clenched with nerves. She wondered why she was feeling so anxious. Most of the people at the ball would be business acquaintances. People she had worked with either in person or on the phone.

True, they'd never seen her like this, but why would they? She'd hardly wear a gown in the office. At any rate, there would be a number of strangers there as well. Her Coyote peered through her eyes, making them glow in the dim light of her bedroom. It was as if she sensed something coming. *Something big.*

She crinkled her nose and sighed, grabbing her evening bag and slipping on the thin heeled shoes she'd splurged on to go with the sinful gown.

Surprisingly enough, they were comfortable and added some much-needed height for her to pull off the entire ambiance of her attire. She'd be mingling with millionaires, powerful businesspeople, and even heads of state, *supernatural and normal alike.* Tickets to the *Worlds Bank Charity Ball* were coveted. At five-thousand dollars a head, they were not easy to come by. Thankfully, her employer paid for hers.

She grabbed her matching sheer wrap and left her apartment. The driver exited the waiting sedan, giving her a once over that made her grin though she chose not to acknowledge the borderline leer. If anything, she was flattered.

There would be no subways for her in this outfit, she smiled. She'd never splurged on the luxury of ordering a car before, but if she were going to play *Cinderella* she might as well go all the way.

Music pulsed as Melody made her way through the crowds. Her sensitive nose picked up on several supernaturals in the room. The ball was an event frequented by both human and supernaturally run banks and companies across the world.

It was her first time attending, however. She was not much for parties. Tom had truly done a number on her confidence she realized sadly. She didn't know why she'd ever taken what he'd said to heart.

They weren't mates in any true sense of the word. He'd played on her insecurities and paid attention to her at a time when she was feeling lost and quite low. She married him believing he'd change and grow to love her for herself in time. But he never had.

The way he griped on about her size was one more nail in the coffin of their marriage. She'd gotten enough of that kind of shit from the snarky females in her old band. She'd been called all sorts of names as a kid and teen. *Fatso, chubs, two-tons of fun, you name it. Bitches.*

Coyotes were social creatures, but the band she'd grown up with was ripe with judgmental individuals who thought they were entitled to criticize those they did not understand. Melody was big, but she was also smart and kind. And she was beautiful in her own way.

It took a long time for her to embrace herself for who she was. Now, at the age of thirty-five, she finally accepted her body as it was, and, to other people's constant consternation, she fucking loved herself.

Every inch, every jiggle, every dimple. Melody Casper was a

confident woman. Even if she repeated that little mantra to herself at least once a day. Her Coyote whole-heartedly approved of her self-affirmation.

Didn't her old math teacher, Sr. Rita, teach her that? She recalled the old, white-haired nun fondly. She spoke with a lilting Irish accent that had been firm, and yet kind. Tears stung Melody's eyes as she recalled her inspiring words.

Repeat after me, Miss Casper. I am good. I am beautiful. I am God's perfect handiwork and God loves me. There now. Pay no attention to the others. God makes no mistakes, child, and He made you. Remember that.

Yes, Sr. Rita, I remember. Melody sighed and got hold of her emotions. She was not a child anymore. And she was not Thomas's scared little wife. She was Melody Casper, Coyote Shifter, management accountant at *Merlin Banking Solutions*.

She felt wonderful in her new gown and, judging from the men breaking their necks to get a glance, she looked wonderful too! She felt her cheeks heat but relished the fact that she could induce that kind of behavior from the opposite sex.

"Melody, my dear" Mrs. Grayson ascended on her like a storm and gave her a great, big hug.

"Hi, Mrs. Grayson," she laughed and hugged the woman back.

"You look beautiful, my dear! Amelia treated you well then, yes?"

"Yes, I just love her store. I bought a few items, but she insisted I wear this gown this evening. I admit it is my favorite."

"Indeed, she was right! Green is your color, dear!"

They chatted a few minutes and Melody smiled. The older woman was charming and lovely. She knew she was retiring this year, and Melody thought what a shame to not have her around to chat with.

"I'm expecting to be a full-time grandmother you know!"

"Congratulations! You'll be a wonderful grandmother. I am more than certain of that fact."

"Thank you, dear, I am so excited!"

Melody nodded and chatted until Mrs. Grayson was cooped up

by her husband who wanted to dance with his wife. She loved that the graying couple was still so obviously in love. They were lucky.

Melody exhaled. She'd settle for a night where she didn't go to bed alone. A little light fun. Sex and no strings. That was all she wanted for herself. Anything else was unrealistic.

She walked up to the open bar and ordered a flute of champagne. She tapped her neat, unpolished nails on the gleaming wood counter and waited for her drink. She noted a platinum-blonde giant of a man walking up to the bar.

She inhaled a deep breath. *Shifter.* But she could not tell what kind. The scent was not *canid* or *feline*, it was something else she was unfamiliar with. Still, he smelled nice enough. She smiled and accepted her drink from the bartender. The stranger looked down at her and did a slow double-take of her breasts before raising his gaze to meet her laughing eyes.

He wasn't the first man in the room to be caught drooling over her ample cleavage. It amused her more than anything that men would stare at her body when the rest of society deemed her over-weight and unattractive. *The hell with them. I look good!*

"Uh, I guess, I'm busted," he grinned revealing a cute little dimple on his right cheek. He was genuinely nice looking, even if Melody didn't usually go for blondes. Still, he might be nice to chat with while she sipped her champagne.

"Yes, I'd say you are! Do you always have a one-track mind?"

"Excuse me?"

"Well, when you consider where your eyes were your choice of words is interesting. *Busted* indeed," she smirked back.

"That is funny, my sweet," his accent held traces of England. She laughed with him even though her joke was kind of lame.

"I would apologize to you, but you'd know I was lying. So, what if I simply tell you the truth then?" He quirked his lips and she nodded, eager to hear him continue.

"You have got an amazing body. And that gown looks as if it has been made for you. Simply gorgeous, love. You could conquer nations in that dress. I was simply appreciating the view."

Melody's eyebrows were raised to her hairline. Talk about a smooth line. Holy cow!

"My name is Cecil, by the way, and you are?" He reached out to take her hand.

"I'm Melody Casper-" she smiled and was about to accept his proffered hand when she felt a powerful urge to turn around. It was as if someone or something was pulling her towards them.

She turned, and her gaze collided with a strange man. He was even bigger than the giant next to her. He had silky, dark hair and wore a perfectly tailored tuxedo.

He looked incredible. *Devastating.* Yet, he was breathing as if he were in pain. Helpless to stop herself, she crossed the twenty feet or so that separated them.

Melody stopped a breath away from the stranger, his intoxicating aroma filled her nostrils and sent her senses a-tingling. She exhaled, feeling the Coyote rise to take a look.

His low growl reverberated from his chest, causing her skin to break out in goosebumps. *He was sex on two legs.* She vibrated with anticipated pleasure but pushed the mental image away.

What kind of person salivated over a man in pain? She mentally berated herself as she fought the instinctive urge to wrap herself around his enormous frame. Instead, she focused on his breathing, looking for injuries as her eyes ran over his large body.

"Are you alright?"

FIVE

Nikolai had handed the keys to his Rolls over to the valet along with a couple of hundred-dollar bills. The man smiled widely and nodded, promising to take care of his vehicle.

He breathed deep, taking in the many scents, most unpleasant, that was New York. The crowded, impatient, beast of city was home to many, though he failed to see the appeal.

Fine for conducting business or taking in the sites, but not as a dwelling place. He'd left his luxury penthouse suite at the exclusive hotel he'd booked and made it across town in record time.

Something tickled his senses as he stood taking in his surroundings. *Bam.* It hit him again. Hard. *Fuck.* He pressed his hand over his chest. He felt odd. He was a predator at heart. His *EnergyDragon* peeked out and looked over his surroundings. He was safe, but something was different.

Nikolai rolled his shoulders trying to dispel some of the tension he felt. He frowned as he entered the stuffy, though beautifully decorated room. They had chosen a terrific venue, he thought idly. Too bad they'd filled it with a bunch of self-important idiots.

He was greeted by a few bank presidents that he was acquainted with. He'd done business with several of them, *supernaturals* and *normals* alike. Some of the faces were new, but the names remained.

Banking in the supernatural world was a family affair, and he'd been around a very, very long time. First, he'd been doing business for the Blackthorn Clan at the behest of his jailor, and now he did it for himself and his brothers.

Indeed, the Falk Clan was already wealthy, but now they were gaining ground in the world of technology. *Taking it by storm*, to hear the head of *Merlin Banking Solutions* tell it.

Daniel Atkins was an older man, an elf to be precise. He was wise and affable. He liked making money, but not as much as he liked his spotless reputation. After a hacker got past their old system using some nefarious spells, he'd come knocking on Nikolai's door for the brand-new magically enhanced firewall he'd spent the past year perfecting.

Nikolai had interviewed him regarding some details about banking that he'd needed for his software. That was how Daniel knew about it. He had volunteered to test the firewall for Nikolai, but he hadn't wanted to pay for the tremendous upgrade until it became clear to him that it was a necessity.

"Yes, my boy, you saved my life! Because of you, we no longer have to change our slogan, we simply are the *most secure bank in the world*! Genius! You, *Falk*, are pure genius," Atkins' voice boomed across the room and Nikolai groaned. He hadn't wanted his presence announced in such a way.

"Excuse me, Atkins, I'm off to get a drink," he nodded and excused himself. Nikolai liked the man, but he was tired of talking business tonight.

He cringed when a familiar woman blocked his way as he attempted to flee the crowd. All he'd wanted was to find himself a quiet corner and indulge in a nice tumbler of *Apple Thyme Bite*. The artisan whiskey was crafted by a neighbor of his, and Nikolai was greatly impressed with the quality of the product.

Angie White reeked of magic. The Witch was using a particularly strong glamour to make herself appear younger than she was in reality. Not that Nik would have approved of her even if she were as young as she'd like people to believe.

He noted her bespelled hair and features with a grimace. He wondered what she would say if he told her he could see right through her glamour. *All the way to the skinny hag underneath.* She'd probably try and hex him, he thought, bored with the idea as he was with her constant presence.

"As I live and breathe, Nikolai Falk of *Draco Fortis*, in the very fine flesh," her beady eyes sized him up and he could only imagine what she saw. Dollar signs? A chance to find out of the rumors she spread were true. He was not letting her get that close to him. Not tonight or ever again.

"Yes, hello Ms. White. Excuse me, won't you?" He pushed past her only to find the irritating Witch following on his heels.

He felt his Dragon surge forward and he stopped in his tracks. *No. Not now.* He tried to regain control of the beast, but something was not right. Whether it was the annoying presence of the Witch who kept babbling in his ear, the way her fake tits pushed up to her throat in that mockery of a dress, or the fact that there were too many strangers in the room, he didn't know.

"I said, have you considered my proposal for a merger between *Draco Fortis* and *Viridi Lux*. I have been trying awfully hard to connect with you all week, *Nicky-boy*, we can make this work. Seal the deal and all that, what do you say?"

"Ms. White, while I'm sorry I didn't return your calls, I have been quite busy, but a merger is not in the cards for us," he was polite out of habit. Normally he'd be thinking of ways to fake his inability to *be with her*, but right then his attention was elsewhere.

"I see. Well, maybe you and I can meet up, after all this, and *talk?*" She smiled at him, her grin showing too much of her teeth and gums. It was a mockery of a smile, one he ignored completely as the scent of something tantalizing reached his nostrils.

The spicy citrus fragrance was driving him wild. His *Energy-Dragon* rippled beneath his skin. He needed to step back and try to rein in his beast for the sake of appearances. Too many normals around for his tastes.

There it is again! Suddenly, everything was *too much*. Too much noise. Too much light. Too many smells. Too many strangers.

Nikolai tilted his head and breathed in deep, desperate to get away from the crowds and the noise of the gala. He stopped abruptly, as if some unseen force had him in its grip.

That beguiling aroma filtered its way through the cloying perfumes and artificial colognes, making his insides tingle with awareness. *Grrr.*

He strode forward, determined to find its source. He picked his way through the throng of partygoers, flinching away in disgust when another bold woman with far too little clothing on rubbed her body against him, her invitation clear.

He growled and, with a single-minded determination he'd never shown before, Nikolai went flying across the room, uncaring of those he shoved out of the way. *Es meus*, his emerald Dragon roared in his mind's eye. Those words stopped him in his tracks like nothing else could. She was here. In that very room. *His mate.*

He inhaled and groaned aloud as the sweet, tempting scent hit him again, harder than before. He opened his eyes to see a curvy goddess dressed in a forest green gown standing before him, concern marring her fiery whiskey-colored eyes.

"Are you alright?" her voice was husky and soft.

It sent chills down his spine. *And more.* For the first time in nigh on a hundred years, Nikolai's cock filled to bursting.

He felt his Dragon surge forward, powerful and hungry.

Nikolai whispered the only thing he could think to say before sweeping her into his arms and lowering his mouth to hers, "Mine."

SIX

oly fucking shit. Melody barely had enough time to register that the gorgeous stranger she'd spied across the room, who'd been trembling and breathing heavily, now had her in his steely arms and was kissing the life out of her in front of everyone!

Well, she knew he was a Shifter. But even her keen sense of smell couldn't discern what kind. He smelled *powerful.* Full of magic, as opposed to animal. *An avian Shifter perhaps?* How could she think when he was possessing her mouth with his own?

He was tall and powerfully built. She noted his pale green eyes and thick, dark hair, the first time his gaze collided with hers. After that, it was kind of a blur. He'd moved with incredible speed. Grasping her by the hand and slamming her body into his.

Her Coyote practically drooled over his manly show of dominance. *Get a grip.* And she did, on his enormous shoulders. *Holy crap!* His body was corded with sinewy muscles. She felt them rippling against her much softer frame as he walked her backwards into the hallway, his lips never letting up for one single moment.

She threw her arms around his thick neck. To keep herself from falling, she told herself. *Yeah. Right.* Melody knew she shouldn't be doing this, but she couldn't stop herself from responding either. He was a total stranger! *A sexy as all hell stranger*, she corrected.

He growled deep in his throat. He wound his tongue around hers, caressing it and her with his lips, and tongue, and teeth. It was driving her wild with need. His kiss was insistent, but tender, as if he were savoring her. *Bullshit. He doesn't even know me. He must be either crazy, drunk, or under some spell.* She'd heard the Faeries in the office threatening to spike the food if they didn't get paid vacation time this year.

Fuck. That must be it. She attempted to pull back, but his arms tightened around her. Her breasts were crushed against his hard chest. Her nipples tingled through the fabric as if she were bare against him, despite the built-in bra.

She appreciated a well-built man. Always had. And boy, was he built really well. His large, strong hands gripped her around her waist and back as he firmly continued to suckle at her oh-so-willing mouth.

This was one of those *greatest-movie-kisses-of-all-time* things. The kind where the hero storms the castle to get his woman at the end of the movie and they live happily ever after. Where they kissed like they were dying for each other. *So romantic!* And so very fucking wrong!

She was no movie damsel, and this wasn't her happy ending! *But it could be*, her Coyote whispered in her mind's eye. *Horny bitch.*

No. Must stop. This time she pushed against his chest with a little more force. Using the strength of her Coyote. Melody straightened her shoulders and looked into his glowing green eyes. She could sense his confusion and sought to address it immediately. *Before this gets any more out of control.*

"I'm sorry," she began.

"Don't be, we can pick right back up," he murmured and bent to kiss her again.

"No! No, none of that," she said and turned her head to avoid his masterful lips.

That was a mistake! He found the exposed skin of her neck and proceeded to kiss, lick, and suck. *Oh fuuuckk!* Shivers ran up and down her spine. Heat pooled in her stomach and traveled straight down to her pussy. Then he went and bit down, not hard enough to break skin but her needy clit twitched in response.

Fuuckkkk meeee!

She moaned against his seeking lips as he made his way back up to her mouth. He tasted spicy with an edge that bordered on fantasy. *Totally out of her league*, she wanted to banish the hateful thought that crept into her mind.

As if sensing her doubt, he increased the pressure of his lips. She swallowed harshly as his hands found the skin at the opening in the back of her dress. *Sensation overload*, she moaned finally understanding the phrase. He was everywhere. His scent, his taste, his touch. And she didn't know his name!

"Mmm, baby, you feel like silk, Smooth and hot to the touch. I can't wait to peel this dress off you."

"Hold on. Wait, please stop," she whispered the despised words, wanting to kick herself when he obeyed. He was breathing roughly and turned his head in wonder as if only realizing now where they were.

The hallway was empty except for the odd person walking discreetly towards the restrooms. He'd at least had enough presence of mind to tuck them in a corner behind a large potted tree.

Melody took a step back and righted her dress. She wiped her mouth and looked at his roving green eyes. They seemed to caress her body like hands.

So expressive in his desire, she gasped. Had any man ever looked at her with such open hunger? She doubted it.

"Um, who are you?"

"I'm Nikolai Falk. You're name, sweet?"

He took her hand in his, drawing circles against the soft part while he watched her with a curious expression on his too handsome face.

"My name is Melody Casper."

"Perfect, as you are, *Melody Casper*," he said, and seemed to savor it on his tongue.

"I'm not perfect," she stated blandly.

"But you are like a song, beautiful Melody. *Poetry*," he said and caressed her face with his fingertips.

She sighed and struggled to hold onto her humanity. Her Coyote barked and yipped in her mind's eye. The furry beast doing circles inside of her. *What the heck?*

"You're a Dragon?" She asked astonished at her own rudeness.

"I'm sorry, I shouldn't have asked that!"

"Nonsense, you can ask me anything. Yes, I am a Dragon, and you are a Coyote, aren't you little one?" His gaze was purely appreciative as he looked her over again.

"Yes, I am," she pulled her hand slightly, but he refused to let it go. A fact that made her want him all the more.

"Look, I have heard about you know," she murmured, rolling her eyes at his confused look.

"Your reputation precedes you, Mr. Falk, and-" Melody couldn't believe what she was about to say, but before she could get a word out, her large, blonde companion approached them.

"Hello, friend, I'm Cecil," he extended a hand to Nikolai who merely looked at the other Shifter and growled.

"Okay, then. Hey Melody, I just wanted to make sure you're okay?"

Cecil's question was firm and direct. She smiled at him, grateful that he'd cared enough to check on her. The big Dragon who was still holding her hand did not seem to like it all that much. In fact, he lifted his lip and snarled at the blonde man.

"The lady is perfectly fine and none of your concern, *friend*," he said the word, but Melody knew he didn't mean it. *Neanderthal.* Okay, it was a little hot.

Still, Cecil waited for her to answer. She nodded and opened her hand up to Nikolai's possessive one. Wanting to soothe him, though she didn't understand why.

She was almost embarrassed at how turned on she was by his blatant show of possessiveness. It was a Shifter thing, she guessed. Her inner Coyote liked that he could take care of her. Feminism was alive and well in the Shifter world, but apparently her inner animal was not feeling it!

"Thank you, Cecil, but Nikolai and I are fine, I do appreciate the concern," she stepped forward to kiss his cheek.

Again, Nikolai growled, but she stepped into his embrace quickly, pressing her back against his chest. The movement seemed to soothe him and his beast. His hands rested on her waist, but she knew his eyes still watched the other male Shifter until he retreated with a wave back to the gala.

"That was risky on his part," Nikolai said as he nuzzled the back of her neck. She arched and sighed, loving the way his hot breath tickled her skin. His fingertips ran down the length of her back exposed by her gown. Stopping to toy with a spot above her left buttock.

"Is that a tattoo?"

"Yes."

"What of? Never mind, I'll find out, later," he turned her around and pressed their lips together in a sizzling kiss that left her breathless.

"Let's get out of here," she said. She felt wild and reckless and so fucking turned on she didn't ever want to think again. Especially if thinking meant talking herself out of leaving this place with that man on her arm.

"Baby, you don't know what you do to me. Come on, let's go," he grabbed her hand and led her to the coat check. She was barely aware of him talking to her, but he smiled and pressed his thumb against her palm.

"I said, stay here and I'll come back for you once the valet pulls my car out front. I won't be long," he kissed her lips quickly and went to talk to the valet.

Melody exhaled. *Holy fuck!* Her whole body was on fire! She was burning for him. She'd never really done one-night stands, but there was a first time for everything. Besides, she was thirty-five and just ripe for a blazing affair.

What if he changes his mind? What if he doesn't like what he sees when he gets my clothes off? Oh no. What if he has a small dick? Wait. *No way.*

She'd felt the evidence of his enormous manhood pressed against her belly when they'd kissed before. Everything about him was big. *Thank fucking god!*

Her thoughts were interrupted by a woman in a short, skin-tight red dress with six-inch stilettos. She was blonde and super thin, with a lot of make-up, and a nasty look in her blue eyes.

"You know, as a fellow woman, I thought you should know, that one has some rumors flying around about him."

"Excuse me?"

"They say he is a fucking pervert. He takes out his afflictions on others, you know what I mean?"

"What are you talking about?"

"Dear, are you that dumb? That one is all show, he can't get *it* up. He is all talk and no action, but worse, he's got a temper too. Just thought I'd warn you, but you're probably not used to male attention like that, can't say I blame you for falling for it," she continued with her unwanted advice and Melody was fuming by the time her rant was finished.

"You know, I don't believe I asked for your opinion. Have a good night."

She walked to the door at the same time Nikolai came back to fetch her. His eyes were on her and so he seemed to miss the unwelcome exchange.

"You ready?"

"Yes," she said. *More than ready.*

SEVEN

Nikolai held her hand and drove like a madman till he reached his hotel. He ignored the doorman in his haste to get her up to his penthouse.

He grabbed for her as soon as the doors to the private elevator slid closed. Oblivious or uncaring of the cameras he was sure were placed there. He growled as the sexy scent of her arousal reached him.

Fuck, his baby was hot as sin. Her face was fucking perfect. *Like an angel*, he thought. Her coloring all golds and ambers. Luminous skin, silky hair with beautiful highlights other women paid a fortune to try and mimic, curves that made his mouth water. And she was his. She just didn't know it yet.

Nikolai couldn't hold back another second. He took her face in his hands, testing the softness of her skin against his fingers. Need overwhelmed him, and he dove in for all he was worth.

Tongues dueled, lips crashed, and bodies heaved with desire in the confines of the small elevator. He pulled fabric out of the way, leaving his tuxedo jacket, tie, and shirt on the floor. The doors opened, and he lifted her up in his arms, never breaking their kiss.

Thank the gods, her dress was flowy, or he'd have ripped it. That would have been a shame. He stood her up in front of the king-sized bed. His body hummed with the need to have her. *Claim her. Es Meus.*

Amazing. His cock was so hard he damn near burst through his slacks for wanting her! Months of nothing and now he was like a rocket about to go off. Like a Dragonling with his first wench.

Nay. No others. Es Meus, his EnergyDragon roared. Nikolai agreed wholeheartedly. This stunning Coyote Shifter was all his. He'd make her see it too. He twined her fingers with his and ground into her with his clothes body. Sucking on her lower lip.

Fuck yeah. He couldn't wait to taste her everywhere. Every curve, every dip, every single inch of her was his. She belonged to him as he did to her. Now he just had to show her.

"Oh yes," she moaned and threw her head back as he sucked on the hollow of her neck.

He sought clasps and zippers and after some clever maneuvering, smoothed the silky confection down her supple body. It pooled at her feet like an ocean of green silk, and he dropped to his knees to nuzzle her sex through the sheer black panties that separated her from him.

He sucked in a breath and tasted her on his tongue. *Citrus bean and bourbon.* Sweet and savory. *The perfect meal,* he thought, and yes, he was going to make a meal out of her.

He nudged her gently and laid her down on the comforter, pulling her until her ass hit the end of the mattress. He draped her sexy, large thighs over his shoulders. Her heat reached him, making him shudder with explosive need. His cock standing up at the scent, he gloried in his reaction to her.

Nik exhaled slowly. He'd missed feeling this way, true, but it was even more now. He was made for this one woman. To see to her every need and desire. He pushed her thighs wide open. Leaving her on display for him. She sat up on her elbows worry creasing her brow, but he smiled and dipped his head, inhaling deeply.

"These are very sexy panties, sweet, but they have to go," he growled as he took them in his teeth and pulled.

Melody's head dropped back once again, and she moaned. He ripped the flimsy fabric off her flesh and growled. She was dripping for him. Her pretty pink pussy gleamed in front of him. Sweet as pie to his hungry eyes and mouth.

"Your glistening, baby, so wet and hot for me. I bet you taste like you smell, all sweet citrus and ripe berries, I can't wait to fuck you with my tongue," he blew on her sensitive skin, and was rewarded with another moan.

"So, fucking beautiful, baby," he growled, and she fisted his hair. His sweet mate was fierce too, he mused as she tried to force him down to where she wanted. He smiled and resisted, giving in only when she whimpered his name.

"Please, Nikolai," she moaned softly.

"Please what? Say the words, baby, and I'll do what you want."

"Please, lick me, Niko."

He liked the way she'd shortened his name. *Niko.* A private little moniker just for her to use. *Yes, I like it,* he thought, and he showed her how much by driving his tongue straight into her tight channel.

Her taste exploded on his tongue and if possible, his cock grew even harder. With every lick and taste, he felt his Dragon ripple beneath his skin. The beast wanted him to mark her. *Claim her. Take her. Es Meus*, he roared.

He wanted to do that. So, fucking badly. But he fought back the urge to claim and concentrated on pleasing his mate. He pinned her to the bed with one steely arm over her stomach while he buried his tongue inside her moist heat. He wanted to plunder her depths, make her scream his name.

Fuck, yeah. She tried to rock her hips, but he wouldn't allow it. She'd come from his ministrations alone. He'd take care of her. *Fuck yeah*, he was born to please her.

He clamped his lips over her clit, sucking hard as his fingers replacing his tongue in her tight, slick heat. She bucked underneath him, moaning aloud. Saying his name over and over again.

Nikolai moaned against his mate's pussy. He pushed his fingers deeper, freeing her body as he used his other hand to roam over her gorgeous ass, lifting it higher as he found her forbidden hole.

He teased as his mouth sucked and fingers plunged. And she loved every second of it. Her body rocked against him, chest heaving, mouth open. She was fucking glorious.

His dick throbbed with the need to be inside her, but he needed her to come first. His pleasure could wait. Hers, not so much. Nik groaned as her pussy clenched around his fingers. Her clit throbbed against his tongue as he lapped at her.

The scent of her musk surrounded him. He doubled his efforts and was rewarded when her body stilled violently against his tongue. Her channel milked his fingers, and she screamed his name, her Coyote in her voice as she came with unabandoned glory.

The first of many orgasms to come, he thought with pride as he calmed her by kissing her swollen sex.

She moved to slide away, but he held her firm. His kisses slowly exciting as they slid up her soft thighs, arousing her all over again. He growled against her. Unable to stem the sound as she mewled beneath him.

His Dragon roared in his mind's eye. She was the perfect mate. Sultry and so damn responsive. He thumped his dick once with his hand, ordering his appendage to behave lest he cum in his pants. But how could he behave when she was glowing with the aftermath of her first orgasm with him.

Nikolai eased over Melody's nude body. Continuing his sensuous assault on her body. Wanting to stamp himself all over her. He used his thumb to tap her clit while he licked his way to her glorious breasts.

"Niko, more," she moaned. She wound her hands around his neck and shoulders, caressing him.

He loved her attentions, his skin heated where her fingers tread.

He raised his head and took her in. He had never seen anything as beautiful as his mate bare and willing beneath him.

His hands roamed her curves stopping with both hands full of her beautiful breasts. Tipped with dark, mauve nipples that puckered under his mouth. *Cherries,* ripe and sweet. He sucked and plucked until she was writhing beneath him once more.

Nikolai hesitated. His gorgeous mate was driving him insane. Her naughty hands ran down his abdomen flicking open his pants. He hissed out a breath as she brushed the closely cropped curls and delved further down.

He'd had performance issues just recently. That was enough to make any man nervous. *I'm not any man, I am Dragon.*

Knowing his body would not work for anyone other than his mate should have stemmed all his fears. *She was the one. His fated mate. Es meus. He felt it, his Dragon knew it. His body would obey.*

He growled and shoved his pants down. He stood before her, growing even longer under her rapt gaze. Heat filled him. *Yes,* he was impressive. He was a Dragon, after all.

He hovered over her for a single moment. She had no idea that she was his mate. Should he tell her first? He didn't know if he could control the beast inside him. Claiming her was all he wanted.

Then Melody moaned and lifted her hands to her own nipples. She looked at him under heavy-lidded eyes glowing gold with the power of her animal.

"Niko, please," she begged and parted her legs wider for him.

His rapt gaze found her smooth sex and he growled. This was more than mindless need. This was acceptance. She was a Shifter too. Deep down her animal knew who he was to her. *Mine.*

"Melody," he growled as she continued to twist and tug her heavy breasts.

"Niko," she moaned, "I need you. Now."

He growled and grabbed his cock. Placing the head at her swollen entrance. His emotions no longer under control, he pushed inside of her reveling in this first step of their mating.

"Mine," he growled as he thrust his hips, pushing further inside her tight pussy.

She was slick with need, her pussy dripping for him as he swirled his hips and ground his pelvic bone against her.

He found her G-spot and hit it again and again. His cock homing in on every erogenous zone she had. Her pussy tensed around him like a vice.

So fucking good. She was made for him. A perfect cushion to his hardness.

"*Baby, fuck, baby*, you're like silk and steel all around me. I want to fuck you until neither of us can move. I want to stamp myself over every inch of you, Melody! You. Are. Mine," he growled and kissed her hard pounding wildly in and out of her yielding body.

He wondered if he should go softer, slower, but his beast rode him hard. She was a Shifter. She could take it. *Fuck*, she wanted it if the claws embedded in his hips were any hint.

The combination of pleasure and pain was almost too much for him, but he needed her to come again one more time before he could find release.

"Come on, baby, come for me," he growled and swirled his hips again and again.

She mewled and arched. Her head thrashed back and forth, nails cutting his skin. *Yes*, he thought, *mark me, baby. Let everyone see I am yours.*

"Melody, mine," he growled, a deep animalistic sound that she responded to.

Her body clenched around him like a vice, tight channel milking his cock as her pussy fluttered and squeezed her release. Only then did he allow himself to reach the pinnacle. Stars burst behind his eyes, galaxies formed, whole universes even, as he bellowed loudly, filling her with his seed.

His body twerked and jerked inside her sweet heat as their combined pleasure spiraled. Their satisfaction seeming to feed off the other's. Such a sacred and profound coming together, momentous even.

His fangs elongated in response, but he bit back on them. Talk, they needed to talk. To bond with something more than sex, but the beast was still riding him hard, even as she squeezed the last drop of cum from his cock. *Soon.*

I will claim her soon. Es Meus.

CHAPTER

EIGHT

Melody opened her eyes slowly. She stretched her body noting soreness in her previously under-used muscles. *Hurts so good.* She smiled lazily, looking over to the large male breathing evenly in blissful sleep right next to her.

Niko's hair fell over his forehead, the hard lines of his face relaxed in slumber. The sheet hung low on his hips and she ached to tug it down lower. To see him in all his masculine nudity before her hungry eyes. She hadn't gotten to taste him last night, that would be her one and only regret.

He breathed deep and the muscles along his tight abdomen rippled with the movement. *Whoa.* That was definitely a sight she could get used to, she sighed.

She supposed she'd just have to live with the single encounter. It's not like they'd made any promises to each other. Hell, they hardly talked. *Yes. You talked the language of love,* her Coyote insisted.

He'd been such an exquisite lover. The best she'd ever had. Tender and affectionate, while exceeding every naughty, rough, and wild fantasy she'd ever dreamed of!

319

She wouldn't make any apologies about her lusty nature. The fact is no man had ever come close to satisfying her the way Niko did.

Shifters were very physical beings. She'd only gone to bed with a handful of men. True, they were all Shifters, but there was no comparison. Like, at all.

He'd given her exactly what she never knew she needed. Filling her in every way, shape, and form. The Dragon Shifter brought her to orgasm again and again. Wringing pleasure out from every nerve ending in her willing body. *And boy, oh boy, had she been willing.* Sun peeked in through the hotel's luxury blinds and she grimaced.

Time for the walk of shame. Pain squeezed her chest as she watched him. The steady rise and fall of his chest, the smooth, muscled skin that she'd caressed and kissed, the man that had loved her so well.

She slid from the fiery sheets, moving away from him. With each step, she felt the cold seep into her, down to her bones. Her Coyote howled in protest.

Melody considered waking him, but she wasn't in the mood for a long, uncomfortable goodbye. *This is what you signed up for*, she told herself firmly. *Then why am I so sad?* She ignored her overactive emotions.

Last night was exactly what she had wanted. Hot sex with no ties. A chance to let her hair down and get buck wild with someone!

An image of the catty blonde Witch who'd stopped her before she left last night sprung to mind. Whatever that woman had been trying to do, Melody couldn't even fathom!

Imagine trying to spread a rumor that his mighty Dragon-ness over here was unable to satisfy in bed? *Yeah. Right.* He probably just turned her down. *Sour grapes and all.*

Well, it didn't matter. Nikolai was definitely not impotent. She could attest to that. Images of the night they'd shared flooded her mind.

Lips touching, hands searching, bodies coming together. Secret sounds and smells, touches and tastes. The air still held hints of their combined passion.

No surprise there. He'd made love to her for hours. Sure, they'd exchanged very few words in that time, but they were sensory creatures. Shifters relied on body language and instinct as well as human forms of communication. She knew he'd enjoyed himself as much as she had.

Her hand went to her neck and she sighed. Her Coyote yipped in her mind's eye, her brownish-gold fur shimmering in the magic of that special place where their bond existed. The beast craved him still. Longed to feel his teeth pierce her skin. *Mate. Mine.*

Whoa there. Easy girl. No marking here. WTH. But no matter how much she wanted to deny it in the cold light of day, Melody had desperately wanted to wear his claiming mark on her skin. She came close a time or two to ordering him to just bite her already. *Uh oh.*

It was just the sex haze, that's all. She could hardly think straight when he was moving inside of her. *No. you wanted it. Mates. Love. Mine.*

Melody growled. It didn't matter what she wanted. Clearly, the Dragon had not been inclined to claim her in the way of Shifters. Whatever she felt, it must not be true for him.

Don't mistake sex, for love. Fuck. Where the hell did that come from? Time to go. She stood and snuck out of bed.

The word *mates* scared her. Thomas had been her husband, but not her mate. Being with Nikolai felt different. But it was one night only, she reminded herself.

She refused to dwell on the fact that she wasn't meant for the big, beautiful man who slept soundly not five feet away from her. *Stupid heart, getting attached.*

She blinked rapidly and snuck out of the room. She would not cry. *Nope. No way.* She grabbed her wrinkled gown and put it on, along with his silk shirt. That would at least cover her almost bear back.

Surely, he wouldn't mind and if he did, she could mail it to him. If she knew where he lived. *Oh, whatever.*

Melody sighed as she realized she'd have to forego underwear. He'd torn her sheer panties to shreds with his teeth. *Grrr.*

She felt her cheeks heat and knew she was blushing furiously just thinking about it. No man had ever wanted her so much. *Not even douchey her ex-husband.*

She glanced at her phone and rolled her eyes. The clock was ticking. Melody jogged down the stairs barefoot to the next floor before snagging the elevator. She hadn't wanted to alert him to her leaving with the pinging noise. He might feel obligated to her in some way, and she didn't want that at all.

Nope. She'd take a cab back to her apartment, soak in a tub to ease her sore muscles, and go back to her life come Monday morning. She'd have the next two days to wallow in the memories of her hot as sin night with her sexy Dragon lover.

If only she were made for happily-ever-afters! *Oh well.* She paid the exorbitant fee to the cab driver and exited the taxi. Ignoring her neighbors' odd looks. It wasn't ever day she returned home at seven in the morning dressed in a man's shirt and evening gown.

Her Coyote beckoned, and she decided she could use a little run. Melody entered her ground floor apartment and pulled down the shades. She stripped out of her clothing and welcomed the familiar hum of magic that settled over her body.

Bones cracked, skin shrank, fur sprouted and soon she was her animal. She stretched and twitched her tail. She loved being in her Coyote skin. She was similar in appearance to grey wolves, but much smaller. Her goldish hue made it easy for her to pass herself off as a dog to her neighbors.

She'd resented it at first, but she lived in a city and stealth was necessary. She even installed a dog door which she used regularly. She gave a quick shake of her fur, then Melody trotted over to the loathsome door. She exited into the small, paved courtyard that sat behind the building she lived in.

Through the wrought iron fence, stood a stand of trees that led to a small, enclosed wood. The smattering of trees was hardly a forest, but it gave her much needed room to run.

Her emotions had been rioting inside her since she woke up that morning. Melody needed the blissful oblivion of being in her other skin. Her Coyote longed to howl, but she knew better than to loose the sound there.

Uniformed police would be there in minutes if she did. City folk did not appreciate the threat of wild animals. She'd learned that the hard way when she'd first moved there three years ago. She moved swiftly as her thoughts through the dried-up grass and over the frozen ground.

The brisk December wind whipped the short bristly fur that covered her elongated snout. Her muscular body was leaner than her human one. She was fast and strong, agile and very aware of her surroundings.

A true predator, she snorted. Melody preferred the running to the hunting, though she wasn't objecting to chasing a squirrel or two on her run. Tongue lolling to the side, she absorbed the freedom that came with being in her fur and shook off the negative feelings she'd had about leaving Niko that morning.

She was being ridiculous. Her Coyote growled at her. *Mate. Mate. Mate.* No. Not mine. He was only interested in the one night. She finished her run and headed back to her apartment. A little scrambled eggs and bacon sounded exactly right.

Melody climbed the stairs and walked through the pet door to the sound of her phone ringing madly. It took her a couple of seconds to change shape. The stretching of skin and bone was fast after years of practice, but it still hurt. She panted with the effort, glaring at her blasted cell phone.

Maybe she should change that stupid beeping ringtone? It was hard on the nerves. It was another few seconds before she could comfortably move. Not that the damn thing stopped ringing. Whoever it was, they weren't giving up.

"Come on, it's Saturday," she mumbled as she grabbed the receiver. *Ugh.* It was work.

"Hello? Slow down, Mrs. Grayson. *Who*? A client. *Okay*. What do you mean I have to travel! No, no, I'm sorry. I didn't mean to be rude, it's just I don't understand. Why me?"

After a few seconds of Mrs. Grayson's brief explanation, Melody realized she had no choice. The bank president, Mr. Atkins, had hand-picked her, Melody Casper, management accountant, to be loaned out to *Graves Enterprises*.

Apparently, their CEO needed a fill in and her boss had generously donated her. They were a multi-million-dollar company and an especially important account. As if she needed the reminder.

Great. All she wanted to do was sit at home and eat something deep fried with way too many calories, while she binge-watched medical romances, and mooned over the last eight hours. *Ugh.*

"Yes, Mrs. Grayson. It's fine. I'll pack a bag right now. Give me one second, and I'll write the address down," she dropped her things and scrambled for a pen and piece of paper.

"Okay. Yes, Maccon City, New Jersey. Got it. Be there tonight at seven? Okay, yes, I can do that. Goodbye, Mrs. Grayson."

CHAPTER

NINE

Nikolai rolled over and inhaled. Fiery citrus and smoky bourbon filled his nostrils, he smiled as he reached out a hand only to come up empty. *What the...?*

He leapt out of bed. His Dragon grumbled unhappily. His mate was gone! *Where was she?*

He pulled on pants and grabbed the phone calling the concierge. It seemed his mate had left an hour ago in a nondescript cab. It would take hours to find her this way. *Shit!*

He had to think. Fuck. His Dragon was growling, scales sprouted along his arms and chest. The beast was furious with him. He wanted to be let out. To hunt. To seek. To claim.

Be calm. My tongue is needed not your claws, he told the beast. Nikolai scrubbed a hand over his face, his stubbly beard scratching his palms. An idea struck.

He grabbed his cell and dialed the bank only to be greeted by a recorded message. They were closed. *Fucking hell!* He paced back and forth, running a hand up and down his face. Then he called Randall.

The man was a computer genius, not to mention an old school hacker. He felt shitty about this for all of a second before his Dragon

325

reminded him what was at stake. Five-hundred years in chains, one hundred without the feel of a woman, waiting for his one fated mate. And she slipped out the door!

Not for long! He'd have her info in no time at all, and then he'd have her. By his side. Where she belonged. *Grrrr. Es Meus. Mate. Mine.*

His heart thundered as he waited for someone to pick up his call. The word *mate* galvanized his actions. Okay, so he was mildly stalkerish. He had damn good reason to be.

She was about five and a half feet tall with honey-streaked hair, with a sexy citrusy scent that made his mouth water, and a body he would never get tired of sinking into for all the long years of their lives.

"Randall? Yes, it's Nikolai, listen I need your help," he spent the next fifteen minutes bringing his friend up to speed. Next, he called his brothers.

Surely, the family wouldn't mind a week away from the castle on him. He needed the privacy and space to woo his mate.

Decision made, he called the family jet, had it ordered fueled and ready to go, and sent a stretched limousine to pick up his three brothers and their wives, not to mention his new niece.

"But Nik, why the rush? What is going on?" Callius bellowed over the phone. His natural dominance causing Nikolai to sway slightly.

"Look Cal, I met my mate-"

"But that's wonderful, after all we heard you, er, had some *problems*, um. Look, Nik, I'm sorry I know rumors are not all they seem, but are you, you know able to-"

Nikolai groaned. *Great.* His brothers had heard about his little problem the last century or so. He waited for his anger to rise, but it never came.

Finding his mate had soothed his beast, as losing her had riled him. His only focus was Melody. *His sweet Melody.*

"Callius! The past doesn't matter now. I found her. *My one true fated mate.* With her, I am whole. I just need some time and the castle free of you lot, so I may woo her without distraction. Please, Cal."

"Okay, brother, then you shall have whatever you need. Besides, Winifred is packed already and sends many thanks for the trip! The spa package you texted really sold her on the whole thing. By the way, where are we going?"

"To *Falk Island*, of course."

"What?" His brother's shock would have, at any other time, amused him. But Nikolai had other things on his mind.

"Yes, I was saving it as a surprise, but what the heck. It is a small, uninhabited island southwest of Cuba. I've had dwellings built along the beach. A series of luxury cabins, an outdoor swimming pool, plumbing, and a discreet staff who will meet you there."

"Wonderful! Many thanks, I wish you well of your mate, Nik. We are all pleased for you."

"Yes, well I still have to convince her she is my *emerald rose.*"

"Just remember to be honest with her."

"Of course, Cal, and thank you."

"My pleasure, now I must see to my mate and young. Until later, brother."

"Aye. Send my love to the others."

Nikolai placed his cell phone down on the table and packed his suitcase. He left instructions with the hotel that one of his employees would come to fetch his car and bag shortly. Being a *Stein Luxury Hotel*, it was a supernaturally run facility, therefore, no explanations necessary.

Callius didn't have any time to lose. He needed to ready things for his mate's arrival. He stood naked at the open window and launched himself into the air. Calling on the strength of his *Energy-Dragon*, he changed mid-leap and took off like a lightning bolt.

Part of his supernatural powers was being exceedingly fast. More so than any of his brothers. His enormous size did not deter him in the least. His wings pumped through the air and he let loose a stream of green fire as he flew furiously through the thickening clouds.

Snow was on the horizon, but he did not mid in the least. *'Tis the season, after all.* Dragons were not Christian, but they'd adapted to the times and had come to celebrate the holidays along with the normals.

Now that his brothers were mated, *Castle Falk* boasted a decorated Christmas tree year-round in the center hall. It was twelve feet tall, its roots in an enormous gilt pot. The thing even had its own gardener! He roared as he thought of his home and hoped with everything in him Melody would find it acceptable.

In the time it took for him to make arrangements and pack, he'd read the file Randall had sent him on his chosen. His Melody was an only child, her parents lived in Florida and were somewhat estranged from their only daughter. Their choice, *and loss*, in his opinion.

She'd been married before. A fact that made him want to tear the head off her ex-husband. The Coyote was an all-around loser and braggart. *Perhaps, I shall have a bonfire with his name on it.* The idea held merit.

Nikolai's oblong scales glittered a brilliant green, like spring leaves on his underbelly, darkening to pine needles on his legs and back.

The winter sky was a blinding white, but as he inhaled, he realized the snow would be hours away. *Perfect.* He flapped harder, pushing himself to get home. At that moment, he'd look more like a green comet than anything else.

Normals would mistake him for a trick their eyes played for staring at the sky for too long. He didn't worry about them. All his focus was on one thing. Claiming his mate.

He landed with a thud on the roof of Castle Falk a mere fifteen minutes later. Naked as the day he was born, he allowed his subconscious to scout the home, and found it empty as promised.

Nik grunted as he headed towards the stairs. He was truly

thankful for his brothers and their mates. Blessed with his family, his clan, and now *her*. There was nothing they would not do for each other.

Nikolai showered quickly and dressed in a pair of blue jeans with a white button-down shirt. He wore his favorite black Aquatalia boots and headed for the main floor of the castle.

His phone beeped, and he noted his car and bag were headed back. Randall loaned him one of his associates, a Shifter who'd worked for the man for years. Nikolai trusted Randall's assessment and didn't spare it a second thought. After all, he had work to do.

Wooing his mate was everything in that moment. He'd never expected it to be so difficult. Especially with her being a Shifter too. But clearly, he'd messed up the night before and now he had to rectify the situation.

Nikolai was used to women fawning over him, but the only one who mattered had run! He could only imagine it was because he had failed somehow. *Not physically. Not with her.*

Actually, the opposite was quite true. He'd been starving for her. He licked, tasted, and savored every inch of her body. She'd moaned his name and opened for him like a flower in bloom. *God*, how he wanted her this very moment. His cock hardened in anticipation.

His Dragon snarled. The beast had wanted, no, he had *demanded* he mark her last night. But Nikolai had resisted. He did not want to take her like a rutting animal.

He'd planned on speaking to her about it once he'd taken the edge off his incredible desire for her. Of course, that had taken all night long and, by morning, she was gone.

This was his only chance to clear things up, and he wasn't about to ruin it. No, he was calling in the big guns! First, he texted Randall to see how things went on his end.

Next, he dialed *Moonlight Blossoms*, the best local florist around. He ordered one hundred long-stemmed, red roses, and told the proprietor, Ms. DeMarco, that he needed them to be the most romantic arrangement she'd ever created.

"For a special occasion then, Mr. Falk? Yes, of course, I can accommodate you," she said and promised delivery within the next two hours.

Next, he got on the phone with *'Iamo Bella,* the best Italian food for twenty miles around and ordered a verifiable feast complete complimenting red and white wines and an array of artisan pastries made on the premise.

The owner, Giovanni, was more than happy to provide chaffing dishes and confirmed the delivery and set up would be handled in a timely and professional manner. *Va bene!*

Nikolai looked around the dining room and sighed. *Flowers, dinner, wine,* what was he missing? *Music!* He'd designed the Castle Falk's entire *inner brain* to be fully functional to the brothers and their mates.

It was a verifiable *smart castle.* What technology couldn't provide, Dragon magic did. As it was, the castle boasted an extremely advanced security system. But he was not concerned with their safety at the moment.

He touched a panel discreetly located behind an eighteenth-century Florentine ebony chest that his brother had acquired at auction recently. The screen lit up and he searched through his options.

From that panel, and similar ones distributed throughout the house, he had the ability to control lighting, temperature, entertainment, appliances, vehicles, phones, and many other features. The same type of system with more personal preferences and additional securities were installed in each of the brothers' private quarters as well.

He punched in a few commands and within seconds the marble fireplace along the far wall roared to life. Next, the overhead lights dimmed and changed in color to a warm, romantic tone that would also allow them to see and enjoy their dinner. Finally, he chose the music, hoping his mate would appreciate the classical beauty of Puccini over dinner.

TEN

Melody sighed as she pulled the company car into the long, winding driveway of the client's home. *Holy shit!* Her eyes opened wide as she took in the size of the structure in front of her. *Was that a castle?*

Sure enough. It was a real-life castle sitting right there on the Jersey shore! Four turrets, or castle towers, rose up against the darkening skies. Snowflakes began to fall, and she shivered inside of her thin coat.

It was astounding! The castle walls appeared to be made out of solid stone bricks. They glowed silver and gray, enhanced by discreetly placed security and landscaping lights.

She noted the cobblestone pathway and the towering evergreens that lined the property. The trees in front of the castle were draped with thousands of white twinkle lights. Huge red bows sat atop them.

Christmas was weeks away, but the scene was set. *Like a wonderland.* The outer perimeter seemed to blend with the pine barrens on one side while standing out against the ocean landscape on the other. Truly beautiful.

She sighed. It was as if she were stepping into the pages of her favorite fairytale. All she needed was her handsome prince. *You already found him*, her Coyote whined, *but you ran out on him!*

Oh shush! She told her animal. Her Coyote had been morose and moody all day. What could she say? She'd gone without a man for a while. *Mate? Nah.* She was mistaken.

Maybe her poor Coyote was confused? Sex did not equal love and mating. Even if she was out of touch with her Shifter sensibilities from lack of a band to run with, surely, *he* would've known.

It didn't matter anyway. Melody had no time to think about Nikolai Falk and the amazing evening they'd shared. She'd been called to go off and help a high-profile client. She had no choice in the matter.

"Now Melody, as a management accountant, your job is to compare and contrast data to determine whether specific projects are profitable for us and whatever company you are sent to work on," Mrs. Grayson had said to her as if she'd forgotten her role.

Melody knew her job and she did it well. She utilized comprehensive analysis to calculate when the company should hire/fire, continue a project, make acquisitions, sell off property, any number of important decisions.

Her job was high-pressure, but she had always enjoyed it. Melody had a keen mind and was excellent with numbers and projections. Her personable nature made it easy for her to work with other departments. They usually felt threatened by people in her position, as she had the power to essentially shut them down.

But Melody had a real knack for working with other departments. She wanted to make sure her firm was simply betting on the right horse. In fact, if she believed in the project, she would help point out pitfalls, so they could be fixed before she made her final decision.

Which was why she supposed she'd been chosen to help this special client. *It's something different at least*, she thought. Things at the bank had felt stale lately.

She was in a rut. A change of scenery was nice. Hey, maybe she'd even get headhunted by this guy! She could get used to living by the beach.

Melody straightened her shoulders and smoothed down the knee length, velvety dress she wore over ankle high boots. The dress was another purchase from *Skin Deep*. The soft velvet covered her skin in a loose dress that hugged her curves when she walked. The neckline was rounded, but modest, and the sage green color flattered her honey hair.

She looked professional enough for a home or *castle* visit, she supposed. She smiled when she stood before the large mahogany door. There was even a mini-portcullis mail slot of all things!

She rang the bell before she noticed the note taped to the frame. *Come inside. I'm expecting you.* Melody frowned but just shrugged her shoulders. The guy was obviously rich, busy, and probably eccentric as all hell.

Good thing she was a Coyote Shifter and could hold her own. Anyone got fresh with her, and she'd take off a finger or too. Shifter justice was hard and swift. *Damn straight! Grrr.*

Melody grabbed her big-girl panties and hurried inside. The lights were dim, yet inviting, and music was coming from further inside. Something smelled delicious. Her stomach rumbled loudly, and she covered her stomach with her hand. Damn, why hadn't she eaten all day?

Oh well. She was human. Sort of. And she was hungry. She smelled food, so obviously her business associate realized it was dinner time.

Damn. *Was that pasta? Ooh, and sausage with sautéed broccoli rabe?* Her supernaturally enhanced sense of smell was working overtime determining the food she scented from the other room.

There was something else underneath it all too. A piney, woodsy scent that she couldn't quite place. Her Coyote was distracting her. The animal was yipping and doing cartwheels in her mind's eye.

Okay, okay, little miss impatient Coyote, we're gonna eat soon, and then maybe a run. Now quit that racket! A growl and bark were her answer. Go figure.

"Hello?" Melody called out. She walked further inside and gasped.

Her fingers ran across the back of an elegant dining room chair while she took in the beautifully laid table. A crimson clothe was set with exquisite flatware and gold utensils. Linen napkins were folded like little bouquets and champagne chilled in a bucket off to the side.

An enormous arrangement of blood red roses sat in the center. Her eyes widened as she mentally calculated how many were stuffed into the gorgeous vase. *Holy cow!*

She gasped and blinked, looking all around her. The highly polished ebony furniture was stunning against the white marble floors with the gold and metallic black veins running through it.

She knew she was gaping like a child. Melody closed her mouth and bit her lip. Everything looked sleek and expensive, but she wasn't put off in the least. Underneath the opulence, was taste and warmth.

Yes, I could be very much at home here, she thought. Melody indulged in her daydream for another moment before going through her purse to find her cell. She must have gotten mixed up. The man who lived here clearly had something other than business in mind. Not with her of course. She was a total stranger. Whoever this was intended for, she was some lucky girl.

Her eyes kept going back to the roses. They were gorgeous! The deep, crimson petals looked superb against the lush, mossy looking green foliage. *So beautiful!*

She did not recognize the names of the accent stems and leaves, but she appreciated their beauty. She'd always been partial to green.

Melody sighed as she scrolled through the confirmation email Mrs. Grayson had sent her. *Hmm.* She had the correct date, but maybe Mrs. Grayson had it wrong?

She cleared her throat and moved to back out of the elegant dining room. Tingling sensations shot up her spine. She'd hoped to at least have dinner, but she'd stop somewhere on the drive back home. The drive would be at least two hours in Saturday night traffic. And it was snowing. *Ugh.*

"Hello, sweet," a deep, familiar voice reached her ears and she spun to find herself face to face with the man who'd rocked her world just a few hours ago.

"What? Who? How?"

He was even more striking than she recalled. His silky dark hair was brushed away from his face. All of the hard lines and angles on brilliant display, making him appear even more handsome. He was larger than life.

Six and a half feet of long, lean, hard male. *Yum.* His body was corded with long ropes of muscle visible through his blue jeans and white shirt. But what struck her the most was his pale green eyes.

They seemed to light up when they looked at her, glowing darker when his Dragon peaked through. *Wow.* She'd lost the ability to speak for a moment. When she did come around to her senses, she found she was actually speechless.

"Um, Niko? What is this?"

"This is dinner, and these," he said plucking a single red rose from the vase and using it to brush the side of her face, "are for you, my Melody."

She tried not to swoon, really, she did, but what was a girl to do? Who was she kidding?

Melody had every intention of caving to any and all persuasion. She took the rose and breathed in the light fragrance. *Another night, maybe two?*

Her chest squeezed. She was falling for this big man. Hard and fast. Could she give him another night without losing her heart entirely?

"Is this from *La Boheme*?" She asked gesturing towards the music in the air.

"Yes! I hope you like Puccini?"

"I do, but Nikolai, what is this? Are you the client I am supposed to work for?"

"Yes and no, I mean I needed to talk to you, Melody, and this seemed the best way."

Anger and outrage made her tremble. Who the hell did this guy think he was messing with her job? She wasn't about to let anyone handle her that way!

"So, you arranged all this for a booty call? You must be out of your mind!"

"*Booty call?* No, Melody, look, I need to talk to you, but I understand your drive was long. Why don't we have some dinner. Please?"

His tone was so repentant she couldn't help but soften. He did go through all the trouble and she was starving. But as soon as she was sated, she'd get to the bottom of this.

One thing she knew, Melody hated games! Especially ones where she was nothing more than a pawn. *Please, at least be honest with me,* she silently entreated.

"Fine. But only because I am hungry."

"Excellent. I had the restaurant set up a little bit of everything family style. We can serve ourselves if you like or I can serve you? Is red okay?"

"Yes, and I can serve myself. I don't mind," she sat down across from him while he poured red wine in two glasses.

He lifted the covers off of several dishes and she smiled widely. He really had ordered a little bit of everything. There was all manner of *antipasti*, multiple small dishes with fresh vegetables, two kinds of pastas, and a variety of meat dishes. It looked amazing and smelled even better!

She sighed over her choices and moaned in delight at the way the fresh ingredients seemed to burst on her tongue. Being a Shifter, Melody loved food, but she'd always been career minded. Cooking was not one of her talents though she did have a passion for eating. *Obviously.*

She wiped her mouth with her napkin and sipped her wine.

Nikolai lifted a forkful of chicken to his mouth but stopped when she swallowed her sip. His eyes glittered at her, and she licked her lips under his intense stare.

"How's the chicken?" She asked breathlessly.

He was watching her as if he'd rather be eating her. *Oh my. Yes please.*

OMG. I'm a total slut for this guy, she grimaced. Melody swallowed again and broke eye contact. Her chest was heaving, just from looking at him.

"I don't know how the chicken is Melody."

"What?"

"I said, I don't know how the chicken is. I can't recall how anything tastes. Anything other than *you* that is. And I want more," he growled the last bit and heat pooled in her belly.

Melody dropped her fork. Her limbs went limp. *Holy shit.* She needed air if she was going to get through this meal unscathed, but apparently, he wasn't done yet.

"You want to know why you're here? Why I called in every favor owed to me to make this happen?" He motioned to the room and between them.

She nodded, and his eyes flashed with determination and possession. Melody felt her body slicken in anticipation. *Oh my.*

"Why am-" her voice cracked. She cleared her throat before trying again, "Why am I here, Nikolai?"

"For one reason. You. Are. Mine."

"You can't just say things like that," she shook her head and looked down. Doubt and distrust creeping through her veins.

"I've been down this road before, Niko, I can't just drop everything for a man who is looking for some kind of minor amusement-"

"Look at me, baby, I want you. You, Melody Casper, are my fated mate. Can't you feel it?"

"I, thought, I mean, are you sure?" Doubt faded, and hope filled her spirit. Shifters knew instinctively when someone was destined for them and she'd hoped to meet her soulmate for most of her life.

She messed up with Thomas. Let her own lack of confidence push her into deciding. But she wasn't that scared little girl any longer.

Melody Casper was a woman. Failed marriage behind her and destined for a life unfulfilled as a workaholic. Unless she took a leap of faith now.

Her Coyote howled inside of her. *Trust yourself. Trust me. He is our future.* She exhaled and lifted her amber eyes to his emerald ones. How had she come to care for this man with such intensity in just a day? *Because the Universe doesn't make mistakes*, was the answer.

"Niko?" She waited with baited breath for him to answer her question.

"Yes, love?"

"I need you to be sure," she licked her lips and watched him. She'd know if he attempted any kind of subterfuge. Her Coyote would scent the lie.

"Oh, baby, I am sure," he growled, the sound sending bolts of pleasure straight to her pussy.

"*Es Meus*."

ELEVEN

Nikolai trembled with the power of his need. Trying to make small talk between bites of food was practically fucking killing him. *Claim her. Es Meus.*

The fight to regain control from his beast was near impossible. The Dragon could not handle having her near and not touching her. Neither could the man.

He accepted her as his mate the second he breathed in her bright, citrusy scent. She was in his blood. Part of his soul. She belonged to him. *Now. Take her. Mine.* His Dragon was burning him alive from the inside out.

Sweat beaded on his forehead as he fought to contain the beast. He sucked in air, getting more of her peppery-sweet scent. He growled deep in his chest. She smelled fucking divine.

He noticed her eyes dilate and her breath coming faster. *Oh fuck. Yes.* She wanted him too. *Mate. Mine. Now.*

"Are you done eating?" he growled the question, unable to keep the beast from his voice.

At her nod he stood, pulling her up by the hand. He pressed her body flush against his. Wrapping her lush figure in his arms as his lips sought hers.

"Melody," he whispered her name. His Dragon stirring under his skin, stretching the limits of his control.

"Open your mouth," he murmured and licked the seam of her lips. His beast wanted a taste of her too.

She hooked her arm around his neck, pulling him down to meet her tongue. *Thank fucking god.* He gave her what she wordlessly asked for.

Both of them mindless in their desire for one another. He pushed the food back off the table and lifted her deliciously plump ass until she was planted on the edge of the sturdy ebony.

With one hand he kneaded her full round breasts while he stroked her thighs apart with the other one. She moaned into his mouth as he found the buttons to the pretty, but too damn confining dress she'd worn.

His brain turned to mush as her luscious breasts spilled from her flimsy lace bra. He hoped it was not a favorite as he lifted one clawed fingertip sliced through the strap.

He growled and tugged on the fabric, freeing her mouthwatering nipples. He pushed his hips closer, allowing her to feel his throbbing cock through too many layers of fabric.

He slid his tongue in and out of her lips. Gathering her unique flavors and storing each one in his memory. His to keep and savor forever. *Es meus ad infinitum.*

Nik dragged his lips from her mouth to one ripe berry and sucked hard. He loved the way she held his head against her moist flesh with nail tipped hands that pulled on his longish hair. *Yes.* She squirmed beneath him, undulating her hips in an attempt to get him closer. *Thank fuck.*

He slid his hand over the front of her body till he reached that oh-so-fucking-hot spot between her legs.

Oblivious to the wine spilling over the side of the table as he rubbed his fingers over her hot sex. Her panties soaked his fingers and if possible, he grew harder.

"I need inside of you, baby," he growled sucking on her neck while his hands did away with her damp panties.

"Yes, please, yes," she moaned arching into him.

Her clawed hands raked down his back and he fucking loved the burn. Loved her. Needed her. Now.

Nikolai had had women in any number of places, but it had been so long since he felt this. Never. Never had he experienced this kind of passion flaring through his body. Only with her.

Dishes fell, wine spilled, and silverware clattered around them as he swept her clothes away with his large hands. She writhed with him, beneath his fingers. Her soft skin hot to the touch. Aflame for him alone.

As it should be, his Dragon roared. Soft and ripe and utterly his. She mewled and gasped, all but consumed by the mating instinct. But did she recognize it for what it was?

That all-powerful need to fuck, to claim, to make her his. *Mine. Forever. Es Meus.* Nikolai's chest heaved with the effort to breathe. He knew what she was to him, but he needed her to accept his claim.

"Melody," he started, his lips grazing her skin as his teeth elongated.

The mixed scents of sex, desire, her fiery citrus fragrance, and his own piney, fresh air smell filled the air.

Nikolai freed his throbbing cock from his pants, as she ripped his shirt off his body. She was just as wild for him as he was for her. He thanked every god he knew for that small blessing.

"Yes, Niko, oh god, yes," she cried out as he pushed the head of his swollen cock into her slick heat.

She was so fucking tight. Her pussy sucked his cock deeper, but he held himself still.

Reveling in the perfection of being inside her superb body. She whimpered and tried to move but he held her with firm hands.

"You feel so fucking good, baby."

"Move, please," she moaned.

"Can I keep you, sweet Melody?" He growled the question and stilled the movement of her hips with his steely grip.

"Yes, Niko, yours, move please," she tried to move him again.

"This body was made just for me," he growled and pumped slowly as he spoke, eliciting a long, drawn out moan from her lips.

"I am keeping you. Not letting go. Yes, love, like that."

Her wide whiskey-colored eyes met his, mouth open, panting for air as he squeezed the globes of her perfect ass and thrust more fiercely.

She could take it, hell, she wanted it. He saw it in those glorious eyes of hers.

"More," she whimpered, her long claws raking down his back.

Perfect. He growled, his own animalistic side begging to be released as he continued to pound into his mate's sweet body.

His movements were measured, yet frantic. His desperation making him lose his focus. *Claim. Mate. Now.*

He wanted to so very badly, but he needed her to come for him first. He reached between them with one hand and teased her sensitive bud. She responded by throwing her head back and moaning deep and low while providing him perfect access to her exquisite breasts.

"Baby, I'm going to feast on you all fucking night long. You want that, don't you? My mouth all over you, my dick inside of you, my cum filling you. I'm going to fuck you until neither of us can think straight. I want you so fucking bad, my mate, mine," he growled and nipped her nipple.

Dominance and possession surged through him as he lifted her hips and slid deeper into her channel. Her answering moan was enough to encourage him. Her eyes glowed with the power of her Coyote.

"Yes," he growled, "Es meus!"

Melody opened her mouth and howled as ecstasy shot through

her body. Nikolai held on by a thread as her pussy clamped down on him, squeezing him until he could hardly breath.

Her scent was everywhere. On his mouth, his nose, his hands, his cock. He fucking loved it. He couldn't wait to sink his teeth into her. To stake his claim for the whole universe to see.

Nikolai nudged her down on the table as he swirled his hips, grinding into her sensitive nub as she rode out her orgasm. He was relentless. Swirling and plundering, quickly bringing her to another peak.

"Niko!" she howled again, and finally, he drove towards his own fulfillment.

Her thighs squeezed him as he slid a hand down the crack of her luscious ass and teased her tight little hole while his thick cock filled her dripping slit. *Yes*, his little mate had a naughty streak! One he couldn't wait to explore.

As her next climax took her, Nikolai slammed into her heat. Withdrawing and pumping, his eyes riveted to the way she welcomed his body with glorious abandon.

She was fucking gorgeous. Streaked hair flying around her flushed face, tits bouncing with every thrust, mouth repeating his name in a litany. *Fucking perfect.*

The sounds of their slick bodies coming together was more beautiful than any music he'd ever heard. Sexy and raw. Erotic as fuck.

Puccini had nothing on the symphony that was the slap of his skin against his mate's. Nikolai lifted her by the waist as he found his completion desperate to sink his teeth into her neck.

"Melody?" the question in his voice distinguishable through his fangs, his eyes searched hers for an answer.

"Yes, Niko. Claim me, make me yours," she growled the words, eyes aglow with her Coyote.

"*Es Meus*," he roared and struck her skin just over her heart.

His dick pulsed as he came at the same time. Her pussy clenched around him. Heat massaging his cock until he was spent.

Nikolai was lost to her taste, her being, her soul as it entwined with his.

MINE! ES MEUS!

His Dragon's ferocious roar was deafening. But Nikolai did not stop pumping his hips until he'd tended her wounds. Lapping at them with his tongue until the bleeding stopped.

He picked her soft, limp body off the table and carried her to his bedroom.

TWELVE

"Does this mean I'm yours now?" her soft voice was unfamiliar even to her own ears.

She felt more than saw his smile. Her face buried against the soft hair that covered his wide chest. He smelled so good, like pine, smoke, and musk. *Utterly intoxicating.*

She finally understood what had her Coyote going nuts the second he'd looked at her with his Dragon in his eyes. He was her one true mate.

Fated and chosen by the Universe to be hers. *A fairytale*, she'd thought as a child, but here was living proof.

Nikolai Falk, sexy Dragon Shifter, genius software developer, and multi-millionaire many times over, was her mate. *Holy crap!*

He not only recognized the fact, but he'd just claimed her on the dining room table of his own fucking castle!

Her. Little Miss Nobody Coyote Shifter from a band who'd rather not acknowledge her chubby existence. *Cinderella ain't got shit on me!*

Not that she was down on herself exactly. She was a confident modern woman. She knew she was smart, good at her job, and definitely worthy.

Regardless of what the prick ex of hers said. Still, there was so much about him she didn't know.

"We should talk," she said as he laid her down on an enormous bed made up with dark green sheets and a heavenly soft comforter.

"Ask me anything, mate," he said as he settled in beside her.

He couldn't seem to stop touching her. Hand on her arm, lips on her skin, fingers tracing her hair. It was something she absolutely loved.

"When?"

"When did I know you were mine?" He guessed correctly. Their bond was already working at making them more in tune with each other.

"The second I scented you at the ball. I searched and found you and it was all I could do not to take you right there on the floor," he spoke without inhibition or reticence of any kind.

"I remember the kiss, but when did you know I was your mate?"

"I told you, sweet mate, that second. My Dragon recognized you, loved you immediately. From that point on, my body, mind, heart, and soul belonged to you. No other, Melody, only you," he lifted a finger and trailed it from her cheek down her neck to her shoulder.

He dipped it further and she frowned. A stinging sensation following his fingers.

Melody looked down and gasped. A mark was beginning to blossom just there, across her left shoulder. A green rose with swirling leaves and vines flowing from it.

It glowed and pulsed on her skin, warming it. *She felt him there.* Tears filled her eyes.

"What is it?"

"It is my marking, my *emerald rose*. See this here," he taped a matching symbol on his chest, it pulsed beneath her fingers. The hum of magic tickling her senses.

"Before I found you, it was shriveled, almost dying. A Dragon's rose is connected to his heart and soul, his sacred bond to be shared only with his fated mate. I thought it was never going to happen for me, that I would despair in my loneliness until rage consumed me, then I found you. I have claimed you, and now, my *emerald rose*, you have accepted me," his cocky grin was almost contagious.

"How can you tell I accepted? Maybe you just made me delirious with your sexy skills," she smiled coyly, and was treated to some sensual wrestling that ended with him towering over her prone form.

He bit down playfully over her claiming mark. The action sending shivers down her spine directly to her needy sex. She could hardly believe how much she wanted him, needed him, burned for his body. *And more.*

"Look," he said and lifted himself up. She mourned the loss of his hot flesh but understood what he was showing her.

He lifted so that his chest was visible and there she saw how his rose reacted to her nearness, the vines swirling and eliciting the same reaction from hers.

She reached up with shaky fingers and traced the glowing lines that marked his perfect body. He trembled at her touch and she grew bolder.

Empowered by his helpless reaction to her hands, she ran them up and down the hard planes of his sculpture worthy form. He pressed his naked hips against hers and she moaned at the sizzling friction.

"We are tied now forever, my Melody. No one can come between us, love," he leaned forward and kissed her mouth with so much feeling and tenderness.

Emotions that could not be reduced to mere words. *Mate. Mine. His heart, his body, his soul. All mine.*

"*Es meus*," he nibbled at her chin and neck, and she felt her body opening for him.

Never before had she felt so confident and bold in her body. The purely lustful look in his eyes when his gaze swept her form removed any doubts she may have had. *Fuck her ex, fuck everyone else. Only he mattered.*

"What does that mean? *Es meus*? You keep repeating that phrase?"

"It is my native *Dracan*, Dragon language, my sweet mate. It means you are mine, my own," he growled and dipped his decadent tongue between her breasts.

Melody sighed and stretched. She was insatiable when it came to him. The way he touched her, worshipped her, was unlike anything in her experience.

Her Coyote yipped, and she knew he was worthy. He would never hurt her. When a Shifter found his mate, it meant forever. *A lifetime of love.*

"Niko?"

"Yes, baby?"

"I love you."

He lifted his gorgeous head and stared at her with eyes like green fire. His grip on her tightened briefly and he bent to kiss her, eyes closed as if the act was painful.

Melody moaned under his masterful skill, but more so because she felt him, in her heart.

His *emerald rose* was blossoming. She swelled with the knowledge. Proud and grateful for having him in her life. All his thoughts, feelings, desires sifted through to her from their newly formed bond.

She felt his promise to keep her safe, his passion for her body and mind, and his love shine through that special connection they shared. A connection only true fated mates could ever know.

She smiled as her own marking warmed her skin and gasped as his long, thick cock found her entrance. Her pussy was sopping wet, hot and needy even after their coming together downstairs only minutes ago.

"Baby, I love you too. I need you," he growled in her ear.

"Push up, yes, like that. Let me fill every inch of you. I'm going to stamp my scent all over you, sweet, sexy mate. Fill you with my cum, and make you scream my name."

God, yes, she wanted that too. He was so fucking hot. Sexy and handsome. She knew in her heart she belonged with her sexy Dragon Shifter as she never had Thomas or any other male of her acquaintance.

"I want to meet your Dragon," she gasped as he thrust in and out of her.

"Yes," he growled, "I want that to. And to meet your beautiful Coyote."

"Yes," she moaned.

"First, I'm going to fuck you every way I can, fill you up with me. You want that, my love, I know you do," his dirty words were just icing on the cake.

Melody's body sang for him. He made her cream just by saying her name. Body and soul recognized him as her other half. *Oh my.* She felt so right, wrapped around him.

"*Grrrr.* My Melody, you feel so fucking good," he growled deep in his throat, more Dragon than man.

She saw the truth shining in his emerald eyes. In ways his words couldn't express, he loved her with his body, claiming her as his very own. She'd never felt such intense pleasure, knowing in her soul she was created for him in that very moment.

This time, she thought, *I will claim him as well.* Melody pushed up against his chest, using a little of her Coyote to help get his attention. Her mate's eyebrows shot up, but he understood without words.

His eyes flared. Nikolai's chest grumbled as he gripped her waist and flipped them over so that he was on his back beneath her.

Melody arched as his cock impaled her, sliding further than ever before. She felt him, *everywhere.*

Oh, fuck yes. She rocked her hips slowly, sliding up and down over his long, hard shaft. His thick cock felt heavenly, a perfect fit.

She squeezed with her thighs and her mate groaned. Her Niko gripped her hips attempting to exact control from her, but she had other things in mind.

She grabbed his hands and pushed them over his head, draping her entire body over him. Her lips crashed into his, tongues swirling as she continued to undulate rhythmically.

Melody growled, her Coyote coming forward as she recognized the call to claim. Her mating instinct was running her now. *Grrr.* She moved frantically, her peak cresting. *Almost there.*

She felt her fangs elongate in her mouth and nuzzled his face, so he'd move and give her room. He did without words, the symphony of their bodies slapping bringing her to even greater heights.

Melody was wild for him. Saliva coated her tongue as she anticipated his flavor. She needed this. Needed him.

A deep growl built up from her chest as she kissed and licked his neck. He growled her name, fingers clawing her hips.

That hint of pain made her pleasure that much greater. She couldn't wait to give him that.

Without warning, she reared back and bit down. Slicing his skin like butter. *Fucking hell,* his rich flavor coated her mouth and tongue, sliding down her throat.

His taste was heady and powerful, like the magical beast he was. *Dragon. Mine. Mate.*

"Melody, mate," he roared her name and grabbed her by the ass. He lifted her up and down at a punishing pace. Pounding his cock inside of her while she sucked and lapped at the wound.

Seconds later stars burst behind her eyes as he struck again over his own mating mark.

The coppery scent of their combined blood met her nostrils. She growled loving the mixed fragrance. Pine and citrus, musk and sex. *Mates.*

Together they reached ecstasy. Their bodies and hearts in perfect time with each other.

It was like nothing she'd ever experienced in her thirty-five years on this earth. Her human side might have doubted had her Coyote not shown her the truth.

This was the way of Shifters. Mating was fast and primal.

Instinct and certainty. No room for fear and doubt. The Universe did not make mistakes.

I will never doubt again, she thought as he wrapped her up in his powerful arms.

"You will never have cause to doubt me, love. I will never hurt you. I love you. You are everything to me, my beautiful Melody."

"I love you, Niko," she sighed.

All of her anxieties eased out of her with that last declaration. Sure, they had some work to do. Getting to know each other and everything.

"I want you with me, here. Will you do that Melody?"

"I want to be with you too. If you're sure," she flicked her gaze down, but he'd have none of that.

"Look into my eyes, mate. You are mine surely as I belong to you. Our matebond is strong, you bear my emerald rose, surely as you wear that dragon tattoo on your back-"

"You saw?"

"You mean the miniature portrait of my dragon? Yes, love," his grin was her undoing, she wrapped her arms around his neck and kissed him again.

"Your Dragon?"

"It is an exact copy, I swear it."

She heard the certainty in his voice and more when he opened his mind's eye to her. His beast was glorious. An enormous green dragon with a long neck and fierce teeth. He puffed smoke from his nostrils and chuffed for her. Love and possession emanating from him. *Beautiful. And yes*, she thought, *an exact replica of my tattoo.*

"Marry me?" She spoke the words before she could stop them, and her Dragon Shifter roared a laugh before kissing her again.

"You took the words right out of my mouth!"

"Mmm, don't worry. I have other uses for your mouth besides words, *mate.*"

She tugged him close, and he willingly went where she led. She lifted her head, monitoring his progress as he slowly licked his way down her body.

Thank god for Shifter resilience, she bit her lip and moaned as he kissed her sensitive inner thigh.

"Do you like that, love?"

"Mmm. I think I can live with it," she teased, then lost all ability to speak as his long, clever tongue snaked out and flicked across her sensitive clit.

"Niko?"

"Mmm."

"You never answered my question. Will you marry me?"

"Yes, love, and I was going to ask," he growled and scraped his fang over her sensitive nub before proceeding to fuck her with his tongue.

"Beat you to it," she moaned.

"Yes, we will marry, mate, and you will bear my young, and we will fill this castle with laughter and life," he growled as he lifted to his knees, spreading her legs wide.

"Yes," she answered, her sex moist and ready for him.

He thrust his ever-ready manhood inside of her hitting her g-spot and grinding his pubis against her needy clit.

He knew just how to touch her to make her scream and moan. He gripped her hips and pushed her down into the mattress. Her pussy clenched around him.

"Niko!" she yelled.

He snatched control then and pumped furiously into her body. She needed that. Needed him like no one else. For the first time in her life Melody truly let go. He was *hers*. There was no doubt in her mind.

Melody's orgasm hit her like a tsunami. A thousand waves of pleasure coursed over her body and she reveled in every single one.

"You are so fucking beautiful when you come," he growled and followed her into oblivion.

Hours later...

"Niko?"

"Mm," her Dragon Shifter grumbled from his spot underneath her limp body.

They'd spent the entire evening in bed. Melody was exhausted, true, but she wasn't ready to slip into sleep just yet.

"The night we met, at the ball, there was a woman, my Coyote sensed she was a Witch."

She lifted herself off his chest to straddle him, aware of his sudden attention as certain parts of him perked up. *Grrr. Later.*

"What?" he lifted a hand to trace the outline of her breast, but she swatted him away.

"Niko, talk first, sexy times, later. Okay?"

"Anything for you," he said, but his naughty fingers continued to trace along her thighs and hips, nearly distracting her.

"The Witch, Nikolai, she said something odd?"

"What did this Witch say, my love, and do I need to hunt her down?"

"No, hush. Listen. She said there were rumors about you."

His grin soon turned into a frown and she guessed he knew what this was all about. He lifted her off him and stood up. His nudity aside, he looked about nervously and paced the room.

"Uh, Melody, are you sure you want to discuss this?"

"Yes? I mean, yes," she said a little more firmly, "She said-"

"I imagine she told you rumors of my inability to perform on command?" His skin burned bright red, and she smiled at his boyishness.

Her big, bad Dragon Shifter was embarrassed. *As if he had reason to be!* She kept a straight face as he ruffled a hand through his har and exhaled. He sat down on the edge of the bed, his back towards her as he spoke.

"The fact is, Melody," he growled and continued though it was obvious he was uncomfortable.

"I have not taken a lover in over a century. My Dragon would not, um, *cooperate*, you see. He was not interested in tasting pleasure with anyone other than my one, fated mate."

Melody's jaw hung open. Was she hearing this correctly? The man who had so thoroughly loved her the past two days had been abstinent for longer than she'd been alive! *Holy cow!*

"This is not something I've talked about with anyone else," he began, but before he could finish, she'd wrapped herself around him from behind.

"Niko?"

"Yes?" Tension rolled off him in waves as she decided what she was going to say.

"You waited all that time to find your mate?"

"I waited all that time for *you*."

"So, that's your big secret is it? And I thought it was gonna be something all bloody and gory,"

"Ha," he laughed, "That's my secret, love, no guts or gore, just a Dragon hopelessly waiting for his love to come to him."

She felt his happiness bloom between their matebond as he reached for her and dragged her across his lap.

"Well, that's a secret I think I can live with!" She smiled as she kissed him. Love, desire, and promise filled her from head to toe. Melody trembled with anticipation for her big, sexy mate.

They tumbled together in their bed and explored one another for the rest of the night. Wave after wave of rapturous bliss engulfed them. Finally, her mate turned to her and smiled.

"So, what now?" She asked.

"Now, there are no more secrets. Just us, sweet mate."

EPILOGUE

Melody strode towards the kitchen in the main part of the Castle looking for her mate. After several days, most of which they'd spent in bed, she'd relented enough to move in with her Dragon.

As if he had to do much arm twisting, she snorted. She couldn't wait to move in, the platinum emerald and diamond ring on her finger was a testament to his sincerity almost as much as the *emerald rose* marking that warmed and pulsed on her skin whenever he was near.

She belonged there, at Castle Falk, with her mate. They'd found their fur and scales together last night for the first time. The two of them anxious for their beasts to meet face to face.

Melody had been in awe of the magnificence of Niko's *Energy-Dragon.* The magical beast was more powerful and majestic as anything she could have imagined. Her Coyote had yipped at his heels and howled in glee when he'd raced through the pine barrens with her.

Yes. She was exactly where she belonged. In fact, she'd just emailed her official resignation letter to Mrs. Grayson at *Merlin Banking Solutions.*

Oddly enough the woman had already started the paperwork, having had an inkling Melody would not be returning after she'd sent her down to Maccon City after Nikolai, unbeknownst to her.

It didn't matter. She had a new job at *Draco Fortis*. She was excited at the prospect of exploring the partnership between her mate and *Graves Enterprises*. They had many projects in the works. They only needed the greenlight from her to begin production.

One thing she did immediately was send a huge NO THANK YOU, to *Virdi Lux* and the vicious tongued Angie White. Followed by an announcement in the local newspaper of the upcoming nuptials. *Take that, beyotch.*

After a honeymoon of course. She'd agreed with Niko on that front. They needed time. Their mating too new for work to intrude.

She stretched her arms and sighed as she padded barefoot across the marble floors. She probably should have donned something more than her towel, but he'd promised her breakfast in bed and she was starving.

"Niko?"

She entered the kitchen and was stunned to see three enormous males each with his arms around a woman, one was obviously pregnant, and another held a squirming baby.

"Uh-"

"Hello!"

"Is this her?"

"Yes, her scent is mixed with his."

"She's naked!"

"Hi!"

Whispered murmurs, wide eyes, and smiles met her confused face as she tried to duck back out the door. But her mate decided to stroll in at that time, wrapping his arms around her and pressing his hard bulge into her ass.

"I had to run to the store, love, but since we are here why don't we pick up-"

Heat pooled between her legs, her constant state around him, she realized. He nibbled her neck, and she was speechless for a second before she recalled their audience and elbowed him.

"Ouch!"

"Nik, perhaps your mate would like to learn our names before you expose her to your family?" Callius' laughing voice boomed in front of them and her mate stilled instantly.

"Oh stop, Cal!" Winifred handed her tall husband the baby before coming over and embracing the nearly naked Melody.

"Hello, ooh you're Coyote, that's cool, I'm a Werewolf, my name is Winifred, but everyone calls me Fred,"

"Damn," Nikolai growled and took off his sweatshirt, sliding the top over his mate's damp curls and tugging it done over her nearly nude frame.

"That's a lovely mate you got there, runt," growled a large redhead followed by a grunt after the short curly-haired woman next to him slapped his arm and rushed forward to take Melody's hand.

"I'm sorry, it will be over soon," Nik kissed her ear and held her close. She was decently covered by his oversized sweatshirt, but embarrassment stained her cheeks.

"I'm Joss, that's my mate Edric. That there is Sander and Noelle, and welcome to the family!!"

Melody smiled and shook hands, exchanged hugs, and learned the names of Nik's three brothers.

She'd had no idea that mating him was going to include an instant family, but her heart felt near to bursting it was so full of happiness.

They escaped back to their bedroom and she stood off to the side as Nikolai entered slowly behind her.

"Baby?"

"You never said you had family," she murmured.

His heart stopped. Was this a game changer? He did not know but he was scared as fuck.

"No, I didn't think it was important."

"I'm sorry, I should have asked if you were okay living here, with everyone. The Castle is designed to be four separate living quarters with only the main halls and kitchen joining them, but Melody I swear if this is an issue for you, we can go, anywhere you like."

She turned her glowing eyes on him and leapt in his arms. He caught her. Ever ready for his sweet mate.

"You gave me a family, Niko," she whispered the words as if they were a secret.

"You are my family, Melody," he said and locked his lips onto hers.

Love and desire burned through his veins.

"Es Meus."

"Yes. Yours," she moaned.

"I love you."

T*he end.*

Thank you for reading *The Dragon's Secret*! I hope you enjoyed it!

For more of The Falk Clan Tales CLICK HERE!

JOIN THE PACK!

Looking for a Paranormal Romance series that is loads of growly fun?

Welcome to the Macconwood Pack!

These stories are split into two series, the Macconwood Pack Novels Series, and the Macconwood Pack Tales.
Each story features one or more Pack members their journey to their one true and fated mate. They can be read alone, though they are better read in order, as characters may show up in each other's stories.

Pack is family for the Macconwood wolves, and when you read their tales, you become family too. What are you waiting for?

Join the Pack today!

https://www.cdgorri.com/series/the-macconwood-pack-novel-series/

BEWARE... HERE BE DRAGONS!

The Falk Clan Tales began as my stories surrounding four dragon Brothers and how they find their one true mates, but when a long lost brother arrives on the scene, followed by a few more Shifters... what can I say? The more the merrier!

Each Dragon's chest is marked with his rose, the magical link to his heart and his magic. They each have a matching gemstone to go with it.

She's given up on love. But he's just begun.

In The Dragon's Valentine we meet the eldest Falk brother, Callius. He is on a mission to find a Castle and his one true mate, one he can trust with his diamond rose....

His heart is frozen. Can she change his mind about love?

In The Dragon's Christmas Gift our attention shifts to Alexsander, the youngest brother of the four. He has resigned himself to a life alone, until he meets *her*.

Some wounds run deep. Can a Dragon's heart be unbroken?

The Dragon's Heart is the story of Edric Falk who has vowed never to love again, but that changes when he meets his feisty mate, Joselyn Curacao.

She just wants a little fun. He's looking for a lifetime.

We finally meet Nikolai Falk and his sexy Shifter mate in The Dragon's Secret.

She doesn't believe in fairytales, until a Dragon comes knocking on her door.

Meet Castor Falk, the long lost brother of our original four Dragons, and his sassy mate Josette. The Dragon's Treasure is full of adventure and laughs.

Nothing can surprise this six hundred-year-old Dragon, except maybe her.

Devine Graystone meets his match in Sunny Daye, an irrepressible Wolf Shifter with a heart of gold. Read their story in The Dragon's Surprise.

He's a hardcore realist until she dares him to dream.

Nicholas Gravestone doesn't know what to think when he spies Minerva Lykos on the property his Dragon covets. Can this unlikely pair come to a truce? Find out in The Dragon's Dream.

Thanks for reading.

xoxo,

C.D. Gorri

*Dragon Mates & Dragon Mates 2 boxed sets are now available in hardcover, paperback, and ebook.

WILD BILLIONAIRE ROMANCE IS HERE!

In producing a brand new contemporary romance series from USA Today Bestselling Author, C.D. Gorri!

These wild billionaire playboys are used to getting their way...

There isn't much money can't buy, especially when it comes to pleasure. But can these curvy women tame these billionaire beasts and win their love? Or will their souls be sucked into oblivion by the wanton bliss their bodies crave more and more with every surrender? Each of our heroes wears a mask on the outside to face the world, but his disguise comes off when he runs into the one female who makes his blood run hot. Need and possessive passion abound in these books, but our heroes know only one way to control their desires. Will they f*ck the feeling they see as weakness out of their systems, or will their needs only grow more wild with every touch, kiss, and plunge into ecstasy with the object of his affections?

Continue reading for info on book 1...

His Wild Obsession

He's a hardened ex-criminal. She's a stranger to his world.

Adrik Volkov worked hard to wipe the slate clean of his criminal past for his sake and his brother's. Bringing Volkov Industries into the 21st century has taken everything he's got. But it's been worth it. His company's patented mining techniques for harvesting rare earth metals used in electronics and smart tech have made him a billionaire.

Instead of breaking legs and taking names, he's attending parties with people he neither likes nor understands. It's all part of his new title. But money can't erase his harsh upbringing. Once a brawler, always a brawler. Those skills come in handy when he sees a woman being accosted at one of the ritzy, booze filled gatherings he must attend.

Sofia DiFalco was more than just a damsel in distress. The curvy stranger made his body buzz with desire and his hard heart beat a little faster. From the second he saw her, Adrik wanted only one thing. *Sofia in his bed.* But after one tantalizing night, she disappears without a trace.

He tries to forget her, but she's an obsession, and he just can't let go.

Also coming soon from...

Merciful Lies by C.D. Gorri

Lies can be merciful. It just depends on the why.

Meredith

I knew the second I saw him, my life would change forever. When my brother offers me as payment to Nico Fury, the king of the Vipers, how can I refuse? Tattooed, built, and tall, he was the only man I saw when I walked into the room. It was like he occupied all the available space, sitting on his throne of blood, sweat, and lies.

Nerves assailed me, but I owed my brother too much to let anything happen to him. One night. That was all. But it would leave me wrecked. Actions always had consequences. Six months later, my

brother was killed by a rival organization, and now they were
after me.

There was only one place I could go to keep my unborn baby safe. I
just hoped the king would be merciful.

***

Nico

Perfect things didn't exist, at least not in my experience. But she was
pretty close. I had her in my bed for one night, and I couldn't shake
the memory. No, I wasn't meant to keep soft things like Meredith
Keller. My life belonged to my crew, and we were a vicious group.

Hell, we weren't called Vipers for nothing.

But she was different. She made me want, and I loved and hated her
for it. Meredith was light in a world of constant darkness. She was all
warmth and beauty like no other. And I craved her like a drug.

Six months had passed since I took her in return for clearing her
brother's debt to me, but that man attracted trouble like honey did
flies. It wasn't long before I learned Sam Keller had gotten himself
killed. Less than an hour later, Meredith came back to me, on her
knees, asking for sanctuary.

I knew the moment I saw the swell of her stomach she was carrying
my baby. Meredith thought coming here would protect her, but she
was walking right into the Viper's nest. Before I was finished, my
little runaway would be begging me for mercy.

**Merciful Lies is the first in the contemporary romance series of
connected standalones, Jersey Bad Boys. This series features
familiar tropes such as enemies to lovers, forced proximity,
arranged marriages, secret babies, and contains some violence
and explicit scenes.**

ALSO BY C.D. GORRI

Contemporary Romance Books:

Cherry On Top Tales

Her Yule His Log

His Carrot Her Muffin

Her Chocolate His Bar

Wild Billionaire Romance

His Wild Obsession

Jersey Bad Boys

Merciful Lies

***

Paranormal Romance Books:

Macconwood Pack Novel Series:

Macconwood Pack Tales Series:

The Falk Clan Tales:

The Bear Claw Tales:

The Barvale Clan Tales:

Barvale Holiday Tales:

Purely Paranormal Romance Books:

The Wardens of Terra:

The Maverick Pride Tales:

Dire Wolf Mates:

Wyvern Protection Unit:

Jersey Sure Shifters/EveL Worlds:

The Guardians of Chaos:

Twice Mated Tales

Hearts of Stone Series

Moongate Island Tales

Mated in Hope Falls

Speed Dating with the Denizens of the Underworld

Hungry Fur Love

Island Stripe Pride

NYC Shifter Tales

A Howlin' Good Fairytale Retelling

Standalones:

Witch Shifter Clan

Young Adult/Urban Fantasy Books

The Grazi Kelly Novel Series

The Angela Tanner Files

G'Witches Magical Mysteries Series

Co-written with P. Mattern

Witches of Westwood Academy

with Gina Kincade

Blackthorn Academy For Supernaturals

Be sure to check out my BUY DIRECT BUNDLES and get 30% off when you buy available only my website.

Click here for The Official C.D. Gorri Reading List

About the Author

USA Today Bestselling author C.D. Gorri writes paranormal and contemporary romance and urban fantasy books with plenty of steam and humor.

Join her mailing list here: https://www.cdgorri.com/newsletter

An avid reader with a profound love for books and literature, she is usually found with a book in hand. C.D. lives in her home state, New Jersey, where many of her characters and stories are based. Her tales are fast-paced yet detailed with satisfying conclusions. If you enjoy powerful heroines and loyal heroes who face relatable problems in supernatural settings, journey into the Grazi Kelly Universe today.

You will find sassy, curvy heroines and sexy, love-driven heroes who find their HEAs between the pages.

Wolves, Bears, Dragons, Tigers, Witches, Vampires, and tons more Shifters and supernatural creatures dwell within her paranormal works. The most important thing is every mate in this universe is fated, loyal, and true lovers always get their happily-ever-afters.

In her contemporary works, you will find fiercely possessive men and the smart, confident, curvy women they are crazy about. As always, the HEA is between the pages.

Thank you and happy reading!
del mare alla stella,
C.D. Gorri

http://www.cdgorri.com
https://www.facebook.com/Cdgorribooks
https://www.bookbub.com/authors/c-d-gorri
https://twitter.com/cgor22
https://instagram.com/cdgorri/
https://www.goodreads.com/cdgorri
https://www.tiktok.com/@cdgorriauthor